No Earthly Treason

BOOK TWO
THE NECROMANCER'S DAUGHTER

GENEVRA BLACK

CHAPTER ONE

THE RIVER VÁN was uncharacteristically calm, its surface like a black mirror that parted gracefully for Sárr's rowboat. Though gray clouds peered over the horizon as always, there was no rain, no thunder. The miserable howl of the wolf was a drone—part of the landscape, now.

But the river was silent. Waiting.

As he worked his long oar through the water, the Wounded leaned over the side and caught sight of his own face: pale, thinner than it had been. He had only just fully recovered from the damned vivid's magic. Shame simmered in his eyes.

But let Marius Eirikson have his small victory. Sárr's goal had never been to defeat him.

He slashed the oar across the water, disrupting his reflection and pulling away, back into the boat.

As the rowboat drifted closer to the cave, he found himself surrounded by ebony rocks jutting from the river, some as tall as thirty feet. They shone like they were made of glass, as if they had grown from the water itself, as if the entire vista was all one smooth piece. The mouth of a cave, slanted and craggy, called to him from beyond the inky sentinels.

He maneuvered the little boat through the breach, slipping in silently. And as darkness covered him, sucking every bit of light from the entryway through which he'd just come, he had only one, warm thought: *Home.*

After a few moments, the tight passage opened into a much larger cavern, and the Wounded hurried his rowing, wedging the bow of his rowboat onto the rocky shore, as he had many times. He stepped out, sabatons scraping against the stone as he tugged the boat further ashore. Darkness filled the cavern and obscured his vision, but he didn't need to see to find his way.

He stepped up to the enormous stone slab of the kinsblood seal and stretched out a hand, stroking its runed surface. He took a deep breath, and when he called to the blood in his veins, his markings—the wounds for which he was named—began to glow, sizzling in a frenzy. Red mist fluttered just above the surface of his skin, smelling heavily of copper.

There were only a handful of beings in the Nine Worlds for which this door would open ... and he was one.

The crimson-flecked mist seemed to take on a life of its own. It oozed, weightless, from his markings and filled the grooves in the stone.

A pause. Then the runes glowed a vibrant gold, and the circular door rolled aside.

For a moment, the wolf's droning cry was cut off. The massive beast strained forward against his loathsome chains, snuffling at the new scents coming in through the open door. When he recognized Sárr's, he grunted lowly and sat back again. Though he had ceased howling, a breathy, faint whine still issued from the back of his throat.

The Wounded stopped in front of the wolf, looking into his red eyes. The aqueducts in the floor around them were overflowing, fuller with slaver than usual. The wolf panted, jowls slicked with saliva.

In pain.

Sárr had to spread his arms wide, but he put a hand on either side of the wolf's enormous head, bringing it in close and resting his forehead against the muzzle. He breathed in the wolf's musky smell, knotting his fingers in his fur. The wolf responded in kind, nudging the crook of Sárr's neck and closing his eyes. *Home.*

After a moment, Sárr pulled away and walked hastily to the wolf's side to survey the manacles. Even one of the outsized links of the wolf's long, long chain was as tall as Sárr himself. He'd tried many times to move them, but they would only give a few inches. As he brushed his hand along the bindings, he noticed that constant straining against them had rubbed away some of the wolf's pelt. It cut into the wolf's skin, and dark, sickly blood matted the fur around each laceration.

Sárr's heart ached. He had never seen such a thing, in all the time he had spent by the wolf's side. "You're bleeding."

The wolf could only respond with a deep yowl. An enchantment had stolen his voice long ago, so he could only cry wordlessly. The Wounded longed to hear him speak.

Soon.

He brushed the fur of the wolf's huge ear, speaking softly, trying to bring him comfort. "Your sons are doing well. They had their first taste of Midgardian battle, and they fought gloriously."

The wolf grunted and exhaled a hot breath.

"They've returned to their hunt for now. But I look forward to calling upon them again."

As he continued to stroke the wolf's fur, the hair on the back of his own neck began to stand up. Every muscle slowly tensed. Someone had joined them from the depths of the river.

He didn't have to wonder who. His body knew before his mind, and his mind knew without having to look.

"I confess," the Wounded murmured as he dropped his hand and turned to look into the shadows, "I didn't think I'd find you here."

A great, black shape stood there, perhaps ten or eleven feet tall, wavering as though on unsteady feet. The wolf raised his head a bit, watching the shape closely, his whimpers quieting.

You did not find me. I found you, said The Shape. The voice, soft, with no discernible age or gender, surrounded Sárr.

"Of course." Sárr bowed his head, gritting his teeth.

You have been avoiding me, said The Shape.

"I couldn't avoid you if I tried."

A pause. *The New Gloaming lives. The culling was successful, and now you can build.*

Sárr said nothing. The Shape wasn't offering congratulations, or a compliment; The Shape was reminding him of his debt.

The hellerune fled.

Sárr clenched his fists. "A certain Auroran vivid intervened on her behalf. But she never raised her own hand in defense. I won't believe she has as much power as you say she does. She *wept*."

She has all of your stolen power —The Shape seemed to look him over, and just that one look caused Sárr's markings and irises to flare and spark with white energy, so painful he nearly doubled over— *and more. Whether you collect her or not makes no difference to me, in the end. But you waste your resources on chasing her.*

The Shape's next sentence began before the previous one had ended completely, two voices working in unison: *If you truly find yourself incapable of capturing her, kill her.*

Sárr's eyes widened, bleached magic still clouding his vision. "But she's mine. You promised her to me!"

The moth uses its tiny frame to escape the clumsy hands of children, but it is not immune to the pin.

She is your *prize. If you want her alive, take her alive. Otherwise, snuff her out. Soon.*

Remember: above all else, the Reach stays dead.

Above power, above haste, the Reach stays dead.

Put your desires aside for the twilight.

Sárr suppressed a snarl. "The Reach is nothing. It's the Aurora that have the power to stand against me ... and not for long."

Ah. The Shape seemed almost amused, though Sárr couldn't tell if it was at his expense or not. *The traitor.*

"Yes, the Auroran. They will help us take it down from the inside."

And how, little one, can you trust that your friend will keep their word? said The Shape.

"I don't have to trust," Sárr whispered. "The traitor's only alternative was unthinkable. There was no chance our demands would be refused."

The Shape seemed satisfied.

Nothing more was said as the darkness engulfing the amphitheater fluttered and thinned. The Shape sank back into the depths of the river.

Color returned to Sárr's face. He was alone with the wolf again.

Sárr turned to him and stroked the fur of his neck, bitter, cursing softly. The Shape was impossible to read, and almost as hard to please. But Sárr held out. Looking at the wolf's raw wounds, he found new resolve.

What they'd been promised was worth the work and ruin.

Above all, it was justice.

CHAPTER TWO

EDIE WAS in the clearing again.

Over the past two months, she'd visited this place so often that she already knew how the dream would play out—the same way it did every time.

She sat up, brushed off her velvet cloak, and stood shakily. Silence stifled her eardrums for a moment, but it didn't last for long. Hoping to expedite the nightmare, she breached the circle of trees and started in the direction she thought she heard the murmuring river. She was sure now that it was a river and not whispers, after being here so many times. A couple of nights, she had almost been able to reach it.

Behind her, a familiar noise: the howl of a wolf. The same howl she heard every time. The beast was waiting, stalking the forest. She wasn't as slow or confused as she'd been the first dozen times, but it would find her eventually. She resisted the urge to follow the howl, to find the wolf, focusing on slowly picking her way through the tightly-packed trees.

The river was getting louder. The further she went, the more heavily the snow fell, like the forest itself was trying to prevent her from finding her way.

It was too cold. It was too white. She couldn't see anything. How was she supposed to reach this stupid river if she couldn't see where she was going?

Suddenly, something horrible was screeching in her ear. Her eardrums clutched, and a shock went through her.

She woke up. Light was pouring in from the window across from her bed.

Edie groaned, pulling her brocade comforter over her head and trying to conserve the warmth she had trapped under the covers. Why was it so freaking cold in her room anyway? It was supposed to be early July.

She got up the courage to poke her hand out of her comforter, and groped around for her phone, pulling it under the covers with her when she finally found it. Ten o'clock in the morning. *Fuck.* She was supposed to have been up hours ago ... but it turned out it was kind of hard to keep any kind of schedule when you were completely unemployed. She'd lost her job at the garage, of course, a while ago, and it was pretty safe to assume she was no longer welcome at Nocturnem.

Edie sighed and finally left the comfort of her blanket hovel. At least in her sleeping nightmares, she knew what was going to happen. In this waking one, she never knew what was coming next.

She reached automatically for her bottle of pain relievers, but stopped short, instead reaching down to rub her ankle. Two and a half months ago, she'd faced off against Hati and Sköll, two demigod wolves who, according to legends, were supposed to devour the sun and moon at the apocalypse. They'd settled for trying to devour her foot instead. Thankfully, Cal had run them over with a hijacked ambulance, but the bite had still been deep enough to need stitches.

This morning, though, she felt fine—completely normal. And the scar was even fading a little, thanks to the bloodmending she'd quickly learned to utilize. It had been really, really gross, but holding the hospital's soiled linens had made her heal faster, so she'd done what she needed to do.

It was the exhaustion that was getting to her; a bone-deep exhaustion since she had brought Mercy back from the brink of death. But there was no medicine for that. As she dragged herself up out of bed, she wondered how her father had dealt with things like this. Then she wondered if she really wanted to know.

Edie looked down at her wrist, at the rune that was now tattooed there: a stout diamond shape, about two inches across. Satara had called it *ingwaz*.

The beginning.

Apart from her whole worldview shattering, her body would never be the same, either.

Clattering from the kitchen pulled her attention away from her wrist. *Mercy.* She rushed out of her bedroom so fast she almost knocked her guitar stand down.

Edie's vision tunneled when she looked into the kitchen and saw her roommate struggling to reach something on the top shelf of the kitchen cabinet. Mercy's bubblegum-pink hair was tied back, and one ergonomic crutch lay on floor.

Neither she nor Mercy was tall enough to reach the highest shelf, so they usually just hopped up onto the counter to get things down or put them away—but, of course, with one arm and her entire lower body in orthopedic casts after the battle, that had been impossible for Mercy. Now that her casts were off, she was testing the boundaries—and the strength of Edie's heart.

"I'll get it!" Edie darted forward and scooped up Mercy's fallen crutch, returning it to her.

Mercy shook her head. "I can get it."

"No—"

"I can make my own tea, Edie." Mercy's tone was grumpy, and she blushed in embarrassment, but backed off nonetheless. "I'm not a total baby."

Edie stretched to reach the tea tin, and glanced skeptically over her shoulder. "*Baby?* Are you even hearing yourself? Let me take care of you. It's the least I can do."

That, at least, coaxed a laugh from Mercy. "Technically, the least you could do is nothing."

"Ha, yeah, I'll take a page from Drake's book," Edie mumbled, rolling her eyes.

After the battle that had left Mercy disabled, everyone had agreed she would probably be safer at her boyfriend Drake's after she got out of the hospital. Unfortunately, Drake had strongly disagreed, and after only two weeks of Mercy living with him, he'd bailed and kicked her out. Edie couldn't imagine abandoning someone when they were as vulnerable as Mercy was—both physically and emotionally. Edie wasn't the only one suffering nightmares.

From the bathroom at the end of the hall, there came a throaty gurgle and some splashing. Mercy looked at Edie and smiled fondly, her dark brown gaze soft. Fiskbein was still making the best of his home in their bathtub, and he and Mercy had become close friends, despite his ... well, despite him being him.

Thankfully, Fisk was awfully protective of Mercy now that she was home, and considering no one could be sure if or when they were all going to be hunted out by the New Gloaming, that was pretty useful. Or, it had been.

Lately, he hadn't had the strength to leave the bathtub for very long. He was resilient, but even he was getting sick without enough space and proper salt.

"Well," Mercy said, adjusting her crutches, "if you're content to mother-hen me, I'm going to go check on our roommate."

Edie grabbed a mug and the kettle, then filled the latter up with tap water. "I won't have to mother-hen you for very long. You'll have better range of motion soon."

This was especially true considering the weird medicine Cal had been bringing Mercy. Her specialists were baffled that she was recovering so quickly.

Mercy thumped quietly down the hallway, leaving Edie to her thoughts. The way Mercy had become hurt—what the Wounded had done to her, for no reason other than he thought it was fun—made Edie's blood boil every time she thought of it. She wasn't sure she'd ever get to kill that asshole, but she fully intended to hurt him—bad—next time they saw each other.

The bathroom door clicked shut, bringing Edie back to reality. She hadn't even gone pee or showered or brushed her teeth yet, but she was used to the bathroom being occupied now, and if she didn't make sure Mercy and Fisk were taken care of first, it would bug her for the rest of the day.

She opened the fridge and carefully unwrapped the huge Atlantic salmon on the top shelf. Edie and Cal went down to the fisherman's market at the marina every afternoon and bought whatever hadn't sold during the morning. Thankfully, he paid for all the fish.

Edie couldn't help but wonder where he got the money, but she was glad he had it. Keeping a seven-foot marine animal fed was a pricey task, and she and Mercy were racking up debt that Edie *knew* they had no hope of ever paying back. Mercy's parents had helped where they could, but she still didn't want to dip into the band fund. Unfortunately, neither of them was in much of a position to go out and apply for jobs.

She grabbed a cutting board from the cabinet and flopped the fish down on it. A couple of months ago, she'd had trouble with tuna from a can, but now she could butcher fresh fare with the best of them. Fisk preferred to eat it whole while it was still wiggling and bleeding, but he was still in *her* bathtub, so he was going to eat raw fish in chunks like a respectable gentleman. She grabbed a cleaver from the knife rack and chopped the giant fish into four pieces, then scraped them into a bowl. Fine dining.

The kettle screeched, and Edie poured the boiling water into the mug, then packed her skull-shaped tea infuser—"Creepy Steepy," as Mercy called him—with tea leaves.

The television was on in the living room, repeating the morning news. Something about *another* riot, this time on the south side of the city. A bunch of prisoners had been broken out of jail by a mob. Edie didn't have to look at the photos flashing across the screen to know who had done it.

The New Gloaming takeover had been absolute. Astrid said Sárr had probably been planting his people for a long time, slowly replacing key Gloaming officials, so that when he began his "culling," it would happen virtually overnight. And it had worked. The New Gloaming was the only Gloaming now.

Now it made sense why no one had heard of the Wounded: he'd done it on purpose. If you had no idea something was coming, you couldn't prepare for it.

His people ruled the night. Instead of hiding, they walked the streets brazenly—so much so that even the unattuned were taking notice. Agents that Astrid and Satara called Watchers patrolled the streets everywhere. Attacks and murders in Anster had risen drastically, and the police did nothing but clean up after them. Between these Watchers and the Aurora still hunting her, going outside for long periods of time had proven dangerous for Edie and her friends.

Maybe it was for the best that Edie didn't have a job. No way would she be able to survive an eight-hour shift somewhere.

She checked the tea, added sugar, then carried it and Fisk's breakfast down the hall.

When Edie entered the bathroom, Mercy was sitting on the edge of the tub, her crutches leaning against the nearest wall. She was looking over Fisk's shoulder, petting his spines as he tried to sound out the words of his soggy copy of *One Fish, Two Fish*. Fisk himself was a considerably duller shade of turquoise than he had been, his gills sallow.

"This is the language of bastards," he said, looking wearily at his book as Edie approached. "The mouth-words sound similar to the Old Tongue, but the look-words are too round."

Edie smiled. "You're doing good, though."

"I knew a little before..." He trailed off, offering no further explanation before slamming the book shut and setting it aside. He eyed the bowl in Edie's hand.

She handed Mercy and Fisk their respective items and placed her hands on her hips. "Remember to keep it all in the bowl this time, okay? No one wants fish bones and guts clogging up the drains."

The vættr had already swallowed one of the pieces whole, and didn't seem to be listening.

After taking a sip of her tea, Mercy hummed and asked, "Have you heard from Satara yet today?"

Edie sighed and took this opportunity to *finally* have her morning pee. She sat across from Mercy and fiddled with her raven ponytail as she took care of business. "Not yet."

Since it had become apparent that Edie needed to step up her game, she and Satara had been hitting the gym every few days, venturing out for a couple hours at a time. They'd gotten to know each other much better. Edie knew Satara and Astrid were trying to figure out where the Wounded had come from and what his next move was, but Satara hadn't mentioned any sort of breakthrough. Their unsuccessful hunt was probably exactly what Sárr had wanted.

"All those assholes did, besides kill people, was grandstand and make lofty speeches," Mercy said, rolling her eyes. "It's hard to believe that they're subtle enough to not leave *any* sort of clues."

"That's probably true for Zaedicus. But I think Sárr was just giving people what they wanted." Edie remained sitting on the toilet, lost in thought. "Or maybe we're not looking in the right places."

"Whoever's funding them probably has some strong feelings about what they should be doing with the money. So if you find those people, you find their driving force. And their plan, hopefully."

Edie considered that. "Satara said they're cleaning out the coffers of all the ousted Gloaming Lords. They're making a ton of noise about it. So they might not need crazy-rich supporters now. But you're right, they will eventually."

Fisk swallowed the fish head whole and asked, "Do you two always bond while relieving yourselves?"

Mercy smiled and patted his head. "It's a human thing."

The vættr thought for a moment, then made a face, gills flaring.

A series of thumps on the apartment door drew Edie from her reverie and, feeling much more relaxed, she finally stood.

Mercy's brows drew together as she asked, "Who is that?" She had expressed some nervousness about letting anyone into the house, which made sense, but the apartment was a safe place for now. Fisk wouldn't let anything happen to her, and Edie only unlocked the door for Cal or Satara.

And considering it was almost time for his morning visit... "Probably Cal. I bet his hands are full. I'll go get it."

She exited the bathroom and closed the door softly behind her. Poor Fisk. But what could they do? He refused to return to Maine, and insisted on being close to them, especially Mercy. There was probably someone in the city they could contact, someone who could heal him or give him the right minerals or something ... that'd be a good thing to ask Astrid or Satara.

Edie went to the apartment door and stood on her toes to look out of the peephole. Cal was on the other side, staring right at her with a sour expression on his gnarled face. Not in a good mood, then. She'd tell him to smile, but he didn't look any better when he did that.

When they'd first met each other—after he'd tried to kill her, that is— she'd learned she was the only one who could effortlessly see through his glamour, and he wasn't pretty underneath. Because of charms her father had put on him years ago, when he'd raised him from the grave, the revenant would always be frozen in a state of pretty grisly decomposition.

Mostly, it didn't bother her. He wasn't gooey or decaying, and he didn't smell rotten. Still, it was pretty menacing to see that face glaring at you.

She unlatched the chain and flipped the lock. The moment there was enough room for him to squeeze past her, he did. He was dressed in light wash jeans, a matching jacket, and a flannel. It had been an unseasonably cold summer so far, and even though the temperature only bothered him on a superficial level, he didn't want to draw attention to himself by being that guy walking around in a T-shirt when it was freezing outside.

In one hand, he held four or five shopping bags; with the other, he shoved a new smartphone into her hands.

"I hate this fucking thing," he snapped, setting the bags on the coffee table in the living room before turning and thrusting a finger at the phone. "There's too much shit on it. I can't find anything."

Edie couldn't help but smile. For a while, she'd found his abrasiveness exhausting, always assuming it was her fault he was such a crab-ass. But nope. That was just how he was, and generally, he didn't mean anything by it.

"You don't have to use the things you don't need," she said. "I can make it so all your important apps are in one place. So you don't have to click around?"

"I guess." He grunted and planted his hands on his waist. "It makes me feel like a fuckin' old man."

"You *are* an old man." Edie approached and set his phone down on one of the side tables, then looked at his bags. "Anything good?"

Cal turned and started to take things out, piling them in her arms as he listed them off: "Bucket of aquarium salt, medicine for Her Highness, and"—he handed her a Styrofoam takeout box—"lunch for you."

Edie set the five-gallon bucket aside and looked at the paper bag that contained Mercy's medicine first. Inside was a tin of ointment about the size of Edie's palm, wrapped in wax paper with a little tag stuck to it. *Crushed brunnmigi teeth & knitbone salve.*

Knitbone was fairly straightforward, but she'd been meaning to ask about the other thing. "What is a *brunnmigi*, anyway?"

Cal snorted. "Technically, it can mean fox, but in this context? Basically a little goblin who goes around pissing in wells."

She made a face and lifted the takeout box. "And this?"

"Quesadilla from that terrible hipster place you like." Before she could ask, he said, "Mango salsa *inside*, not *on the side*."

Edie raised a brow at him. A couple weeks ago, Cal had taught her how to control their mental connection and put a wall between their minds. She had been able to erect a good, sturdy one, but still wasn't great at letting it come down. Now they were stuck in a weird place where she could still feel some of his emotions, but he couldn't feel any of hers. He said she'd get more fluid with it, but at this point, it seemed like they barely needed their connection—he still finished her sentences half the time.

The revenant might have a hard shell, but he sure did a lot of nice things for her without being prompted. Especially lately. Whenever she asked him about it, or took issue with him running errands or paying for her groceries, he acted all dodgy and guilty. She didn't understand why. It wasn't like it was his fault she was struggling, right? And she didn't want to use up all his money.

"I figured you hadn't eaten anything yet," he said, shoving his hands in his pockets. He tossed his head in the direction of the bathroom. "What with having to take care of them."

"I don't *have* to take care of Mercy. I want to. I like to." It was true— and no matter what Mercy said, it was the least Edie could do. She set her quesadilla aside for now, gesturing to the other bags and hoping to change the subject. "What else?"

He'd only picked up a few groceries and other odds and ends, but she brought them into the kitchen and began helping him unpack.

"You heard anything from the Norn yet?" he asked, elbows deep in the top shelf of the cabinets. "Indri-whatever?"

Edie sighed. "No."

"Astrid's been buggin' me about it."

She hesitated. "There's nothing I can do until she contacts me again. Besides, she didn't want to talk to Astrid, she wanted to talk to me."

"I mean, if she's gonna join up, she's gonna have to face Astrid at some point," Cal said, stacking pasta boxes with alarming speed. "That oughta be a catfight to remember. 'You sent my boyfriend to Valhalla, you bitch!'"

Edie rolled her eyes. Indriði had abandoned the Reach because she'd had a "fixation"—that was the word Astrid had used—with a soldier whom Fate had chosen to fall on the battlefield. A soldier whose soul Astrid had to collect. "Yeah, somehow I don't think an ancient spirit of Fate and a millennium-old valkyrie are going to have a catfight, Cal."

"Whatever." He opened a container from the fridge and sniffed it, then chucked it, Tupperware and all, into the trash. "The lady *said* she wanted to see you, so she better turn up soon. It's been over two months."

Edie sighed, glancing over the kitchen counter and out the living room window. The sunlight was pale and weak, barely peeking through an iron cloud cover. The buds on the trees surrounding the playground across the street had bloomed in the spring but had died quicker and younger than usual. She was sure a soul-burning heatwave would turn the tides any day now, as they tended to do lately. Of *course*, on top of everything, she still had to worry about freaking climate change.

"Cal?" She turned to look at him.

He was putting stuff in the freezer and didn't look back at her. "Hm?"

"Astrid still hasn't found anyone who can teach me how to use my powers." After a pause, "I'm starting to think she's not going to be able to."

He was silent.

Edie took a deep breath. "But you seemed to know what to do, when I had to help Mercy. Right?"

He still said nothing.

"I was thinking—"

A strange noise cut her off—a faint shriek, as though some passing car had a loose fan belt. Then there was a strangely weighty thud against the living room window, like someone had thrown a small child.

What the hell? Edie whipped her head around just in time to see a *pug-sized*, fuzzy, blue—

—*spider.*

CHAPTER THREE

Edie screamed, and wasn't sure she'd ever stop screaming, as she watched the thing—literally the size of a full-grown pug—struggling for purchase against the windowpanes, its eight little feet working hard to keep it from falling into the shrubs.

In a flash, Mercy and Fisk were out of the bathroom, and Cal was by Edie's side, staring into the living room. Out of the corner of her eye, Edie could see Mercy start to ask her what was wrong.

Then Mercy spotted the spider and let out a shriek of her own. "What the hell is that thing?!"

The horror only escalated when the spider managed to find steady footing and carefully moved two sets of its hind legs along the windowsill. Before any of them could process what was happening and rush out there to stop it, it had wedged its feet under the bottom and opened the window.

With the tips of its feet, it oh-so-delicately touched the bottom and the side jamb to make sure the window wouldn't close on it, then slipped into the apartment. It was a streak of cobalt as it hopped up onto the coffee table.

Then, unexpectedly, it hunkered down and chilled there.

Though she felt like she could probably go on screaming for a thousand thousand years, Edie was able to stifle her screams and stand, frozen, staring at the unwanted visitor.

It stared back at her, its tiny eyes glinting in the weak sunlight. It sat there like it was expecting something.

"Well." Cal put his hands on his waist and tilted his head. "You don't see that every day."

Mercy stared at the spider for a long time, then looked at Edie, perplexed. "I ... I think it's waiting for you to say hello."

Edie grimaced. Of course the horrifying giant spider wanted to talk to her, specifically, because why wouldn't it?

She didn't mind spiders *too* much. She wasn't scared of them, really, and some were even beautiful. But she liked them over *there*, away from her. And not nearly as huge.

Should she even risk getting close to it? She glanced at the others for reassurance. Cal shook his head; Mercy looked wary. Fisk was nodding in enthusiastic encouragement.

It seemed she didn't have much choice. She couldn't just let it sit there and go about her day.

Edie exited the right-hand entryway of the kitchen and moved into the living room as slowly as she could, afraid that quick movement would frighten the spider into jumping at her. It didn't, though; the spider only shifted slightly to face her and sat patiently, rubbing its third set of legs against its abdomen.

Now that she was closer and not quite so horrified, she couldn't help but notice what a lovely color it was. Its sternum and back legs were a light cobalt, but the two front sets of legs were a glossy sapphire that almost seemed to twinkle. Its abdomen was covered in fiery orange fuzz.

What did you even say to a spider? Edie fumbled for a moment before trying, "Hello?"

To her great surprise, it raised one of its pedipalps—the tiny not-quite-legs near its fangs—and waved.

The room fell silent. After a long moment, Edie asked, "Did you just ... wave hello?"

The spider did it again.

She couldn't help but smile. It was huge and horrifying, but it was clearly friendly—or at least well-trained—so there was that. She still wasn't gonna get any closer, though. "Well, aren't you smart?"

It covered its fangs with its pedipalps like it was hiding its face bashfully.

"Who are you? Why are you here?"

Dutifully, the spider turned around and reached under itself with its third legs. It produced a small object that Edie hadn't noticed was fastened to it before, shaped like an acorn and made of brass. The spider turned and flipped the top open with its foot, producing a tiny piece of paper. It used its front feet to slide the paper across the coffee table, toward Edie, then stepped back and hunkered patiently down again.

"Uh ... it has a note," she said, looking back at her friends.

Mercy tilted her head, eyes wide. "Huh!"

Edie desperately wanted to know what it said, but it would require her moving even closer to the giant spider. And though the spider seemed very nice, she didn't feel like taking her chances. "Cal, go read it."

The revenant didn't say anything. He simply threw his hands up in defeat before exiting the kitchen and grumpily grabbing the note. He read it slowly, mouthing the words. When he finished, his face twisted as he turned it over, then turned it back and scanned it again.

Edie's brow furrowed. "Who is it from?"

He exhaled hard through his nose hole and flipped it over so she could see. It was written in fancy, feminine script and signed with one name:

Indriði.

Edie looked up at the massive townhouse, then back down at the piece of paper in her hands. *3 Olive Street, Alderdeen.* She glanced over at Cal, who was sitting on his throne: behind the wheel of his white 1963 Cadillac Eldorado, affectionately named "Ghost," for the spirit who possessed it. Ghost had taken a pretty serious beating on their way to Maine a couple of months ago, but since then, Cal had fixed her up good as new. You couldn't even tell that she'd had some of her leather upholstery and a big chunk of her dashboard melted by a witchwolf's primal fire.

Edie took a deep breath and said, "This is the place."

The huge building took up a good portion of Olive Street. The upper floors were mostly hidden by the honeylocust trees lining the sidewalk, but Edie could see the entrance: cherrywood double doors on a roomy stoop, flanked by what appeared to be a doorman. The outside of the building was meticulously clean stucco, the ground floor windows had neat little planters in them, and she could make out balconies further up, surrounded by intricate wrought-iron railings.

Cal squinted at the house. "Well, la-di-da, how hoity-toity."

Edie turned and sighed at him. "She is, like, a demigoddess. What did you expect?"

"Whatever." He put Ghost in gear. "I just don't know why they have to flaunt it."

"If you had that much money, you'd probably want to flaunt it, too." She grinned.

He didn't respond.

When she'd received the letter the day before, her first thought had been that it was a trap—the Gloaming, trying to lure her out of the house, to an address where they could jump her. It had only taken a quick call to Astrid to confirm that the blue spider was, in fact, the lesser Norn's personal pet, and that it wouldn't have delivered a message for anyone else.

Still, she wasn't completely comfortable with the fact that Indriði would only meet with her alone. So, she'd come prepared: a hunting knife was hidden in her jacket and a bone-handled machete was sheathed at her hip, both borrowed from Mercy. Sure, she had no idea how to wield either of them, but how hard could it be? They would have to do until she learned how to use her own magic. Maybe she should get one of those runic staves.

Cal pulled around the corner and circled the block again. He stopped at the end of the street and parked the car in the only available space.

"I'll be here." He didn't look at her as she unbuckled and got out of the car. He slipped his new smartphone out of his pocket. "I've got Astrid on speed dial just in case."

"I'll text you when I'm done," Edie said warily, checking to make sure her weapons were in place. Despite the equipment, she didn't feel prepared.

She took a deep breath and turned, starting down the block. With her jacket pulled tightly closed, she could hide about half of the machete, but she still glanced around her as she approached the townhouse's front stoop, hoping that no one would look her way and decide she didn't belong in this part of the city. Fortunately, the street was largely empty, aside from a woman walking her dog on the opposite side and a runner who wasn't even using the sidewalk.

She could feel someone's gaze on her, though. As she approached the big front doors, she realized they were the eyes of the doorman she'd noticed earlier. He *looked* human, but Edie had long since learned to doubt her senses in that regard. He kept his eyes trained on her as she made her way up the front steps and stopped before him.

"Hi." She waved awkwardly and fumbled in her pocket for the Norn's note. She wasn't exactly sure how to address a doorman—it wasn't often she went to a place that had one. "My name's Edie. I'm here to see Indriði."

"Good for you." The doorman looked her over, his gaze slowing when he spotted the machete at her hip. "What makes you think I'm going to let you in?"

"Er, I have this note." She drew it from her pocket and smoothed it out before handing it over. "A giant blue spider gave it to me."

That definitely wasn't a sentence you said every day.

The doorman examined the note, eyes darting quickly as he read its contents. Edie had read it so many times that she could practically recite it word for word: *Dear Ms. Holloway. Please forgive my delayed communication. During that awful party, it came to my knowledge that you were looking for me. If you still wish to speak, I'm ready. Come to my home at 3 Olive Street, Alderdeen, and present this note to the guards. All the best, Indriði.*

Mr. Doorman still didn't look particularly thrilled to be dealing with Edie, but his brow smoothed. He nodded and handed the note back to her before wordlessly moving to the side and opening one of the doors.

A wave of cool, fragrant air greeted Edie as she stepped into the foyer. It was sweet and earthy, like flowers and cinnamon, and she couldn't help but feel a sense of calm wash over her as she entered. Unlike the classical exterior, the interior of the house was shockingly modern. Shining white floors, slate walls that glittered like real stone, an imperial staircase with steel balusters woven into the shapes of spiders' webs. In the center of it all, over a dozen silver pendant lamps, dripping with crystals, were arranged in the shape of a chandelier.

On the left side of the room was a sleek horseshoe desk, behind which sat two men wearing gray shirts and badges. One of them was clicking around a massive computer screen in front of him. Beside his keyboard was a black baseball cap with a "Security Officer" patch on the front. Behind them, an elevator with platinum doors stood between two long hallways.

The man behind the computer looked up at her expectantly as she approached the desk. Suspicion rolled off both guards in waves. Even though she knew she was supposed to be there, she suddenly felt like a trespasser.

She mumbled a greeting and slid Indriði's note across the desk. Both of the security guards seemed to be human, just like the doorman. She managed to make eye contact with the one she was standing in front of now, but there was no change, no telltale sign of a revenant or wight.

"What's this?" the guard behind the computer asked, like she'd handed him something worthless. His voice echoed off of the walls even at normal speaking volume.

"It's a note from Indriði." Edie tried not to let uncertainty creep into her voice. "The doorman already let me pass, so can I see her?"

The security guards exchanged glances, then the second one leaned forward and picked up a silver desk phone from its cradle, holding it between his ear and shoulder as he pressed a couple buttons. Edie looked around the foyer as he had a brief conversation with someone on the other line, wondering why all of this security was necessary.

"Okay, fine. She'll be here." The guard finished his call and set the phone back down, then looked up at Edie. "The lady's steward will be down to meet with you in a second. You can wait over there." He jerked his head in the direction of a white-cushioned bench next to the elevator, but never took his eyes from Edie or the machete at her hip.

"All right. Thanks." Thanks for nothing, more like. She was starting to think she'd never meet this woman. So far, she'd had to go through the doorman, security guards, and now a manservant was going to come escort her to the lady of the house? Was never moving a muscle part of being a weird rich person or part of being a demigoddess?

Edie took a seat on the bench and drew her cell phone out of her pocket. A notification from Satara was already waiting for her. Someone had made a group chat with her, Edie, and Cal—probably Satara herself, considering how useless Cal was with a smartphone.

[Satara Izem]: How's it going?

Edie couldn't help but smile. Despite their rocky beginnings, Satara and Edie had become friends. It was hard not to like someone who had put their life on the line for you, and Satara had turned out to be a lot more understanding of Edie's many failings once it was made clear that Edie didn't even *want* to be the Reacher. Edie was beginning to understand Satara more, too. Everyone kept trying to convince her that she had to be a fierce, fearless warrior, but there was so much more to her than that. She could be as vulnerable and uncertain and loving as anybody else.

It seemed to Edie that living with Astrid, fighting for her since she was sixteen, had been so intense—maybe so traumatic—that Satara tried to quash those feelings.

Did Astrid see that?

Edie doubted it. The valkyrie didn't strike her as cruel, only oblivious to the fragility of humans after having not been one for so long—if she ever had been. Edie had never actually gotten a straight answer from anyone on how valkyir were made. Still, it didn't change the facts.

Satara had also been brave enough to offer to be Edie's gym buddy, even though she hated being in public—which Edie could definitely relate to—so they had socially-awkward solidarity.

[Edith Holloway]: it's going... weird... I'm not dead yet but it is weird

[Cal Bonjovi]: WEird ho w,,

[Edith Holloway]: Did you seriously make your chatsapp name Cal Bonjovi?

[Cal Bonjovi]: it ask ed 4 a last nmame,.

[Satara Izem]: I can change it...
[Satara]: There.

[Cal]: duck you
[Cal]: duck
[Cal]: DUCK
[Cal]: lissen.

[Cal]: IF,,, bonvoji ask ed me 2 mary him i wolud

[Edie]: I'm sitting in the foyer right now... had to get past like 47 thousand people just to get to talk to Indriði's butler. I'll let you know how it all pans out

[Satara]: Good luck. Astrid and I can be there in a second if you need us. Cal, do you have a bead on E?

[Cal]: I nnow when edie so much, as has. To pee ,,,,, i got this
[Cal]: sttupid ducking fone

Apparently, he hadn't had the heart to tell Astrid and Satara that Edie's brain was temporarily completely closed off to him. Edie hoped it wouldn't be a problem.

Ding.

She quickly put her phone in her pocket, careful to keep the knife in her jacket concealed. When she looked back up, the platinum elevator doors slid open, revealing—

no one? Wait, no.

Her eyes darted downward. Just a very *short* someone.

CHAPTER FOUR

THE MAN in the elevator couldn't have been more than waist height to Edie, but he carried himself like a much taller individual. He was wide, stocky, and so muscular he looked like he could suplex Cal. His head was square, his brow and nose smashed in like a boxer's, but the neat black suit he was stuffed into suggested he wasn't at all interested in fighting.

Though he was humanoid, he was clearly not human: his impressive copper beard glinted very much like a penny in the bright foyer. His skin looked like polished silver nickel, dinged and scratched here and there like an old piece of machinery. The color and sheen of it shocked Edie for a moment.

He fixed her with flintlike eyes, his expression one of mild distaste. "Edith?"

It took her a moment to find her voice. After a pause, she stood. "That's me."

The man didn't hold out a hand to greet her, but he reached forward and stopped the elevator doors from closing, beckoning her closer. "I'm Roggvi, Indriði's steward. Come with me, if you please. She's expecting you upstairs."

Edie nodded and stepped into the elevator with him. Unlike the others, Roggvi didn't seem a bit worried about her machete—in fact, he didn't even seem to notice, looking rather bored as he pressed a button and let the doors slide shut.

Edie glued her gaze to the numbers counting up on the digital floor indicator, trying to distract herself from the awkward silence. She glanced at Roggvi. He was all dressed up. She was sure she looked like hell, despite having tried really hard to apply her makeup in a way that made her look less dead. Should she have worn something nicer to see Indriði, or were ripped jeans acceptable? Fuck. She'd been so focused on preparing for a crisis that she'd forgotten to make a good impression.

Oh, well. She was never battling in heels again—not after last time.

Finally, the elevator came to a stop and dinged pleasantly. The doors opened to reveal a long hallway, lit with natural sunlight coming in from floor-to-ceiling windows in the rooms to the left and right. The honeylocust trees in front of the street-facing windows blocked the harshest rays, so the light coming in was gentle, but bright enough for Edie to see comfortably.

Roggvi stepped out of the elevator and continued down the hallway unceremoniously. Edie followed, but slowed for a moment to look into the softly lit rooms. To the left was what looked like a lounge, with luxe white couches and chairs, a sleek bar with high stools, and a shimmering silver harp. To the right was a spacious study filled with bookshelves, a large glass desk with a wide-screen computer, and a couple of ergonomic kneeling chairs. On display between bookshelves were glass enclosures, the contents mostly obscured by thick white webs. She didn't even want to know what kinds of arachnids called those home.

Edie's gaze touched every piece of furniture in awe, taken aback by how *modern* everything was. She had imagined the Norn would live somewhere upscale, but she'd envisioned something more … *Lord of the Rings*? Rivendell, maybe? She had to admit, she was pretty intrigued to meet this person.

She picked up the pace and turned forward again, only to find that her guide had left her behind. For a short guy, he sure walked fast.

"Excuse me? Wait up," she called out, continuing to walk ahead though she had no idea where she was going. Hopefully, she could figure out her way around the mansion, or else he'd notice she had lagged behind and would come back to retrieve her.

Hopefully.

Her semi-confident stride stuttered to a halt as she reached the end of the hallway and realized that it split into another, longer hallway. Left, right, or straight?

"Hello? Sorry, I got behind..."

No answer. She listened hard, but she couldn't hear anyone walking or speaking nearby. Somewhere to the right, though, there was a distinct shuffling sound. It probably wasn't Roggvi—he'd have heard her if he was that close—but perhaps it was another staff member who'd be able to put her on the right path.

As she turned down the right-hand hall, she rested a hand on the hilt of Mercy's machete. This could just as well be some kind of trap. Who the hell walked that fast unless they were purposefully trying to lose someone? Edie gritted her teeth, every muscle tense as she continued down the hall. After ten feet or so, the hall forked again, and she stopped to listen. Right again.

Her pace was slow as she made her way down the hall. She had become completely turned around. There were no big windows illuminating this hall; it was almost as dark as if it were night. The shuffling had turned into a steady scratching, like someone was trying to scrape something off a surface.

A few feet ahead stood the only open door in this hallway, and Edie crept closer, listening for a while before saying "Hello?" again.

The scratching stopped, resumed softer and faster for a moment, then stopped again. An odd slinking sound followed, like something very heavy was being dragged across the floor. Before she could register what was happening, a hulking black shape had squeezed out into the hallway.

Edie's breath hitched. She took a step back, looking up.

Two enormous yellow eyes stared back, pupils dilating as they met

Edie's. A long, pink tongue darted out from the darkness, and a wave of steamy bile breath hit Edie as the creature exhaled.

She took another step back, coughing, trying to collect herself. "Wrong way," she finally choked out. "Wrong hall. Sorry."

The creature didn't seem to care. It slank forward, shaking the floor as it thumped a wide, clawed foot right in front of her. As it shifted, she could see scales glinting. Then a rumble deeper than anything she had ever felt—somehow both soft and soul-shaking—emitted from the creature as it began dragging itself toward her. The dim light caught a pointy black tail whipping behind it.

Edie didn't know exactly what she was looking at, but she wasn't about to stick around to find out. She took a gulp of air, turned tail, and sprinted back from where she'd come so fast that the soles of her combat boots squealed against the wood floors.

Behind her, the creature issued another wave of heat and a reptilian bark, and pursued.

The floor below her trembled as the creature tore after her. Breathing hard, Edie hazarded a glance behind her and saw that it had four powerful legs and a muscular chest like a pitbull. Its giant tail skimmed along after it, and its huge nostrils flared as they made eye contact again.

Edie faced forward again and focused on running.

Cal, Cal, Cal, Cal!

It had been a trap. If she could get to the elevator, though, maybe she could get downstairs, fight her way past the guards, and flee. She turned left, and hope blossomed in her chest as the elevator doors came into view.

But the hope was only momentary. The floor shuddered as the creature used all four of its legs to pounce. Enormous claws punctured her leather jacket and grazed the skin of her back as the thing toppled her over. She rolled forward, and the creature wheeled around with her before turning, rolling her over, and planting a foot on her chest.

She looked into its eyes, and it looked into hers. In the light pouring in from the windows, she could finally make sense of what it was. A dragon.

Cal! She mentally shrieked his name, but it was no use. Damn this stupid wall!

The dragon was pressing her into the floor so hard that it felt like one wrong move would either sink its claws into her or break a rib. She lay there, breathless for a moment. She expected to feel hot jaws close around her head at any moment, but the dragon seemed to hesitate. It ducked its head a little, looking almost uncertain.

There wasn't any time to analyze its actions—this was as good an opening as any. Edie slipped one hand down to her side and gripped the hilt of the machete. With a loud cry, she drew it from its sheath and slashed upward, pushing against the force of the dragon's paw. The blade connected with its underarm, and all at once, the enormous pressure on her chest was gone.

She sat up and rolled over, trying to ignore the pain radiating down her back as she slammed the elevator call button. Then she turned on her knees and watched as the dragon took a few steps back. It blinked its eyes —tiny compared to its huge head—and huffed in confusion before letting loose a pathetic yowl of pain. Yellowish blood pattered onto the wood floor. The dragon's nostrils flared as it sniffed at the wound, the wings tucked against its back fluttering.

After a moment, it reared its head around to look at Edie, pupils dilating. She clutched the machete tighter. *Come on, elevator!*

Unexpectedly, a woman's voice rang out. It was soft, but filled the hall, as if the speaker were standing right next to them: "Augustus! What do you think you're doing?"

The dragon's ears flattened against its head. It hunched a bit, hopping to one side and twisting into a U to look back down the hall. Loosing a little honk, it lowered its head further.

Edie leaned to one side, breathing hard, to see past it.

A short woman stood there, probably no more than an inch or two above five feet. She wore a houndstooth-patterned pencil dress, her fiery red hair close-cropped and slicked back with a streak of white peeking out at the front. Edie wasn't sure who she was looking at, but she sure was glad she'd arrived—as long as the woman wasn't going to change her mind and sic the dragon on her, anyway.

The woman barely looked at Edie as she beckoned the dragon closer with a stern look. "Exactly what are you doing, sir? What have I told you about chasing, Augustus? It scares humans."

The dragon ducked his head even lower, chin almost grazing the floor. He quirked one ear at the woman, sat on his haunches, and planted his front feet wider, exhaling hard. His thick tail slapped the floor in annoyance.

"Don't take that tone with me."

The woman stepped forward and grabbed the dragon's head with both hands—despite resistance on his end—lifting it so that their eyes were level. Edie had to wonder where this small woman found the strength to manhandle such a creature. His head alone—a boxy, canine shape ending in a lizard nose—was wider than her torso.

"That is *not* how we treat guests! And look, you made a mess of the floors. That was a *bad boy*."

Augustus recoiled when she said the words *bad boy* and sank lower to the floor, looking between Edie and the woman with sad, shiny puppy eyes. Edie relaxed a bit and stood slowly.

"Apologize," the woman commanded.

The dragon grunted at the floor stubbornly.

"Ugh." She shook her head, pointing down the hall, away from them. "Go see Percy, you naughty lizard."

Augustus glanced back at Edie one last time before huffing and thumping his way down the hall, back legs bowed and tail swishing back and forth. Under normal circumstances, the image of him grumpily shaking his giant ass would have been cute. As it was, Edie shivered, limbs numb and heart thundering.

The woman watched him until he disappeared around a corner. Then, she turned and looked at Edie, tilting her head. One corner of her maroon-painted lips quirked up as she took a few steps closer, offering a pale hand. "Sorry about him, hon. He just likes to play."

Edie exhaled incredulously, but accepted the woman's hand nonetheless. "Play? He nearly mauled me."

The woman shrugged and held Edie's hand for a moment before letting it go. "He's still a baby, and when you're that big, it's hard to play gently. In the wild, he'd be chasing his friends and tackling them just like he did to you. You can tell he wasn't trying to hurt you because he didn't poison his claws."

"Oh. I guess that's good news." Edie sheathed her machete, wincing as she felt a bit of blood trickle down her back. Thankfully—apparently—he hadn't been trying to kill her, and her leather jacket had taken the brunt of the damage, so she probably only had scratches. Still, they stung like fire.

She wriggled out of her jacket and held it up in front of her to assess the damage. A little whine issued from the back of her throat. The jacket had two ragged holes and two rips in the middle—he'd completely torn through the leather and most of the lining. *Should have worn a sweatshirt under this.* Now she was feeling rather chilly in her purple tank top. And she'd have to spend some nonexistent money on another jacket.

The redhead's eyes widened, and she sighed hard. "Oh, that little *griss.*" She reached out and touched the jacket, fingering the leather with a mournful expression. "I'll replace it, if you like."

"It's fine," Edie lied. She grimaced as she twisted an arm to wiggle her fingers under her tank top and brush the wounds there. "Sorry I, uh, hurt him."

"He'll be fine. His kind regenerate quickly. Did he hurt *you?* Can I get you something?" The woman stepped a little closer.

"It's okay. I can heal it." She'd been practicing healing herself with blood magic for the past couple months and was getting pretty good at it. She could staunch bleeding and close up nicks from kitchen knives in a couple of minutes now. The most bothersome thing about the scratches on her back was the pain—and the fact that her shirt was now spotted with blood.

The woman smiled a little. "Well done. You must be Edith, then."

"Yeah." Edie threw her jacket over one shoulder and smoothed herself out. "I'm here to see Indriði."

The woman laughed. "Open your eyes, babe, because here I am."

This was Indriði? Edie had expected someone with pointy ears and a gown, not a chic businesswoman. There was also the distinct lack of a crazy Icelandic accent. Edie nibbled on her lip. "It's good to, uh, finally meet you."

"It's good to finally meet you, too, Edie. Can I call you Edie?"

Edie exhaled. "Please." Glancing down the hall, she added, "Is that a *pet* dragon?"

Indriði turned and started toward where the dragon had disappeared, motioning for her guest to follow. "He's a drake. They're a much smaller class of dragon. He's technically an adolescent, but won't get too much bigger." The Norn looked at Edie as she caught up with her, quirking a red brow. "They make excellent guard animals. In theory. A well-trained drake will only listen to its master, but you saw how sassy he can be."

"I guess giant teeth and claws would make an intruder think twice about his life choices. And poison, apparently."

"Yep. He's a Venomgut, so his breed is known for their poison powers. They're also immune to mind-control, sleeping, and confusion spells. Useful, no?"

They reached the end of the hall, and Indriði led her around the corner, then took an immediate left. This hallway was shorter, with a pair of white double doors at the end. Edie felt like she had completed a trial and was finally being led to the center of the labyrinth. Hopefully, her luck would continue.

The Norn strode forward and opened both doors simultaneously.

CHAPTER FIVE

IT TOOK a moment for Edie's eyes to adjust to the much brighter room. It was a spacious two-story great room with floor-to-ceiling windows looking out over the city. The dark wood floors were polished to a shine. On one end was a beautiful dining table lined with high-back chairs, and on the other, a sleek electric fireplace sizzling with blue fire. In the middle sat a glass coffee table and two white armchairs facing each other. To their right as they entered, a staircase climbed up to a loft.

As Indriði led her to the armchairs, Edie craned her neck to see another, more richly furnished living area.

Indriði settled into her chair. "Augustus is very smart, but he would rather chew on furniture and play than patrol the halls for intruders. Maybe I spoil him too much. There's also the fact that he's going to want to try his wings soon. He didn't come with them clipped."

As soon as she said the drake's name, a rustling, slinking noise came from the loft. Edie watched with a quickening pulse as Augustus himself eyed her from the overlook, then minced down the stairs. In the bright light, his black scales looked iridescent—emerald, gold, pink. He thumped closer, head down, tail curled close to his body as he sniffed the air around her.

Edie stood stone still, glancing to Indriði. "What do I do?"

The Norn waved a hand. "Ignore him. He'll get used to you. He's just being a touchy little prat."

It wasn't quite as easy as ignoring a temperamental cat or a nasty dog, though, was it? Nonetheless, Edie trusted that Indriði knew what she was talking about—for the moment—and eased into the seat opposite her.

Augustus slank behind Indriði's chair and horseshoed around it, fixing Edie with an unwavering stare. Even as he craned his neck to lick his wound, he glared at her.

Great. Leave it to her to get off on the wrong foot with a poisonous drake.

"I hope Roggvi didn't give you any trouble, besides leaving you behind." Indriði crossed her legs and relaxed into her seat. "He's very protective of me."

"It's … fine, I guess. It's just— I lagged behind for a second and he was gone all of a sudden." Edie fingered the ruined leather of her jacket and tried to figure out how to word her next question politely. "What exactly is he? Roggvi. I'm kind of new to all this."

The Norn smiled and reached out to stroke the top of Augustus's head slowly. "He's a dvergr—sorry, a dwarf. He's been my steward for … gods, ages now. Over three hundred years. I can't say he was pleased when I decided to join civilization. Dwarves aren't known for their outgoing personalities."

"Is he made of metal?"

Indriði nodded. "Convenient, right? Long-lasting and durable." She laughed, then waved a hand. "You want something to drink? Tea, coffee?"

"Just water," Edie replied. Though her throat was dry as hell, she wasn't sure if she would actually risk drinking anything she was offered. Indriði *had* saved her from the drake, and she did exude a calming energy, but better safe than sorry.

Indriði plucked a little bell from the glass coffee table and rang it. A moment later, a small door next to the dining area opened and a silver trolley rolled out, seemingly of its own accord. It stopped right beside

Edie, and after a moment, a familiar creature scuttled out from behind it: the blue spider.

"Thank you, Percy." The Norn grinned and gestured to the spider. "Edie, you've met Percy."

The spider looked up at her with sparkly eyes, rubbing its fangs.

"Uh, yeah, I have." Edie shifted uncomfortably, but still smiled at the spider. He seemed nice. It wasn't his fault he was scary. "Hi again."

"As you can see," Indriði said, patting Augustus before standing and going to the trolley, "I'm a bit of an animal lover. Spiders in particular. They're *so* misunderstood. They're just weavers trying to survive in this world like everyone else—like Norns." She held up a crystal water jug as she said it, then poured Edie a glass and handed it to her.

Edie accepted it, trying to keep smiling politely. "Yeah, they're pretty."

The room was quiet for a while. Edie had been watching closely when Indriði poured the drink and hadn't noticed anything suspicious, so she hazarded a little sip. It was easier to use bloodmending when she was hydrated and well-rested. She could try for at least one of those things.

Eventually, Indriði finished fixing her tea and went to sit in her chair again. Percy left the trolley where it was, disappearing behind the ever-staring Augustus, then reappearing on the drake's back. Now they were *both* staring.

"But anyway," the Norn said, adjusting the silver tea strainer over her cup, "I know you didn't come here to chat about spiders and drakes. You must have wanted me for something important, considering the lengths to which you went to contact me."

Edie grimaced, thinking about the party. In some ways, it was good that she had been there to witness Sárr's takeover. On the other hand, they had walked right into a trap that Astrid had been so sure the Gloaming couldn't possibly set. How had Zaedicus known they were looking for Indriði, or even that they would show up?

That thought still haunted Edie, and she knew it must bother the others, too. Was someone watching them, or was it more unthinkable than that? Was one of them a mole?

She cleared her throat. "Yeah, well, we didn't know it would turn out to be such a big deal. All I wanted was to talk to you."

Indriði took a sip of her tea and opened a hand. "Here I am. And I can finally ask what exactly you wanted me for."

Now came the difficult part. She took a deep breath, knotted her fingers in her ruined jacket, and said, "We ... I wanted to ask you if you would join the Reach."

If the Norn was fazed by this, her expression didn't give anything away. Her tone was less cordial, though. "Of course you do. You really are your father's daughter."

Edie grimaced. "I know it's a lot to ask, but we need you. You saw what happened. The Aurora and the Gloaming are going to start fighting, and they're going to sweep a lot of innocent people up in it. We've got to protect them. Or stop it."

"Who is *we?*" the Norn asked flatly.

Edie got the feeling she already knew the answer. "Listen..." She floundered for something professional, something diplomatic and profound to say, but gave up. There was no sense in dancing around the truth when she didn't know the dance steps. "I know why you hate Astrid."

Indriði was quiet, staring.

"I'm not going to try and convince you to like her. The fact is, you don't have to like her to help us, and we *need* help." She paused. "I get why she wants to bring the Reach back so much. Attuned people's options shouldn't be between genocide and complete domination and slavery. And now the New Gloaming are hurting unattuned people, too. They've murdered a bunch of people, and caused riots and chaos for no good reason."

"Do you really think a handful of Reach are going to make the difference?"

"No ... but we can get more people. We can start, with your help."

Indriði smiled thinly. "You say *we* so confidently, but do you even know who *we* is?"

Edie opened her mouth, then closed it again, unsure of what to say. What did she mean by that?

The Norn took another sip of her tea before leaning forward and placing it on the corner of the coffee table. She was silent for a few moments, too, before she clasped her hands and looked up at Edie. "Have you ever had your runes read, hon?"

"Uh ... I had my palm read by a drag queen once."

Indriði chuckled and snapped her fingers, and a bag appeared in her hand. Made of deep navy silk and studded with tiny white stones, it looked like the night sky. She smiled slyly at Edie. "Cool, huh?"

Edie laughed nervously.

The Norn shook the bag, and something inside rattled. "First step of runecasting: you have to ask the runes a question. I'm sure you have more of those than you know what to do with. You can ask anything you want, and we'll see if they answer."

She was right about Edie's number of questions. In fact, Edie had so many that she wasn't really sure which to start with. Honestly, some of her most pressing questions were also the most broad.

As if she had read her thoughts, Indriði prompted, "You can ask anything, from the most obscure questions to the most specific."

Edie hesitated for a moment before crossing her legs uncomfortably, looking at the bag in the Norn's hands. "Okay ... hi, I guess, runes?" She paused. "What's, uh ... what's my general situation looking like?"

Indriði smiled and handed the bag to Edie. "Shake them up, then dump them out."

Edie shook them until the Norn looked satisfied. Then she loosened the drawstring at the top of the bag and emptied it onto the coffee table.

Royal purple tiles cascaded onto the glass surface, clinking. They were roughly oblong, etched with angular characters that Edie, through the little bit of studying she'd done since spring, recognized as the Elder

Futhark, the oldest runic alphabet. The letters, painted gold, glittered as they came to rest.

The Norn snapped again, and the tiles began moving by themselves. They scraped against the glass as some of them arranged themselves in a three-by-three square in front of Edie with dizzying speed. Once they came to a stop, Indriði smiled and brushed the other runes off to the side. "And here's your answer. You want me to tell you what it means?"

Edie nodded silently.

"This row represents your past." Indriði pointed to the row of tiles closest to Edie, indicating the first tile in the row. The character sort of looked like a cup on its side. "This rune, perthro, represents your hidden past. It tells me there was a secret in your past, maybe secret even to you. Perhaps coming into a magical power?"

Edie chewed her bottom lip. "My dad never told me about what I— what *we* were. He didn't tell me anything about the world."

The Norn cocked a brow and nodded. "And there might still be something hidden from you. Who knows?"

Edie didn't like that thought.

"This one"—she pointed to the next rune—"represents your general past, what happened to you. It's laguz, but it's inverted, see? *Merkstave,* which means the original meaning of the rune is reversed."

"Okay..."

"This one is telling me about a time of confusion and sadness. You made bad decisions. You were afraid, going around in circles, trying to avoid addressing things that hurt too much. I see you sick, withering away."

Edie frowned. When her dad had died, it felt like the whole world had collapsed. Like there was no meaning to any of it.

Indriði pointed to the final rune. "This is ingwaz, the beginning and end."

Edie reached for her wrist, touching the ingwaz tattooed there.

"This tile represents your current feelings about the past. Ingwaz has no merkstave, so there's kind of..." The Norn made a vague gesture. "A duality. It tells me, on one hand, you feel a sort of peace, knowing the truth about yourself and your father, like an *a-ha* moment where questions you didn't even know you had were answered. But on the other, there was labor, sacrifice. You've had to give up a lot because of what happened, including your old life ... or maybe the way you used to see your dad."

Damn, a little on the nose, runes. Edie sighed and rubbed her tattoo.

They moved on to the middle row of tiles, and Indriði pointed to the first one. But she didn't say anything—she was silent, and eventually creased her brow as if she didn't quite understand what she was seeing.

"Is something wrong?" Edie asked quietly.

"This row," the Norn said, "represents the present. This tile symbolizes hidden forces at work now."

"Okay..." She peered at it. Maybe she had a secret admirer who would start sending her money and flowers any day now. The money, at least, would be nice.

"Thurisaz. It's merkstave."

Oh. Bad, then.

"It's telling me that there's danger—hidden danger. You're defenseless somehow, in a way you've yet to realize." Indriði squinted at the rune. "You're being betrayed, and whoever is betraying you knows what they're doing. They're doing it to hurt you."

Edie felt her face go numb. God forbid she was right about how Zaedicus had gotten his info. "Could it mean the Gloaming?"

"No, this is someone you've yet to discover is evil. They're taking you for a ride, Edie, and they enjoy dominating you."

Edie gripped her ruined jacket tighter and said nothing. Could one of her friends really be lying to her? Surely the runes were up for interpretation, and they could mean something else. Although ... Indriði was a Norn, and supposed to be more in tune with Fate than anyone else. "What else?"

Indriði watched her for a moment before moving onto the next rune. Again, she paused. "This one is merkstave ehwaz. It's not necessarily bad.

It's mostly used to confirm the runes around it," she said carefully. "Considering the rune before it, it probably means contention. Mistrust. Betrayal."

"Okay, what's the next one?" Edie pressed, desperate to hear some good news. The palm-reading drag queen had told her how old she'd live to be and how many kids she'd have, not any of this heavy shit.

"The next one represents your attitude toward present events, and it's merkstave, too, I'm afraid." Indriði frowned and clasped her hands, eyeing the last tile in the row. "Berkana. It says you're having domestic problems, anxiety about the people close to you. You feel like you're losing control." She paused, then added, "It can also indicate that you're lying to yourself."

Edie ran a hand through her hair and took another tiny sip of water. "I don't suppose the future is any brighter."

Indriði moved on to the top row. "The first is the hidden forces that will act in your future. The rune, isaz, tells me that you're going to have a hidden challenge in your future. It's also saying that betrayal, illusion, and deceit will follow you. There's going to be some sort of ambush, or a plot against you. Someone sly and cunning will trick you."

Wow. She really couldn't catch a break, could she?

As Indriði continued, she seemed to become increasingly disturbed by what she saw. "This, hagalaz, represents what you will see in the future. It can't be reversed, so it's not merkstave—"

Edie's shoulders sank with relief.

"—but it still symbolizes crisis."

"Fuck me!"

"Specifically, crises involving nature. Like … a natural disaster. It could also symbolize chaos in general. Maybe both. Catastrophe, pain, suffering, and loss."

"I assume the next one is my … what, reaction to the catastrophe? What I'll do?"

"Yes—" Indriði cut off as she moved onto the next tile, and glared at it. "What the hell?"

Edie looked, too, and saw that it was blank—a smooth tile with no rune.

"Why the hell is this here? I *never* use a blank tile." The Norn plucked it off the table like she was picking up a particularly gross piece of rotten food and flicked it across the room.

Edie frowned, looking down at the other tiles. "What does the blank one mean?"

"'Fate will decide.' Of course Fate will decide. It's garbage. Useless. I was sure this set didn't even have one."

Edie leaned back in her chair, hugging herself around the middle. She had the feeling that Indriði had been trying to comfort her with the runecasting, but it had only made her infinitely more upset. Apparently, there was nothing but betrayal in her past, present, and future.

The Norn rose from where she was sitting and went to Edie, crouching next to her seat and taking her hand. Augustus gurgled in protest, but she ignored him. "Listen, honey … you seem like a nice girl. But you're confused, and you're going through a lot of change. Some people are like leeches. They can sense that you need guidance or you're vulnerable, and they take advantage of that."

Edie closed her eyes and thought of all the people who had guided her the past couple months. Astrid. Cal. She frowned, her heart sinking as she remembered something that had been bothering her. She opened her eyes. "My friend Cal has been acting really weird lately. Like … guilty and shifty."

Indriði raised a brow. "Cal?"

"My dad's revenant. He ran away when my dad died, but he came back when I got my powers because he thought he'd have to kill me. He's not a huge fan of hellerunan." When Indriði only stared at her, she continued. "He's the one who took me to meet Astrid in the first place. He thought she'd help me figure out my powers, but she just wanted me to do work for the Reach."

The Norn was quiet for so long that Edie wondered if she'd said something wrong. Then she squeezed Edie's hand and said, "Let me get this straight. A revenant showed up at your door, attempting to kill you. He hated your father, he hates hellerunan, he dropped you into the lap of a spirit of death ... and you trust this person?"

Edie was still. She had never considered that Cal might not be trustworthy. Sure, he'd shown up with the intention of killing her, but he'd saved her ass a ton of times since then. "No, he hates the Gloaming. He would never." She shook her head hard, like that might get the idea out of it.

"He doesn't have to be Gloaming to betray you," Indriði scoffed. "You think the Gloaming and Aurora are the only ones who have hurt people? The only ones who have condoned slavery and war? The Reach isn't the bastion of peace and civility Astrid would like you to believe. Especially not while she's in it."

"But Astrid wants me to be the Reacher. I could make it better."

The Norn huffed and shook her head. "Edie, Astrid and I were very close, for many, many years. I know her better than anyone. Trust me when I tell you this: She doesn't want a leader. She wants a scapegoat."

CHAPTER SIX

Marius wrenched open the top drawer of his dresser and yanked the towel from his waist, balling it up and throwing it at a nearby chair. He tossed things aside carelessly as he searched for his warmest underclothes, then he balled those up, too, and pitched them at his bed.

At least he wasn't feeling as fatigued as he had for the first month after Zaedicus's party. He had been in the midst of battle before, but to face someone like Sárr one on one had been harrowing. In the end, he'd won, but the cost to himself had been great. He'd been almost as injured as his opponent, and had been confined to his bed for weeks after. Not that he had been in much of a condition to fight or train anyway. Unleashing his aura of light didn't ordinarily take so much out of him, but then again, nothing about that night had been ordinary.

His father had been displeased to say the least. When Marius had finally come to, Radiant Eirik had been right there, watching over him. For the first couple of days, Marius thought maybe he'd gotten away with it. His father seemed so genuinely frightened at his condition that he hadn't brought up the party; he simply sat with him, prayed with him, and instructed him to rest. But that hadn't lasted long. Once Marius could stand up and move around more properly, he'd gotten the lecture of a lifetime.

Marius gritted his teeth against the thought and tugged on a shirt, ignoring the unpleasant feeling of linen clinging to wet skin. Grabbing a comb and the gel he used to slick his curly hair out of his face, he focused on the reflection in the mirror before him. He'd saved people—just the wrong people. And worse, he couldn't stop wondering if they were okay.

Especially Edie.

He'd been having dreams about her. They never seemed to happen at night. Since he'd been laid up in bed, he had gotten used to waking later than usual and skipping first light prayers. The dreams only came in the early morning, when the sun was just filtering into his bedroom and he was beginning to stir. He swore he felt someone in bed with him, warm, barely touching him across the mattress. When he reached for her, the dream would become hazy, only to come back in full force an instant later. She'd turn and smile, her stormy eyes sleepy little crescents.

She didn't quite look like herself, an imperfect memory. Nonetheless, absolute contentment enveloped him every time. When he pulled her close, there was nothing but peace.

The feeling made it all the more painful when someone inevitably came in to wake him. For the past few weeks, he had made a concerted effort to get up before dawn to avoid such dreams. At first, it had been a relief to avoid them … but sometimes, he found himself longing for that feeling again.

Marius pulled on his breeches and boots, putting *her* out of his mind and instead turning his thoughts to his mission for today, the first his father had allowed him to go on since the party. Ynga's testament to Marius's behavior and her careful extraction from the battle had pleased the Radiant, and he'd nominated her as a candidate for Tyr's Rite shortly after their return to the temple.

Since the New Gloaming's Watchers had begun parading openly around the city, she had been deployed often, and had even successfully commanded a small squad of adherents quelling riots and raiding Gloaming hideouts. Those things were impressive, but today, her real proving would begin. Under Marius's supervision, they would see if she really was cut out to be a vivid.

Exactly what her trial was would be a mystery to both of them until they met with his father. Marius crossed the room to his armor rack and slipped into his arming doublet. Most of the vivids' gear was modified in some way to make it easier to put on with one hand, and he'd had almost three years to practice. He fastened it closed without missing a beat and moved on to his greaves.

Even with the modified gear, without help, donning his heavier armor was a long process, and he might not get the right fit. He stepped into the hall for a moment and flagged down one of the pages running back and forth in the dormitory corridors. Marius and the boy worked in silence as they secured his breastplate and pauldron, and finally, the wolf's head vambrace. He studied its snarling mouth, staring at it for so long he almost forgot to dismiss the boy.

By the time he was dressed, it was half past seven. He was supposed to be standing in front of his father *now*. Hopefully, showing up late wouldn't result in more punishment. The last thing he wanted was to be sent to the Golden Crypt again and forced to polish Radiant Ellander's armor, or the Lance of Hidden Stars, or the Puretongue's stupid dagger of truth, which always left him with cuts all over his fingers, without fail.

From his bedpost, he grabbed the cloak he'd worn to the party, the one with the sunburst clasps. He'd become fond of it. If he held it close enough, he swore it still had the lingering smell of—

Marius shook his head. He threw the cloak over his shoulders, locked his door, and hurried across the grounds toward the pyre of translocation that the Radiant had ordered built the night before.

His still-wet hair frosted a bit as he stepped out into the early morning. Winter rarely touched the temple grounds, but it had been so unseasonably cold lately that Marius was starting to wonder if something was wrong. His father hadn't acknowledged it, so it was probably nothing, but...

Marius slowed as he walked along the dormitory veranda. A stone mural there depicted Tyr with his right hand in Fenrir's mouth, a resigned look on his bearded face. Marius's heart clenched for a moment, remembering Sárr's wolf companions. There was little doubt that they were Hati and Sköll, sons of Fenrir. Though Sárr hadn't revealed any plan beyond dominating the Gloaming, anything involving the devourers of the sun and moon had to be catastrophic.

The New Gloaming was taking over, changing the landscape of their centuries-old conflict—but the Aurora hadn't adapted. They were only meeting the Gloaming, inconveniencing them, not pursuing them. And despite the clear threat Sárr posed, Edie Holloway remained their primary objective.

Marius was alarmed, but he couldn't say he was surprised. For as long as Marius could remember, Radiant Eirik had had a gift for predicting the future. It was a gift from the dís—a spirit of Fate, usually a lesser Norn—that had presided over his birth. Every newborn was attached to a spirit of Fate who led them through the weave and weft of their life, and they often gifted them with aptitude for certain things. Eirik's dís had been especially generous.

Because of this, Radiant Eirik often worked at problems from angles no one else could understand. Maybe he'd seen a near future where the hellerune joined the New Gloaming and turned the tides, or maybe she was simply more dangerous than any of them realized.

Marius just wished Eirik would share his plans with others—with his son, at the very least. He could *help*. Eirik didn't have to do it all alone, but he certainly seemed to think he did.

When Marius finally reached the temple grounds courtyard, he followed the stone path to the pyre. The structure that held the raging bonfire was a twenty-foot spherical frame of scorched steel, shaped to depict a scene of warriors with banners and swords kneeling under the sun. The base on which the sphere sat was a massive, ancient tree stump, and a short stairway upward disappeared into a break between metal warriors—a sort of doorway leading directly into the fire.

Standing a few feet in front of the first step were Ynga and his father. As far as Marius could see, they were the only three people in the courtyard.

"My apologies," he said simply as he hurried to Ynga's side, keeping his head bowed. He was only a few minutes late, but he was sure the Radiant had noticed. His father always noticed things like that, even if he didn't say anything.

Eirik was quiet for a moment, looking him over. Then, as though nothing had happened, he crossed his arms behind his back and looked at Ynga. "Adherent, do you accept Vivid Marius as your escort during your proving?"

"I do," Ynga said, though she didn't even look at Marius. He'd had such hopes for their friendship, but she hadn't said a word to him in the past couple months. Everything he knew about her progress was from his father, or else overheard from other adherents and vivids.

"Very well." The Radiant nodded and gestured between them. "You will be taking the pyre of translocation to a heimdyrr in the White Mountains, nearly 200 miles north of here."

Ynga tilted her head. "A door to one of the other Worlds? I've never been anywhere but Midgard." Her tone was reserved, but Marius could see a glint of excitement in her eyes.

"Few adherents have ever left Midgard, but a vivid must be prepared to answer Tyr's call to any of the other eight Worlds. Some humans don't acclimate well to the journey through the heimdyrr." The Radiant smiled. "So, you see, the going through is a test in itself. Marius journeyed to another World for his proving, too."

Ynga turned her head and asked, "Where?" The first word she'd said to him in months.

"I went to a forest in Vanaheim," he said. "I killed a huge, mad boar who was ruining a landvættr's garden. She made me a drinking horn from his tusk." He patted his hip, where the horn hung from his belt.

"You will be going to Jotunheim, land of the giants."

The Radiant produced two leather satchels that Marius hadn't noticed before and handed one to each of them. Marius immediately slung his onto his back, but Ynga opened hers and began to sift through its contents.

"There is a troll there, residing in a network of caves near where you'll enter the realm. He stole an artifact from a runepriest during a pilgrimage—a prophetic mirror that he blessed in Mimir's Well. You are to destroy the troll and retrieve the mirror." Eirik pointed to their packs. "You'll find everything you need for the journey in there."

He turned away from them and withdrew a small pouch from his armor, then took a pinch of its contents and threw it in the fire. Though Marius couldn't see what it was, he'd translocated many times before. The fire would only take you where you wanted to go if you offered it something from the land around your target destination, usually a certain plant. The Aurora had a large greenhouse filled exclusively with materials for translocation, carefully potted and tended by botanists.

The fire within the sphere flared up for a moment, the blessed flames reacting with the material. If Marius shifted and squinted just right, he could almost see a gray, rainy scene on the other side of the fire—not at all like the crisp morning in the courtyard.

The Radiant turned back to them. "You step through first, Adherent, and Vivid Marius will follow you shortly."

Ynga slung her satchel across her chest and pulled her cloak tighter, then stepped up to the first step of the pyre stairs. She glanced back at Eirik and Marius for a moment before ascending. Marius could sense her hesitation, and he couldn't say he blamed her. He still remembered using the pyre for the first time. The flames were as sweltering as any other fire until the second you stepped into them. It was still a bit disconcerting.

The adherent took a deep breath before hurrying through. Her form disappeared into the flames, then was gone.

Marius stepped up to the stairs without hesitation, ready to follow her. The moment he'd been feeling better, he had gotten back to combat practice, but the real thing was so much different, and he ached to *do* something. However, before he could climb the first step, a gentle touch on his forearm stopped him.

He turned toward his father with a questioning gaze. The look on Eirik's face was unusual, almost pained. Concerned. Apprehensive. But Marius had known his father long enough to know nothing scared him.

"Marius," he said, "are you sure you're feeling up to this? I can always send another vivid."

Marius frowned, resisting the urge to jerk his arm away. "I can do it, Your Grace."

"Perhaps, but are you feeling up to it? Will you be okay if something goes wrong, if you start to feel weak?"

After all this, his father still doubted him. Marius's chest ached deeply, and he couldn't look at his father's face anymore. After everything, after proving time and time again that he was an accomplished vivid, his father still thought of him as a child. Nothing he did would ever be good enough, would it?

"Marius, please. You worry me." Eirik squeezed his arm gently. "I can't lose you."

"Don't worry. I'm fine."

His father studied him for a long moment. Then, he released Marius's arm and eased back. "Very well. Go to your task, then."

Without saying anything else, Marius turned back to the pyre and climbed the stairs. As he passed through the fire, he thought he heard his father whisper a prayer.

CHAPTER SEVEN

MID-MORNING LIGHT FILTERED through the windows of the cozy apartment above Harbinger Trinket & Tome, the scent of a newly lit vanilla candle and fresh laundry wafting through the living room. Curled up on her couch, book in hand, Satara listened to the quiet noise coming from the street and the nearby harbor.

It was a modest apartment with small rooms, but it was private, clean, and quiet. Most importantly, it was all hers—the only one in the building besides Astrid's, which was on the first floor. The living room was decorated simply, with a comfy couch and overstuffed armchair, a television on the far wall, and some shelves and side tables for plants and knickknacks. A handful of decent paintings hung on the wall at intervals, a testament to one of Satara's long-time hobbies.

A few weeks ago, Edie had come for a visit and expressed surprise that a shieldmaiden lived so normally. Satara thought that was silly. Just because Astrid was old-fashioned didn't mean they were both completely cut off from the world. Satara might not have any social media, but she had a cell phone; at home, she watched movies and some television. And while Shipshaven was small, there was still a library, an ice cream stand

and diner, a hairdresser, a comic book store, and plenty of shops owned by craftsmen and artists.

Of course, even though Satara had lived here for a decade, she still preferred to socialize as little as possible. It had been like that since she was a child, well before she'd come here. She was much more interested in scouring the library for something good to read, whether it be history or adventure or simply a good romance.

The warriors her parents had expected her to train with bored her. She much preferred the warriors who lived within the pages of her favorite novels. She had the skill to be a shieldmaiden, but not the passion. Her mother and father's twin vocations, death priestess and undertaker, had always appealed more to her—but after what had happened with Darras, she'd had little choice but to follow the path her family preferred.

Darras. She pushed him out of her mind quickly and tried to focus on her book.

Aevana turned with a small gasp as she heard someone enter the library, but her view of the doors was obscured by the tall, ornate bookshelves. Who could it be, she wondered? No one but her was supposed to be in the reliquary tower at present. Her master would be furious if he found out someone had gotten in on her watch. She would have to scare them away.

The tome-keeper lifted the hem of her robe—rendered sheer from the rain she'd run through on her way to the tower—and started toward the end of the aisle to confront the interloper.

She halted abruptly when he stepped around the corner instead, his frame filling the space between the shelves almost completely. He stared her down, cobalt eyes as frigid as the grave as they searched her face. His countenance—bluish and gaunt, yet somehow impossibly, beautifully preserved—struck Aevana's heart with an emotion she could not begin to describe.

Satara winced as she realized she had bitten her thumbnail to the quick, the pain pulling her out of her story. She had thought reading something would calm her nerves or at least distract her from her current anxiety, but no such luck.

Edie had called yesterday to tell Satara and Astrid that Indriði had finally contacted her for a meeting. Valkyrie and shieldmaiden were now on standby should something go wrong. Satara had been texting Edie every so often, checking up. Though Astrid had assured her everything would be fine, she couldn't shake the feeling that something would go wrong.

Her eyes scanned the page, but she didn't retain any of the words. She set her book down for a moment to send a quick text to Edie, asking her how it was going. Then, she set her cell phone down, trying to put it out of her mind.

Aevana had traveled so far to separate herself from him. There was no use being close to a man she could never have; the pain was unbearable. That was why she had come to the Court of Stars in the first place. And now he was here. Against impossible odds, he had come for her. Why?

"Commander Coldheart," she finally breathed. Beneath her wet robe, her whole body shivered, and she could feel her nipples harden as his freezing aura caressed her skin.

Coldheart's eyes fell down her body, and her blood heated at the thought of what might be visible to him. The proper thing to do would be to cover herself as best she could ... but she could not bring herself to do it.

She kept her eyes locked with his. "You're not supposed to be here."

He rasped, "I know," and swiftly closed the gap between them.

Satara's cell phone buzzed on the coffee table in front of her, and she almost jumped. Of course Edie would answer right when Commander Coldheart was about to forsake his deathless army for the woman he loved (surely he and Aevana had to end up together).

She picked the phone up again, and after assuring that Edie was okay and wishing her luck, dropped it into her pocket. As she was about to go back to her book, however, she felt a slight pull. Somewhere downstairs, Astrid needed her for something. Her connection with Astrid was of a different nature than Cal and Edie's—and it probably wasn't as strong—but Satara's instincts hadn't steered her wrong yet.

She slipped a bookmark into her novel, set it down, and headed out of the apartment. After descending a couple of flights of stairs and opening the old wooden door, she stepped into the shop.

Astrid was near the front. Her face and posture were rigid with stress, but she was busying her hands setting up a display of candles she'd poured herself a few days previous. A salesgirl was nearby, ringing up a pair of customers.

When Satara approached, Astrid looked up. "Ah, hello."

"You needed me?" the shieldmaiden asked, smoothing out her shirt.

Nodding, Astrid straightened and waited for the two customers to leave before explaining. "I need to take care of something in town. Can you stay by the phone in case Edie calls?"

Satara suppressed a sigh. "All right."

She had long given up trying to convince Astrid about cell phones; the valkyrie often forgot Satara even had one. Satara herself was no obsessive lover of modern technology, but it was silly to pretend that it didn't have its uses. Astrid was just that stubborn.

"Are you sure it's safe?" Satara asked after a pause. It was far from the first time she'd asked. The answer was the same every time, but she couldn't shake her anxiety.

"The worst Indriði can do is say no." Astrid walked to the sales counter and shouldered a leather bag that had been sitting off to the side. She turned, saw Satara's uncertain look, and returned with an earnest one of her own. "I promise you, there's no danger. There is even a chance she will say yes. Her anger toward me must have subsided by now, at least a little."

Something was wrong, though. Satara could see it in the way Astrid fiddled with the rings on her fingers, how she kept pushing her hair back. Stress created lines in her face. Then again, Satara had seen her stressed many times before, and it was never like this. Something strange was going on.

She didn't say anything, however. She watched through the shop's gritty windows as Astrid left, then drew her phone from her pocket to check on Edie. No update from her or Cal. Gods willing, that was a good sign.

"Satara?" said a soft voice from beside her. When she looked up, the salesgirl was looking at her from over a huge stack of art prints. "I'm sorry—do you mind helping me with stock? Jonne called out with a cold today, so I'm alone."

"Sure," Satara agreed after a moment's consideration. She put her phone back in her pocket, grabbed a notepad and pencil from behind the sales counter, and got to work.

She worked in silence for a while. The salesgirl didn't attempt to make small talk, for which Satara was grateful. Some people assumed that Satara was quiet because she was unfriendly or aloof, but that wasn't true. She didn't think she was better than anyone else, but she certainly wondered why she wasn't allowed to be shy or private without being hassled.

She'd been working for about half an hour when she went into the back room to look for a box of items that needed restocking. As she lingered next to the door of Astrid's living quarters, she swore she heard movement on the other side.

She stopped dead to listen. The sound was subtle, but ... yes, that was definitely shuffling. Dread filled her chest. Someone was trying to keep quiet in there, and they would have succeeded if she hadn't caught the noise at the right second.

Without another moment's pause, she lifted the latch and threw the door open to confront the intruder.

Satara stopped inside the doorway, taking in the scene before her.

A tall, willowy figure stood by the far wall, looking over its—his?—

shoulder at her. The intruder was dressed head to toe in battered black leather with several scarves of black gauze wound around his neck and arms, and a bulging cloth bag was slung across his chest. It took a half-second longer for Satara to realize the thief was poised to grab Astrid's shield and spear.

Satara cried out and ran forward, but before she could reach him, the thief had started for the nearest window. She followed him closely, dodging to the side at the last second and just barely catching one of his scarves.

The thief was jerked back for a second as the scarf tore, but his reflexes were astonishingly quick. Seemingly without having to think of it, he seized a chair from the nearby table and turned, shoving it into Satara's chest.

The shieldmaiden staggered back, breath knocked out of her for a moment. She recovered quickly, though, and grabbed the legs of the chair, which the thief still held in his gloved hands.

For a moment, Satara and the thief were locked, both straining against the chair. He wore a hood and a cowl that covered the lower part of his face, but a pair of slightly-too-large, narrowed beryl eyes glared out at Satara. A low, even voice hissed from behind the cowl: "You should never have pledged your loyalty to Astrid."

Satara was so taken off-guard by the comment that she eased her hold on the chair—only slightly, but enough to break the deadlock. The thief shoved the chair into Satara's chest again, then dropped it, darting away. He threw open the window and slipped out before she could stop him.

Adrenaline still coursed through Satara's system as she picked herself up. She could try to go after him, but he had already proven to be a lot faster than her, never mind his head start. Trying to control her breathing, she glanced around the room to make sure everything was in place. Her heart stuttered as she realized that the hall door and the door to Astrid's room were both open.

She rushed into the bedroom and nearly gasped at the sight of it. Everything was upturned, all the drawers and the wardrobe flung open, their contents strewn across the room. It looked like a cyclone had swept through.

Hastily, she crossed the room, locked the bedroom window, and drew the curtains. She moved through and did the same for every other window, too. If the thief had set off any of the shop's wards, Astrid was probably already on her way back. Until then, Satara had to make sure the intruder didn't come back.

As she hurried into the shop, the door swung open with a chime, and Astrid stepped through. A look of confusion twisted her face, but when she saw Satara's expression, it turned to anger. They didn't exchange a word as the valkyrie hurried into her rooms, shieldmaiden at her heels.

When they reached her bedroom, Astrid stood in the doorway for a few moments, scanning the damage. Then, she began to rifle through the mess, probably trying to determine what had been stolen. As she did, she asked, "What exactly happened?"

"I was helping Keir with stock, and I came into the back room to get something." Satara glanced behind her, into the hearth room, as she recalled the scene. "There was a person dressed all in leather. He—I think it was a he—was reaching for your spear, but I interrupted him before he could take it, and he disappeared out that window."

"Did you see what he looked like?"

She racked her brain. "He was tall and slender ... and had vibrant blue-green eyes. The leather was dyed black, scratched and worn in some places ... he wore scarves the color of shadow. I couldn't see anything other than that."

Astrid was practically panting in frustration as she tossed things over her shoulders. "I will find him. A shade can't hide from me." She looked up from where she was bent and fixed Satara with a serious stare. "No one is to know about this, understand? Do not tell anyone what happened."

The shieldmaiden nodded. "Did he take anything?"

"I don't know yet. Dammit." Astrid cursed again under her breath and stood. "I'll need some time to figure this all out. Go wait for Edie at her apartment. See what Indriði said, and report back to me soon."

Satara nodded and left for her apartment. With a head full of questions about the mysterious thief's motives, she donned her armor and set to her task.

CHAPTER EIGHT

MERCY FLUTTERED her fingers in the afternoon light streaming through the living room window, admiring the shimmery violet nail polish as she filed the edges. Fisk was curled up in the bathtub, napping, so she'd decided to do her nails before her mom came to pick her up for dinner. After the hospital, it hadn't taken her long to figure out that the armrest of her wheelchair was the perfect height for nail-painting ... so at least there was that.

Besides occasionally going out with Mom or Dad, who had come up from the Cape to be with her, she didn't have much to do anymore besides stay home and take care of Fisk. She'd adapted to the accessibility issues of going out pretty early on, but she found herself fatigued easily, and now that those Watchers were walking around? Yikes. She was doing her best to avoid another run in with one of those cuckoos lest they crunchify her upper half, too.

Besides Edie and their new friends, Mercy visited with her family only. It was a shame that *they* could never visit *her*. What if they had to use the bathroom? Too risky. She just told them her landlord was weird about visitors.

Satisfied with her nails for now, she screwed the cap back on the nail polish bottle and hoisted herself out of her chair. Her crutches were never far away, and she'd become pretty good at getting around with them. She was certainly getting a workout. Soon, she might only need a cane on good days.

Mercy smiled a little, looking down at herself. Yes, she was hurt—maybe permanently—but she'd done a lot of thinking. Honestly, her accident had brought her closer to her friends, and even more important, it had chased away all the fakers in her life. The people with her now? They were worth keeping around.

She was about to go check on Fisk when, suddenly, someone began pounding on the door. It was so loud and close that she started, nearly dropping herself in the process. Her heart fluttered, but she took a deep breath. It was probably Satara, or maybe Cal coming to pick something up. Neither of them had a key—everyone had agreed it would be too risky to have so many apartment keys floating around.

Considering Satara knocked like a normal person, it was probably the stupid meathead. Mercy still hadn't completely forgiven him for the way he'd treated her when they had first met, or how tedious he was in general.

"Coming," she called out, crutching over to the door with a sigh. Just to be sure, she stretched her neck to look into the peephole. Sure enough, Cal stood there, staring at the door with his arms at his sides.

Mercy sighed again and flipped the lock, unlatched the chain, and nudged the doorstop out of the way. Then, she opened the door.

"Hi," she said wearily, turning as soon as he was in view and going back toward the couch. "Is Edie still at her thing? Did you leave something behind?"

Cal shut the door, but didn't say anything.

Mercy paused, turning to look at him. He was a jackass, but he didn't usually ignore her when she was talking to him. Either something was wrong, or he had reached a new level of assholery. But he didn't look angry or even anxious about something. He just stood there, staring at her. Then, he took a step closer.

"Are you okay?" she asked, looking him over. Bizarrely, he was wearing a T-shirt, not the same thing he'd been wearing this morning.

He took another step closer, and Mercy took one back.

"Are you all right?"

As she watched in horror, his eyes traveled down from her eyes to her lips, then to her chest.

Mercy was suddenly gripped with panic. She couldn't imagine why, but for some reason, Cal was going to hurt her. Her heart thumped against her ribcage like it was trying to get out; her breathing came faster, shallower.

Cal's eyes widened as he watched her chest rise and fall. Then, he dove forward.

She didn't have a hope of escaping—he was too fast. He grabbed her throat, squeezed so hard that she couldn't make a noise, and kicked her crutches out from under her. They crashed into her wheelchair and jostled it, scattering her nail kit across the floor.

The zombie didn't even seem to notice, focusing solely on her. With her still struggling in his hands, he carefully laid her out on the floor under him.

Before Mercy knew it, his face was inches from hers. She tried to raise her arms to push him off of her, but he was like a solid wall of muscle. She opened her mouth to scream—

Nothing. She couldn't. In fact, only a little whistle emitted from her mouth as the air was sucked right out of her.

The thing above her didn't quite look like Cal anymore. Its face and form seemed to shift and change—man and woman, human and creature, young and old. Features whirled like a cyclone before her, but she could see that its mouth was open, gaping. Faint streaks of white light were being sucked from her mouth into the monster's.

Mercy struggled against it, trying to find her voice. If she could just call out, she could get Fisk's attention, and even this strong thing was no match for a giant fish man. But she couldn't. No matter how she worked her jaw, her mouth wouldn't close completely, like a strange force was keeping it open.

Beyond not being able to shout, Mercy found that she wasn't able to *breathe*, and struggling was only making her lightheaded. She had a limited amount of energy left before this thing completely emptied her of whatever it was it wanted. She had to spend it wisely.

Mercy turned her head to the left first, trying to break the connection, but she could only move for a second before the strange force suctioned her back into place. She tried jerking her head to the right instead, but the suction pulled her back again. Though she tried to close her mouth, the whistle of air escaping never stopped.

She couldn't feel her face anymore, or most of her torso, or her shoulders. Her vision became dark, and cloudy with tears. She felt like she was standing on the edge of a black tunnel, about to fall down. Was she really going to die here, after everything?

Then, something caught her eye. There, on the floor—the purple handle of her nail file.

Mercy worked her fingers against the carpet, only barely able to catch the corner of the metal file with one of her nails. She gaped and bucked. Pain radiated through her hips and legs, but she was able to slide the file into her hand. The little white lines and the darkness closing around her were the only things she could see, now. White stars exploded behind her eyes.

She drew in the tiny bit of energy she had left, gripped the nail file, and thrust it into the monster's side.

Suddenly, it was like she was smacked in the face. All the breath the thing had stolen rubber-banded back inside of her, pinning her to the floor for a moment with its intensity. Her lungs were paralyzed. They were going to explode—

Mercy jerked again and exhaled in a hard cough, the tears in her eyes finally pouring down her temples. She gulped in more air as her lungs settled.

No explosion. She was going to be all right.

Something squealed and scuttled across the living room, out the door, leaving it hanging open.

A shuddering breath, another cough. The reality of what had happened finally dawned on her, and she sputtered and burst into tears.

Mercy kept her fist clenched around the file, barely sobbing anymore, instead wailing like she was making up for that torturous minute of silence. She could feel heat blooming on her lower stomach. Her clothes stuck to her skin like someone had poured hot water on her. She didn't care. She just wanted to scream and scream until her voice didn't work anymore.

The front door flew open. Mercy stopped for a second, hiccupping and clutching the file tighter—but when she saw a familiar face, she let her head fall back onto the carpet, sobs burbling up from her chest and out of her mouth like a geyser of pain.

"Blessed Mare, Mercy! What happened?"

Satara's warm, soft hands caressed her arms and helped her into a sitting position. Though the world swam through her tears, Mercy locked eyes with Satara, then threw her arms around her. The shieldmaiden seemed taken aback for a moment, but she returned the hug.

"I'm— he— I can't—" Mercy breathed in short little gasps, nose dripping.

Satara placed a hand on the back of Mercy's head, cradling her securely. With her other hand, she searched Mercy's body, patting her down for injuries. She stopped short when she reached the warmth on Mercy's stomach, and pulled back a little. "You're covered in blood."

"I hur— hur— I hurt— him." Mercy pulled back, too, and brandished the nail file. She was sure she looked like a psycho, covered in blood and tears, but she couldn't quite grasp the will to calm down. She felt like she was in a car spinning out of control, and no matter how hard she slammed the brake or worked the wheel, she was still spiraling into a ditch.

"Hurt who?"

Mercy shook her head, suddenly remembering something. "Where's Fisk? He should have heard me. He must have heard me!"

Satara cursed under her breath. She stood without saying a word, trotting to the bathroom door and wrenching it open.

Edie approached Ghost with leaden feet and a leaden heart, dreading having to talk to Cal. What Indriði had seen in her runecasting was jarring, to say the least, but the longer Edie thought about it, the more sense it made. Why on earth was Cal helping her if he hated who she was so desperately? She should have seen that before. And why had he been acting so guilty lately?

He had to have some ulterior motive, and that fact put her on edge. How was she supposed to face him now that she wasn't even sure she could trust him?

As she opened Ghost's passenger door and slipped in, Cal looked up from his phone. "Hey— Jesus, what's with the jacket?" He nodded to the big leather mess in Edie's arms as he started the engine.

"Nothing. There was a dragon situation. I'm fine." She'd been so preoccupied by the rune reading that she had forgotten to heal her cuts, and they stung like hell. The water Indriði had given her had helped a little, so she'd been sure to drain the glass before she left. She dropped the ruined jacket by her feet, trying to look casual as she watched out the car window.

"A dragon? Fuck, kid." He gritted his teeth, pulling away from the curb. "We really gotta get rid of that wall. I coulda helped."

"Yeah, well ... luckily, it turned out to be a pet, not a trap."

Cal snorted and fished a cigarette out of his pocket. "She better fuckin' be paying to replace it."

"I don't *know*," was Edie's abrupt reply as she looked pointedly out the window.

The silence that followed was like the silence that followed a hard smack. Cal shifted in his seat and didn't say anything for a while, didn't even light his cig, and Edie's heart sank. She hadn't meant it to come out so mean, she'd only wanted him to stop talking.

Eventually, they left hoity-toity Alderdeen, and Cal spoke again. "Uh … I'm guessing by the attitude that she said no."

Indriði hadn't *technically* said no out loud, but she'd made her answer pretty clear. Edie glanced at him and simply shrugged in response.

Cal pressed, his tone becoming impatient. "Did she say *anything?* Did she talk to you?"

"She just— She didn't want to join."

"Is she really still that mad at Astrid?"

"I don't know."

Cal threw a hand up, and it came down hard on the steering wheel. "What *do* you know? You were the one who talked to her, for Christ's sake!"

Edie looked out the window again, suddenly more focused on where they were headed. Not toward the apartment. Her heart seized for a moment. "Where are we going?"

"Uh … I thought we'd stop by the marina and pick up fish. It's a little early, but while we're out—"

Edie leaned forward to grip the dashboard. "I want to go home."

"Are you kiddin' me?" Cal looked over at her, practically gaping. "Shamu needs to eat, Holloway!"

They were getting farther and farther away from her neighborhood, and her stomach was starting to hurt. "Then go and get him something to eat later. I want to go home."

"What the hell is—"

Apprehension, annoyance, and exasperation mingled. She didn't want to go anywhere with him until she figured a few things out. "Cal! Just take me home!" she finally snapped.

With a growl, Cal threw the wheel around and pulled a U-turn right in the middle of the street, almost hitting a parked car in the process. He sped down the road, toward her apartment.

There was a heated silence before he spoke. "I'm not your goddamn servant and I'm not your chauffeur. *Don't* forget that. If you fuckin' insist on making me run errands, I'm doing the errands *my* way, got it?"

Edie didn't respond. She crossed her arms and looked out the window until they reached the apartment. Once they were parked, she hopped out without a word. She could hear Cal behind her, slamming the car door and pocketing his keys.

She entered the apartment building without him and walked to the end of the hall, where she was surprised to find her door standing open— surprised, then panicked. She hurried inside. "Mercy?"

Mercy and Satara were sitting on opposite ends of the couch, Fisk sandwiched between them. He looked bad. The vibrant teal of his skin was much duller, his gills were gray, and even his eyes weren't the deep, sparkling obsidian they usually were. Mercy looked almost as sick, hair tangled, eyes and nose red.

Edie sniffed the air. She'd become more attuned to the scent of blood, and it was heavy here. When she looked down, she saw a trail of crimson spotting leading out of the apartment. She looked back up at her friends. "What's going on? Are you guys all right?"

"Fisk is sick from the tub," Mercy said through clenched teeth, clinging to a slimy arm.

Edie rounded the couch and knelt in front of her friend, taking one of her hands—shaking, pale. Under it, on her T-shirt, was a huge blood stain. Edie squawked and touched it, but as soon as her fingertips made contact, she could tell it wasn't Mercy's. She knew the feeling of Mercy's blood intimately at this point.

Her eyes wandered next to the coffee table, where a bloodied nail file sat. "What happened?" Her tone was darker now.

"I ... I let ... him in, and he attacked me." Mercy looked down at her hands. "He pushed me down on the floor—"

Edie blanched. "Who? Did you see who?"

She nodded and opened her mouth to reply, but was cut off as Cal shouldered through the apartment door and stepped into the room.

Unexpectedly and rapidly, Mercy moved closer to Edie in an effort to distance herself from Cal. "Him!"

Edie exchanged confused glances with Satara. She might be questioning Cal's motives, but he'd been either waiting for her or with her the entire time, and he couldn't be in two places at once. She looked up at Cal, who had frozen in the entryway of the living room.

For once, he didn't have a smartass comment. "What?"

The sickly Fisk managed to turn and look at Cal with a half-hearted, disoriented rage. "Villain!" he slurred, trying to claw his way over the back of the couch. Satara stopped him with a firm yank. The vættr groaned, wavered, and didn't try to move again.

Edie eyed him, then looked back at Mercy. "Cal couldn't have attacked you. He was in the car with me the whole time."

"But it looked like him," Mercy insisted. "I *saw* him. I'm not making things up!"

Edie looked at Satara. "Do you have any idea what's going on?"

The shieldmaiden shook her head. "I only just got here. I was to come meet you about what happened at Indriði's, but the apartment door was open, so I came in. Mercy was on the floor and Fisk was unconscious in the bath." Then she looked to Mercy. "Can you tell us what happened? Don't leave anything out."

Mercy swallowed, avoiding even turning her head in Cal's direction. The story she relayed made Edie's pulse race and she hadn't even been there. Cal didn't say a word in his defense the entire time.

"You said this thing was sucking the breath from your mouth?"

Mercy nodded.

"Any ideas on what it could be?" Edie asked Satara.

"My first thought was that it must be a mimic," she replied thoughtfully. "The shifting faces and the fact that it was wearing different clothes than the real Cal would confirm that. But the fact that it sucked all the air out of her lungs... It must be an andi-stelari. A breathstealer. They often take on the form of someone close to their victim."

Edie grimaced. No part of that sounded good, least of all the (admittedly badass) name. "What was one of those doing here?" She dreaded the answer she already knew was coming.

Finally, Cal spoke up, though his arms were crossed tightly over his chest. "And how the hell did it get my face?"

"It's been a while since I read about them," Satara said, smoothing down her shirt as she spoke. "I think I remember that breathstealers lurk a bit before attacking. So, it must have been staking us out for a while, waiting for an opportunity. Perhaps it saw you come and go and thought your glamour was as good a face as any. As for who sent it..." She turned up a palm and sighed.

"The Gloaming," Edie murmured, looking down at Mercy's hand still in hers. "The only question is whether they were targeting me or Mercy."

It didn't matter who they were trying to hurt. Either way, it was Edie's fault—and it was becoming rapidly clear that this place wasn't safe anymore.

Edie released Mercy's hand and went to stand in front of Fisk instead. She leaned in and touched his gills, shuddering at how scaly and bloated they felt. "Do you know what's wrong with you?"

He tilted his head an infinitesimal amount and burbled, then said, "The water is not right, and there is not enough of it. I tried to endure, Edie, but I do not think I can continue much longer."

"We're probably being watched even as we speak," Satara said. "It's not safe here anymore."

"But where could we even go?" Mercy murmured hopelessly.

Edie closed her eyes, thinking hard. Half-formed plans swam around in her mind, trying to piece themselves into a rational shape. What were they supposed to do? They couldn't just crash at Astrid and Satara's. To do that, they would have to tell the valkyrie that Mercy *knew*, and they had already *very* narrowly avoided revealing that Mercy had been at Zaedicus's party. Astrid would be beyond furious if they dropped that bombshell now.

Mercy could go stay with her parents, but Edie doubted Fisk would let himself be separated from her. In any case, that might put the Cedenos in danger, and they would definitely have questions about the seven-foot-tall fish man in tow. Maybe if Mercy got a new place by the bay—but how safe would that be, really, and where on earth would they get the money to do such a thing?

Where was she supposed to find someone who had the means and the inclination to take care of her friends' needs? Who in this city could she even remotely trust?

The answer came to her like an electric shock, so sudden and brilliant that she gasped out loud.

She whipped around to face Cal. He returned her exuberant look with one of confusion, then dawning horror.

"No," he said. "No way."

Edie pointed at Mercy. "Pack your bags."

CHAPTER NINE

MARIUS TOOK a deep breath as the portal sizzled shut behind him like a wound being cauterized. His ears clutched as the pressure changed, and he felt dizzy for a moment before acclimating.

A canopy of pines covered their entrance, but it was windy. Rain sprinkled against his face as he took a deep breath of mountain air. Ahead of him, sitting on a damp log, Ynga had pulled up the hood of her cloak. She hugged her satchel close to her chest.

Marius came closer and dropped into a crouch, setting his own satchel down on the forest floor before him. As he opened it, he asked, "What's in yours?"

"Healing potions, some rations, a whetstone, bandages, and a blanket. You?"

The vivid sifted through his bag before answering. He had all the same gear—but shoved deep into the bottom of the pack, wrapped in cloth, were two holy boons and a peculiar amulet.

He fished the amulet out and held it up, turning the stone over to read the inscription on the back. The rune was one he remembered studying. "It's an amulet of invisibility." Imperfect invisibility. If the wearer moved too much, you could see the light ripple around them. Still, it could be useful.

"Will you have to use it?" Ynga asked, raising a brow.

Pride burned inside of him, and he thrust it at her. "You could use it more than me. When you want to activate it, empower the rune with a bit of your energy."

She accepted the amulet without comment and slipped it on.

Marius stood, pulling a small map from one of his satchel's outer pockets and unfolding it. "According to this, there's a pass ahead that we should cut through, then once we hit the river, it's a long hike up the mountain." Looking forward, he squinted. Through the fog and rain, he could make out the adjacent mountain peak, dark against the steely sky. He pointed it out. "That's where we'll find the heimdyrr."

Ynga stood, cracking her neck. "Let's not waste any time, then."

Already shivering from the freezing rain and wind, they made their way out from under the canopy. The path down into the pass was steep and muddy in this weather; both of them spent most of the journey sliding and inching down so as not to fall. Shivering breaths were the only thing that filled the silence between them.

Their way down ended abruptly in a small drop-off. Ynga sat on the edge to scoot off, falling only a few feet before she landed and quickly regained her balance. Marius followed suit. There must have been a storm recently, because the pass itself was littered with fallen trees and debris. Heavy wind raked its fingers through the grasses and scared up pebbles, but the two worked against it and the rain the entire way through.

Finally, they crested a hill. About a hundred yards out, Marius could see the unquiet river. He unfolded the map again, holding it taut against the wind.

"Let's turn here." There were no other mountains beyond, closer to the river, so this must be the one they were supposed to hike. He looked to the side. Dread filled his heart as he realized just how steep their hike would be.

Ynga sighed, too. She went before him and started to scrabble on hands and knees up the beginning of the rocky incline. It wasn't a dignified way to do things, but they had no choice. Marius tucked the map away and followed after her.

Gradually, the hike became a little easier. It was no less steep, but there were more rocks to climb, more area for proper footing. After some time, they found themselves on a relatively flat shoulder. The summit was in sight, but they wouldn't have to go that far. Marius could feel the vibrations of the heimdyrr nearby.

His companion must have noticed the change in him. "Are we close?"

He responded with a noncommittal grunt and picked up his pace, leaving the rocky path and slipping into the thick pines. Pinecones and needles crunched as Ynga followed him closely.

After a few minutes of picking through the tightly packed conifers, he finally found what he was looking for. The feeling was almost an audible hum, and it drew him toward a craggy opening jutting from the mountain's face. An old tree had been ripped from the ground, its robust root system exposed, and was leaning against the brow of the cave, partially obscuring the entrance with dead branches.

Marius approached. The breach was small, barely big enough for them to slip through. He traced the doorway with two fingers, and the vibration was so strong he had to clench his jaw to keep his teeth from chattering. "In here," he said, ducking so he could slowly ease inside.

He had no idea if Ynga followed him. Once he was enveloped in darkness, the White Mountains fell away. The smell of earth surrounded him, and he could feel soil and roots under his feet as he carefully felt his way forward. After a minute or so, the path widened, and he was eventually able to stand to his full height. Behind him, he could finally hear Ynga, her armor jingling as she straightened up.

"It's well dark here," she whispered.

Marius hadn't thought about it. There wasn't much to see besides dirt, so he hadn't cared. He shifted his pack and conjured a ball of yellow light with his left hand. It floated above their heads, bobbing between them as they made their way through the earthen tunnel.

The tunnel, which had been declining steadily, suddenly swung up and became smaller again. By the time natural light reached them, they were on their hands and knees. The last few feet of the tunnel were nearly vertical, and Marius realized they would be emerging not from a cave but a hole in the ground. He squeezed himself out, then turned around to help Ynga do the same.

The forest around them now was similar to the one they had left in many ways. Evergreens were packed tightly, fog settled all around them, creatures sang and scuttled between nurse logs. The notable difference, however, was that everything was massive.

Jotunheim was not only the land of giant beings—it was a land of giant everything. Even the skinniest trees were thicker than Marius was tall, and it would have taken at least five or six people to make a ring around one of the trunks. Their branches started so high up that they formed a canopy themselves. Boulders were more like hills. Even the creatures were bigger. Marius squinted as, in the fog, he observed a pheasant that had to be at least the size of him dart into a nearby bush.

When even a place's woodland creatures could eat you for a snack, you knew you were in danger.

Ynga picked up on it right away. She brought her lips right next to Marius's ear before speaking. "Where do we go next?"

He turned a little. "How do you feel? Was the transition okay?"

"I feel fine. Where next?"

Seemed she was eager to get this over with. He couldn't say he blamed her. He didn't want to spend any more time in this place than he had to. Vanaheim had been one thing; this was quite another. He didn't like the feeling of everything being so much bigger than him.

Hastily, he drew out the map and flipped it over. The path from the heimdyrr to the network of caves his father had mentioned was almost a straight line, cutting right through the forest. How long it would take, though, he had no idea.

He started forward without answering her, dismissing his ball of light. The sun was so shadowed by so many enormous branches that it was practically nighttime at their level, but he couldn't risk an animal—or worse—finding them. If a full-grown giant happened upon them, he wasn't sure they could bring it down.

He was so focused on the fog ahead of him that he was taken off guard when the earth began to tremble, and he stopped mid-stride. Ynga pulled up close to him and loosed half a gasp before covering her mouth.

A hulking shape loomed ahead, and the ground continued to shake as it got closer. Thankfully, with the heavy fog, it hadn't spotted them yet. Marius grabbed Ynga's wrist and pulled her behind a nearby boulder.

As the form passed, Marius got a better look at it. It was about three times his height, hunched, with disproportionately long arms. Where worn pelts didn't cover its limestone-colored skin, a veritable carpet of moss clung to it like fur. Tangled hair fell down its chest, which was adorned with necklaces of beads, shells, rocks, and clattering junk.

A troll. And judging by its jewelry, one who liked to collect things. There was a good chance this was the creature they were looking for.

Marius tapped Ynga and gestured for her to follow him. They stalked the troll on light feet, hiding when they got the chance, relying on the fog to conceal them otherwise. Eventually, the hulking creature approached what would have appeared to be a normal hill, had smoke not been curling out from the top of it. The troll ducked into a cave in the side and disappeared.

As they followed, they soon learned that Radiant Eirik hadn't been exaggerating when he'd said it was a *network* of caves. There were so many twists and turns that they soon lost the troll, and Marius had to rely on its mildewy musk and a footprint here and there to finally locate the central chamber. As they approached, warm orange light flickered against the tunnel walls.

The chamber was small but cozy, with a fire burning hot in the center of it. Charms made of sticks and crystals hung from the ceiling. There was a mass of hay and rotting animal hides off to the side, patted down into a little bed. On either side of this were heaps of seemingly random objects, ranging from mundane things like tankards and bowls to embroidered silk, jeweled cuffs, even a golden tiara on top of one of the piles. Marius eyed the piles as he peered into the chamber. Being solitary creatures, trolls didn't have much in the way of culture. Most of this was likely stolen.

Far into the chamber, its back to them, was the troll. It was sitting down, leaning over something it held in one of its disproportionately huge hands. Something that twinkled in the firelight. A mirror.

Marius observed as the troll combed its knotted hair to the side and touched the reflection. This behavior struck him as so odd that he found himself standing there, staring. As the troll shifted the mirror to the side, the vivid saw his face reflected back at him, right over the troll's shoulder.

In an instant, it lowered its mirror and turned, affording them their first good look at its face. A short, wrinkled forehead sloped into a triangular slit that served as its nose. Crooked canines poked out of its wide mouth. Impossibly huge, round eyes of solid, softly glowing ivory studied Marius.

Behind him, Marius heard a quiet *woosh* as Ynga's amulet of invisibility cloaked her in the shadows. The troll didn't seem to notice her.

"A human?" It spoke in Old Norse—and its voice was deep but surprisingly soft, as though it was not angry to see him standing there, only mildly surprised. The ivory eyes searched him, lingering on his drinking horn briefly.

Marius was unsure of how to respond for a moment. Then, "Yes. Sorry to bother you, ma'am."

"Sir!"

"Sorry. Sir."

The troll narrowed his eyes, but made no move to attack. Considering that the runepriest it had stolen from had survived to tell the tale, Marius got the feeling this troll wasn't interested in bloodshed—only his shiny things. It was rather funny that a blessed oracular mirror was now being used as a vain troll's looking glass.

"Are you lost?" the troll asked.

"No, sir. I came to see you about something you ... collected." Marius glanced toward the troll's piles of knick-knacks.

Finally, the creature hauled himself up to his feet. He was standing an appreciable distance from Marius, almost six feet, but was still able to reach over and stroke the shiny plate of his pauldron. "I've never seen such a pretty human. Your skin is like deer's fur."

"Thank you?"

"Your eyes are like coins."

"Thank you."

The troll peered at him. "Maybe I should add *them* to my pile."

Marius moved his shoulder away from the troll's massive hand. "I can't stay for long. I've come to get that mirror you're holding in your hand, there. It belongs to a friend of mine."

The troll looked down at the mirror, then clutched it with both hands. "Are you here to kill me?" he asked, sounding slightly concerned but mostly unimpressed.

Marius considered. A few months ago, he would have come in with his weapon already drawn and separated the troll's head from its shoulders without a word. But he'd had a lot of time to think. Not everything had to come to violence—and not *everything* that seemed monstrous really was.

He was still getting used to the idea, but he'd resolved not to attack this troll unless he had no choice. He folded his arms behind his back. "I don't want to kill you if I don't have to."

"Hmph." The troll held the mirror to his chest and glowered. "I'm not giving you the looker-glass, ever, unless you cut it out of my dead hands."

Marius sighed and ran his hand through his hair. "We can do this another way. How about a bargain?"

The troll seemed unsure. "You don't have anything I want."

"Nothing?" Marius raised a brow as he unbuckled his boar tusk horn from his belt. It was a treasured possession, but he could see no other way to avoid battle and secure the mirror Ynga needed for her proving—though he hadn't failed to notice that she hadn't been doing a thing, simply lurking in the shadows behind him. He tried to staunch his annoyance for now.

The troll peered down at the horn and tilted his head. "Is it special?"

Marius held it up, turning it so that it glinted in the firelight. "It's made from a Vanaheim boar's tusk. It was created by a landvættr there as a gift to me. You can drink out of it, or you can uncork it and blow it, if you wish."

This seemed to please the troll greatly. He held the mirror up and gazed into it one last time before setting it on the packed earth and toeing it toward Marius.

A strange sense of satisfaction washed over the vivid. He had done what he had set out to do without killing anyone, and now—

A cry pierced the air, and before Marius understood what was happening, Ynga flew past him in a white streak. He stared in horrified confusion as she launched herself at the troll, sword bare, and plunged the blade into his jugular.

"No!" Marius sprinted forward and pulled Ynga off the troll, but the damage had already been done. The troll wrapped his hands around his own neck to try and stop the spurting blood, but he was already on his knees. It was only a few more seconds until he thumped dead at their feet, the glow fading from his eyes.

There was silence. They were both covered in blood, and more was spreading across the floor of the chamber. Ynga moved forward, planting her foot on the troll's head and wrenching her sword out of his neck.

Marius took a step back, staring at her. "Why did you do that?"

She wiped the blade on the troll's worn furs and turned to Marius, her face red. "Why did you pull me off of it?"

"I didn't want you to kill him."

Her nose and brow wrinkled in confusion. "I thought that was your plan. You would trick it with a bargain, and then I would strike and surprise it."

Marius raised his voice, tone firm. "I really *was* making a bargain."

"You're more of a fool than I could have ever imagined," she scoffed, bending to pick up the mirror before thrusting it at him. "Radiant Eirik told us to kill the troll and take the mirror."

He couldn't contain his anger, as if the size of his frustration was too big for his body to hold. "I was working on another way, dammit!"

But, as he looked down into the mirror, his anger faded away in an instant. The sight greeting him was not his own face, but rather an image of a room he recognized as the temple's chapterhouse. In the vision, his father was delivering some kind of speech. Then, without warning, a blade fell, cutting him down. Marius watched in horror as Eirik's steadfast, reliable form crumbled to the stone floor.

He looked up from the mirror in shock. Ynga hadn't noticed him stopping, hadn't noticed the mirror's image. She was digging through the troll's piles, probably looking for a trophy.

A faint but niggling screeching sound like nails on a chalkboard drew his attention back to the mirror. Something was appearing, as if etched into the glass itself—seven runes spelling one word. *Svikari.*

Traitor.

CHAPTER TEN

"RIGHT HERE," Edie said as she looked up from her phone. "This building."

"I *know* which building it is." Cal grumbled and pulled up to the curb, but kept the car running. "Get out."

Edie couldn't help but sigh at him.

When she'd called Matilda, the wight had been more than accommodating, even excited at the prospect of having house guests for an indefinite amount of time. That was more than could have been said for a lot of people in her position. Edie knew this was a huge favor, but even though she and Matilda barely knew each other—and Matilda had been a member of the Gloaming until very recently—Edie had a good feeling about her.

The only problem was Cal. He hadn't spoken a word to Matilda since he'd dumped her and skipped town ten years ago, after Dad's death. When they'd met again at the party, things had been ... awkward, to put it lightly. It had become clear to Edie right away that Matilda still had feelings for the revenant, but she still wasn't sure if he reciprocated.

At the moment, he was throwing a hissy fit over Edie even *talking* to her. When it came to how her dad had treated him, Edie understood his moods. There was no polite way to talk about the guy who had kept you as a slave for over a decade. But with this, he was being a big drama queen.

"Aren't you going to come in?" Edie asked, shoving her phone into the pocket of her quilted sweatshirt, the only clean piece of outerwear she had after the destruction of her leather jacket.

Cal looked at her like she'd grown an extra head, then quickly looked away, gripping the steering wheel. "No, I'm not gonna stick around. Just text me when you're done."

Edie glanced into the back seat and exchanged a look with Mercy, then sighed. "Okay, fine. We probably won't be longer than an hour."

Sitting next to Mercy, Fisk was bundled up in a huge hoodie layered over a black bed sheet, the only two things in the apartment that had covered him even semi-adequately. He wasn't as alert as usual, though he did peer out the window at the tall building they'd pulled up to. "New home?"

"Hopefully," Mercy replied. She sounded marginally better than she had that afternoon, and had finally stopped shaking.

It had taken them a few hours to arrange everything and pack a few things, so it was evening now. The lights of the office buildings, hotels, upscale boutiques, and penthouses twinkled in gray light and freezing rain. Thankfully, almost no one was walking the street at the moment; most people were still working or had taken refuge from the chill.

Edie climbed out of the passenger seat, then turned to help Fisk and Mercy out. "Let's get inside before anyone sees us," she murmured.

The building before them stretched up taller than most of those surrounding it, a sleek rectangle of shiny steel and glass. Matilda lived in a penthouse consisting of the top three floors, and Edie could make out its massive windows and terrace. There would be more than enough room for guests there, but it wasn't the size of the penthouse that had sealed the deal—it was the fact that Matilda had a pool.

Matilda had told apartment security to expect them. Edie and Mercy were able to hustle Fisk through the lobby and into the penthouse elevator without much fuss, despite him being dressed like a clinically depressed Grim Reaper.

Once actually inside the elevator, Fisk leaned heavily on Mercy, who in turn leaned heavily on Edie. "Water?" he croaked.

"Yes, baby," Mercy said, "water soon."

Baby? Edie eyed her with a sly smirk, but didn't say anything.

The elevator slid open, revealing a carpeted vestibule. To their right was a small side table with an arrangement of white and purple flowers on it, and in front of them was the door to what must be Matilda's apartment. It was smooth, black-painted wood with a highly-polished silver knocker shaped like a fox head. Edie was so nervous she might smudge it that she opted to use the doorbell instead.

They stood silent and crowded in the vestibule for a while. Edie was about to try the doorbell again when the lock clicked audibly and the door finally opened.

Standing in the doorway was not the petite woman Edie had expected, but rather a *very* tall, very thin man, with sickly olive skin and long, dark brown hair. He wore a black turtleneck and matching pants, several sizes too big and hanging off his body. He regarded each one of the visitors with a steady but uncertain gaze.

"Uh ... hi," Edie ventured.

The man jerked his head to the side slightly to look at her, hair hanging in his face. He looked like a drowned person. It was clear to Edie that he wasn't human—or, at least, not a living human. She just had to hope that he was supposed to be here and hadn't done anything to harm Matilda.

"We're, uh, looking for Matilda Ardelean. Is she home?"

The man stared her down for a few seconds. Just when it seemed he was never going to answer her, quick little footsteps echoed from somewhere deeper in the penthouse and a familiar voice called out, "I'm coming! I'll be right there!"

It was only another moment before Edie recognized Matilda coming into view behind the man, though she didn't look quite as glamorous as when Edie had first met her. She'd traded her elaborate hairstyle and diamond-encrusted gown for capris, a simple ponytail, a casual button down over a tank top, and pink latex gloves.

"*Mulțumesc*, Antoniu," she said as she touched the man's shoulder and gently brushed him out of the way.

Antoniu lingered for a moment, staring at Fisk in particular, before he disappeared.

"Edie!" Matilda's smile was enormous, exposing her elongated canines as she drew Edie in and gave her a kiss on both cheeks and a tight hug. She did the same to Mercy, careful not to disturb her crutches. "I'm so happy that you're here. I hope you traveled well?"

"Hi, Matilda. We caught an Uber," Edie lied. Probably best not to say, *Your ex brought us but he can't stand the sight of you so he didn't even come say hi.* "You're not that far from my neighborhood."

"Please, call me Tilda." The wight waved an over-sized, rubbery hand. "And don't mind me, I always ask about the journey. I suppose it's left over from the days when you could get eaten by a wyvern or impaled by a Catholic while traveling to the next town over. Please, come in!"

"What is a Catholic?" Fisk stage-whispered to Mercy as the three of them stepped into the penthouse.

She patted his arm. "I'll tell you when you're older."

The penthouse that stretched out in front of them was a bizarre mix of cutting-edge technology and very old personal effects. Three of the four walls featured floor-to-ceiling windows, with giant oil paintings, maps, and tapestries hanging in the remaining space. Unlike Indriði's place, there were no mazelike hallways, just an open plan that started in an enormous living room. The floors were sleek black wood; couches and a long sectional surrounded a shiny entertainment center, while in the leftmost corner was a white grand piano on an elevated platform. Not an inch of the place wasn't luxe or lush, whether the fittings were modern or antique.

Edie looked around as Tilda walked through the living room, into a kitchen-and-dining-room big enough to fit a chef's dream kitchen *and* a formal dining table. The table itself, scratched and pitted, looked like it had been hewn from a tree in one slab. Its legs were ornately carved, intertwined in a way that reminded Edie of a Celtic knot. It definitely wasn't from the last century or two; it might have been even older.

Paired with those tapestries, the paintings... Edie had never thought about it before, but Tilda must be ancient.

"We were just finishing up draining the pool," the wight said, stripping off her gloves and laying them on the counter. "I'm having some nice boys come and get the saltwater and everything set up tomorrow."

Mercy grinned, though her eyebrows shot up in surprise. "Tomorrow? That soon?"

"You'd be amazed what mortal men will do for an extra thousand dollars and a pretty Eastern European accent," Tilda said, then laughed humorlessly. "Or maybe you wouldn't. Either way, a saltwater pool! How chic!" She seemed genuinely excited, which was fortunate, considering they didn't have anything to offer her in return for her help.

Edie smiled. "Was that your roommate?" she asked politely, nodding to the stairway down which Antoniu had disappeared.

The wight looked confused for a moment. "Oh! Him? No, he's just an old friend. He runs errands for me and helps me around the house a couple days a week."

"Is he a vampire like you?" Mercy asked, ever-curious about the world into which she'd been thrust.

"He's a wraith, actually."

Edie blinked. If she remembered correctly, wraiths were what wights left behind when they sucked an enthralled human dry, killing them. The last wraiths she'd tangled with had turned into twisted, ghostly humanoids with branchlike limbs—and even before they had transformed, they'd been creepy and animalistic. Antoniu hadn't exactly been the picture of hospitality, but he hadn't looked like he was about to kill them. "He just … helps you?"

"The high-wight that turned him died a long time ago. Wraiths don't typically last long after their masters die. Most go mad, unbridled, and cause chaos and are put down." Tilda leaned against one of the kitchen's black quartz counter tops. "In the early stages of panic, he ran through the village and ended up at my home. I took him in and taught him to live on his own. So, the years go by, and this and this"—she gestured vaguely—"and I move here around the turn of the century. After a while, he wrote me telling me he was moving here, too, and he's been helping me with little things ever since."

It was a nice story, but Edie noticed that Tilda's smile didn't quite reach her eyes. It wasn't until her next statement that she understood why:

"He knows I get lonely."

There was a period of silence where Tilda turned and carried her gloves to the sink so she could hang them over the edge. Edie watched her shoulders rise as she took a deep breath. Then, she turned around and smiled at Mercy and Fisk.

"I don't think we met formally at the party." She came forward and offered her hand to Mercy first. "Matilda Ardelean."

Mercy shook her hand and said, "I love your accent."

The vampire smiled, then took a step back to take in all of Fisk. "Wow," she said playfully, "so many muscles."

Fisk managed a smile, gills flaring up a bit. He was looking a lot better now that the promise of saltwater was in his immediate future. In the imperious tone he reserved for people who didn't yet know what a dingus he was, he said, "You stand before Fiskbein, Matilda Ardelean."

"I certainly do." She chuckled and brushed past them. "I say let's not waste another moment, eh? Come, come. I have a little elevator just around this corner if you need it, Mercy—I'm happy to see it finally get some use. I have all the latest wards installed on the penthouse, so you'll be perfectly safe, and your parents are welcome to come by all they like. The pool is downstairs, your rooms upstairs..."

"You coming?" Mercy asked over her shoulder when she noticed that Edie hadn't moved an inch from the kitchen.

"I'll just stay here, thanks. I have to make a phone call anyway."

Mercy gave her a suspicious look, but said nothing more as she disappeared after Fisk and Tilda.

Edie wasn't much of a snoop—she didn't usually feel the urge to unlock other people's phones or open their bathroom cabinets or look at their internet history—but a special opportunity had just been dropped in her lap. What Indriði had said earlier ... she supposed she wasn't surprised that Astrid might be keeping things from her, but Cal was so frank. Why would he lie?

She had to know. And if she wanted to know why he was lying and what he was lying about, she had to learn more about him. What better place to look for a clue to his true past than his ex's home?

Unsure of where to start, she slowly made her way back into the living room. Besides a few select pieces and the tech, most of the furniture here was antique, ranging from Edwardian to straight up ancient-looking. She opened the drawers of a sideboard that kept a bowl of keys and other miscellanea, but found nothing except letter-writing materials.

She closed the drawer, careful to make as little sound as possible as she stepped up to the piano and fingered the keys. She wasn't Mozart, but she knew how to play a few things—though drunkenly plunking the intro of "The Phantom of the Opera" on a Casio keyboard wasn't quite the same as tickling the ivories of a grand piano in a millionaire's penthouse apartment. With her left hand, she worked of couple notes of the bass line of "Bela Lugosi's Dead," which seemed appropriate, considering.

As she did, she peered past the piano's cover and noticed a small wooden trunk nestled between a bookshelf and the frosted glass doors of the terrace. Something about it drew her, and her fingers stilled on the

keys. A moment later, she hopped down from the piano platform and
went to it, testing the ancient lock.

It opened.

Inside was a veritable treasure trove of documents. Edie flipped
through letters of inheritance, immigration papers, certificates of all
kinds—death, marriage, degrees—some so old that they were barely
legible. She carefully sifted through the papers, moving them aside until
she found something that called out to her. It looked like a thick, leather-
bound book, and when she opened it, she discovered it was a photo
album.

When Edie turned the first page, which was stuffed with more
miscellaneous documents, a tintype stared back at her. Though her
hairstyle and makeup were different, Tilda hadn't changed that much—
she still had the small, heart-shaped smile and big black eyes. The frilly
get-up she wore made her look like a little doll. Edie peeled back the edge
of the picture and found a date: 1857, although, judging by some of the
other decor, Tilda was much older than that. A ticket to something called
The Rose of Castille accompanied the portrait, along with a pressed
daisy and a hand-painted postcard of a river.

The next couple of pages were more of the same, though the dates
changed along with what Tilda wore. A slimmer, less frilly dress in 1882;
a bathing costume that resembled a tent more than anything in 1896;
puffy trousers and a bicycle in 1901. The page after that featured a picture
of Tilda bundled up in furs and grinning in front of the Statue of Liberty.
Pictures of her in a World War I nurse's outfit followed; then dancing in
a jazz club, with cropped hair and dark makeup, her mouth open in a
gleeful shout.

Glamor shots with perfectly coiffed hair, smoking in her SS Tourer,
the Great March on Washington, kissing another woman in a sparkly
pantsuit, Polaroids of clubbing in neon fishnets and hoop earrings. 70s,
80s, 90s … each decade passed. The people in the photos changed, grew
older and disappeared, but Tilda's face was constant, as young and fresh
as in that first tintype.

Finally, Edie found what she was looking for.

Cal's face jumped out at her the moment she turned the page. It was a dark photo, and the disposable camera had caught his glamour, but she recognized the eyes even when they weren't clouded with decay. Tilda was leaning in to him, holding a glass of red wine and smiling. He wasn't smiling, but he had a playful twinkle in his eye. He looked almost content.

Edie pressed her mouth into a hard line as she shifted this picture aside to look at the one tucked behind it. Some kind of party was going on. Cal was sitting on a couch with his arms stretched up above his head, shirt riding up a bit. Tilda was standing in front of him, talking animatedly to someone out of the shot. And the look on his face ... he was looking at her with the world in his eyes.

The next page almost made Edie drop the book. Slate eyes stared back at her—a familiar pointy chin, a full goatee, high cheekbones. Dad. Cal sat next to him, glancing away.

"Edie, what are you doing?"

The voice startled her so much she nearly threw the book out the window. She shut it and tried to stuff it back into the box, but it was no use—Tilda had already caught her snooping through her things.

With dread, she looked over her shoulder. "Sorry, I was just..."

Tilda was looking at her with a drawn expression. "I left Mercy and Fiskhein to explore the upstairs by themselves," she said carefully, coming a little closer and looking down at the leather-bound book. Her expression evened out a bit, and she sighed. "If you wanted to look at that, you only had to ask."

"Sorry." Edie looked down again. "You have a lot of really awesome photos."

"Ha, if you think that's a lot, you should see all the paintings I have in storage." Tilda smirked and sat on a nearby settee, resting her arm along the back of it. "I should probably get rid of some of them ... but it's not because I want to look at my own face all day! They let me remember the people who painted them, my friends. If I ever miss this or that paramour or confidante, I can go back and touch their brushstrokes or read their letters." Her smirk faded.

"Right." Edie dared to open the photo album again and flipped to the back. There were other photos of Cal here, too—most of him working on her SS Tourer. The edges of many of them were faded, much more so than any of the others, even the old ones. Edie got the feeling they were well-loved.

"What made you want to look through my photos? I'm really not that interesting."

Edie begged to differ. Still, she answered, "I was looking for pictures of Cal. You know ... even though we spend a lot of time together, I don't know that much about him."

"If you wanted to know more about Cal, why not ask him?"

"I dunno if you've noticed, but he's not very forthcoming." She sighed and turned to the picture of her father, lingering. "I didn't know you all hung out together."

"Hm." Tilda shifted. "I wouldn't say I *hung out* with your father. I just wanted to be where Cal was, and mostly, he was with Richard."

"Right."

Edie turned the page back and fingered the plastic over her dad's face. He was smirking. Had Mom known where he was when he was going to these parties or doing whatever necromancer stuff he did? Had she known about Cal? For that matter, did she know about the supernatural at all?

Edie hadn't seen her mom in a long time. No one had even called to tell her Edie was in the hospital, and maybe that was for the best. Edie didn't know why, or what she'd done wrong, but she and her mother didn't speak anymore. There hadn't been a falling out or a fight, they had simply parted ways and not spoken for over a year. They weren't even friends on social media. Not that Edie had time for social media these days.

After a while, she looked at Tilda and asked, "What was he like, to you?" She hadn't had the balls to ask Astrid in-depth questions about their relationship, and she already knew full well how Cal felt on the subject. It would be interesting to know what Dad had been like in the eyes of other attuned beings. There must be a reason everyone had been so scared of him.

"He was..." Tilda sighed, humming as if searching for the word. "He was different. He had many sides to him. He could go from friendly and caring to calculating and focused in a second, but whatever he was doing, he was *intense* about it. Those eyes pinned you where you stood and demanded the absolute truth from you."

"He sounds scary." Edie didn't remember him like that at all, but she knew better by now.

Tilda nodded. "He was intimidating. And I was 600 years older than him! You never really knew what to expect because of his ... *self-serving* nature. He might do something wonderfully generous and good one day and then something dreadfully evil the next—as long as it suited his needs."

Edie closed her eyes for a moment. She knew he was bad, but the reality still stung every time she heard it again. It hurt partially because, even though she now knew he'd been a garbage human being, she still loved him. She still found herself missing him.

She was, apparently, the only one. Even Astrid, whom he'd been close with, didn't seem particularly broken up about his violent end. After what Indriði had told her, Edie almost found herself wondering if the Reach had caused his death, not the Gloaming.

"I'm sorry, Edie," Tilda said genuinely, her voice soft. "I know it's not easy to find these things out about someone you care for."

She shook her head and flipped the subject. This wasn't what she was here for, anyway. She needed to learn more about Cal. "What about Cal? What was he like back then?"

The vampire shifted in her seat, frowning. "Hm ... he was quiet. Somber. He wasn't permitted to smoke or drink, but he sometimes did secretly. When he first started fixing my roadster, he didn't say much to me, even though I really did want to make friends. There was something about him." She smiled wistfully. "I could tell there were big things going on inside of him; huge, complex thoughts. It made me ache that he couldn't express them. I tried to be a refuge."

Something Cal had said to her a while ago came back to her: *You don't know the things your father made me do.* He was right, but he'd never expanded on it. Edie looked up at Tilda. "What exactly was Cal's job, anyway?"

Tilda shifted again. "Ah ... a servant, I think. Probably other things. I couldn't tell you the particulars."

"But didn't you date him for a long time? Like, five years?"

"He didn't like to talk about it." Her tone was harsher. "Like I said, I was a refuge."

"Do you know who he was before he died?"

"No idea."

Edie could see that Tilda was getting uncomfortable, but she couldn't stop now. She had to gather as much information as she could. "Did he know about me? Did I ever meet him before?"

"Your— your father kept you very secret, far away from everyone else. I knew he had a child, but nothing more. I'm not sure if Cal ever knew you." The wight crossed her arms. "I really think you should ask *Cal* about these things, not me."

"Maybe." Edie chewed on her lip. "But I don't think he'll tell me the truth."

"He takes time to open up."

No, I mean, I think he'll lie to me. And I think you're lying to me, too. She doubted Tilda was lying out of malice—she was probably just protecting Cal—but Edie didn't mention it. Best not to anger the only person who could keep her friends safe.

She risked one last question. "Cal ... he had to have some kind of income in Vegas, right? Do you know where he gets his money?"

Abruptly, Tilda stood from the chaise and began walking toward the kitchen. "I ... I really have a lot of housework to do today, so I should probably get back to that, but it was so nice to see you, Edie, so thanks for stopping by." She didn't make eye contact. Instead, she shifted some stuff around on the counter and grabbed her rubber gloves again.

Edie blinked, stunned for a moment. Message received. She mumbled a quiet goodbye and drifted toward the door.

As she left, foreboding clenched around her body. Things were not adding up.

CHAPTER ELEVEN

Satara descended the stairs to Astrid's hearth room, boots clanking with every step. She could hear the teakettle screeching—or, at least, what she assumed was the teakettle. After the week they'd had, she supposed it could be steam coming out of the valkyrie's ears.

It had been two days since the last time Satara had seen Edie, and she was beginning to wonder if the necromancer was ever going to follow up on her meeting with the Norn. The last time they'd seen each other, Edie had been more focused on taking care of Mercy and Fisk than talking about Indriði. It was understandable, considering, but Astrid was not known for her patience, and it was Satara who had to deal with her.

Thankfully, however, Astrid had been distracted with trying to hunt down the mysterious thief. The shade hadn't succeeded in taking her shield and spear, but he had stolen something else—something apparently important, if Astrid's rage was any indication. The valkyrie had been vague on what, but Satara supposed she'd find out once they took it back.

A tug in her subconscious had compelled her to don her armor and head downstairs. Now she walked into the hearth room to find her battlemother pouring boiling water into two cups. This was Astrid's ritual before anything and everything, and she had a different blend of tea for a surprising array of occasions. When Satara sniffed the air, she could faintly smell chamomile, thyme, and nasturtium. Most likely something for going into a fight ... which must mean it was time to track down the shade.

"Here, drink this," Astrid said, placing one of the cups on the table as Satara took a seat.

"What news?" asked the shieldmaiden.

"Lylirion For-Shadow." Astrid sat in the chair across the table, arctic eyes intense. "Our thief. He's a light elf blackguard. We're not the only ones who have run into trouble with him recently. With my eyes around the city, he wasn't hard to find."

"Maybe this is what they call hiding in plain sight?" Satara raised her cup to her nose and inhaled the aroma. This was an angry tea.

"He's what *I* call a cocky show-off. But not for long."

"It's strange..." Satara frowned. "Why would an otherworldly being like that bother to come to Midgard to steal from a valkyrie? Whoever hired him must have paid him a great deal."

"By all accounts, he has lived here for a while," Astrid said. "Perhaps exiled from Alfheim. Or *slumming* it. Light elves are talked up to be nothing but sun and goodness and beauty, but they can be just as spiteful and self-serving as anyone else. Perhaps more so, considering how powerful they are."

"But he stole something specific from you, didn't he?"

"He did."

"If he had what he was looking for, why would he stop to get your shield and spear?"

"Whoever hired him probably offered a bonus if he brought them back."

"With all due respect, Battlemother ... why? They are old, but what's so special about them?"

"They are unique weapons." Astrid sighed and took a long sip of her tea. "I suppose I've never told you their history."

Satara looked up, already listening intently. Even though she had lived with Astrid for a decade, she knew little about her past. What she did know, she held close to her heart. Even though her passion didn't lie in being a shieldmaiden, she loved Astrid like a second mother.

"I am ancient," Astrid began, "but I am far, far from the eldest of my kind. After the Aesir-Vanir war, Freyja and Odin turned a handful of his familiar spirits into valkyir as a sign of the Pantheons' truce. In the beginning, there were six—the Riders—then eleven more to keep Valhalla. But Freyja's most trusted valkyrie is the Rider-General and youngest of the Mother Norns, Skuld.

"In old times, Sváfa, my battlemother, helped Skuld and the other Riders win a difficult battle and was given two gifts: a spear, crafted and enchanted by the dwarves of Niðavellir, and Skuld's own shield."

Satara's eyes flew wide, and she looked at the shield hanging on the wall. It was well-made, and she had seen it glow in battle before, but she'd hardly expected a Mother Norn and one of the first valkyir to wield something so plain. Still, it certainly answered her question. Stealing such a legendary relic would ensure Lylirion For-Shadow never had to work another day in his immortal life.

Astrid had already finished her tea when Satara looked back at her. "When Sváfa fell in battle," she said as she rose from her seat, "the weapons passed to me. I won't give them up so easily."

Astrid suited up in her silver half-plate armor, and by the time they grabbed their weapons and exited Harbinger Trinket & Tome, the sun had set.

The valkyrie scanned the dark blue sky for a moment before loosing an unearthly whistle. From the horizon slipped three blue forms that solidified into black birds as they veered from the sky, landing all in a row on Astrid's shoulder and outstretched arm.

Satara watched as the one on her shoulder leaned close and croaked softly in her ear as though it was whispering. Astrid tilted her head, nodded, and lifted her arm to send the birds off. They disappeared as quickly as they had come.

"He's staying in a small apartment in Strongfair, in Anster, but he's

packing his things. Someone must have told him I was looking for him."
Astrid reached into her armor and pulled out one of her wolf whistles,
attached to a chain around her neck. She blew it, and the great beast burst
forth to greet them with a howl and its usual stench.

"Are we going there to kill him?" Satara asked as she climbed onto the
wolf behind Astrid.

"Not if he cooperates. It's always a shame to take an immortal life …
but I've done it before, and I'll do it again if I have to."

The night air whipped Satara's face as the wolf bounded down the
dark street, gaining momentum before a portal that looked more like a
deep wound opened and swallowed them whole.

A split second later, they were in Anster. The fresh air of their seaside
town was replaced with the strange, bitter smell of the city. The alley in
which they'd appeared smelled particularly bad. An overflowing
dumpster sat against the brick building to their right; grime crawled up
the walls, and under a dense cloud of light pollution, shattered glass
shimmered against the concrete. After living in small villages her whole
life, Satara chose to see the ruin of the city as a beautiful display of chaos
and order. She didn't mind the ugly parts. But she could not imagine a
light elf feeling the same way.

She and Astrid slipped off the wolf, and as it disappeared, she
murmured, "Why here?"

The valkyrie peered up at the building as if willing it to tell her its
secrets. "Who would expect a graceful fox to live in a hovel of dirt?" She
pointed to a railing on the fire escape, and Satara noticed one of her birds
perched there, staring into the window across from it. "He's there. The
third floor."

Quietly as they could, so as not to alert the shade of their presence,
the two women snuck around to the building's front door. The lock
broke easily, and as they slipped inside, darkness enfolded them.

A number of the apartments on the bottom floor seemed to be
abandoned; as they climbed the cramped and creaking stairs, only a
handful of doors were locked—a few weren't even intact—some with

faint light seeping from under the doors and some as dark as their surroundings.

When they reached the third floor, they made their way to the alley side of the building. Astrid listened closely at each closed door until she came to one toward the end of the hall. The sounds of a window being wrenched open and a bird flapping and crowing told them this was the right apartment.

Unceremoniously, Astrid reeled back and kicked down the door.

The room beyond did remind Satara of the fox dens to which Astrid had compared it. It was one small, dark room and bathroom. A tiny cot sat under the one window. Clothes and miscellany were strewn about, and a full bag of belongings sat open on the floor. Standing before them, slender hands still clutching the window's casing, was a familiar figure. Lylirion For-Shadow.

The elf had jerked his head over his shoulder at the sound of their entrance. He was dressed in the same battered leather as before but had discarded the shadowy scarves, revealing his face. Satara stared in surprise; she'd been expecting him to be an exiled elf like Zaedicus, one who had lost nearly all their elven features, but that clearly wasn't the case.

A sheet of ash-blond hair fell to the small of his back, and his pale gold skin—covered with a barely-visible layer of peach-fuzz—almost seemed to have its own luminescence, shimmering slightly on his razor-sharp cheekbones, nose, and forehead. In lieu of human eyebrows, two thin, black antennae twitched angrily along his elegant brow. Familiar beryl eyes narrowed to a glare as he unsheathed a knife from his belt.

Before he could use it, however, the room flooded with a terrible, cold light. Satara murmured a spell to help her see through the glow of her battlemother's unveiled form and drew her own weapons, watching Astrid strike the knife from her opponent's hand with a small blast of energy.

The knife clattered to the ground, and Lylirion grasped his wrist with an audible groan. Still, his glare didn't waver; not even the blinding light rolling off Astrid made him flinch.

"I'd ask what in Yngvi's name you want," he said through gritted teeth, "but we both know the answer."

Astrid reached him in a single stride and grabbed him by the collar. Her voice echoed as if it was coming from the bottom of a well, dark and demanding. "Where is it?"

He clamped his mouth shut. After a moment of silence, the valkyrie lifted him off the floor, then yanked him down with great force. Satara's heart sped as she heard the crack of his legs breaking, but he made no sound.

"Where is it? Tell me." Astrid enunciated each word this time, voice growing louder.

He hung loosely in her grip, mostly leaned against the edge of his cot. The sweat beading on his face was the only indication that she had hurt him at all. "It doesn't matter if I tell you. You're going to find it either way."

"Don't die over it, then."

Lylirion said nothing, but for a fraction of a second, his eyes darted to the left side of the room. Without having to be asked, Satara followed his gaze and began to overturn anything she could get her hands on.

Though she didn't know exactly what he had stolen, she knew she had found what she was looking for when she saw it. In a wardrobe cabinet filled with various food items, a large horn of burnished brass sat partially obscured behind some cans. She drew it out, and the runes on its surface glistened in the light emitting from Astrid.

"You're going to regret this," the elf muttered, closing his eyes.

The valkyrie leaned in and jerked him. "Who contracted you? That isn't worth dying over, either."

"I don't *freelance*."

"What organization are you a part of, then? Are you with the Gloaming?"

"It doesn't matter, does it? You have something shiny to bring back to your nest." His snarky attitude was somewhat weakened by the fact that he was panting through his teeth now, exposing small fangs that curved inward. "And you've got your bloody shield."

Satara cut in, her tone more even than Astrid's. "We need to know who's after those things. If you tell us, you can go home."

"Home?" Lylirion scoffed. "You're even more miserably lost and confused than they said." He looked at Satara. "Especially you."

Before the shieldmaiden could reply, Astrid had discarded her spear and drawn the broad bladed throat-cutting dagger at her hip. "I will use your severed head to weight my loom, elf. Do not test me on this. Tell me who your people are."

"No," he said, almost primly. "But don't worry; I'll take heart in the fact that I was on the right side of this conflict."

A million more questions sprang to Satara's mind with that statement, but Astrid's hand was quick. Before she could ask him what he meant or even react, the valkyrie had slashed his throat open and dropped him to the cot.

A strange fluid—viscous like blood but glowing like molten gold—seeped onto the sheets beneath him. Satara watched in awe as his body shriveled up, drained of all its blood almost at once. She had been around dead bodies her entire life, but it had never occurred to her that an elf would die any differently than a human.

She tore her eyes away from the rapidly desiccating body, still holding the brass horn to her chest. "We could have gotten yet more from him, couldn't we?"

"He wasn't going to tell us anything," Astrid replied as she shifted back into her human form. "I could see it in his face. At least we got what we came here for."

Satara nodded and handed their prize to her mentor. "I wonder what he meant."

"Hm?"

"I wonder what he meant when he said he was on the right side of the conflict," she clarified.

"I don't know." Astrid looked around for a moment before snatching up a heavy canvas bag in a corner near the bathroom. She wrapped the horn in a discarded shirt and placed it inside. "He most likely meant the winning side. The New Gloaming are even more arrogant than their predecessors."

Satara frowned. From what she knew, the light elves were no friends of the Gloaming, however mischievous or unkind they could be. Was Lylirion simply a defector, or an exile? If so, why had he retained the elves' insectoid features? What if more was at play here?

"What is that, anyway?" she asked, eyeing the bag Astrid had strapped across her chest.

There was a pause. Astrid didn't look at her, simply held the bag closer. At length, she replied, "I'll tell you some other day."

Satara was still for a moment, disappointed but not surprised by that answer. As Astrid turned to leave, the shieldmaiden stepped closer to the elf's body and noticed a chain around the withered neck. She slipped a pendant out from within the armor and snapped the chain, bringing it closer so she could study it. It was tarnished, etched with the image of a sun and two crossed daggers. It looked almost like an insignia.

"Shouldn't we—" Satara began.

Astrid cut her off. "There will be plenty of time to figure out more about him another time, my dear. Let's go home."

The shieldmaiden took one last look around the room and at the glittering blood pattering to the floor beneath the dead elf. Tucking the pendant into her armor, she turned and followed Astrid into the hall.

Thirty-three ... thirty-four ... thirty-five. Edie released a puff of air as she finally finished the set of curls she was doing. Her bicep ached, but it was a good, burning ache that told her she was getting stronger. The fact that she was adding weight onto her equipment nearly every day was proof positive of that.

It was approaching eight o'clock at night, but to her, eight to midnight was the perfect time to go to the gym. Hardly anyone else was here, and it was a huge facility, so no one bothered her. Though, to be fair, it was a safe bet that anyone whose lifestyle required they go to the gym in the dead of night wasn't interested in speaking to her anyway.

Understandably, Satara had been skeptical when it came to investing in a gym membership. Edie wasn't sure where it was, exactly, shieldmaidens trained, but she was willing to bet it wasn't Fitness Galaxy. She'd been a trooper. For now, though, it was probably best if Edie avoided her ... at least until she figured out what was going on with Astrid.

So, she'd asked Cal to give her a ride—not a much better option when it came to potential betrayal, but a lot better than riding the T drenched in sweat. The revenant sat on a bench nearby now, jacket hung over one shoulder, looking at his phone disinterestedly.

"You done yet?" he asked while Edie was trying to decide which machine to do next.

She was definitely done with this day, but probably not in the way Cal meant. She'd had to fight off a dragon two days before and was *really* feeling the bruises. "I want to get a few more things done," she said, wiping the sweat from the crease of her arm and grabbing her water bottle. "I can't rely on revenant powers to make me strong and durable."

He grumbled and looked back at his phone.

They hadn't talked about her adventure at Tilda's yet, and he didn't seem curious, but Edie's brain had been swimming with questions for the past couple days. How much could she really trust someone who told her so little about himself?

Maybe she could approach it from another angle. Fiddling with the cap of her water bottle, she ventured, "So ... Tilda's doing okay."

Cal just grunted.

"I, uh, guess that's no surprise, though. I mean, she has the money for a fancy security system, so ... the Gloaming or Aurora probably won't catch her by surprise. If they care about going after her."

"Seems like they care more about going after us." He put his phone down, but didn't say anything about the wight.

Edie studied him carefully as she added, "The guy who answered her door seemed nice." There was probably nothing going on between Antoniu and Tilda, but she wondered how he would react.

Cal stared straight ahead for a moment before saying, "Good for him," and picking his phone up again.

She suppressed a heavy sigh. Maybe she'd need a more direct approach if she was going to get him to talk about this. "Are you *ever* going to get up the nerve to talk to her?"

The revenant finally looked her in the eye. He had a familiar expression on his face—the *drop it* look. "It ain't about nerve, kid. We have nothing to say to each other, that's all." After a pause, he continued, "Shit, you saw that fiasco at the party. There's no point in it. It's been ten years. We're ... y'know. Different people."

Edie wondered just how different. "She was nice enough to let our friends stay with her for free. She's good."

"Speaking of that," Cal said, quickly changing the subject, "you still gotta find somewhere to stay, too. Guess it'll have to be with Astrid."

He was right that she had to find somewhere other than Tilda's. She already attracted so much trouble, and since that probably wouldn't change any time soon, it was for the best that she and Mercy stay far away from each other, at least until they were more secure. But staying with Astrid now, after what Indriði had said?

"Right..." She tried to play it cool. If Cal found out that she was suspicious, who knew what would happen? Their relationship seemed so tenuous to her already. Would he decide whatever he was trying to get out of this wasn't worth it—cut his losses and kill her? "I might just take my chances and stay at the apartment."

Cal looked at her like she'd turned green.

"It would be nice to get the apartment to myself for a while."

He snorted, raising his voice a little. "Uh, yeah, and freakin' dangerous."

"I don't really feel like hanging out with Astrid day in and day out, to be honest. She's a little … much." Okay, that part wasn't a lie. She didn't know how Satara did it. Astrid seemed super overbearing—she couldn't imagine how much worse it would be living with her as a mentor.

"She is kinda intense, but it ain't worth getting *raided*. Those everfuckin' Watchers are getting closer to *your* neighborhood, kid. Who knows when they'll decide to cut the crap and come after you directly? Sounds like they already sent someone in to test the waters the other day." He jerked his thumb back in the direction of her apartment.

He was right. No way the breathstealer was a coincidence. Or had it really been a breathstealer at all? A million conspiracy theories had already formed in her mind in the past couple days. She didn't think Cal had powers like the ones Mercy had described. Then again, since *he* barely trusted *her*, she didn't know everything about him.

"I'm not ready to see her," Edie said truthfully.

Cal made a face. "Not ready? Not ready for what?"

"I'm going to have to tell her Indriði said no."

"So?" He threw up a hand. "Just do it. It's not your fault the stupid Norn's got beef."

Edie thought back to Astrid's reaction when she had told her that Tiralda refused to join the Reach. She'd probably be more prepared for Indriði to say no, but then again, Indriði's answer seemed especially important to her. Edie didn't want a repeat of *that* tantrum. "I don't want her to get angry at me."

"Why are you so scared of her?"

Edie took a long sip of water to buy herself some time. Her stomach was starting to hurt again. "Uh, where do I even begin? She's *terrifying*, for starters. And..." Jesus. How to put this without coming out and admitting she didn't trust *him*, either? "I'm not sure she, you know, has my best interests in mind. Even if she thinks she does."

Cal raised a brow. "So, what, you don't trust her?"

And there it was. Edie floundered for a moment before shrugging.

"Listen," Cal said, "she's not perfect. And yeah, she can get overzealous about things. But she'll listen, and she means what she says. She's trustworthy. You've got my word."

That doesn't mean much if I can't be sure of your word, Cal.

"But..." Edie began tentatively. "It's just, I'm so new to this. There are still so many nuances that I don't have any idea about, you know? I can't make informed decisions when I don't know what the hell is going on or what she's talking about."

"That's what I'm here for," the revenant insisted, standing, almost squaring up to her. "I can translate all the Norse bullshit."

He wasn't getting it. And Edie knew she should drop it before he realized she had found out he was lying to her. "Okay," she said noncommittally. "I'll talk to her soon."

When she glanced back up, he was wearing an expression that mirrored how she felt: *I don't believe you.*

Their staring contest was interrupted as a guy with two of the tiniest dumbbells Edie had ever seen and extremely tight shorts did moving lunges past them.

"Fuck sake," Cal mumbled, "I can see what religion that guy is."

Edie snorted loud enough to cut some of the tension.

After a moment, he looked back at her warily and gestured around the gym. "So? What next?"

"I, uh ... I dunno." She tried to keep her tone light. *Keep playing it cool.* "I feel stronger, but I can't really defeat monsters by deadlifting them."

"Well, I can't teach you offensive magic," Cal replied tersely.

"I know, but since I'm thinking we're probably going to get into more fights before we can find someone who *can* teach me, I need to learn different stuff. A knife and a machete aren't going to cut it."

The revenant crossed his arms, rubbing his chin thoughtfully as he looked over each machine around the gym. Finally, his gaze stopped on the punching bags in the corner of the cavernous room. "I know where we can start."

Edie followed his gaze and frowned. The few times she'd seen people using those, it was always huge, profusely sweaty men who screamed and smacked the poor heavy bag like it owed them money. That wasn't really her style. But Cal had already turned around and started toward them before she could protest, so she followed.

He positioned himself slightly behind the heavy bag and motioned for her to stop a couple feet from it. "You know how to punch?"

"Kind of. Mercy taught me a little."

Cal rolled his eyes. "Has Mercy ever actually punched anyone?"

"Considering how often you piss her off, she may soon."

"Okay, what d'you know?"

Edie curled her fist and punched the air—basic, if a bit limp. Then she turned her hand up. "That's it."

His shoulders fell a little, unable to hide his disappointment. "Jesus Christ, we have a lot of work to do."

"I could've told you that."

He pointed up and down at her. "The first and most important thing in a fight is keepin' your hands up in front of your face. You want to block the chances of your opponent pounding your noggin as much as possible. So put 'em up. Try to stand straight and firm, but keep relaxed."

"Okay," she said, getting into position and glancing at him. "Now what?"

"'Kay, important thing to keep in mind when you're using one of these suckers." He sidled up next to her and raised his fists. "You wanna *work* the bag, not attack it. You're not pushing, right, you're punching. Thrusting your entire arm through this guy is not what we're aiming for. Here, watch."

Cal planted his feet and began to strike the bag. It was mostly a hail of small punches that snapped back to him each time, shaking the bag instead of swinging it. Occasionally, he'd come in with a stronger blow. He moved with the bag the little it did move, keeping the distance between him and it roughly equal the whole time.

"You kinda want it to be a continuous, uh ... flow, I guess. Always keep your hands up and keep the punches coming. We're not looking to strike with max force every time. You wanna—"

"Work the bag."

"—work the bag, right." He touched the bag to steady it, then backed up. "You try. Remember, punch like a … like a cobra. Strike in and let it rebound back to you. Keep your arms relaxed and your feet ready to move."

Edie raised her hands. "Shouldn't I be wearing gloves?"

"If you do it right, you won't need 'em." He crossed his arms, waiting expectantly.

"I really think you underestimate my tenderness." Nonetheless, she planted her feet and threw a few punches. They didn't make quite as much impact as Cal's, but he was right—even after a few cycles of punching, her arm muscles felt fine, and her knuckles only stung a little.

"Pretty good. Try and use your middle knuckle, not the two smaller ones. It's stronger. And keep your hands up, for god's sake!"

She adjusted herself and focused on the bag again. At intervals, he'd bark out an order and remind her to keep the distance between herself and the bag equal. Eventually, it became a pattern that started to feel more natural, and she found herself more comfortable with moving around the target.

As Edie thought she was starting to get the physical aspect, she felt something familiar come over her. It was like electricity stroking her arms, waves of energy beating at her skin, eager to be released into the world. It was the same feeling she'd had during the battle with Sárr, when she had been so dazzlingly angry that she had almost, *almost* been able to tap into … something. But she wasn't so much angry, now, as focused on her punches.

Slowly, it occurred to her that this feeling was magic. Not the kind she'd used to heal Cal or Mercy or herself—not even the kind she'd used to raise her poor hamster, Hervey. This was a different feeling, like her blood was heated from battle. Her body felt ready to deliver magical blows instead of physical ones.

If only her brain was.

"Good!" Cal practically shouted. "Keep movin'. The power in the punch comes from all the muscles in your trunk, not your fist. *Don't leave an opening. Let them flow into one another.*"

The feeling inside of her built up until it was a constant, almost painful buzz in her limbs, like static. It was overwhelming, made her bones ache. *Agony.*

She was about to call a time-out so she could find some way to release all this confused energy when she was suddenly aware of someone approaching them. In the corner of her eye, she watched as whoever it was stopped just short of the mats and waited. Both she and Cal turned their heads to the newcomer.

The girl standing there couldn't have been more than sixteen years old. Her features were round, wide, and smooth, her hooded brown eyes crinkled into half-moons as she smiled expectantly at them both. She wore a fleece-lined sweatshirt, skinny jeans, and men's combat boots. As she tucked a lock of dark, chin-length hair behind one ear, four or five piercings from her lobe to her helix were revealed. In her arms was a large, white box.

"Are you Edie?" she asked, presenting the box abruptly.

Edie backed away from the bag and lowered her hands, taking a slow breath. "Yeah?"

The girl shook the box a little. "She only said you'd be the lady with black hair, so, not very helpful, to be honest."

Edie chuckled uncertainly and took the box, testing the weight of it. It was heavier than she'd anticipated, and she tried to guess at what was inside. Cupcakes? She really hoped so, but it didn't smell like baked goods. She picked at the tape on the side of the box, looking the girl over. "She?"

"Yeah." The girl shoved her hands in her sweatshirt pockets and continued without elaborating, "I was supposed to bring it to Edie Holloway at the 24-hour Fitness Galaxy. And I did, so … tip?"

Coming out of anyone else, Edie would have thought the way she said it was pretty rude. But the girl was so charming with her earnest smile, holding out her hand, that Edie didn't have the heart to scoff. Still, she didn't have any cash on her, so she shook her head. "Sorry, nothing."

The girl didn't seem particularly bothered, at least. She shrugged and stuffed her hand back into her pocket. "It's all Gucci. Do you have any gum?"

Edie raised a brow, but walked a couple feet to her punk-patch-covered backpack and produced a couple sticks of fruity gum. "Uh, here."

"Sick." The girl immediately unwrapped them both and started chewing, then turned and left with a wave and a spring in her step.

Once she was gone, Edie sat on the nearby bench, and Cal joined her. "What the hell was that about?"

Edie snorted as she peeled the tape from the sides of the box. "Gen Z is even weirder than the generation before it. And now I sound like an old man," she mumbled, finally lifting the cover of the box.

A familiar smell hit her the moment she opened it, and though the contents were still wrapped in a layer of white tissue paper, she already had a feeling she knew what it was. She carefully picked up the note resting on top.

> *Edie,*
>> *Come see me soon. I've been thinking about our meeting. I have something I want to talk to you about.*
>> *Indriði*
>> *P.S. You'll be needing this.*

She slipped the note into her pocket before Cal could see it and unwrapped the tissue paper. Sitting there, folded neatly and glittering with silver studs, was a new leather jacket.

CHAPTER TWELVE

Now that Indriði had replaced her jacket, Cal assumed that they washed their hands of her and moved on. Edie, however, intended to answer that note.

Getting to the Norn's place without letting Cal know what she was doing was a delicate process. When she finally worked up the nerve, it had been almost a week since the breathstealer incident, and Mercy and Fisk were completely moved out of the apartment. But the revenant hardly let Edie out of his sight anymore. He said it was because he was trying to protect her, but ever since she'd confessed that she didn't quite trust Astrid, he'd seemed quieter than usual, more cautious around her.

She supposed she *could* tell him that Indriði wanted to talk to her again, but the last thing she wanted to do was make him suspicious of the Norn. If he knew she'd told Edie not to trust them, who knew what would happen?

Her efforts to shake Cal had started the night previous, when she'd complained about not feeling well. She'd even skipped dinner and fallen asleep on the couch to make it seem extra believable. She only had to get him out of the house for maybe an hour. He wouldn't let her leave, sure, but once she was out, what was he going to do, drive around the city looking for her?

Trying to appear as tired and weak as possible, she offered him the impossibly long shopping list she'd prepared that morning.

"Uh … s'cuse me? What the hell is this?" From the look on his face, you'd think she had just offered him roadkill.

"It's a shopping list." She forced out a groan of mock-pain. "I know it's a lot to ask, but it really needs to get done, and I don't feel well. I can pay you back…"

Cal rolled his eyes. "You can't wait another day? Who am I, your mom?"

This wasn't working. She had to bring out the big guns. She looked up at him and stuck her lip out, forcing her eyes to water.

Cal just growled.

"Please?"

He waffled for a moment, then snatched the list from her, glaring as he read it over. "Okay," he said, "fine. But you owe me one, sister."

Twenty minutes later, she was riding the subway uptown, knives tucked into both inner pockets of her new jacket. The Watchers wouldn't quit their jobs just because she had somewhere to go, so better safe than sorry.

When she reached Indriði's townhouse, she found that the doorman —a different one than before—knew her by name, and the security guards didn't even make her wait for Roggvi. Edie rode the elevator up to the fourth floor again.

As she exited, soft, twinkling music met her ears, and a familiar voice called to her from the lounge to her left: "Edie, is that you? I was wondering when you'd show up."

Edie turned to see Indriði, dressed in a silk blouse and trousers and playing her harp in front of the large windows. A corona of afternoon light hugged her form.

As she approached, Edie teased, "I thought you could see the future."

"I knew to find you at the gym, didn't I? Give me a little credit, here."

The Norn smiled, dark-painted lips parting. "The future isn't so cut-and-dry, babe. I knew you'd come see me, one way or the other, I just wasn't completely clear on when." She lowered her hands and stood, smoothing out her trousers. "I see you got the jacket I sent. It really suits you."

Edie couldn't help but smile. She touched one of the spiked lapels. "It's really great. Warm, too."

"It should last you a while, unless Augustus decides to jump on you again." Indriði laughed and moved to the lounge's bar. "If he does, the next jacket will be made of drake skin, I can guarantee you. You want anything?"

"No, thanks." She sat on one of the swiveling bar stools as Indriði busied herself behind the bar. "Thanks, by the way. You didn't have to buy me a new one. That was decent of you."

"Bah." The Norn waved a dismissive hand as she poured vodka, orange liqueur, lime juice, and cranberry juice into a cocktail shaker. "Stuff gets damaged; it's a fact of life. But stuff also costs money. Money is time, and most of you humans don't have much of that in the grand scheme of things. I break something of someone else's, you better believe I'm using my own money to replace it."

Edie cracked another smile.

"Anyway," Indriði said as she shook her cocktail, "you didn't come to chat about how flipping fantastic and generous I am, I assume?"

Edie dug in her pocket and produced the note that had come along with the jacket. "Your note said you had something important to talk to me about."

The Norn turned to grab a martini glass from a refrigerated compartment behind the bar. "Oh, yeah. I wanted to know how everything went with Astrid."

"It ... didn't really go." Edie bit her lip. "I haven't gone to see her yet."

"She won't like that."

"Yeah. Her shieldmaiden has been blowing up my phone, wondering when I'm gonna make it down there. She's probably going to show up at my door someday soon." Edie ran a hand through her hair, raven strands falling in her face. "I just … last time I told Astrid that someone refused to join the Reach, she went apeshit and tried to quit altogether."

Indriði raised her red brows as she poured her Cosmopolitan. "Someone else?"

"A sorceress named Tiralda. They were close friends, I guess."

She wrinkled her nose. "Tiralda, really? She *must* be desperate." With a laugh, she added, "I guess she'd have to be if she's trying to send you after me. Ymir's bones."

"I can tell that me asking you means a lot to her. So if telling her about Tiralda was bad, I can only imagine the blow-up that's waiting for me when I tell her about you." Edie scrubbed her face. "So I've been avoiding it. It's not like I could defend myself if she lashed out at me."

She thought back to the horrible pain she'd felt when she and Astrid had first touched. She'd been sure she was about to die, and that had been an *accident*. How could she protect herself against that, especially considering she didn't know how to manage any of her powers?

Indriði looked confused. "What do you mean you couldn't defend yourself? She's a valkyrie, but you're a hellerune. That counts for something."

Edie rubbed the back of her neck. "Ah … well. The thing is … I kind of don't know how to use my powers. The only times I've ever really used them were—" She paused and thought. "When I accidentally raised my hamster, when I healed a bad burn on Cal's face, and when I kept Mercy from dying. And I guess bloodmending. But that's it. I don't know anything that I could use to defend myself."

The Norn leaned against the bar, sipping her drink thoughtfully. At length, she said, "Damn. I hardly expected that. Astrid's really left you defenseless? Now, of all times?"

"She said she would look around for someone who could help me."

Indriði snorted. "Not sure where she thinks she's going to find a hellerune around here. You're most likely the only one in New England. I suppose she could find one trainer for each school of magic; blood, plague, shadow, death…"

Edie had to admit, that made her spirits lighten. Of course—there were people who weren't hellerunan who practiced those things individually. "That sounds okay. Why hasn't she done that?"

The Norn shrugged. "To be fair, I'm sure she's hard-pressed to find people who practice the ebon magics and *aren't* part of the Gloaming." She straightened, swirling her glass in thought. "You shouldn't even need teachers, though. That's the beauty of being a hellerune. You should just know how to do it."

"Well"—Edie spread her hands palms up—"I don't."

Indriði was quiet for a while, as if mulling over their dilemma. She pursed her lips. "Hmm. What are you finding so difficult about it?"

That was a good question. She thought back to the gym, when she'd tried to tap into her powers. It wasn't the energy she was having trouble with, but rather knowing how to release it. It was probably easier for people who had grown up around magic, seen what could be done with it. She was starting from zero. A painter might have all the talent and innovation and genius in the world, but if they'd never seen a tree in their life, how were they supposed to paint one? Someone describing a long brown log with sticks and leaves coming out didn't really cut it.

"It's like," she began slowly, "I know I can do it, I can feel it inside of me, but I can't seem to get it out. I don't even know where to start. Hell, I don't even know what it should *look* like." Edie sighed, starting to regret not accepting a drink.

She watched as Indriði knocked back the rest of her Cosmo and emerged from behind the bar, crossing to look at the honeylocust trees through the huge windows. After a long period of silence, she sighed and spoke. "You know ... I try not to involve myself in these politics. It's been a hell of a long time since I believed the Reach could fix anything going on between the Gloaming and the Aurora. It's too late for that, you know?" She looked over her shoulder. "The Reach worked during the Dark Ages for a reason. It's done. It won't do anymore."

Edie's voice was quiet. "So what happens now?"

Indriði smiled. "Just because the Reach is done for, doesn't mean there's nothing we can do. Something stops working, you tear it down; you salt the earth and you start over, with new requirements and measurements and leaders." She finally turned fully toward Edie and approached, stopping only a couple feet away. "And you know what? I think you could do it."

"I— *You* think I could lead the Reach, too?"

"Not the Reach. Whatever comes *after* it. I believe in Edie Holloway."

Edie couldn't help but snort. "I can't imagine why."

"You've got it all, kid." Indriði spread her hands. "You're kind, bright, cautious but open-minded. People respond to that. Every leader starts somewhere. Talent is tempered with experience. See?" She crossed her arms, assessing Edie. "The only thing you're missing that people will *really* respond to is power. To protect yourself and to, you know, give you legitimacy. Prove your birthright and all that."

"Yeah." Edie scrubbed her face. "So, the important stuff. I don't suppose you know anyone who can help me?"

The Norn skipped a beat, but then picked right back up. "That's the thing—I don't think training is what you need. And why put in all that work if you don't need it? You don't need someone who isn't a hellerune telling you how to control your powers. You could probably level the city right now, if pressed." She laughed, going behind the bar and starting to mix another drink. "No, what you need is a … push."

"A push?"

"You're like a balloon. You know, the pressure is building and building. If you wait too long, let it build too much, you'll explode, and no one needs a feral hellerune on their hands right now. You need to be dealt with before dealing with you at all is dangerous."

Edie envisioned a balloon with her face on it, and Indriði holding a giant thumbtack, getting ready to stab her. If the pressure was low enough, a pinprick would let the helium out gently. If she waited until she was full to bursting, a pinprick would tear her apart.

She couldn't be sure exactly how accurate the analogy was, knowing as little as she did about magic, but Indriði was right about the pressure.

That was what it felt like … and the Norn definitely had more experience in these things.

Edie drew herself up, sitting straighter. "Okay. I wanna let it out." She chewed her lip and looked at Indriði. "Can you help me? Is there something you can do? I'd— I'd make it up to you somehow."

Indriði was going wild with the cocktail shaker again despite the pensive look on her face. "Funny thing, actually. I was just reading about these particular artifacts and wondering if I could get a hold of one—as a curiosity, but maybe it could help. Please tell me you know what a fylgja is?"

Great, more stuff to learn. As if she didn't have info leaking out her ears already. She cringed apologetically. "Sorry, I don't."

"It's sort of…" Indriði tilted her head back and forth as she poured her second cocktail. "It's a spirit, usually an animal, that watches over you. A guardian. But it's you, too—part of you. It dies, you die, and vice versa. Sometimes it takes form depending on your character, like a fox if you're exceptionally clever, or an owl if you're serene and wise, a wolf if you're loyal and protective. That kind of thing."

"Like a Patronus?" The second she blurted it out, Edie felt like an idiot. Who the hell talked about their Patronus anymore? What year was it, 2007?

To her surprise, though, Indriði pointed at her and nodded enthusiastically. "Yes! Exactly like that." She sipped her drink and shrugged one shoulder. "Generally not as fun, though. See, fylgjur usually travel before you. They're about a day ahead of you in your timeline, give or take, so they pretty much go where they please. They might come back to warn you about what's about to happen, might not. Sometimes, other people's fylgjur will come visit you, to sort of feel you out before they meet you."

Edie swallowed, dread filling her stomach as she thought of her recurring nightmare. "Do they show up in dreams?"

"More often than not, that's where you'll see them. A sleeping brain is more open to nonlinear time than a waking one. Why?"

"No reason."

Indriði motioned for her to wait for a moment, then set her drink down and crossed the hall to her study. When she came back, she was holding a book browned with age, its bindings fraying at the corners. The spine had clearly been gilded at one point, but now the title was only etched into it in a slightly darker shade of brown.

Hauling all five feet of herself onto the barstool next to Edie, Indriði opened to a bookmarked page and began flipping back. "Since fylgjur travel ahead of us, it's damned difficult to make them appear. They'd have to come all the way back to our present to reveal themselves. Still, there are some rituals that can sort of pick them out of the future, drop them right in front of you. Lucky for you, you have a Norn on your side. We're good with time."

She finally stopped flipping the well-loved pages, smoothing the book out. It was written in an alphabet Edie couldn't even begin to comprehend, but she leaned over to look at it anyway. The passage staring back at them featured an illustration of a diamond-shaped prism.

"This is called a keeper paragon. If you drag a fylgja back through time and let go, it will only slingshot back where it came from, maybe even get hurt in the process. You have to make sure it stays put long enough to do whatever it is you need to do. So, that's where this comes in."

"Does it hurt the fylgja?" Edie asked, struggling over the Norse pronunciation a bit.

Indriði shook her head. "Nope, not at all. It's only a receptacle."

"So what does this have to do with helping me with my powers?"

"Good question." She skimmed a paragraph with the tip of one neatly manicured finger. "You're having trouble making the magic happen, but your spirit, your soul already knows what to do. You wouldn't be a hellerune if it didn't." A smile bloomed on her face. "Maybe the perfect person to train you *is you*."

"My fylgja?"

"If we can focus it in the keeper paragon, once your spirit is right in front of you, maybe things will become clearer. And if nothing happens, there are other things we can try. I can empower it. Make your spirit stronger. Maybe that's the push you need to let it all out."

Edie pushed a lock of fallen hair behind her ear and peered at Indriði. "You'd really do that?"

The Norn smiled again. "Like I said, I believe in you, Edie. I'm not Astrid's or the Reach's biggest fan—you know that. But you could really make a difference."

She sounded so genuine that Edie felt a little embarrassed. No way she could ever be that important ... but at the same time, she found that she believed Indriði. If anyone knew what it took to make a difference, it would be a Norn, a literal weaver of Fate. If Indriði really thought she could do this, and do it without Astrid and the Reach, maybe she was right.

"Thanks," Edie said, barely louder than a whisper. She ran a hand through her hair, untucking the strand she'd just fixed. "Really. Thank you. But I don't have anything to pay you back with."

Indriði sighed and closed the book, stroking the spine. "Tell you what ... like I said, I was wondering if I could get my hands on one of these things anyway. I've been researching who I could get one from around here, and I have a name. Khenbu." She stood from the bar, holding the massive tome to her chest. It was almost as big as her torso itself. "The problem is, he's a collector, and these things are rare. I don't think he's going to give it up easily."

"Oh." Edie was pretty sure she knew where this was going, and braced herself.

"If you can convince him to give the paragon to me, you can consider us even." Indriði turned and started walking back to her study.

Edie slipped off the barstool and followed so they could continue their conversation, giving the spider tanks a wide berth. "I assume he won't just give me the thing because I ask nicely? He'll want money or something for it, right?"

The Norn wrinkled her nose as she shelved the giant book. "No, he doesn't care about money … but you're right, he'll want something in return." She tapped her fingers against her mouth as she turned, going to a display case a few feet behind her desk chair. She unlocked it with a tiny key from a nearby shelf and began to sort through the things stored there.

Edie watched as she withdrew a small black box and opened it. Inside was a piece of silk, and as the Norn unfolded it, Edie caught a glimpse of a skinny white cylinder.

As Indriði plucked it out of the bed of silk, it left behind a dusty residue. "This is gátt-krít—doorway chalk. Tracing a complete, connected, three-sided doorway on any surface will allow you to use the surface you outlined as a door. Essentially, you can use this to go through any wall. With powerful magic, you might even be able to make a heimdyrr."

Edie eyed it. "Is it rare?"

"Very rare. Once you use it up, it's gone forever." She tucked it back into the silk and took the bundle out of the box, handing it to Edie. "I'm willing to bet this is one of the only pieces out there."

"What if he wants something else?" Edie asked as she took it and slipped it into her shoulder bag.

Indriði sighed. "Then I guess I'll have to go to him and get the paragon myself." She went to her desk and jotted the address down on a scrap of paper, then handed it to Edie. "Let's try and make it so I don't have to do that, m'kay?"

Edie sighed. *Right. No pressure.*

CHAPTER THIRTEEN

As Edie stepped out of the elevator and into Indriði's vestibule, she clicked her phone screen on to check her notifications and barely held back a grimace. There were so many that they couldn't all fit on the screen at once. Probably all from Cal, wondering where she was.

After this most recent visit with Indriði, Edie didn't want to get him involved. She trusted him less and less with each passing day, and the fact that he seemed constantly on-edge didn't help matters.

She made sure her phone was on silent and tucked it away in her back pocket. Even though she didn't want to be around Cal, she didn't want to run into any Watchers, either. She had to be alert when she went to visit this collector. With a sigh, she drew the bundle of silk out of her bag to look at it.

It probably wasn't a good idea to go alone. Maybe she could ask Tilda for help? Tilda could hold her own, as she'd displayed at Zaedicus's party. Then again, if something did go wrong, Edie didn't want to paint an even bigger target on the wight's back. She was supposed to be protecting Mercy and Fisk, after all, and a high-tech anti-magic security system could only do so much.

Edie was so preoccupied in figuring out her next move that she almost careened right into someone as she was passing through the front door. They both stopped just short of collision.

"Sorry," she said absently, side-stepping to avoid them.

To her surprise, they side-stepped, too, blocking her way.

It was then that she finally registered the person. Her confused gaze began at their untied combat boots and went up their velvet leggings, over-sized plum sweater, and choker necklace. The face was familiar.

"Oh, fuuuuck." The girl's half-moon eyes crinkled as she smiled. "What's up, Edie?"

The girl from Fitness Galaxy. Edie assumed, based on her tone, that *oh, fuuuuck* was a good thing in this context.

"Uh ... hi?" It came out a lot more confused than she had meant it to, but she'd never expected to see the girl again. "What are you doing here?"

The girl motioned to the building behind Edie with one hand, sticking the other in her pocket. "Indriði's the only person who lives here, so. I was coming to see if she had any errands for me to run. Don't have anything better to do."

Edie looked her over again and raised a brow. "Shouldn't you be in school?"

The girl grinned, threw a *hang loose* sign, and said, "Online classes, babeyyy."

"Oh. Cool." If only Edie'd had that option; maybe she'd have done better in school.

"I'm Sissel, by the way." The girl gave a more subdued smile. "Sissel Inuusuttoq."

"Edie Holloway, but I guess you already knew that."

Sissel snorted; then her attention was drawn to the bundle of silk Edie was holding, and she tilted her head. "What's that?"

Warily, Edie pulled it a little closer to herself, almost trying to hide it behind her back. It wasn't that she thought Sissel would try to take it; she just figured the fewer people who knew she was transporting it, the better. "Uh, something Indriði wanted me to deliver to a friend."

Sissel drew her mouth smaller, and the movement made the tip of her nose dip down slightly. "She's supposed to call me if she needs something delivered. We have a system worked out."

"A system?"

"Yeah! I'm a courier, right, for magic people? She kinda knows my dad so she tips me extra. Like, extra-extra." She drew her hand from her pocket and rubbed her ear lobe, muttering, "She better not be phasing me out."

Edie shook her head. "No, it's a special delivery. A one-time thing."

"Where to?" The girl stood on her tiptoes to try and peer at the bundle, though she wasn't all that much shorter than Edie.

Most people weren't this insistent on knowing her business. Normally, she'd make it clear it had nothing to do with them, and they'd let her go about her day. This girl didn't seem to be taking the hint, but Edie found herself more bemused than annoyed. "Oh. Um. I have to take it to a guy named Khenbu in, uh, the Financial District, I think."

The teen drew back and sucked in air through pristine white teeth. "Oof, that's gonna be rough."

Anxiety crept up in Edie's chest. "Why's that?"

"I know Khenbu. Sort of." She paused. "I know someone who knows someone who couriered for him. He's a fuglfolken, so he's really finicky and doesn't like letting people near his treasures. So even getting in is gonna be a hard sell."

Great. On top of not knowing what the hell a fuglfolken was, she might not even get to meet him in the first place—but if she had a chance to unlock her powers without a trainer or Astrid's "help," she had to try anyway. At least she had something that might entice him, and it was from the private collection of a lesser Norn. That was probably more than most people could say.

She ran a hand through her hair and glanced down the street, starting to feel a little exposed standing in the doorway. "Thanks for the heads up. I guess I should get going."

"Hey, hold up," Sissel said, holding her hands out like she might need to stop Edie bodily, even though neither of them had moved an inch. "I can go with you!"

"I'm not sure that's such a good idea."

Edie expected her to be offended, but the teen looked less indignant and more genuinely confused. "Why not?"

"How old are you?"

"Fifteen?"

Wow. Younger than she'd expected, even. "Well, uh, not to be ageist or anything, but I'm not sure this particular ... journey, I guess, is suitable for a teenager. Honestly, I'm not sure being a courier at all is suitable for a teenager," she added.

Sissel laughed, her face lighting up. "Okay, *Dad*. Real talk, though, I can get you in. So let's go!"

Narrowing her eyes, Edie asked, "How?"

"I just can. Okay? I can't guarantee he'll tip you well, but I can at least get his guards to listen."

Edie was about to reply, but something caught her eye. Across the street, a group of people rounded the corner—four men packed tightly around one taller woman in the middle, all clad in suspenders, flannels, and lensless glasses. Hipsters, which checked out, considering the bougie location, but...

There was something not quite right about the way they were observing their surroundings, like snakes slithering through tall grass. Not one of them seemed to have a cell phone, and they weren't talking to each other.

Edie had long since figured out that a lot of Watchers looked much different from the usual black-and-silver clad New Gloaming. Instead, they dressed in whatever would let them blend in: suits, sportswear, leathers. She had seen some dressed as businessmen, construction workers, cops. If you knew what to look for, you could pick them out.

"Come here." Edie grabbed Sissel's upper arm and began pulling her down the street.

The teen resisted, digging her heels into the pavement, but Edie's weightlifting had paid off and she was able to power through. "What the hell is going on?"

"We should get inside before they see us," Edie replied shortly, tossing her head in the direction of the group.

Sissel followed Edie's motion, expression twisting, but said nothing. They turned a corner and scurried into the nearest storefront, a cafe and bookshop. It was small but well-lit, and as they entered, the smells of vanilla and paperbacks washed over them. Somewhere nearby, an espresso machine ticked and hissed. Edie immediately felt more at ease. They had avoided being spotted, and everyone here seemed to be minding their own business.

Sissel shook her off and took a step away, frowning. "Why did we run from them? Are you allergic to craft beer or something?"

Edie made her way past the cafe area and disappeared into the stacks, and thankfully—after lingering in front of the pastry display counter for a moment—Sissel followed. As the teen approached, she put one hand in front of the book spines Edie was examining, wordlessly demanding an answer.

"They were Gloaming," Edie said. "New Gloaming. You know, the people who've been roving around and starting riots?"

Sissel's brown eyes widened in realization. "Oh, word? Those buttholes have been making running a lot rougher lately. By the time I figure out who they are, they're already harassing me."

"They haven't hurt you, have they?"

Sissel snorted. "Nah. I have my ways."

Edie was curious as to what exactly those ways were. With a raised brow, she realized that although Sissel had confessed to couriering for magical people, she'd never mentioned if she was magical herself. "Inuusuttoq is a cool last name. Where are you from?" she asked, hoping to get some answers herself.

The teen's posture shifted—only slightly, but Edie noticed. She stood a little straighter, seemed a little guarded. "My family's Kalaallit Inuit. That's West Greenland. Except I was born in Ottawa."

"I thought I detected an accent, *eh?*" Edie teased.

Sissel rolled her eyes. "Oof, I'm hysterical. Don't unleash another one of those knee-slappers on me or I'll perish on the spot."

"Okay, okay. Do your parents know you're doing this?"

Sissel turned her head, gazing longingly toward the pastry display. Then she looked back at Edie. "My dad doesn't like it very much, but he's busy all the time. He's a professor at U Anster." She paused. "My mom's been missing since I was little."

"Oh." Edie tried not to grimace, but Sissel seemed to notice her falter.

"I figured if I was going to find any information on where my mom went and why, it would be doing this kind of job." Sissel shrugged. "And it kind of worked, I guess. I know pretty much everyone around here, or I know someone who knows them. Except none of them have ever heard of Kass Inuusuttoq before."

"She just disappeared one day?"

She nodded. "Dad told the human police and everything, but … you know, human police. They never found her."

Edie considered. Then, after a moment, she motioned for Sissel to follow her, stepping up to the pastry counter. She paid for two eclairs, and they took a seat near the back of the cafe area, avoiding both of the big windows. The teenager was already mostly done with her pastry by the time Edie came back with napkins and a couple ice teas.

"Are you and your dad human?" Edie asked as she sat down, unscrewing the cap of her tea.

"Yeah, why do you ask?"

"Just wondering what I'm getting myself into."

Sissel laughed, her eyes sparkling. "My mom was, too, but she was mad weird. She was an ice mage, and she could do crazy stuff with her mind, like hear what living creatures were thinking or make them do stuff. She and my dad met when he was researching Greenlandic legends." She took a long sip of tea, shrugging. "My mom never tried to hide magic or whatever from me. She didn't want me growing up all confused."

Edie felt a pang of jealousy. If only her father had extended her the same courtesy. "My father died when I was thirteen, so I know how you feel, a little bit."

"That sucks." Sissel pursed her lips. "I've heard about him. I've heard most things."

"Lucky you. I only just found out I was a hellerune a couple months ago. I didn't even know any of this stuff existed."

"That's nuts." The teen raised a skeptical brow, brushing some hair behind one ear. "How did you not notice?"

"My magic wasn't activated, I guess. No one knew about it—or no one could find me, anyway—so no one bothered me."

"What about your mom?"

Edie looked away. "We don't talk much. I have no idea how much she knew or didn't know."

"No wonder you're so weird," Sissel said, tearing the remaining half of her eclair into smaller halves. "Your parents were wack."

The statement was so unexpected that Edie wasn't even offended. In fact, she laughed out loud. "You're not wrong."

They talked for a little longer, chatting about their living situations. Edie told her about Mercy, Cal, Fisk, and Satara; she summed up meeting Astrid and their first adventures at her behest. She also mentioned Zaedicus's party, and filled Sissel in—the "tea," as Sissel called it—on what was going on with the New Gloaming, and about Sárr.

Sissel told her about herself, too. She lived with her dad and a fat tabby named Shorts in a cozy apartment near the University of Anster, where Professor Inuusuttoq kept long hours. Sissel did her schoolwork in the mornings and couriered in the afternoon, then spent evenings cooking or watching movies with her dad. It sounded like a pretty peaceful existence, and it warmed Edie's heart to hear it. This was the kind of person she was trying to protect. This was why, Reach or no Reach, she had to fight against the New Gloaming.

Eventually, Edie finished her eclair, and Sissel looked over her shoulder, peering out one of the shop's windows. "You think the evil hipsters are gone now?"

Edie turned in her seat and said, "No, this neighborhood is still gentrified to hell."

That drew a laugh from Sissel. "Wow, woketh. I meant the murderous ones."

"Probably."

"Good." She leaned forward and planted her hands on the table in front of her. "So, do you want my help getting to Khenbu or not?"

Edie hesitated, reaching into her bag to touch the bundle there. "I don't know..."

"Do you even know where you're going?"

"She gave me an address, but I don't know the building."

Edie took the little piece of paper from her bag and handed it to Sissel, who glanced at it for only a second before standing up.

"I do. Let's go."

CHAPTER FOURTEEN

"AH ... so that's where she is."

Zaedicus raised his eyes from his scrying basin, letting Holloway's image fade away in the flickering candlelight. For the first time in months, a genuine smile spread across his face.

Scarlet's pet breathstealer had visited the hellerune's apartment earlier that day, but there had been no answer at the door, no signs of the zombie. The Watchers, too, had not caught a glimpse of Holloway's friends in that area for nearly a week. But they couldn't hide from a Gloaming Lord.

When the high-wight looked up, he met Scarlet's cold gaze, staring into him from the other side of the stone bowl.

She quirked a brow. "She's quite bold. Or stupid. I thought she would hide away with her friends."

A certain warmth touched him, one he couldn't quite describe. Something adjacent to anger. He reached across the basin and closed his hand around Scarlet's, resisting the urge to jerk her closer.

Despite her being a lowly human-wight, the memory leech's infuriating beauty and strange nature had enticed Zaedicus against all odds. Where he had kept her at arm's length before, now, with every interaction, he toed the line. Desire burned in him, and her refusal to lie with him—either out of spite or because she wasn't picking up on his cues —only made him burn hotter and deeper.

She allowed him to touch her for a moment, then shook him off and turned away, brushing back one heavy curtain to reveal the closet's door. "Has the master spoken to you yet?"

Zaedicus clenched his teeth. Sárr had appointed Scarlet as the leader of the Watchers, and she seemed to think only of her duty. She was good, and she knew how to incite chaos and sow fear, but she largely ignored Zaedicus unless they were talking business.

The high-wight found it difficult not to succumb to jealousy. In the past, impulsive wrath had gotten him exiled from his homeworld, and after that, his first coven. He would not be thrown out again. As he reminded himself frequently now, he was the Gloaming Lord, and should be tending to his duties, not focusing on the maddening presence of some vampire.

"The Wounded Lord has not spoken to me directly, but he has sent word. We proceed as planned."

"Brilliant." She looked at him over one shoulder covered just-so with a lace shawl. "And the Auroran?"

"Complying, as always."

She took a breath. "Good. Between us and the traitor, the Reach can't hope to hide for long. We'll root them out."

Scarlet left the closet, and Zaedicus followed her into the VIP room slowly, sinking into his favorite wingback chair. He glanced around for a thrall, then gestured for him to bring something to drink.

Scarlet perched on a nearby couch. "I'll have my Watchers spread out immediately."

Ah, she may have ensnared him, but there were still things he knew that she did not. Zaedicus smirked. "Tell the Watchers to do what they will with the civilians, but let Edith Holloway go about her business for now. I have something in mind."

The vampire raised her fine black brows, expression stunned. As she twisted her plump mouth, he could almost taste her anger. She was offended. "What? What is it you're keeping from me this time?"

He kept his gaze trained on her even as his thrall returned and set a tray between them. Her anger, and the fact that she couldn't possibly take it out on him, were intoxicating. "Holloway isn't the problem here. When it comes to her, the Wounded can't see the forest for the trees, as it were; he chases her like a dog with a bone. *I* am focusing my power on the Reach. A calculated strike at the head of the beast is all we need to dissolve it completely."

The thrall handed Zaedicus his drink. When he offered Scarlet one next, she hissed and stood, launching it out of his hand with a firm smack. The thrall scurried away to clean up the mess.

All the sparkle was gone from Scarlet's black eyes. "You didn't bother to tell me about this?"

"You were doing just fine with your little riots."

"I was ignorant!" She stomped over to him, and he felt his blood—such as it was—begin to heat. "You wanted to keep me in the dark so that you could get all the credit for whatever brilliant turn of fate you've come up with. You're desperate for the master's approval now."

"Ha!"

She pointed at him. "Do you want a repeat of last time? It was because *you* kept your *ingenious* plan from me that I ended up dumping the zombie when I was done collecting its memories. How was I to know you wanted to keep him to lure the hellerune? *Your* clumsy fault—and I was punished for it!"

Zaedicus set his drink aside and stood up. He towered over her, but he certainly didn't feel very big. "Am I obligated to tell every detail of my plans to nonessentials?"

Scarlet set her jaw, fingers twitching almost imperceptibly. He could tell that she wanted to lash out, but even she knew there were limits to her torment. He'd see her killed, and he'd deal with whatever punishment the Wounded Lord dealt later.

Instead, she simply slapped her hands onto his shoulders and forced him to sit again. Bent over him, her hair snaking over her shoulders, her breath in his face, she whispered, "You are pathetic."

Fury mixed with arousal, sending chills shooting through his limbs. He could almost feel his dead heart shudder to life. He clutched the arms of his chair and fixed her with a silent glare as she backed up and left the VIP room.

Gods, he despised her. So much it burned.

At least he could take comfort in the fact that, if everything went to plan, the Reach would crumble.

It was almost rush hour by the time Edie and Sissel reached the Financial District in downtown, and Edie was starting to wish she'd eaten something more than an eclair in the past 24 hours.

The teenager led her out of the subway and down Foundation Street, pointing at a tall building a few blocks down. "Khenbu lives up top."

More rich people to deal with? Edie was starting to feel out of her league. But she supposed it made sense for a collector to be rich. How else would he afford all his cool stuff? "I've had my fill of penthouses for a lifetime."

"It's a condo, technically," Sissel corrected her. "And, you know, fuglfolk. So he likes high places."

Edie slowed a bit. "Oh, yeah. I forgot to ask you what a foogle ... volk ... what that is."

"*Fugl* means bird, so..."

"He's a bird person?"

The teenager nodded. "Hence the collecting and urge to be up high."

They hurried to the door of the building and passed the doorman without incident. Edie had to admit she was eager to see what a bird person actually looked like. She was so wrapped up in imagining it that she barely registered the apartment lobby, which was set up like a museum with expensive-looking modern art and paintings carefully placed around a spacious white room. She followed Sissel past a desk, toward the chrome doors of an elevator.

"Hey!"

The voice cut through her reverie, and both she and Sissel turned to look at the person who'd stopped them.

A lady with glasses and a blond bob had risen from her seat behind the front desk and was walking after them now, black heels clicking on the tile. "Where are you going?"

Edie started to stick her hands in her pockets, and the woman came to an immediate halt, staring at her. It was then that Edie noticed the woman had a gun holstered at her hip.

She opted to keep her hands at her sides instead. "We're visiting a friend, uh, Mister Khenbu."

Sissel nodded. "Which apartment is his?"

The woman frowned, eyes narrowing. "You won't be able to use that elevator without an ID. Myself or the resident will have to let you in. Anyway, Mr. Khenbu isn't staying here anymore."

Sissel pulled a face and glanced from the woman to Edie, then back. "We're couriers. A friend of mine dropped something at this address just last week."

The woman had already turned slightly and was motioning for them to step back in front of the front desk. "You can leave your package here, and I'll make sure it gets to him."

Edie closed her jacket tighter. "No, we have to give it to him in person."

A look of annoyance crossed the woman's features. "I'm afraid that's impossible, as he no longer lives here. But I have a forwarding address, and I'll make sure he gets the package." She patted an empty space on her desk expectantly.

Edie looked at Sissel with growing panic, unsure of what to do.

The teen rolled her eyes, sighed, and went to the edge of the desk. She reached out and touched the woman's shoulder, forcing eye contact. A subtle flash of steely silver light passed between the two in a fraction of a second.

Sissel kept her hand on the woman's shoulder as she said, her voice firm and commanding, "Tell me where Khenbu's apartment is."

The woman replied calmly, "30th floor. First door down the hall to the left."

Sissel nodded. "Go to sleep."

The woman's eyes slid closed.

"Edie, get her ID."

Edie jumped into action as though Sissel was controlling her, too, and unclipped the woman's ID from her waistband.

"Good. Also, if you could find a master key around there somewhere, that would be *utterly* clutch."

Despite her casual wording, Sissel's tone was urgent. Edie dug through the desk for a moment before coming along a manila envelope in the bottom filing cabinet labeled *Master*. She pulled out a white card and shoved it into her back pocket. "Got it."

When Sissel released the concierge, the woman slumped in her chair, head lolling to the side.

Their eyes met. Edie released an anxious breath and said, "I guess your mom's not the only one who has mind powers."

The teen smiled. "Yeah, well." Her smile didn't last long, however. She took the ID from Edie and hurried to the elevator, swiping the card. "We gotta hurry. She's not going to sleep forever."

"You think she was lying about him not being here?"

"Why would he move without warning like that?" Sissel shrugged and shoved the ID into one still-untied shoe.

They rode the elevator up to the 30th floor, both of their gazes glued to the floor indicator. Every second that passed was agony, turning Edie's stomach. How long would the spell work? She didn't know much about Sissel's powers, and considering she was a teenager, Edie assumed that Sissel didn't know much about them, either. For now, they were stuck hoping that everything would work out okay.

When they finally reached the 30th floor, Edie paused before poking her head out into the hallway. She checked both ways, and when she was sure the coast was clear, motioned for Sissel to follow as she started down the hall.

As they made their way to apartment 30B, Edie glanced at her companion. She was suddenly acutely aware of the girl's age—only barely a teenager, really. "You should probably head home. I have a feeling this isn't going to be the safest situation ever."

Sissel looked at her like she had told a bad joke. "Bruh, you wouldn't even be up here without my help. What are they going to do, shoot us?"

"They might." When they reached the apartment door, Edie quickly swiped the master keycard through the lock, eager to get out of the hall. "Also, breaking and entering is wrong, and I don't want to be responsible for corrupting the youth."

"I'm staying."

Edie twisted the doorknob so it wouldn't relock and fixed Sissel with what she hoped was an authoritative glare. "The moment something dangerous happens, you run, okay? Don't stay. I can handle it on my own."

Sissel gave her a skeptical look.

"Promise me."

"All right, all right." She rolled her eyes. "You remember from three minutes ago that I have, like, mind-control powers, right?"

"Yeah, but can you stop bullets?" Edie raised a brow in return and finally opened the door.

The room beyond wasn't what she had expected. She'd seen clean rooms before, but this looked downright unlived in. She felt like she was walking into a fresh hotel suite, not someone's house. As she stepped in and looked around, she could see indents in the carpet where furniture had once been, though there were only a few nondescript pieces left now.

Sissel separated from her, going to search the other rooms. When she returned a handful of seconds later, confusion was written across her face. "There's nothing here."

Edie threw up a hand and let it fall against her thigh. "I guess she wasn't lying about him leaving."

In a last-ditch effort to find any sort of clue, Edie made her way onto the balcony off the living area. As she skimmed her hand across the stone surface of the parapet, she noticed a thousand little scratches there, as if made by claws or talons. She supposed that would make sense if a bird person had been living here.

Behind her, she could hear Sissel moving things around, looking under and around the few pieces of furniture that had been left behind. After a moment, Edie joined in.

Nothing.

Where *was* he?

Without warning, the door slammed open. There was a beep and a gruff voice: "Found 'em."

Edie and Sissel looked over their shoulders in unison to see a man in a black security uniform standing in the doorway, staring them down.

Shit. Of course—they must have seen Sissel put the concierge to sleep through one of the security cameras, or had at least noticed Edie stealing her keycard. Edie tried to reach into her jacket discreetly.

Sissel, however, simply sighed and rolled up her plum sleeves. "Nothing can ever be easy," she tutted, planting her feet as the security officer stalked toward her.

"Sissel—" Edie made a move as if to step in front of her, but the teen slid to the side, blocking her again.

The security officer clipped his walkie-talkie back to his vest and pointed a beefy pink finger at them as he came closer. "You can't be in here. Keep your hands where I can see them."

Sissel laughed and raised her hands. "No, you."

Her palms flashed with silver magic, eyes locking with the security guard's. He was stunned for a moment; then, he mirrored her movements, lifting the Christmas hams attached to his arms in surrender.

Boot steps rang out from the hall. A second later, two other security guards were flanking the first. Edie watched from behind as Sissel drew her shoulders closer, shaking with effort as she barked, "Stop!"

A halo of silver traced her body. The new security guards stopped, but they were agitated. Edie could tell without being told that they were fighting against Sissel's control—she was spreading her power a little too thin, and was beginning to pant and sweat.

Edie stepped forward and touched Sissel's elbow. "We have to go."

The teen's voice cracked as she loosed a final command: "Tell me where Khenbu is now!"

The frontmost officer trembled as he fought against her, but he still obeyed her order. "On Cardinal Street. In Springwich. That's all I know."

Sissel didn't look at Edie, but managed through her teeth, "He's telling the truth."

Edie nodded. "Let's go."

The teen struggled for a moment longer before lowering her hands. Another spark of silver announced the end of her spell, and without missing a beat, she barreled forward and shouldered past the officers. Edie followed suit. The two were sprinting down the hall before the men had time to recover.

"Stairs," Edie breathed, pointing down the hall. A plain white door stood at the end, next to a sign that said *In Case of FIRE Use STAIRS* with a stick figure running from flames. She practically pulled Sissel through the door and down the stairs after her, praying to god the whole way that the girl wouldn't trip on her untied boot laces.

Security was only a flight behind them as they pushed through the fire exit door, setting off the alarm. But by the time the guards followed them outside, they had already turned a corner and disappeared into the rush hour crowd.

CHAPTER FIFTEEN

IT HAD TAKEN ALMOST a week for Marius to decide whether or not he should tell his father what he'd seen in the mirror. The Radiant hadn't been interested in his complaints against Ynga's killing of the troll, so why would he care about anything else Marius had to say? Then again, wouldn't he want to be warned of a possible attack?

Though Marius had lost many a night's sleep deliberating, the choice to tell his father seemed obvious after he had decided. The only problem was, the Radiant seemed far more interested in the paperwork he was leafing through.

"Your Grace—Father. I saw you fall. The mirror showed it to me." Marius clenched his fist on the desk in front of him. "The mirror is prophetic. You said it yourself."

Radiant Eirik sighed. "It is."

"I saw what I saw."

His father didn't look up, carefully signing his name at the bottom of a document in front of him "I don't doubt what you saw, Marius, but like with all foresight, outcomes are unpredictable. They may change at any time."

"Where is the mirror now? You can see for yourself." The vivid glanced at the magical safe adjacent to his father's desk. In there, perhaps?

The Radiant's voice took on a more amused tone. "I don't need to use a mirror to see into the future, Marius."

"But you don't have the same insight into your own fate," Marius protested. "You said so yourself once. How can you be sure? We should take every precaution available."

"That's what I have Tiralda for now, among other things." Eirik looked up at his son, mouth drawn tight. "Marius, you know that we have more important things to deal with. You know better than anyone what this New Gloaming is capable of, don't you?"

Marius clenched his jaw. In some ways, even though his body had healed, he was still suffering from the after-effects of battling Sárr. Nightmares were frequent and intense. "Are those things more important than ensuring the safety of the Radiant of the Rising Divine?"

"Yes." Eirik set his pen down and sighed, looking up at Marius. "Vivid, innocent people are dying at the hands of these animals. Every day, there's some new riot or attack or murder. The unattuned police are powerless, and their fear and anger are only encouraging the Gloaming. In some precincts, they aren't doing anything at all."

"Probably bought out ... or infiltrated by Gloaming."

"This *Wounded Lord* was more prepared than any of us gave him credit for." The Radiant scrubbed his face with his hand. "I think—it must be—that he's been planning this for years."

"He can't be any older than I am," Marius mused. "*How?*"

"I don't know, but you see? We have not only our own people to protect, but the rest of the city, and the towns surrounding it. Our temple's jurisdiction stretches 200 miles in all directions. On top of that, the hellerune is still running loose. Spread this thin, I can't even manage to press the Gloaming. I have to focus on the matter at hand: saving lives. I cannot stop for one moment."

Marius's heart leapt in his chest. "But if you die, we'll be without a leader."

"In the unlikely event that I do die," Eirik returned, "the Aurora will have you."

The vivid couldn't deny the fear that lanced through his heart. He had dreamed of being a leader, making his father proud; he had studied hard to try and make sure he was ready for it when the time came. Now that the situation seemed so plausible, however, all of his hard work didn't feel like nearly enough. He said nothing.

After a moment, the Radiant motioned for him to stand, and he did. "Now, please. I have a lot of work to do."

Marius left the conversation feeling no more at ease than he had before—less, in fact. The mirror had not lied to him. Runepriests didn't carry around bogus artifacts.

For now, there was nothing to be done. If his father wouldn't take this seriously, then Marius would investigate it on his own.

He exited the main building of the temple and made his way to the dormitories. A three-by-three group of adherents, led by a vivid, jogged past him on the veranda, probably on their way to answer a summons. The temple hadn't slept in two months. There were always several combat-ready groups awake and prepared to answer the call if the New Gloaming caused trouble.

Marius, predictably, hadn't been allowed to join any of the raiding parties. His father had refused to let him face the New Gloaming until he was in fighting condition, then had given him a number of excuses after that. Typical. He couldn't tell if his father was punishing him or simply didn't have faith in his abilities anymore.

Marius eyed the joggers as they passed. Could one of them be the traitor?

In his mind, there were two obvious leads: Ynga and Tiralda. He had seen Ynga around before they became friendly, but she had always laid low, blending in with the other adherents. For her to rise in prominence, grab his father's attention, and secure a rank in such a short time felt odd to him. And then, of course, there was Tiralda, the sjóvættr. No one here really knew her that well. His father had confessed to him once that he'd only allied with her on the recommendation of another Radiant. She might have been a seidr-woman, a practitioner of Freyja's Craft, but who knew what sort of motive she could have to bring his father down?

Almost without consulting his brain, his feet were taking him in the direction of the sorceress's dwelling. Since she was an esteemed guest, she didn't have a standard dormitory; rather, she had been gifted the solar at the top of the mage's tower, just on the edge of the small canal that separated the temple grounds and the annexed campus.

No one stopped him as he entered and began to climb the great spiral staircase. The fire and light mages that inhabited the tower were a solitary bunch, and a vivid coming into their tower on an errand wasn't uncommon. The higher up he went, the fewer people he glimpsed in the rooms he passed, until finally he was completely alone. A small landing was all that separated him from the arched wooden door of Tiralda's solar.

Marius was surprised to find it unlocked, but thought nothing of it as he stepped through and closed the door behind him, as softly as he could.

For the most part, the room was unchanged from the last time he'd seen it several months ago; the ancient wooden bed, table, chairs, wardrobe, and chest of drawers were still in the same places they'd always been. However, it looked like the sea spirit had tried to make herself feel more at home. The bed's canopy had been replaced with diaphanous curtains of turquoise, teal, and pale seafoam; the sheets were crisp white, devoid of any of the furs and quilts that had been there before. Strewn around the room, especially in the corners and the cracks of the stone, was silty, light brown sand. In the window nook sat an intricately carved spinning wheel; the color and luster of it reminded Marius of shell and bone.

Marius found himself overwhelmed by the room for a moment, unsure of where to start looking. He went to the bed first, smoothing out the sheets and checking under the mattress, the pillows, anywhere something could be hidden. He checked behind the silver mirror above the washbasin. Finally, he moved to the chest of drawers and pulled out the top drawer.

What few underclothes the sorceress used seemed to be stored here, along with a large collection of wooden and gold jewelry arranged into several boxes. The bottom drawer stored a number of small personal items, including books, hand mirrors and fans, a collection of sea shells, a few talismans and charms, and several extra spindles for her wheel. He checked both drawers for hidden compartments, but found nothing.

He moved on to the wardrobe, a medieval oak piece with wrought-iron ring handles. It opened with a creak, and he was faced with a mess of sheer fabric in a range of pastel colors. Below the dresses was a trunk filled with little slippers and pearly sandals that looked so delicate Marius didn't even dare touch them.

Again, he checked for any hidden compartments. Again, he found none.

"That's not right," he whispered to himself, standing from where he'd been crouching in front of the wardrobe. Even if she wasn't the traitor he was looking for, everyone had at least one hidden—or at least deeply personal—thing in their bedroom.

He knew he did. Two years before he had become a vivid, he'd raided an apartment while helping in the hunt for a local slaver. The apartment had been filled to the brim with every sort of document you could imagine: newspapers, flyers, books, magazines. A pile of old *Rolling Stone* magazines had caught his eye, the covers plastered with pictures of bands like R.E.M., The Cure, Alice in Chains, Metallica, and Nirvana.

For some reason, he'd been drawn to them, and had squirreled one away in a trunk under his bed. Over the past few years, he'd read it cover to cover a hundred times, fascinated by the unfamiliar things within its pages. He still took it out every so often, but the feeling was different now. Instead of enchantment, he felt only bitterness; a deep, abiding resentment for the world outside the temple. He was not normal like them. All he had ever known was the order, and this temple, and that was all that could ever be.

He tried not to dwell on it—but thinking of it had given him an idea. He quickly made his way to Tiralda's bed and sank down, peering under it. Sitting there, shoved toward the wall, was a dark oak box with a latch.

Perfect. Marius reached in, sliding it out and unlatching it in one motion

The box was so full that its contents nearly overflowed the moment he opened it. Stacked and bound together with twine were years' worth of letters, some loose, some tucked away in yellowing envelopes. Little bits of multicolored wax had crumbled off of them and collected in the creases and at the bottom of the box. Marius held his breath and carefully untied the first bundle of letters.

Some of it was interesting. He noted, as he shuffled through, some correspondence between Tiralda and Astrid Fengrave. A lot of it was unreadable, water-damaged or in languages he couldn't read. The ones he could read seemed to be normal, if a little boring—letters about drama in Freyja's hall or in other Worlds. By the time he got to the third bundle, he stopped reading closely; and when he was finally done, the last of the letters in his hand, he hadn't seen a singular mention of the Wounded or Sárr or the Gloaming or even the Aurora.

The vivid laid the last letter down and searched the box for a secret compartment. Nothing. He felt his shoulders sink. The thrill of finding the hidden trove was completely sucked out of him.

If he wasn't missing something here, it would have to be Ynga. He tied the letters together and shoved them back in the box.

Behind him, the solar door squealed, slamming against the stone wall as it was thrown open. "Ah!"

Marius turned quickly, trying to shove the box under the bed—but she had already seen. Tiralda stood there, staring him down, her usually beautiful face twisted, angular like a sea serpent about to strike.

"You worm," she snapped, coming forward and seizing him by the back of the neck like he was a misbehaving pet. "What in Njord's name do you think you are doing, Vivid?"

Marius didn't resist her. It would only cause him more trouble, make her more likely to hurt him. He said nothing, either; there was no excuse he could give that wouldn't just make her angrier. He simply grunted in pain and glared at her.

She dragged him down the stairs and out of the tower, shouting the whole way and demanding what business a lowly mortal had rifling through her things. As they crossed the green to the temple, people stopped to stare at them. Some were wide-eyed; others simply watched, wary, as if unsurprised that the Radiant's only son had finally snapped and disobeyed their laws. A couple scurried ahead of them, probably going to alert his father of the situation. Marius grimaced.

Tiralda's ranting only continued as she yanked him up the stairs toward his father's private library. "I ought to remove your other hand and feed it to you!" she said, throwing open the library doors and tossing him in.

His father was already descending the stairs to the library's first floor, and Marius fell at his feet. Eirik looked from him to Tiralda, brow drawn tightly. "What in the Wolfbinder's name is the meaning of this?"

The sorceress glided over to Marius once more and took a fistful of his hair, jerking him around. "Eirik! You should be ashamed of yourself."

"Excuse me?"

"For conceiving such a stupidly audacious failure of a son!"

Eirik motioned sharply for her to let Marius go.

After a moment, she obeyed. Her piranha-like underbite was becoming more prominent the angrier she got, her needle teeth gnashing as she shouted. "I caught your whelp pawing through my belongings. Touching my things! Going through my personal documents like a lowborn rooting for treasure! I had forgotten how primitive humans were."

The Radiant bent slightly and braced Marius's arm with his left one, lifting him to his feet. He looked in his son's eyes for half a second before looking back at Tiralda. "You have my apologies. Did he take anything?"

"No," Marius whispered.

"And how are we to believe you, *Vivid*?" She gestured to him, glaring at his father. "Where I come from, he would be mutilated. Scrounging around for something to take back to his den. Perhaps sell!"

"I didn't take anything," he snapped back.

"Stop." The Radiant's tone was severe, and it shut both Marius and Tiralda up. He drew himself up a bit, mouth in a tight line, and walked past Marius to open the library door for the sorceress. "I will deal with my son privately. Thank you for bringing this to my attention."

She paused before gliding past him with a last imperious sneer at both men. "Very well. I need not speak of this any further. I dismiss you." She turned and left, head held high.

Radiant Eirik shut the door softly after her, then ran his hand over his carefully twisted hair. After a moment, he turned to look at his son, and Marius stiffened, bracing himself for the severe admonition to come. His father wouldn't yell—he never did—but the disappointment would be so heavy that Marius would wish he had. He'd been through it a thousand times before.

To his surprise, however, the reproach never came. Eirik simply walked past Marius and sank into a nearby leather chair, then motioned for his son to sit in the chair next to it.

"Marius..." he began after a period of silence.

Before he could go on, the vivid answered: "I'm sorry, Father, but I didn't take anything."

"I know." Eirik sighed. "Is this the investigation into your *traitor?*"

He nodded stiffly.

"Can't I convince you to drop this crusade?"

His father looked more tired than agitated, so Marius told the truth. "No."

Eirik looked at him solemnly. "Really?"

"Yes."

He sank back in his chair a little. Marius watched his expression go from concern to deep thoughtfulness, then even out. "What made you suspect Tiralda? What would be her motive?"

"Money, an old grudge?" The vivid shrugged one shoulder. "Perhaps it isn't her. She was only my first choice because she was an outsider. It could be anyone."

The Radiant watched him, gaze soft, brows drawn together. "Marius. Trust me when I say I thoroughly vet anyone I let within our temple. If she had any connection to our enemies or anyone that might want to hurt us, I would know."

He leaned to the side slightly. It looked like he wanted to reach out for Marius, but he didn't. He breathed a long, thoughtful sigh, then looked into his son's face. Marius wasn't prepared for his next declaration.

"My Aurora is your Aurora, don't you see? You are my light. I would never, never let in someone who might hurt you. I would die first."

On a realistic level, Marius knew his father loved him. His father was overbearing and expected much; they bumped heads, and Marius often wondered if his father was truly proud of him, but of *course* he knew that he loved him. It was just that he rarely said it so explicitly.

Marius wanted to look away from his father's earnest gaze, but found he couldn't. "The title of Radiant isn't hereditary," he murmured. "Someone else could take the job. Someone else *should*. I'm not ready."

After fighting his father for so long, it felt strange to admit that.

Eirik nodded. "When the mantle was passed on to me, I felt the same way. How could I live up to the Radiant before me? How could I dare? I was only a vivid, and your mother died so soon after I was appointed..."

Even though Eirik was dignified and battle-ready in his gleaming armor, he suddenly looked very weary; haunted, as he always did when he spoke about Mother. Marius couldn't blame him. Eirik had been the only one to survive the siege that had killed her and the innocents they had sworn to protect.

"How did you get through it?" Marius pressed after a moment.

Eirik looked past him, at something drifting in time, something only he could see. Then he looked back at his son. "It was you."

Marius raised a questioning brow.

"When you're called to lead, it is because someone needs you. You

were still a baby. You needed me. The Aurora needed me. Radiant Geir
was dead, Kata was dead, but there were things I still had to do."

Finally, he reached out and grasped his son's wrist, drawing his gaze.

"Marius … there are so many things I wish I could tell you. There are
so many mistakes I wish I could rectify. But for all I've done, I have
learned this: When you aren't sure you can carry on, when you don't
know if you can do what you need to do … you do the things you know
you *can*. You try to be the person they loved. You try to be the person
they trusted. Most important of all, you keep the ones still alive safe at
any cost, and you never let them go."

Marius looked down, silent for a few moments. When he raised his
head again and searched the Radiant's face, he detected a hint of
desperation in his expression. With a sigh, Marius placed his hand over
his father's. "That's what I'm trying to do; that's why I'm searching. I'm
trying to keep my loved one alive."

The desperation prevailed, then … fear. It was jarring to see. Nothing
scared his father. Eirik's gaze was almost pleading, and he lowered his
voice to a tremulous whisper. "*So am I.*"

CHAPTER SIXTEEN

Since Edie had fucked up her connection with Cal, she'd been able to keep him out of her head; she couldn't get into his brain, and he couldn't get into hers. Today, though, that certainly didn't stop him from freaking trying.

As she and Sissel rode the subway into Springwich, there was a familiar, insistent niggling in the back of Edie's mind. She had gotten used to what it felt like when he'd tried, unsuccessfully, to break through the walls himself.

He hadn't made any progress then, and he wasn't making any progress now. Still, it meant he was definitely looking for her. They only had a limited time to do this thing.

When they exited the subway station, Sissel paused outside to tie her boots while Edie had a look around. They were surrounded mostly by four- and five-story brick buildings, though a few single-family houses meandered here and there as the streets curved downward, toward the more suburban parts of the city. This was the last stop on the Yellow Line.

In some ways, Springwich reminded Edie of her own neighborhood. The smoky green stains creeping up the bases of buildings, the litter compacted into the potholes lining the road, windows painted shut. It all spoke of a low quality of living for moderate rent at best.

At least *her* neighborhood was central. She could walk a couple blocks and pick up anything she needed, have any kind of food she wanted to eat. Parks, museums, and a college were only a stroll or a train ride away. A "bad" neighborhood this far away from the center of the city? No one cared if the people who lived here could get where they needed to go, or buy what they needed to buy, or if they had had a vegetable in the last month. No one cared that most of the buildings here had wooden fire escapes, if they had any at all.

Edie hugged her new jacket closer, thinking of the medical bills she kept getting, like the hospital thought she wasn't acutely aware of how much she owed. She and Mercy weren't even living good lives, and they were still lucky to be where they were. There was something so screwed up about that.

Sissel straightened. "Okay, where are we going again?"

She brought Edie back to reality with her cheerful voice. All right, cheerful and a little strained, but that made sense. After exerting most of her energy controlling those security guards, she'd practically fallen asleep on the subway.

Edie squinted, looking up at the sky. They would lose daylight in a couple hours, and Sissel was already weakened from their ordeal.

"You really should go home," Edie said, glancing at her young companion.

The girl shook her head, standing her ground just as Edie had known she would. "No way, bro, I'm seeing this shit through. You'd have already got arrested, like, twice if it weren't for me."

"Yeah, but it's only going to get more dangerous from here. This guy clearly doesn't want to be found." Edie sighed. "You need to go back home to your dad and forget about me."

"I've been through way worse stuff." The smiling teen either didn't pick up on or was ignoring the seriousness in Edie's voice. "I'm not leaving, so you may as well accept it."

She couldn't exactly force Sissel to leave. Clearly, nothing anyone said would deter her, and there was no way Edie was going to physically remove her from the situation. *You said you wanted to protect the innocent*, she thought with a sigh. They'd just have to be extra cautious.

"Which street are we looking for?" Sissel continued. "Cardinal?"

Edie nodded, already walking, and the teen quickly fell into step with her, cell phone at the ready. She was already pulling up directions to Cardinal Street, chattering about how she had to have an unlimited plan because she used the GPS app for work. Edie zoned out a little, glancing at street signs and letting her eyes rove over the area. It was the tail end of rush hour, so people were pouring out of the subway station after them; others were walking home, some hand-in-hand with their kids. Everyone was way too busy to acknowledge the two lost-looking girls roaming around their neighborhood.

Except...

As they rounded a corner, Edie noticed a subtle change on the sidewalk across from them. A group of people she had assumed were strangers on their way home paused all at once. The one in the middle made eye contact with Edie when she clocked the movement, and the others followed suit.

Edie looked away quickly, touching the back of Sissel's arm. "Don't look behind you. There's a group of Watchers. Can you find another route to Cardinal?"

The teen didn't look up from her phone, simply nodding and tapping a button, instantly rerouting. Without warning, she turned sharply down an alley, and Edie followed. She wished she had a way to hide her appearance a little. She usually wore a hoodie under her jacket for warmth, but the new one was high quality with quilted lining, and she'd figured she didn't need the extra bulk. She was regretting that decision now.

They emerged onto another busy street, and this time, Edie stayed alert, looking closely for any anomaly or pattern in the crowd's movement. As people reached their homes, the rush was thinning, which meant the Watchers wouldn't have anywhere to hide. Unfortunately, the same was also true for Edie and Sissel.

Edie spared a glance over her shoulder and watched as the group emerged a mere thirty feet behind them. Sissel led her around another sharp corner, across the street, and down another alley, keeping her head lowered the whole time.

"Have you done this before?" Edie asked, looking the kid up and down.

"I'm a fifteen-year-old girl who walks around by herself for half the day, almost every day of the week. What do you think?"

She shrugged. "Your home life sounded pretty wholesome. How the hell did you learn this?"

"Practice." Sissel grinned. "Besides, my dad isn't the only person I talk to in the whole world. That would be freaking boring. I have friends! I know a lot of older couriers who taught me stuff."

"Huh. Thank god for that, I guess."

The teen nodded wordlessly and pointed to another side street.

Edie caught the barest glimpse of their pursuers as they turned down it. Nervously, she muttered, "Let's pick up the pace."

Sissel obliged, at a trot now. "Cardinal Street is after the next right. So we better lose them before then."

Losing them was going to be pretty hard when Edie didn't even know which house Khenbu was staying in yet. There was no time to go door to door and ask, not that anyone would answer them truthfully. Edie's hairs began to stand on end.

Finally, they reached Cardinal Street. It was lined exclusively with brick buildings. Balconies and fire escapes covered the faces of the apartments, though most of the buildings' ground floors were occupied by businesses. At a glance, Edie noticed a pawn shop, a corner store, and something called DE LITES, outside of which a greasy redheaded kid sat ripping obnoxiously enormous clouds from his vape pen. No sign of Khenbu.

"Maybe the pawn shop?" Sissel suggested, glancing behind them to make sure their "friends" hadn't shown up yet.

"No ... he's a collector, not a pawnbroker. And I've never found anything rare and magical in a pawn shop, have you?"

They only had a handful of seconds, at most, before the Watchers joined them on Cardinal. Edie cast her eyes upward, trying to get a peek inside some of the windows for a clue, though she had no idea what she thought she'd see.

She was about to give up when, as she scanned the apartment building next to her from the top down, she caught something. There, on the edge of the roof, barely visible—and on the edge of the stone balcony, too ... scratches. She clenched her fists, remembering the scratches on the balcony in Khenbu's downtown apartment.

"There." She pointed to the building without further explanation.

Sissel followed her gaze and, though she seemed confused, followed Edie as she hunched under cover of the arched doorway.

Edie tested the door handle and found it locked. "Dammit. Stupid bird."

"I'll check the back. There's probably a window open."

She nodded, but glanced down the street. Their friends would be turning the corner any second. "Hurry up."

The teen was already gone, sprinting around the corner without another word. Just as she disappeared, the Watchers emerged from the side street, scanning in both directions.

Edie's heart leapt into her throat. She turned away and wedged herself into the corner of the stoop, praying to god they wouldn't notice the half of her arm she couldn't hide from view.

She closed her eyes. Sounds of footsteps scraping slightly against the uneven pavement reached her clutching ears, but she breathed slowly, determined to stay calm.

The footsteps stopped. Then, a voice: "You."

Her breath hitched.

"Did you see two girls walking down this street? Dark hair, one of them wearing a leather jacket?"

Edie assumed the next voice belonged to Greasy Vape Kid. "Uhh, yeah, I guess."

"Which way did they go?"

"I dunno, man. I think they, like, went into one of the apartments or something."

Whoever was speaking for the Gloaming group sounded agitated. "Which building?"

"I don't fuckin' know, man. That way, I think."

More footsteps.

Edie almost gasped when she heard a click next to her—then relaxed when Sissel opened the apartment door. She practically fell in, and together, they closed and locked the door as softly as they could behind them.

Edie looked at Sissel. "How'd you get in?"

"There's a laundry room in the back. They left the door open."

They were standing in a hallway with a staircase immediately to their right, a peeling door labeled *1* to their immediate left. Edie leaned to the side, looking up the stairs. "There must be a dozen apartments in this building. How are we supposed to find Khenbu?"

"Yeah," Sissel said, "but look." She gripped the doorknob of 1 and turned it. The door opened with only a slight push, and when she glanced in, Edie could see it was empty. The only thing left was the lingering smell of something stale.

"Abandoned?"

"There were a couple apartments back there that I checked. I think they're all empty."

Well, that certainly made things easier. Hopefully, they'd just have to open every door until they came to one that was locked. They split up and tried every doorknob, but Edie was troubled to find that *every* apartment seemed to be empty.

She waited on the second landing as Sissel thumped down the stairs, finished with her own search. "Any luck?"

"Nothing." They descended the last two flights of stairs, ending up in the main hall again. "They're all empty."

"Could his apartment be cloaked or something?"

Sissel paused and considered this. "Some people do that, but it's kind of hard to maintain. You can only hide so much from people, you know? If they know what to look for, they can just feel their way through." Another pause. "I didn't sense any of that stuff while I was searching. Maybe he's hiding behind something non-magical."

Thoughtfully, she walked down the hall, and Edie followed close behind. "Like a secret door or something?"

"Yeah, something like that."

Edie looked at the wall closest to her. Every so often, there were cracks or gouges that exposed the horsehair plaster beneath. She reached out, running her hand over the walls and knocking softly on them. They had a particular denseness to them; once the noise went in, the walls absorbed it, and there was no echo.

As Sissel led her back toward the laundry room, Edie kept knocking. The teen glanced back for a moment and gave her a look, but seemed to catch on quickly. She moved to the opposite wall and started to do it, too.

Nothing changed as they came to the laundry room. It was a tiny, dirty, tiled room with flickering lights the color of pee. A washer and dryer stood haphazardly on one side of the room, but they weren't actually hooked up to anything, and the dryer seemed to have an abandoned squirrel's nest or something in the drum of it. A laundry cabinet in one of the corners had been reduced to a pile of timber, its wire hangers strewn all over the floor.

Most notably, the far wall was made entirely of stone. Rough-hewn stone, like that of a medieval dungeon.

"Oh, yeah." Sissel came out from behind Edie and stared at the wall. "I didn't really notice that when I came in."

Edie couldn't help but gape at her.

"Look, my dude, I either notice every small little detail, or I'm completely oblivious to everything. There's no in-between."

"Fair enough. At least we're here now." Edie walked up to the stone wall and touched it. There were minute cracks between the stones, and when she ran her hand over them, she could feel a draft coming through. She'd have bet anything that there was a passageway on the other side. "I guess start looking for a button or something that can open this."

Sissel hummed, looking around the room. "I know where I hide stuff I don't want my dad to find." She walked along the right-hand wall and crouched in front of a ventilation duct with an ornate wrought-iron cover. Hooking her fingers through the cover, she dragged it out and reached in. Something clicked inside of the vent, echoing.

Edie was surprised how silent the secret door was. With another faint click, it whispered open. It had only shifted slightly, so the entrance was small and cramped, and Edie had to turn sideways to edge her way in. Sissel followed close after.

The passageway beyond was so pitch-black that even the yellowish light from the laundry room did little to illuminate it. Both Edie and Sissel took out their cell phones, swinging the flashlights around to try and find a switch to close the door. Edie found it first: a heavy-duty flip switch attached to an electrical box.

She hugged her jacket tighter. It was freezing in here already. She kept her phone trained on the floor while Sissel kept hers focused straight ahead, but it was like the darkness down here had substance. The light could only cut through a few feet ahead of where they stood.

Slowly, they made their way through the secret passage. It ended in a flight of switchback stairs, packed tightly in a narrow shaft. No noises from the street reached them, though a small tremor came from the subway every now and again. They must have been several stories beneath street level.

Finally, the stairs ended, and they found themselves in the middle of a long hallway. The ceilings were decently high, but the tunnel had become so narrow that both girls standing side by side nearly filled it.

Edie looked to the left, then the right, and whispered, "Which way?"

"I dunno. I'm also not a hundo that he's going to be happy to see you, even if you brought him something he wants."

She cut Sissel a look. "That's why I told you not to come."

The teen shrugged. She was trying to act cool, but she was clearly anxious, wiping her hands on her leggings. "To be honest, I didn't think we'd get this far."

Edie sighed and picked left, starting down the hall. Left was as good as right. These passages couldn't go on forever; she'd find Khenbu eventually. "You can still leave."

"I— I dunno," Sissel mumbled, lingering a few paces behind Edie. "It's getting dark out, and I *guess* my dad will want me to come home for dinner..."

Just as Edie was about to turn around and send her back, she spotted a blue glow at the end of the corridor. Had that been there before?

No ... it was around a corner, coming closer. Quickly.

Before Edie fully registered what was going on, the clink of armor echoing down the hall reached her ears. Heavy footsteps.

She sprang into action, turning on her heel and hurrying Sissel down the hallway in front of her. "Go, go! Someone's coming."

But before they could reach the stairwell and turn back, light washed over her shoulders, illuminating the hall on either side of them and casting long shadows. *Shit.*

They both turned to see what was waiting for them at the other end of the hallway.

CHAPTER SEVENTEEN

THERE WERE three or four of them, and Edie could tell by their armor that they were guards. They were tall figures, almost big enough to touch the ceiling of the corridor, their forms vaguely humanoid. But instead of human features, the beaks and beady eyes of ravens stared back at her. They were big-headed, covered in black feathers that shimmered purple under the sky-blue lanterns floating around them. Their legs bent backwards at the knees like a bird's, and instead of feet and hands, Edie could see talons—talons holding sharp glaives and halberds.

"Fucking run!" Edie shouted, pushing Sissel harder, barely able to rip her eyes away from the unfamiliar beings. Her heart was beating hard, blood hissing in her ears as she sprinted toward the stairwell only a few feet away—

Sissel, running toward the stairs ahead of her, careened into another one of the bird men. It seemed he had been in the shadows, standing still as a stone wall, with his sword at the ready.

Sissel screamed and dove just in time to avoid the downward swing of his blade. Edie dodged the teen, then clutched her by the sleeve of her sweater and hauled her up off the floor. Together, they stumbled down the right-hand hall, their breaths loud and echoing in the corridor.

Edie's eyes had better adjusted to the darkness, but she still staggered and almost fell over the uneven stone floor. The bird men were gaining on them, shouting in deep, croaking voices like something from a nightmare, ordering them to halt.

There had to be another way out. This hall had to lead to something. Maybe they could find a patch of darkness to conceal themselves—but then the birds would investigate every inch of this place, and they had those lanterns.

She and Sissel had to find Khenbu. That was the only way they were getting out of this. God willing, he was down this hall and not the other one.

The two quickly became accustomed to the pits and swells of the stone corridors. Fortunately, they were also much smaller than their pursuers, who had to squeeze themselves through the passages, brushing their feathers against rough walls in the process. It took a minute or so of running to put distance between them, but it would still only buy them a handful of seconds if one of them fell or made a mistake.

They came to another fork, and Edie paused for a half-second to consider. Though she couldn't make out much in the darkness, she thought she saw a break in the stone wall on the left side, and—yes! A tiny sliver of soft orange light glowed in the darkness. The gap of a doorway.

She grabbed Sissel's hand and sprinted in that direction, but when they reached the door—heavy, old, with an iron ring handle—they found it latched and locked with a large, modern padlock.

"Fuck!" Edie banged on the door, shoving it back and forth, but neither the padlock nor the latch would give. She raised her head and saw sky-blue fill the corridor only fifty feet from them. Looking at Sissel, she asked, "Can you make them stop?"

Sissel looked up at her with shining eyes, gulping hard. She shook from exhaustion. Edie could sense that the girl was running purely on adrenaline. "I could maybe control one for a second, but not all of them." She turned to look at the wall next to the door and pounded on it with a fist, shouting in frustration, "I wanna break down this freaking wall! *Let us in!*"

The birds were at the end of the hall now. The echoes of Sissel's shouting had disoriented them, but it would only take them a second to spot the two in the dark.

Break down this wall. Edie's stomach was doing flips as she reached into her shoulder bag and grabbed Indriði's piece of chalk.

She trotted a few more feet down the hall and, with shaking hands, started to trace the outline of a doorway. The wall was so bumpy that she had to go painfully slowly so as not to break the chalk in half.

Sissel screamed when the birds turned and spotted them. "Edie!"

"I just need a second!" Sweat ran down her back, her palms, her forehead as she meticulously traced the doorway, making sure it touched the floor on both sides.

A complete, connected, three-sided doorway. Before her eyes, the chalk lines began to hiss and sparkle with a dull light.

The bird man leading the charge stumbled, nearly falling over. Whether it was by chance or Sissel's doing, it bought Edie one more second. She pushed against the stone door with all her might, growling with effort as she did.

It barely moved. She wasn't strong enough.

Before the misery of her failure even hit her, Sissel was beside her, pushing along with her. Grunting, their shoes slipping against the gritty floor, they managed to budge the wall.

Then, without warning, it swung in easily and dumped them both into the room beyond.

"Close it!" came a mangled cry. From her or Sissel? She was so panicked she couldn't tell. They scrambled to their feet and positioned themselves on the other side of the stone. The blue of the lanterns became brighter and brighter as they pushed, trying to get the slab closed again.

Finally, the glow filled the doorway. The bird men were here.

One of them reached a clawed hand inside to grip the edge of the door.

"*Close it!*" Sissel screamed.

In a sudden blessed moment, the stone gave way under the girls' weight. It slammed shut and took a few talons with it.

Edie turned and slid down the wall, her entire body shaking. She scrubbed her face, wiping away hot tears of relief. Beside her, Sissel followed suit and buried her face in her knees.

Behind them, the doorway sizzled out of existence, and Edie focused on the room into which they had stumbled. She was surprised, to say the least.

It was a stone room not unlike a dungeon, but it was well-lit by various ornate oil lamps and wall sconces. It was richly—if a bit haphazardly—furnished: Vibrant orange and gold tapestries hung from the ceiling alongside royal-blue curtains. A chaise supported by stout legs squatted in one corner, covered with red-and-white floral silk. Cherrywood chests, a wardrobe painted with yellow and burnt orange, and other intricately painted furniture were placed randomly around the room as if they had been strewn there.

Most notably, sitting in front of a fireplace was an overstuffed sofa big enough to be a bed. It was surrounded by piles of glittering knickknacks: Ornaments of gold, silver serving dishes, platinum rings and cups. When Edie squinted closer, she noticed that the sofa wasn't even on the ground, and in fact seemed to have been thrown on top of the mound of precious metals as an afterthought.

Distracted as she was by the glittering room before her, sudden pounding on the door made Edie jump. She whipped her head to look at the door—the proper door, not the one she and Sissel had come through. Deep-throated squawking was coming from the other side.

Of course. They had managed to shake the bird men in the hallway, but they were still pursuing them. Now she and Sissel were trapped in here, and it was only a matter of time before someone cracked that padlock open. *Dammit.*

Her body protested as she hauled herself up to her feet and reached out a hand to help Sissel. If they were quick enough, they could use the chalk to slip back into the passageways while the bird men were distracted, then sneak back up the stairs and out. Screw Indriði's paragon.

Edie's brilliant plan, however, was quickly foiled. Just as she helped Sissel up and turned, the door burst open and the raven guards piled in. It took only half a second for them to get their bearings, and Edie watched, frozen in horror, as the one in front raised his sword.

"At ease!" cried a voice.

The guards turned their heads, and it took Edie a moment to realize that she hadn't been cut in half. She blinked hard, then turned her head, too.

A man had entered the room through a curtained doorway and was studying the scene before him with soft brown eyes. He had short-cropped raven hair, high cheekbones, and a strong chin that flushed pink against his tawny skin. Shoulders back, posture perfect, he was wrapped in a long smoking jacket with alternating black and white layers. The thick velvet sash around his waist looked black, too, but as he shifted, the light hit it and revealed dark blues and greens. He held a steaming mug featuring clip-art of a carrion crow and the words *Ambulance Chaser.*

The man's eyebrows shot up as he surveyed his guards. "If you could try not to break down the door, that would be great. And in the name of Odin, be careful with those stupid polearms!" He waved his hand around, gesturing to the various tapestries hanging from the ceiling. His guards shuffled and hastily lowered their weapons as he added, "Those are worth more than your year's salary."

Once the guards—all significantly bigger than him—were thoroughly cowed, the man turned to observe the two intruders. His glare eased a bit, but he still looked wary. Uncertainly, he said, "Greetings," before raising his mug to take a sip.

The girls stood there, practically shaking from fear and fatigue. It was another moment before Edie managed, "Khenbu?"

"Yes...?" He tilted his head. "Who are you? More importantly, what are you doing here?"

Sissel huffed, brushing some hair behind her ear. "What are *you* doing here, man? We looked all over for you. What the hell is this place?"

Khenbu tilted his head the other way. His upturned brows gave him a perpetual look of amusement, and Edie wasn't sure if she trusted it. He clearly didn't trust them. "There are hidden tunnels all over this city. I simply figured I'd make use of them."

Edie glanced around. "There's a lot of furniture here ... not enough to fill an apartment, but a lot. I'm guessing the moisture down here isn't good for any of this stuff." She looked at him. "Where's the rest of it, in storage?"

Khenbu tilted his chin up at her. "It's none of your business where I move my things and why. But if you must know, yes, my less valuable furniture is in storage."

"Birdfolk would never live underground unless they were forced to," Sissel mumbled, crossing her arms.

"Before I tell you anything," the collector said, taking another sip and placing a hand on his hip, "you tell me who *you* are."

"I'm Sissel." She gestured beside her. "This is Edie. We're couriers, and we've got something for you."

"*Couriers?*" Khenbu crossed the room and waded through his mound of treasure before jumping up to perch on the edge of the sofa, making the couch's beaded tassels tinkle. He gave a bemused grin, holding his mug in both hands now. "Whatever it is, couldn't you have just sent it to my P.O. box?"

"Well," Edie cut in, rolling the chalk around in her hand, "*I'm* not a courier. A mutual friend sent me to offer a trade to you."

"A mutual friend, eh?" Khenbu crossed his legs, looking more intrigued. Now that he wasn't so angry, he was more animated, smiling. It put Edie more at ease. "Who?"

"Indriði."

Khenbu's eyes twinkled. His grin faded as he addressed his guards: "Go on, go!"

The bird men seemed hesitant at best, but they followed orders. Once they were gone and Edie could finally relax without those beady eyes on her, Khenbu spoke again.

"Sorry for that. I was forced down here because I was receiving death threats from the New Gloaming. Most of my collection is contained here. Where I can keep an eye on it."

"That?" Edie pointed at the piles of treasure under and around his sofa.

He glanced down and chuckled. "No, this is just decoration. Baubles. The real collector's items are hidden safely from view."

"New place, new nest," Sissel said.

"Exactly." He twisted himself this way and that, running his eyes over the piles as though looking for something. "You might actually find some sticks and bottle caps among all the gold, somewhere. I prefer the finer things in life. But a bird is a bird."

Khenbu laughed, eyes crinkling, perfect teeth bared. It was the kind of genuine laughter that made Edie want to smile, too. She was becoming more comfortable the more she talked to him. It helped that he was easy on the eyes, if too old for her. Mercy would call him *distinguished*.

"If you're a fuglfolken"—Edie said the word slowly, followed by an apologetic grimace—"then why do you look … you know, like a human? Those guards really looked like giant ravens."

If the question offended him, he didn't show it, but Edie sensed that he was surprised she didn't know the answer. "Ah, I have a human form. They don't." He flashed a big amber ring on his right middle finger. "Being a giant bird is fine and all when you're in flight, but I much prefer this. The ring is enchanted so that I can look and function like a human. And thank Odin for that," he added. "Do you know what a cloaca is? Ugh. Just no."

"Ah…"

Khenbu rolled his eyes. "Plus, they're giant ravens! Perfect guards.

Intimidating. A human-sized magpie, me"—he gestured to himself—"is not nearly as impressive. Dorky."

"I guess that makes sense."

"Now," the collector said, smoothing out the sofa cover's geometrical flower pattern, "tell me about Indriði's trade. What is it she wants, exactly?"

"A keeper paragon." Edie wished she had a copy of the page that the Norn had showed her. She tried to make a diamond shape with her hands. "Like—"

Khenbu stopped her. "Oh, I know what a keeper paragon is. Used to capture powerful spirits. Very rare. A few years ago, I collected my second one. Pristine condition. I held a viewing party." He smirked. "She's going to have to offer me something good if she wants it."

"You have two?" Edie frowned. "Do you need two?"

"Yes. One in green and one in blue."

She exchanged a glance with Sissel, who rolled her eyes almost audibly.

"So, what did you bring to trade?" He set his mug on a nearby coffee table, which was also swimming in the heap of treasure.

Anxiety churned in Edie's gut. She avoided eye contact as she held up the piece of chalk.

The room was silent. After a moment, Khenbu said, "Okay. Good. I will give you my priceless magical artifact, and in return, you give me art supplies."

She sighed harshly and turned. "This is how I got in. Watch."

Carefully, Edie traced the shape of a doorway on the stone wall. The chalk lines sizzled and sparked, and with Sissel's help, she shouldered the wall open just as she had before. Stone grated against stone and shook the room slightly, making the lanterns interspersed among the drapery dance.

Once the door was fully open, she turned to Khenbu and pointed at him with the piece of chalk. "See?"

The collector rubbed his chin thoughtfully, but she could tell he wasn't convinced. "Is it rare?"

"Indriði said it's rare now. Once you use the chalk up, it's gone, so this is one of the only ones left."

"And you just used it twice," he returned flatly. "For no reason,"

Edie threw up a hand. Now he was starting to annoy her. "Pardon me for not wanting to be stabbed to death by your guards. And you really think you would have believed me if I hadn't shown you proof?"

The look on his face said he couldn't argue with that. Still, he didn't look satisfied. "Hmm. It's not *pretty*, is the thing. It's not shiny or shimmery or glassy. You know? I don't want to look at this boring piece of chalk."

"It's not for *looking at*," Sissel cut in. "It's for using. It's useful! Come on, bro, you have *two* paragon thingies."

Edie wasn't sure why Sissel, who had no stake in this, was going to bat for her, but she was grateful.

Khenbu, on the other hand, was clearly irritated. "Yes, but if I use it, then it gets used and goes away."

"So you use it in emergencies." Edie raised a brow. "Like hiding from the Gloaming emergencies."

For a split second, the collector looked shaken at that. He glanced away, eyes roving the room, but after a moment of considering it, he shook his head. "No, no. I really can't."

"It's *rare*. Probably rarer than your keeper paragons. Have you ever even heard of something like this before?" Edie pressed, holding the chalk up again.

He hummed uneasily.

Maybe what they needed was something to sweeten the deal. Edie opened her bag and began to dig through it. If something shiny was what he wanted, something shiny was what he'd get. Surprisingly, Sissel caught on to what she was doing and followed suit, patting herself down.

Edie grabbed a handful of things from the bottom of her purse. She always had such good intentions of wearing jewelry, then halfway through the day, she got tired of it and threw it in her bag, never to wear it again. The chains were all tangled, but she withdrew a pair of diamond earrings and an engraved pendant watch decorated with blue enamel. Next to her, Sissel came up with a bracelet of ivory and obsidian beads. Both of them offered the jewelry to him, hands outstretched.

"Here," Edie grumbled. "You can look at these while you use the chalk and pretend it's pretty."

Khenbu crossed his arms as he leaned over, peering at what they were offering. He didn't look impressed, but there was something in his eyes... Edie suspected she had struck a nerve with her Gloaming comment.

After a long, silent deliberation, the magpie heaved a great sigh. "Fine."

Thank god.

Sissel flashed Edie a smile, then looked back at Khenbu slyly. "Tip?"

CHAPTER EIGHTEEN

As THE TWO girls rode the elevator up to Indriði's living area, Sissel flipped her newly acquired gold coin over and over. Technically, Khenbu the Magpie had given the tip to Edie, but Edie was perfectly content just having the keeper paragon in hand. Plus, the teen deserved it for all the hard work she'd done.

As if on cue, Sissel yawned. "Let's get this bread," she mumbled—the same phrase she'd been repeating at intervals since they had left the collector's place.

"You should head home soon," Edie said. "It's probably past dinnertime now."

"I will, I will. But I wanna see what Indriði does with the thingy." Sissel nodded to Edie's bag, where the keeper paragon was safely wrapped in the silk that had previously held the chalk.

Edie supposed she could let her stay a little longer. The ritual probably wouldn't take too long, and it had already been proven that she was going to do what she wanted and to hell with anything any grownups had to say about it.

The elevator dinged, and they both stepped out.

"Wow, I've never been up here before! Indriði usually meets me downstairs," Sissel said, peering into the lounge. "It's pretty."

"Wait until you meet Augustus."

They didn't have to look for the Norn for long; Edie spotted her sitting at her desk when she poked her head into the nearby study.

"Hey, you're back!" Indriði smiled and rose, coming to the doorway. She paused, apparently surprised when she saw Sissel standing next to Edie. "And I see you brought a tagalong."

"She was actually really helpful. I wouldn't have been able to find Khenbu without her."

Sissel grinned up at Edie.

The corner of Indriði's smile twitched a little. "Miss Sis is very talented, isn't she?"

"That's why you pay me so much," the teen said. "Can I stay for the ritual? What does this thing do, anyway? Edie wouldn't tell me."

Indriði gave Edie a strange glance, and she got the feeling that the Norn didn't want the girl to be involved. Maybe it was dangerous. "To be honest, honey, I'd rather you didn't. The paragon is for capturing fylgjur, so it's a really ... personal process."

Sissel tried to hide her disappointment with a casual head toss. "Oh, okay. I'll wait out here, then."

Before Indriði could tell her no to that, too, Edie said, "That's fine." She wanted to make sure the girl got home all right, if nothing else.

The Norn looked between Sissel and Edie with an unreadable expression.

A skittering noise from down the hall drew Edie's attention, and she watched as Percy emerged from the labyrinthine halls. He skittered up to Sissel and greeted her by sitting on her feet.

She didn't seem remotely bothered, or even that surprised. "Whoa, sick! Hi, big boy." With a grin, she crouched and busied herself petting him.

Edie glanced down the hallway, searching the shadows. "Where's Augustus?"

"He's in time-out for biting the cleaning lady," Indriði replied. "In his room."

"Who is this Augustus?" Sissel asked.

"A baby drake. The one that cut up my jacket."

"Aw, man, I wanna meet a drake..."

Edie snorted. "Maybe some other time."

Indriði watched them with the same unreadable expression as before. Then, wordlessly, she gestured for Edie to follow her and started down the long hallway.

Leaving Sissel behind with Percy, they began to navigate the confusing halls of the living quarters. Edie wondered who on earth had built this house. Maybe Indriði had had the inside completely renovated? Making a maze of one's house seemed ill-advised, but maybe it was a Norn thing.

Eventually, they came to a hallway that had only one door at the very end of it. From far away, it looked like any other door, but as they approached, Edie could make out myriad runes carved into the door frame, and a protection stave carved into the ceiling just in front of it. She was willing to bet there was one under the floorboards in the same position.

Indriði seemed a bit happier now. She opened the door. "Welcome to my ritual room."

For the most part, it was a regular empty room. The walls were plain, the floor was hardwood. However, there were no windows; the only light came from a wrought-iron chandelier in the center of the room, its candles flickering with an eerie dark blue light. Shimmering webs hung from the ceiling, crawling with little twinkling shapes that resembled spiders, though as Edie came closer, they seemed to be made of twigs and gems. Shrines of sticks and bone were clustered in each of the corners. A black spinning wheel sat on one side of the room, flanked by nearly transparent curtains. In the center of the room was a small table covered with a black cloth.

Edie took a deep breath before stepping into the room, but once she was inside, she was surprised. It didn't feel any different from the hall. It looked mightily intimidating, like it should be mega-energized—but besides the creepy-crawly feeling from the spiders, it felt completely normal ... so at least there was that.

She relaxed her shoulders a bit and watched as Indriði went to stand on the opposite side of the little table. "What do we do first?"

The Norn held a hand out for Edie's bag, eyes sparkling, mouth drawn like she wanted to smile but didn't dare. "Did you really convince him to give it to you? Can I see it?"

Edie obliged, reaching into her quilted bag and setting the paragon on the table.

The Norn reached forward eagerly and unfolded the silk, exposing the crystal. It didn't look quite like it did in the book; somewhere along the line, someone had turned it into a necklace, with an ornately etched bell cap connecting one of the points to a silver chain. Hopefully, it would still work.

Indriði was silent as she took in the sight, inhaling deeply. Then she smiled brightly up at Edie. "It's pretty, isn't it?"

"It's nice." Edie wrung her hands. "It's not, like, glowing or anything, though. Is it broken?" If Khenbu had two keeper paragons, maybe one was perfect and one was junk. She'd go back there and pluck every last one of his feathers if he'd given them a shitty one.

"Oh, it's only empty. It should only glow when it's full." The Norn raised her brows. "Are you ready to start?"

She didn't feel ready, but if this ritual would finally unlock her powers, she had to do it. She had to do *something* if she wanted to be independent from the Reach and start making a real difference, hopefully with Indriði's help. She clamped her mouth shut and only nodded her consent.

"Wonderful. Here." Indriði took Edie's hands and covered the paragon with them.

Edie hadn't touched the bare crystal yet. When she did, a strange vibration began to thrum through her palms, up her arms. It echoed in her bones almost like a song. She was barely able to tear her gaze away as Indriði produced a book from under the table—the same one she'd shown her before, with the detailed illustration of the paragon.

"Now, I've never done this before," the Norn said, "but the incantation is pretty straightforward. Fylgjur and Norns are both spirits of Fate, anyway, so if anyone is qualified to work with one, it's me." She chuckled, then spread the book out before her, tracing the lines with one finger.

Edie continued to cover the paragon. At length, Indriði straightened up and spread her hands palms up, muttering softly in a language Edie didn't understand. Then, she began to chant in a monotonous, entrancing voice, one word at a time.

"*Ansuz ... ansuz ... ansuz...*" Ansuz went on for at least another forty seconds.

The Norn paused to whisper, then continued.

"*Perthro ... perthro ... perthro...*

Kauna ... kauna ... kauna..."

Edie recognized some of the words from their runecasting session. The more she said them, the more relaxed Edie felt; eventually, it was almost as though she forgot where she was.

"*Raidho ... raidho ... raidho...*

Mannaz ... mannaz ... mannaz..."

Edie's ears clutched in an oddly familiar way, and she could feel something fluttering against her ear and face. Strangely, though, she didn't feel startled. She simply let her gaze rove to the side, following the faint blue outline of something that hadn't been there before but was now swooping around the room.

Indriði's voice rose in volume. "*Algiz ... algiz ... algiz...*"

The faint blue mist emitted something like a ... scream? It seemed like it was shouting as it circled Edie. Somehow, she could feel that it was drawn to the paragon.

"*Ehwaz ... ehwaz ... ehwaz...*

Othala ... othala ... othala..."

She couldn't help but gasp slightly when the thing collided with her, but she felt no impact—it simply melded into her shoulder, and she could feel its cold presence as it rushed down her arms and into the paragon in a flash. Not a moment later, the crystal began to glow.

Indriði put her hands over Edie's and whispered more. Then, they both pulled away, looking down at the full keeper paragon.

Edie was struck with the feeling that she was looking at something she wasn't supposed to see. She grimaced and crossed her arms tightly across her chest.

"There," Indriði said. "It's bound. Let me see if I can empower it."

She began to chant the rune *dagaz*, hovering her outstretched hands over the paragon. But nothing seemed to change, and soon, her expression turned to one of frustration.

"Is something wrong?" Edie asked, quietly so as not to break the Norn's concentration.

"It doesn't feel like it's working." After another moment of trying, Indriði looked up. "Is it? Do you feel anything?"

"No?"

She lowered her hands for a moment, took a deep breath, then raised them and tried again. "*Dagaz ... dagaz ... dagazv ...* dagaz, dammit."

Nothing. Edie didn't feel so much as a ripple.

Indriði tried an incantation next, in Old Norse. Nothing. Then, in English: "Spirit, I summon you to this place that we may attend to the empowerment of your master..."

She continued, but it made no difference. Edie's heart sank.

After another long pause with no reaction, Indriði lowered her hands, then brought them to her face, cupping her own cheeks. "I don't understand why it's not working."

Edie hugged herself tighter, rubbing her arms. She felt strange; anxiety roiled in her gut as though a terrifying monster was just out of view in the shadows. She felt naked. "To be fair, you've never done it before."

"But I'm a Norn," Indriði said, frustration evident in her tone. "Magic *is* me. I'm never wrong about things like this."

"I'm sorry." Edie looked down. Had she done something to screw it up? She wasn't sure what that could be, but she wouldn't put it past herself.

With a sigh, the Norn waved her hand over the keeper paragon. *"Tak ór bọndin."*

The glow fled from the crystal, and Edie only caught a glimpse of it before it snapped out of sight with a faint glint. Her anxiety dissipated almost at once; she felt normal and safe again.

Still, it hadn't worked.

Indriði put a hand to her forehead, sounding miserable as she said, "I'm so sorry, Edie. I was sure there was something I could do."

"It's okay." It wasn't. It was far from okay, but what else could she say? Indriði had tried her best to keep her promise. It wasn't her fault that nothing could be done.

The Norn closed the book slowly and put it back, then left the paragon on the table as she crossed the room to open the door for Edie. In silence, they walked back to where Sissel was waiting in front of the elevator doors, petting Percy.

"How'd it go?" the teen asked when they approached.

Edie shook her head.

"We'll figure something out," Indriði said softly, disappointment etched in her every feature. "I won't let you be powerless forever, Edie. It's not fair. Astrid has no right to keep you down like this."

She disappeared into her study for a moment, then emerged with a purse. She drew out a small pocketbook, rifled through it, and handed Edie a couple hundred in cash.

Edie didn't want it. She handed it to Sissel. "We'll figure something out," she echoed quietly, taking a deep breath. Another day without her magic.

The Norn ran a hand over her hair. "I ... need some time to work through this." She pressed the elevator button, keeping her eyes trained on Edie and Sissel. "I have a lot to think about."

Edie shuffled nervously as she entered the elevator. She had found herself becoming attached to Indriði. It seemed like the Norn was the only person in the world who told her the truth, who really wanted to help *her* instead of helping her to help *them*. "When will I see you again?"

"I'll send for you when I'm ready." Indriði leaned over to press the button again, nodding somberly to them as the doors closed.

As they descended, Edie couldn't stop a couple stray tears from leaking. She didn't usually cry in public like this, but the stress from the past couple months was starting to break her down. What was she supposed to do now? How was she supposed to protect herself and others if she was completely powerless, save for the borrowed knives in her jacket?

If Sissel noticed her crying, she didn't say anything. A small blessing. Edie had already carefully wiped her eyes by the time they came to the lobby, taking a deep breath to calm herself.

But her calm didn't last for long.

As they exited the building together, Sissel asked, "What now?"

Edie was about to answer when she looked up from her sneakers and saw a white convertible parked at the curb. Leaning against it, arms crossed in front of his chest and a glare plastered on his face, was Cal.

CHAPTER NINETEEN

"Hey there, kid," the revenant said through his teeth. "Been lookin' all over for ya."

Edie's stomach sank. She was supposed to be in charge of him, but she had never felt as powerless as she did in this moment. She shuffled from foot to foot like a child caught stealing from her mom's purse. "Uh … hi."

Beside her, Sissel said nothing, staring between them.

Cal didn't acknowledge her presence anyway. He pushed off the car and stared Edie down, his voice no more than a growl. "Just wanted me to run and get some groceries, huh? Didn't feel like inviting me on your whirlwind city adventure?"

Anger burned inside Edie, mingling with fear, disappointment, and sheer exhaustion. He wasn't supposed to be here. Why was he so fixated on following her? It did nothing to help his case. She flexed her jaw before mumbling, "It was none of your business, Cal."

His heavy brow shot up. "Ex-fuckin'-*cuse* me? *Not my business*? The only goddamn reason I'm here is to keep you out of trouble. You remember that, right?"

Keep me out of trouble or keep me in the dark? Her cheeks burned. "I don't need help," she shot back. "I'm fine. Just take me home."

She made a move for Ghost, but Cal stopped her with a firm hand to the shoulder.

"No fuckin' way." His voice rose. "You don't get to brush me off all day and then order me to take you home like I'm your christing chauffeur!"

Edie glared at him. "Fine. What do you want, then?"

"I want a goddamn explanation."

"I don't want to talk about it." With a rough jerk, she pulled herself out of his grip and turned, starting to walk away. If he wouldn't bring her home, she and Sissel would find their own way.

"See," Cal said from behind her with a bitter chuckle, "that's the thing about you. Somethin' you and your old man have in common. If *you* don't wanna do something, it's not worth doing it at all, and to hell with everyone else!"

Edie stopped and looked over her shoulder. "Screw you."

"I deserve to know what the fuck is going on!" He stabbed himself in the chest with a mottled forefinger. "Me! The bastard who's been keeping you alive for the past two and a half fucking months."

"*You* want to know what's going on?" She turned on her heel, raising her voice, too. "Join the club! You have been lying to me and keeping me in the dark this *entire* time."

Cal's expression changed. The angry glare was replaced by shock for a moment, then uncertainty as he asked, "What— what do you mean?"

Edie felt a surge of vindication. She'd caught him right in the middle of a lie; his face said it all.

So, it was true. He was the betrayer that Indriði's runes had warned her about—or at least one of them. *Whoever is betraying you knows what they're doing. They're doing it to hurt you. They're taking you for a ride, Edie, and they enjoy dominating you.*

No more.

She bared her teeth. "You and Astrid have been misleading me. What do you people *want*? Do you just want to use my power like the Gloaming does, or am I some sort of sacrifice? Or does Astrid want to make me the Reacher so she can blame all the horrible shit she wants to do on me?"

"Huh?" Cal's face twisted, and he shouted back at her, "What the fuck are you *talking* about?"

"Why the hell would you even stay here if there wasn't something in it for you, Cal? It's pretty hilarious that you're calling me selfish, because that's all you care about—you."

He drew himself up, shoulders tense, fists clenched at his sides. "You don't know the first thing about me."

"Answer the question! Why would you even stay here if there *wasn't something in it for you?*"

"Because I want to help!" he exploded, spit flying. "You fuckin' think, after all the fuckin' times I saved your useless ass, there would be any other answer?"

"You're *lying*! And I don't need you, and I don't want your help. I was so, *so* stupid for ever thinking I could trust you and Astrid."

"Trust me?" He pounded his chest with one hand. "*Trust me?* After everything I've put on the line for you, you don't have the goddamn decency to *trust* me?"

"I've seen the way you look at me, all guilty. For a guy who lived in Vegas for ten years, you have a shitty poker face, Cal!"

The revenant lowered his arms, eyes gleaming with rage. He breathed hard as he stared at Edie, grinding his teeth. For a moment, it seemed like he was going to keep arguing; then his gaze deadened. Finally, he said, "You know what? Fuck you. Fuck you. And fuck this."

He rounded Ghost's front bumper and slid behind the wheel, slamming the door hard. Once the engine started up, he fixed Edie with a look she had only seen directed at her once, when they'd first met: pure hatred.

There was a challenge in his eyes, too. He was daring her to reach with her mind and force him to stop.

She broke eye contact.

The engine revved, and Cal sped off. Edie knew it would be the last time she ever saw him.

When it was done, she felt empty. She let her bag slide off her arm and fall heavily next to her as she sat on the curb, looking down at her shoes. The street felt eerily silent now that the yelling was over, filled only with the soft noises of traffic and birds singing. A cold wind ripped through the street, but she didn't move, letting it play with her hair and sting her face.

After a while, Sissel came to sit down next to her. "Well. Just as I thought. Trash."

Edie glanced at her. "Huh?"

"That guy had *big* bastard energy."

"Kinda." She sighed and scrubbed her face, and when she opened her eyes again, Sissel was looking on sympathetically.

"You wanna stay at my house tonight?"

Edie furrowed her brow. "We just met."

"So? We're friends, right?"

"Uh, I guess, but I'm not sure your dad would be cool with a strange adult having a sleepover with his fifteen-year-old child."

"You can lie about your age."

Edie stared at the kid for a second, sighed, then shook her head. "I'm good. I need to go home."

"Oh, okay." Sissel shrugged it off and stood, putting her hands in the pockets of her sweater. "Let's go catch the train. I'll buy you some chicken nuggets on the way."

Edie's stomach grumbled as she hauled herself to her feet. At least Generation Z knew how to make the best of a miserable situation.

CHAPTER TWENTY

REGRETTABLY, Edie was waking up.

She turned over and hugged the covers around her face, trying to let herself be lulled back into sleep, but it wasn't working. The sunlight had already woken her brain, and her thoughts wouldn't grant her rest.

A groggy moan escaped her. She uncovered her face, turning it a bit to glare at the sunlight coming through her window. As she turned over again, she avoided her phone. She didn't need to know the time. It didn't matter anyway.

It had been a few days since the fight with Cal—or at least, she thought it had. If she was honest, she'd been in a stupor. Alcohol was the only thing that put her to sleep when she found herself up in the wee hours of the morning. Being alone in the apartment was already nerve-racking enough without lying awake, replaying the fight over and over in her head.

At first, she had dared to hope that maybe Cal just needed some time to blow off steam and would come back. Maybe explain himself. But it wasn't long before her first instinct—that she would probably never see him again—had started to seem more likely.

She was left feeling like she fucked everything up. No matter what she did, it seemed to make someone, somewhere, angry at her. So she had withdrawn, isolated herself from everyone for the last few days. Even Mercy. Her friend texted her every so often to check on her and ask if she wanted to come over to Tilda's to hang out, but she didn't. After everything that had happened, it was best for Mercy to stay away from her, anyway. She had already suffered far too much because of Edie.

With a sigh, she dragged herself out of bed, still dressed in what she had worn the day before. A little disgusted, she stripped and headed for the bathroom. It was still weird to be able to take a shower without hauling Fisk out of the tub. She hoped he was doing okay.

After her shower, she dressed, started some coffee, and got a pan to make an egg sandwich. She hadn't eaten well in the past couple of days, and her stomach was letting her know about it.

The house was completely silent as she cooked. No Fisk moving around in the bathtub, no Cal watching TV, no Mercy typing away on her laptop or Satara coming through the front door. The house felt empty without them. It didn't even really feel like her apartment. But what could she do? Those that she wasn't trying to keep safe were associated with the Reach; she couldn't trust them.

Unexpectedly, she missed Cal most of all. The strange magic of their connection was absent, and it left her feeling empty. Without him nearby, the nightmares had gotten worse. She regretted some of the things she had said to him, but he was obviously guilty of something. She wasn't that stupid, and he wasn't that good an actor. He and Astrid were hiding something from her, just like Indriði had said.

The smell of burning reached Edie's nose, and she snapped back to reality, quickly transferring her slightly blackened bread to a plate. Her movements felt mechanical as she stacked an egg and a slice of cheese, then meandered into the living room. She finally retrieved her phone and checked the time; it was 9:04 a.m.

Three days was long enough for wallowing. She still hadn't heard from Indriði, but there must be something she could do. Without "help" from the Reach, Edie had to get back into the swing of things herself—

she just wasn't sure where to start. Finding someone to train her was probably top priority. She could call Tilda and ask her if she knew of any neutral practitioners of the ebon magics. It was a long shot, but...

Edie stared out the window, thinking. She hadn't seen Marius in months. He'd probably have a clue, but then, he might not tell her.

Whomp. A big blue mass suddenly thumped onto the surface of the window, making the pane tremble. Edie was so tired that she was more startled by the sound than the sight, and she took a few steps back, still holding her sandwich.

Once she registered who it was, she relaxed and set her plate aside, going to the window. She bent slightly to open it, letting Percy in. He had his little acorn strapped to him again, and he opened it for her. Edie retrieved a letter while he investigated what was left of her sandwich with his pedipalps.

"Welp, that's yours now," she mumbled as she unrolled the letter. It was in Indriði's hand.

Edie,

I hope you're feeling well. I'm sorry about how long it's taken me to get this letter to you, but I had a lot to think about. I hope you can appreciate that I've thought long and hard to come to my conclusion, and I hope you won't be upset with me.

Edie's blood went cold.

I tried to help you come into your powers myself. I failed you. I didn't want to admit it before, but I realize now that the only way we can find you the training you need, from the right people, is if we combine Astrid's and my contacts.

Although I still don't trust Astrid or her Reach, I think the best thing we can do now is cooperate with them. Therefore, I'm prepared to accept her request that I join.

You, personally, would be stronger with me there. I know all of

Astrid's tricks. With me as your adviser, you would have a real voice in the Reach, someone to advocate for you if she attempted to make you do something questionable, or if she did something questionable herself and then blamed it on you, "the Reacher."

Edie lowered the note for a moment and sat on the couch, emotions in conflict. Her stomach twisted with anxiety, and her head reeled. On one hand, she had finished what she'd set out to do months ago at the party: recruit Indriði. She'd be happy to see Satara again. On the other hand, she couldn't deny that she was still wary about Astrid and the Reach, even if she'd have someone there to advocate for her. To boot, the chances of Cal coming back were not good, even with Astrid's help.

What did Astrid have in store for her—or Indriði, for that matter, considering their long-held grudge? And on the off-chance Cal *were* to come back, it wouldn't be a comfortable confrontation.

In fact, he might already have told the others what happened. Maybe Indriði's decision had come too late, and Astrid had already been alerted of Edie's ... betrayal, for lack of a better word. Maybe they wouldn't even be welcome.

She looked down at the note again.

Since I have no idea what Astrid has planned for me, I'm not comfortable traveling to Shipshaven to meet her. Tell her she can meet me at my place to settle the terms of the agreement. I've enclosed a second, official letter you can give to Astrid. Obviously keep this one to yourself.

And don't worry, Edie. Remember, she needs you. She needs both of us. Between you and me, we can make her agree to anything.

Give my people a call when you know what time she's going to be there. The number for my security desk is 555-9999.

Indriði

Edie's eyes wandered from the page to Percy, who was scarfing down the last of her egg sandwich. "All this trouble just because her boyfriend died?" she asked the spider.

He turned his whole body to look at her, then scuttled over to the window to be let out. She opened it, and he zoomed off. She was alone again.

With her heart in her stomach, she looked up the next commuter train to Shipshaven.

It had taken Satara over a week of combing through Astrid's book collection to finally find something that even half-explained their ljósálfr shade's behavior. *Land of Spirits: A Study on the Nature of Ancestors, Offerings, the Hidden Folk and Their Ways* sat open in her lap, as thick and meandering as its title. Though Astrid had invited her to search for whatever information she could find, the valkyrie had barely spoken a word about Lylirion since they had brought the horn—which Astrid had also refused to talk about—back home. So, Satara studied on her own.

She'd much rather be curled up reading about Aevana and Commander Coldheart, but having something to keep her busy had been a blessing this past week. It had become clear that, for whatever reason, Edie was avoiding them, and Astrid was less than pleased.

This morning, the valkyrie had pledged to give Edie one day more before she went knocking at her door in person.

For Edie's own sake, Satara hoped she came forward before that happened.

In her cozy apartment, the television provided the comforting drone of noise. *Total Recall* tonight. Nothing could focus a crowded mind like Arnold Schwarzenegger shouting, though truth be told, Satara preferred Bruce Willis. As she skimmed the page before her, she opened another package of tea cookies, drawing the attention of Astrid's smaller cat, Brenda, who had come upstairs to visit her. The TV's flashing colors danced on the cat's gray fur as she pawed at the cookies' packaging.

Satara had given up trying to convince her that she wouldn't like tea cookies. She simply let the cat curl up to lick the crumbs, and went back to the passage she had been reading.

Astrid had been right when she'd said that not all light elves were good, kind creatures. According to what Satara had read so far, they had once been known to spread disease and kill crops whenever the mood struck them, especially when they didn't feel like they were getting enough respect from Midgardians beyond their World.

The lines between ancestors, land spirits, elementals, and elves had once been blurry and complicated—complicated enough to fill half this damn book—but now that humans were strong enough to rule an entire World, they influenced the universe, and their influence had made things more concrete and tangible than before. These days, elves and other hidden folk tended to stay as far away from humans as they could possibly get, but a few old-timers still existed. In empty fields that somehow exuded energy, in stubborn stones and trees and roots, in the beautiful and isolated corners of the globe, their presence could still be felt.

For most of the elves, however, things had changed. And those things had changed them. The bone-deep belief they had once fed on was now rare among unattuned humans, so the elves had adapted. They weren't just part of the Yggdrasil's flow anymore; they were their own real civilization.

One chapter discussing their culture had stopped Satara in her tracks. When she'd turned the page, the insignia of a sun and two crossed daggers had glared back at her—the same symbol etched into the pendant Lylirion had worn.

The Shadowborne were a light elven rogues' guild whose philosophy made her shiver. Whenever the sun shone on an object, it cast a shadow, and within those shadows lurked the soul of their order; still products of light, but hidden. The harsher the light, the starker the shadow. The guild was a mix of thieves, assassins, and other brigands, and though most of their crime was sanctioned by the nobility of Alfheim, they were their own independent body. Despite being outlaws in theory, most of them were loyal to their people.

Throughout history, the Shadowborne had usually been allied with the Reach. Apparently not anymore, though, as Satara had never heard of them. Their turning to the Gloaming still didn't seem likely, however. What elf, comfortably employed and protected by nobility, would take orders from the Gloaming? There was no reason. Humans' worship was no longer vital to their survival; they had all the power they could ever want.

But if all that was true, who were they working for?

A knock at the back door of the apartment startled Satara from her train of thought. She looked up from the massive volume with a frown. Usually, people came in through the front door of the shop. The only people who used the fire escape entrance were people who specifically came to see her, and those visits were few and far between.

She stood uneasily and went to the door, peeking through the blinds. A second later, she opened the door to Edie standing there.

"Hello," Satara said, unable to hide the surprise in her voice.

The necromancer was shuffling from foot to foot, seemingly nervous. "Hi."

Satara glanced beyond her, right to left. "Is something wrong?"

"I didn't want to come in the front ... just in case."

Warily, the shieldmaiden stepped aside to let her in.

Edie pointed at her chest. "I like your shirt."

Satara had barely noticed her clothing as she was getting dressed. She looked down at her T-shirt, a graphic of three jolly cartoon evergreens with the words Happy Little Trees under them. Embarrassed, she mumbled a thank you.

"You know who Bob Ross is?" Edie asked.

"I have a television, remember?" Satara nodded to it and closed the door softly behind Edie, adding sarcastically, "I even know about horseless carriages and moving pictures."

Edie ran a hand through her ponytail. "Right. Sorry."

Satara longed to sit back down in her chair, but she felt awkward. She wasn't used to sharing this space with anyone. "I feel like I haven't seen you in a month. What are you doing here?"

It came out a bit more accusatory than she had meant it to be, but really, the way Edie had practically shooed her off after the breathstealer incident, plus all the texts she had ignored since then? It was clear that something was wrong. After Indriði had already waited two months to contact them, it was annoying to have to wait for her answer. Edie was lucky she'd reappeared before Astrid could come after her.

Edie took a note out of her backpack. "I have a letter for Astrid. From Indriði."

Satara tilted her head. Better late than never, she supposed. She swept her braids over one shoulder, fingering them thoughtfully. "That's good. She'll be happy about that. Come on."

Edie followed closely as she made her way down to the shop, but it was empty save for a couple of customers milling around, Kier behind the counter, and the orange tabby, Meowlnir. Astrid was nowhere to be seen.

Satara went to the back room instead and knocked on the door. When no one answered, she opened it anyway. Now she could hear buzzing coming from Astrid's workshop. With Edie close at her heels, she walked down the hall and into the small room.

Astrid sat under the workshop's one window on the far side of the room, head bent over what she was doing. On the wooden bench next to her was a lacquered black horn tankard, and she was carefully working away at a block of pewter, carving decorations for it.

She wore safety glasses and earplugs, but took them out when she sensed Satara and Edie's presence. "I hope you've come back to finally update me on what's been happening, Edith. I do not like being left out of the loop."

Beside Satara, Edie shifted, clearly uncomfortable. "Yeah. Sorry it took so long. It wasn't very easy to convince Indriði to even talk to me after I told her what I wanted."

"And?" Astrid turned her power chisel off and finally turned, setting her glasses aside. "What was her answer?"

The necromancer hesitated for a moment before holding out the letter in her hand. "She told me to give you this."

Astrid stood and took the letter from Edie. She discarded the envelope on the floor in front of her, eyes glued to the page the second it was unfolded. Satara could see it was a short letter, only one sheet of paper, but her battlemother was rapt. The shieldmaiden frowned, wondering why. She knew Indriði had been an old friend, but Astrid read this letter like a parched man drank water.

It took her a long time to read the entire thing, longer than it should have. Then she lowered it, looking at Edie like she had just come out of a stupor. Slowly, her expression became normal again, and her brow furrowed. "Where is Calcifer?"

"Oh..." Edie seemed even more uncomfortable with that question. Satara observed closely, as always. "He's— he's, uh, busy."

A lie. Satara looked to Astrid, hoping to catch her eye, but the valkyrie was completely distracted by the letter. She looked it over one last time, seeming ... pleased, almost hopeful—if a bit shocked. Satara watched as she folded the letter and tucked it in her back pocket.

"So," the valkyrie said after a moment, "she's ... she has finally come to her senses. This is good." She cleared her throat, her tone becoming more businesslike and terse. "She has agreed to join the Reach. She wants us to go to her home for an official meeting."

Dread snaked its way through Satara's body. She wasn't really one for meeting new people, even if she had a talent for diplomacy. Fortunately, it was likely that neither Astrid nor the Norn would be in the mood for lengthy introductions.

Seeing the two ancient women interact was bound to be an awkward experience. Satara looked to Edie, who seemed as wary as she did, and assumed that was what the necromancer was worried about.

"Well?" Astrid brushed past them to the workshop door. "What are you waiting for? Satara, dress in your ceremonial armor."

She turned. "My ceremonial armor? Why?"

Satara and Edie followed the valkyrie out of the room, watching as she took Skuld's shield and spear down from the wall. "We have to make an impression. We must project a certain eminence, even though there are so few of us. Indriði will respond to it."

Her ceremonial armor certainly was eminent. And old-fashioned, and stiff, and pinchy. She preferred her more flexible gear. Nonetheless, she nodded. "What about you, Battlemother?"

Astrid sighed, pushing back her mane of blond waves and braids. Her cheeks and forehead were strangely pink. "I will be wearing mine, too."

Satara exchanged a look with Edie. This was sure to be interesting.

CHAPTER TWENTY-ONE

THE AIR outside the Alderdeen townhouse shifted. A red tear opened in midair, bringing with it the heavy scent of a grisly battlefield. Astrid's huge gray wolf bounded into existence, along with the three women riding it like the weirdest, bloodiest Uber ever.

Well— Edie thought back to a cab she'd taken last New Year's Eve. *Second* bloodiest.

The smell reminded Edie of her battle with Sárr, and that made riding this thing even worse. As she slipped from the wolf's back, she looked at her shaking hands, which were even paler than usual.

It had only taken her a few minutes to call Indriði and let her know they were coming soon; it had taken Astrid and Satara almost two hours to put on their armor, with copious amounts of help from one another.

Astrid's armor had been the most difficult. She was in a full suit of it, a formidable figure in a winged helmet, looking not unlike her true valkyrie form. The armor was silver-white, polished to such a shine that she almost looked like she was wearing mirrors. The blue from the sky and the yellow from the honeylocusts, reflected in the armor, gave it an almost opalescent sheen; and if she hadn't been wearing a blue cape, she might have almost blended into the background.

The cuirass was intricately engraved with feather patterns and an ornamental peak just under the breastbone, extending down the stomach in subtle tiers like a spine. The tasset flared dramatically, with a blue sash and a sturdy triangle of chainmail in the center, covering her crotch and barely touching the cuisses. In her hands were her spear and shield, which, despite their simplicity next to the complex armor, still awed Edie with their strange energy.

Satara was dressed similarly, though her armor was leather. Instead of full arm coverage, she wore only a mantle and vambraces, trimmed with falcon feathers. Under her cuirass and chainmail, she had donned a shirt and a scarlet overdress that split in the center, revealing leather breeches. She had wound her braids into a thick bun, and she held a spear and shield of her own, considerably less ancient than her battlemother's.

Edie wore a T-shirt with a faded image of Garfield on it.

Astrid held her spear tight, looking up at the building before her like it was some great beast she was here to conquer. Her expression was hard, almost unreadable, but Edie detected something startlingly vulnerable. Fear, hope? Maybe a little of both. She looked like she'd spent years traveling through a wasteland and was seeing civilization for the first time, unsure if it was a mirage or not.

Satara was the one to break the silence. "We should go inside before someone sees us."

With the frequent Aurora-Gloaming clashes, seeing someone in armor was no longer uncommon in Anster. But they weren't the Aurora, so it was best that they didn't call attention to themselves.

With Astrid leading, they ascended the steps to Indriði's home. The doorman didn't even bother to stop them; he simply reached over and opened the door, eyeing the two armored women fearfully. When Astrid entered the vestibule, the attendants at the security desk had pretty much the same reaction. One of them grabbed the phone from its cradle and began mumbling into it; the others stared as Astrid came to a stop in the middle of the room, stalwartly waiting to be acknowledged. Without having ever met her, Edie assumed, these people knew full well who Astrid was.

A particularly brave security guard cleared his throat and said, "Just a moment, ma'am," his voice sounding comically small in the big room.

Astrid nodded at him, and he averted his eyes. Edie looked on from behind Satara, conflicted. Being feared came with advantages, as she was reminded every time she invoked her father's name. On the other hand, you were seen as a monster. What were the odds that you would turn into one?

After a few moments, the platinum elevator opened. Roggvi stepped out, hands folded behind his back. Unlike the others, he didn't seem a bit scared of Astrid, his expression passive and unimpressed as ever.

He bowed. "Astrid, *valmey*. We are honored to receive you."

Astrid bowed her head in turn. "Blessings of the fjord-bone be with your house. How does your mistress fare?"

"She awaits," he replied gruffly, turning on his heel and thumping back into the elevator.

With the weird Norse greetings out of the way, the three women followed without another word. Edie's heart was thudding hard. What if Indriði said something Astrid didn't like, or vice versa? What were the chances that a fight would break out, and Edie would be caught in the middle? And if she survived being stuck in the middle of *that*, where would she stand then? She shoved her hands in her pockets and began ripping up a cough drop wrapper she had in there, trying to focus her anxiety.

The elevator ride up to the Norn's living quarters felt like it took a million years. Once the doors opened again, the three followed Roggvi as he navigated the disorienting corridors. This time, Edie was able to keep up, and thankfully, there was no Augustus to be seen. Indriði had probably locked him up again so he wouldn't eat her visitors.

When she was sure she wouldn't fall behind again, Edie mumbled to Satara, "What are they even going to talk about that involves bringing weapons?"

"Astrid is standing on ceremony. More so than usual," Satara replied in the barest whisper. She pursed her lips, looking as unsure as Edie felt. "There's something she isn't telling us. She's nervous about this."

"But Indriði already agreed to join. She doesn't have anything to be nervous about."

Satara shrugged and faced forward again, eyeing her battlemother. Edie did the same. What exactly was going on here?

There was no time to stop the presses and ask. They were already in front of the doors to Indriði's living area, and Roggvi was pulling them open.

The Norn stood at the other end of the room, her back to them. She looked like an angel in her white pantsuit, hair like fire against the afternoon sun pouring in from the huge windows. Astrid took a few tentative steps inside, then stopped, stiff as a statue. Satara and Edie waited off to the side behind her. Roggvi shut the doors, leaving them alone.

Eventually, Indriði turned her head to glance over her shoulder. "You came."

"Are you surprised?" asked Astrid.

"No. I knew you would come."

The valkyrie barely smiled. "Of course you did. You know everything."

Indriði turned, wearing an expression Edie had never seen before. Her lip was curled, eyes hard, nostrils flared. Even her tone was different, no *hon*s or *baby*s. It was like having Astrid in her presence put a bad taste in her mouth.

After a moment, she looked away, adopting a softer expression when her gaze met Edie's. She nodded in greeting, then looked to Satara. "We haven't been introduced."

"My shieldmaiden of the past ten years," Astrid explained, turning slightly to present her. "Satara Izem of Mare Island. Satara, Indriði."

The Norn didn't even glance at Astrid. "Mare Island is a beautiful sanctuary. I believe I met the woman you were named for. She was a battle-healer, wasn't she?"

Satara curtsied deeply, her expression one of surprise. "My great grandmother, my lady."

"Excellent. She was a fine woman." The smile left the Norn's eyes as she looked at Astrid again. "You didn't have to dress for battle, but I'm not surprised you did. Nothing's worth doing in half-measures, is it?"

Astrid flexed her jaw.

"I guess we should sit down and discuss the terms of our agreement," Indriði said. She came away from the window and settled in one of the white armchairs, crossing one leg over the other.

Astrid didn't sit, didn't come closer. Edie closed her eyes and silently begged the valkyrie not to start any shit … but no such luck.

"It's been a century and you have nothing to say to me?" Her tone was terse, like she was trying to rein her emotions in.

Indriði fixed her with a warning gaze. "I have plenty to say to you, Astrid, but despite everything, I've agreed to help the Reach. That's what you wanted, isn't it? Why aren't you satisfied?"

The reins snapped. Astrid's tone shifted, but she didn't shout. On the contrary, much to Edie's surprise, she sounded small and hurt. "I thought time would have soothed your ill will for me."

"You were wrong."

Please, let this conversation be over, Edie thought. Astrid said that she wanted Indriði's help, but she seemed to be doing everything she could think of to derail her own progress. She just *had* to bring up the one topic that would collapse the whole meeting. Typical. Edie was starting to wonder if Astrid *liked* having screaming fights.

The valkyrie stood up a little straighter, tone still uncertain. "I was doing my duty."

"I don't care why you did it," Indriði said dismissively, hands clamped tightly in her lap. "Let's not talk about it. I'm doing what you wanted. I'm submitting to your request, helping you after eighty years of radio silence. Not even a single apology."

Astrid huffed, almost a laugh. "I have nothing to apologize for."

The Norn finally stood from her seat. For a split second, Edie thought she saw the world billowing around her, almost, like waves of heat coming off hot tarmac. "Kolya!" seemed to be the only word she could manage, and she spat it at Astrid.

"Kolya was dying. I had no choice."

"I defy that logic, *Chooser of the Slain.*"

Astrid banged the butt of her spear on the tiled floor, impassioned, shouting all of a sudden. "You of all people should know Fate guides my sword, not my own will! You're not the only being in the Nine Worlds who's ever lost something."

All at once, Indriði's shoulders relaxed. When she looked at Astrid now, she no longer looked *angry* as Edie understood the word. She was bright-eyed, almost amused; her body was unnaturally still, like a predator about to strike its prey from the bushes. Her voice was a cool river of ice as she said, "Oh, I'm going to enjoy doing this even more than I thought I would."

Edie realized how apt the description of a predator was a second too late.

The Norn raised her hands, bringing them together as if to clap, and the world rippled again.

A sizzling *snap* filled the air, like a firecracker had gone off. The next second, Indriði was a couple of steps closer, and the room was full of a strange smoke.

Another snap.

Astrid was gone—there one second and gone the next. Satara was on her knees, hacking, compulsively inhaling more smoke as she did.

Indriði brought her hands together again. *Snap.*

Edie had taken half a step toward Satara, but now she was sitting slumped against one of the windows. Her body stung and ached all over. Smoke filled her lungs. She coughed, throat spasming as she inhaled desperately, but there was no air to inhale.

Snap.

Familiar figures in black and silver armor had converged on Satara, each wearing an opal amulet around their necks.

Snap.

Gone.

It was as though someone had turned on a cosmic strobe light. When it went dark, Edie, her friends, her life, nothing existed; when it flashed on, they did again. On and off, rendering everything choppy, like a series of photos taken in quick succession, with nothing happening in the order it should.

It took Edie a moment to realize what was happening. The world seemed to stop because it *was* stopping—for everyone but Indriði and the New Gloaming warriors. The Norn was bending the tapestry of time to her advantage, navigating the creases they couldn't to catch them off guard.

Edie was the only one left. About ten feet behind Indriði, she attempted to sit up, choking, shaking.

Snap.

The Norn had jumped halfway across the room and was standing over Edie. She planted a foot against her shoulder, pinning her where she sat.

"Thanks for everything, hon. I couldn't have done it without you."

Snap.

Existence stopped.

The first thing to pierce through the darkness was the impossible cold. The area around Edie was freezing; it seeped through her clothes and numbed her skin, sapping her of the energy to do anything but curl up and shiver and try to preserve a modicum of warmth.

Eventually, slowly, sounds stood out in this void. Somewhere nearby, water was dripping. There were shouts and laughs coming from far off.

She had been underground enough recently to recognize how the noise bounced off the walls. *There are hidden tunnels all over this city,* Khenbu had said. Well, she was sick of being in them.

Finally, she became aware of someone breathing raggedly near her. It took her a moment to realize it was herself.

How long had it been since Indriði's assault? A few minutes, days, a year? They all felt the same.

Edie cracked open an eye.

The room around her was very dark—but the barest light coming from somewhere down the corridor was enough to make out that she was sitting in a cell, surrounded by three walls of stone and one of iron bars. She turned her head slightly, teeth chattering. Shackles were riveted to the walls and floors all around her, and a fold-up bunk, wooden and bare, was suspended from a chain across the room.

A tingle of hope went through her. If she could get up and lie on that instead of the floor, she wouldn't be so cold. Standing was out of the question; her body felt so weak. She shuffled onto her knees and tried to crawl her way over.

A jerk on her ankle stopped her short. When she looked back, she noticed that she was shackled to the floor, just out of reach of the bunk.

Edie closed her eyes for a moment and took a deep breath. The oxygen in her lungs was healing, and after a few minutes of deep breathing, she finally mustered the strength to stand and go to the bars of her cell.

"Hello?" she whispered into the darkness.

It swallowed up her words. She might as well have been talking to a black hole. Was this real? Was this even time? She started to wonder.

"Hello?" she tried again.

Suddenly, as if in answer, an orange light flooded the corridor. It came closer, accompanied by footsteps. Edie leaned into the bars eagerly, desperate to come face to face with Indriði. She had a thing or two to say.

But when the figures finally emerged, she deflated completely. It wasn't Indriði standing there. In fact, it was two people. One was Scarlet, holding a torch in front of her smiling face. When she saw the other, Edie's world began to spin, and she sank to her knees again.

Her father.

CHAPTER TWENTY-TWO

EDIE COULD NOT TAKE her eyes off Richard Holloway's face as Scarlet approached the bars of her cell.

"Hello, little thing," the wight said, watching Edie's expression with relish. "You still have a paycheck to pick up. And by the way, you're fired."

Edie's voice was like a tremulous wind when she spoke, searching her father's face. "I don't understand."

He said nothing, simply stared back at her with those familiar slate eyes. Her own eyes. Her own face.

"Aww, what a happy reunion." Scarlet showed her teeth. "Papa," she said to Richard, reaching out to pinch his cheek, "why don't you give your little girl a kiss?"

Edie scooted away from the bars, pressing her back against the far wall. The wight's eyes shone with glee as she produced an iron ring of keys, picking one out with precise movements. She opened the cell and made way for Richard.

Aside from the horrible, alien hunger in his eyes, everything was so familiar it hurt. He looked exactly as he had ten years ago, down to the tiny wrinkles around his eyes, the severe cut of his beard, the salt-and-pepper starting at his temples. But something was wrong...

He hadn't changed at all.

That was impossible.

Fake Dad crouched and grabbed her by her shoulders, bearing down on her. When she fought against him, he gripped her throat and jerked her down, pinning her to the flagstones. A cry started to leave her but was cut short as he brought his face closer to hers. His mouth was open, eyes rolling back in his head as he inhaled deeply.

Realization slammed into Edie. So this was the breathstealer that had attacked Mercy.

Her throat spasmed, her lungs aching as the life was sucked from her. White streaks flickered in her quickly darkening vision, pulled from her and into the creature holding her down. Edie struggled as hard as she could against the strong grip. The feeling of having no obstruction in front of your face or in your throat but still not being able to breathe was maddening, and try as she might, she couldn't keep her mind from switching into panic mode.

If she couldn't get out of this soon, she would pass out. And lord knew what they'd do then. She couldn't let it happen.

Its face was mere inches from hers, if that; but, blessedly, the creature had switched from looking like her father to looking strangely amorphous. Its appearance whirled and shifted as it focused fully on stealing her breath, her life.

She attempted to jerk her head to the side, but she was almost immediately pulled back by a strange gravity. As if to make extra sure she wouldn't be going anywhere, the breathstealer grabbed her by the chin, clutching, forcing her jaw to stay open and facing forward.

Her extremities began to go numb, but still she fought, trying to kick and push her assailant away. Her attempts must have been pretty pathetic, because it didn't move even an inch.

Darkness clouded her vision; her movements slowed, then stopped. There was no point in fighting. She couldn't see or feel where it was—

where *she* was—anymore. There was nothing in this darkness. The world was gone. Did she even exist? Had she ever existed?

Suddenly, her lungs filled with oxygen, a primitive sense of awareness coming back to her. A woman was saying something in a harsh voice, echoing all around her. The blackness receded like ice fractals thawing on a windowpane, giving way to a yellow light. Bars, and two forms, but they were swimming in double vision...

Her muscles ached. Her throat ached. She rested her head on the cold stone floor. From the corner of her eye, she watched the breathstealer turn into her father again and slink out the cell door, its back to Scarlet.

"That's enough entertainment for now," the wight said with cruel satisfaction as she locked the door. "I'll come back with another face soon, Edie. I found lots of good memories to use while you were sleeping."

Disgust and violation curled up in Edie's stomach and bled like dying animals. Edie followed suit, hugging her knees to her chest and turning away until Scarlet and the light were gone. She squeezed her eyes shut, trying to focus on her ragged, fast breaths, trying to calm them before her lungs collapsed from strain.

She lay there blearily for a while before she mustered the strength to sit up and scoot over to the bars. She gripped them, testing their strength. They were sturdy as hell and close together. Even at peak performance, she wouldn't be able to move them.

Slowly, she stood, examining her surroundings. The chain around her ankle allowed her to reach the back wall, and she pushed against it and the adjacent one, trying to find a weak stone. They were all perfectly aligned, however, the mortar between them still good. She'd never be able to get out this way. If only she still had that stupid piece of chalk.

Her heart sank. The only way she was getting out of this cell was if someone *let* her out.

Going back to the bars, she decided to test her voice. It sounded fine, if a bit strained. "Hello? Is anyone here?"

"Edie?"

It was Satara's voice, barely above a whisper. Edie watched with relief as the shieldmaiden crept out from the shadows of the cell across from her, leaning against the bars. Scarlet's voice must have woken her.

"Are you okay?" Edie asked.

"My head hurts, and my muscles." Satara's overdress was damp and torn in a few places, and her hair was half-down from its bun, but other than that, there were no outward signs of injury.

Edie was able to relax slightly. At least they were both intact, though god only knew how long that would be the case. "Where are we, do you know?"

Satara shook her head. "I have no idea. Somewhere underground, obviously."

Edie looked up at the ceiling as though it would provide her with some clue. Every so often, the dungeon seemed to tremble as though an earthquake was rippling through. She'd been in enough underground clubs to have an idea of what it meant. It had happened in Khenbu's tunnels, too. "I think we're still in the city. That shaking is probably foot traffic on the streets above us, or maybe the subway."

The shieldmaiden frowned thoughtfully as she listened to the laughter and movement coming from the nearby corridors. "This place sounds enormous. How could it be under the city without anyone knowing?"

"I was, uh ... in a place like this recently, running an errand." Edie looked back at her. "The person who lived there said there are secret tunnels like this all over the city." She pointed to Satara's dress. "Do you still have your dog whistle?"

"It won't work. Astrid said the Norn's home is filled with anti-teleportation wards." Satara sighed hard and tried the bars.

"They're sturdy," Edie said. "I checked mine, too."

"Someone's been maintaining this place."

"I checked the walls, too, but there weren't any loose bricks or anything." She nodded to the wall behind Satara.

The shieldmaiden followed her gaze and disappeared into the darkness for a few moments. When she came back, she shook her head.

"None in mine, either." She glared down the corridor. "I can't believe that witch tricked us. She drew us in and didn't even let us put up a real fight."

Edie closed her eyes and rested her forehead against the bars. Satara was right, of course. How could she have been so stupid? She should have seen the lies. No one helped for nothing in return. She should have learned that by now. With a sigh, she said, "The people that dragged you away, did you see them? They were New Gloaming."

"Damn." Satara loosed a breath, shaking her head uncertainly. "But Astrid said spirits of Fate don't care about factions. Why would that change now?"

"Maybe she hates Astrid just that much."

"Do you think Zaedicus recruited her at his party?"

"He must have."

Satara leaned closer to the bars, peering to her left, deeper into the dungeon. There were other cells, but they seemed empty—no noise came from them, anyway. "Where do you think Astrid is? She disappeared."

"Maybe she's dead," Edie replied miserably.

The shieldmaiden shook her head. "You can't kill a valkyrie."

"What?"

"Not like you're thinking." She sighed. "They occasionally die in battles in other Worlds, but even then, they may not stay dead. Getting rid of them is doubly hard in Midgard because they're already..."

Edie squinted at Satara. That was right—neither she nor Astrid had ever actually gotten around to telling her how one became a valkyrie. In fact, she knew next to nothing about them. "They're already ... dead?"

"In a manner of speaking." The shieldmaiden sighed again and rested her head against the bars, avoiding eye contact. "You'd have to obliterate one, wipe her from existence so entirely that she could not come back. I would know if that had happened to Astrid."

Edie stared at Satara for a moment, wanting to ask more questions. There would be time for that later, though—for now, they had to think of some way to get out of here. They needed to find Astrid and make sure that she *stayed* not-obliterated.

"Did you see Scarlet?"

Satara shook her head. "I heard a familiar voice. Was that her?"

"Yeah."

"Then Zaedicus and Sárr can't be too far away."

Edie rubbed her face. "Maybe next time she comes by, one of us can trick her into coming into our cell, and we can grab her keys. That's the only way we're getting out of here."

Then, a thought donned on her. *Cal.* A couple of months ago, he'd been held captive, too. The only way she'd known to go looking for him was because she could feel his mind subconsciously crying out for help. If she could finally bring her walls down, maybe she could lead him here. Even if he had already made it to Vegas, he'd been able to sense her from across the country before. Why not now?

Of course, after their fight, maybe he wouldn't come even if she *could* reach him. But it was a chance she had to take if she wanted to get out of here before something really bad went down.

She closed her eyes, felt around for the walls ... and was shocked to find that they weren't there. Panic turned into wild hope. They must have fallen while she was being attacked by the breathstealer, or sometime earlier. Her mind had had her back without her even knowing it. *Could've used that sooner, but I'll take it.* She refocused and searched her mind for some hint of Cal.

She couldn't feel anything. Still, she had to try.

Usually, when he was close, she felt a tiny bit of resistance as feelings passed from her consciousness to his, like diving into the ocean slowed your movement—but as she sent some thoughts out, she didn't feel anything. Her voice simply echoed into the void.

Terror made her heart skip a beat, and she opened her eyes. Had he heard her? Was he blocking her out, or was she not doing it right? She hadn't actually ever conveyed her emotions like this on *purpose.*

She'd just have to keep trying. There was no other choice.

"She's coming," Satara whispered from the cell across from her.

Edie turned her head to see yellow torchlight coming toward them again, and her blood pumped faster as familiar footfalls echoed off the corridor walls. She didn't want Scarlet to come back, especially not with that breathstealer. She wasn't sure she could handle another session of mind-crushing blackness, or seeing her father's face in the flesh—or whatever other appearance Scarlet had stolen.

To her surprise, though, she didn't recognize the person walking with the wight. He was a young black man, an inch or so under six feet tall, sporting a low fade and silver and brown splint armor. Though baby-faced and with concerned eyebrows, his resemblance to Satara was immediately apparent. They had practically the same eyes, cheekbones, chin.

Edie shifted her gaze to the shieldmaiden. She looked petrified; and from her lips, one word trembled. A name, spoken with the greatest terror.

"*Darras?*"

A bad thing. Something Satara didn't want to see.

Edie's protective streak flared up. It made sense that Scarlet would want to torture Edie—it was almost fair, considering the upset she'd caused in the Gloaming. But Satara? Now she was just being cruel.

"Satara," she barked, trying to refocus her attention. "Don't believe it. It's not real! It's one of those things that attacked Mer—"

Scarlet lashed out, then, smacking the bars of Edie's cell with the torch. "Quiet!" The flame flickered and spat embers that fell in Edie's face, burning her eyelids and cheeks.

Edie pulled away, but didn't relent. "Satara, it's not real! Don't believe anything they say to you!"

The breathstealer lingered impatiently, looking between Edie and Scarlet.

"I said *quiet!*" The wight moved to block Edie's view of Satara. "Do you want me to bring your daddy back? You have a lot of catching up to do."

Terror gripped Edie's heart, but she couldn't sit back and let her friends take the heat. She'd done that enough already. "Do whatever you want to me," she mumbled. "Just leave her alone. She hasn't done anything to you."

Scarlet sighed and looked over her shoulder at the breathstealer. She handed him her iron keyring and motioned for him to go to Satara.

"No!" Edie threw herself against the bars, reaching her arm out as far as she could to grab the wight's. With a strength she didn't know she had, she yanked Scarlet forward. The vampire hit the bars with a dull clang.

But her reaction was quicker than Edie could ever have anticipated. She leveraged Edie's hold against her, twisting her arm painfully so she lost her grip. Before Edie could regain control or back away, Scarlet had grabbed her shoulder and jerked her forward. Her face smacked against the iron bars.

Pain exploded. Her ears rang. Her head was suddenly filled with pressure, and a pervasive confusion entered her mind, such that all she could think to do was go limp and fall asleep.

Her back hit the stone floor. Maybe she lost consciousness, or maybe she lay there in a daze she would later forget. Either way, darkness set in.

CHAPTER TWENTY-THREE

CAL WAS USED to losing things. He was used to drifting from distraction to distraction—different people, same bullshit, same outcome. He was used to friends scattering to the winds and never speaking to him again. He was used to relying on his anger to carry him into the next day, or week, or year.

Above all, Cal was used to being alone, and he told himself he liked it that way.

It'd been three days since Edie had blown up at him, but he hadn't left Anster yet. He'd only gotten a couple of miles down the highway before turning back. He told himself it was because he still had a score to settle here. That Scarlet bitch was still walking around with the memories she'd stolen from him when he'd been kidnapped. He intended to get them back from her, killing her for them if he had to.

That was the only reason. That was the safe explanation for turning around and coming back.

But there was no explanation for what he was doing now: sitting at the bar of some crummy Irish pub, drowning himself in the middle of the day. And that pissed him off.

Two months ago, he had promised himself he would run. Sure,

maybe he wanted to stay and help the Reach, but he'd silently sworn that the second Edie Holloway inevitably showed her true colors, he'd leave her behind before she could stop him. And he'd kept that promise.

And he'd—

He...

He buried his face in his hands, thinking of when he'd woken up in that alley. He was used to the feeling of people looking at him but not seeing shit, frozen into their own little worlds. Everyone he'd known in Vegas used each other to their own ends and nothing more, and that was the bargain. He had thought he was okay with that.

But that day, she'd shown up right away, protected him, *seen* him. He hadn't been seen in so long.

Stupid fucking girl.

He had been an idiot to fall for her trick. Her apparent earnestness to be *good* had lulled him into a false sense of security; he'd let himself relax, let himself think it felt nice to be a part of something.

She'd lied. Even if he didn't know why, that was the only explanation. How else could she have changed so quickly, suddenly not trusted him or Astrid anymore?

That Norn. Don't fucking trust her. No one goes to Zaedicus's parties who doesn't belong there.

What about Tilda? What about me?

Fuck Tilda. And fuck me.

His heart twinged a little at his own reply, and he twirled his empty glass. He didn't want anything to do with the Reach anymore, but ... maybe he should go tell Astrid, just to warn her. If it was the Norn's fault, maybe she could fix it. If it wasn't...

Screw it. He didn't feel like seeing Astrid. He didn't feel like seeing anybody. He was busy licking his wounds, and it made him feel weak. Edie had been playing the long game, and he'd fallen for it like a little bitch. While he'd been getting comfortable, she'd gotten comfortable, too. Turned out she was comfortable hurting people.

Is that really true, though? Her?

Cal tapped the bar to ask for another refill, but the bartender shook her head. He sighed heavily and refrained from laying his head on the bar. Instead, he half-turned, glancing out the window.

Across the street, a preteen girl sat on a bench next to her dad. Her arm was in a cast—probably fresh considering how vibrant it was—but she was swinging her legs and smiling. For some freaking reason, Cal found himself transfixed. She and her dad held matching ice cream cones, and though Dad looked tired as hell, he was smiling, too. Whatever crisis had caused the broken arm had been dealt with, and this was their prize: a second of peace.

Cal glared. Fucking Hallmark movie bullshit. No one really had a life like that, all happy and secure. It was a lie they told to make themselves feel better, an act. Chances were her dad had been the one to break her arm in the first place.

That was what people did. They hurt each other.

He turned back to the bartender. If she wasn't gonna serve him, he'd go somewhere else and start fresh. But might as well try. "Hey, one for the road?"

She glanced at him, and her smirk made her septum piercing flip up slightly. "I saw you driving around in that Eldo. That's a nice car. I wouldn't want you to wreck it."

He groaned. "Ahh, I'm not even drunk. You can tell, can't you?"

"That's kind of my job, yeah. Also my job to make sure you don't drink yourself to death." She glanced around the room, sighed, and looked back at Cal with a shrug. "Okay, fine. You can hold your liquor. One more."

"Thanks." Cal tipped the glass appreciatively once it was filled.

"So"—the bartender crossed her arms on the bar, leaning forward—"why the day drinking?"

"It's past five o'clock in Ireland."

Her eyebrows disappeared behind her bangs. "Wow, I've never heard that one before."

Cal lowered his glass, glaring at her. With all the piercings and dark makeup, she reminded him of Edie. He hated that he was lowering his guard because of it. Edie was the enemy now. She'd put *herself* in that position. "Oh, so are you gonna do the barkeep thing where you pretend to care about my problems, now?"

"Sure." She shrugged, peering at him deeply. "Let me see if I can guess."

He huffed incredulously. "Seriously?"

"Is it a girl?"

"No. Well ... kind of. She's a kid. A girl kid." Cal knocked back his drink. He'd need it if this chick was really going to insist on talking to him about this.

She didn't look convinced, but conceded nonetheless. "All right, so what happened?"

"We had a ... fight. She doesn't *trust* me."

"Why?"

He threw up a hand. "I don't even fuckin' know. She thinks I'm using her or tricking her or somethin'. She says I don't do anything unless I get something out of it, so why would I be helping her?"

"Hm ... kinda sounds like she's been let down in the past," the bartender said thoughtfully, checking her nails. "Maybe someone who didn't turn out to be who they said they were."

Well ... she was right. It wasn't the first time someone had lied to Edie about who they were. "But I'm not lying to her. I've *never* lied to her, only tried to help her."

The bartender looked up skeptically. "Never?"

Fuck. Cal looked down at the bar. There were still things he was keeping from her. Edie wasn't stupid. She'd begun to notice.

"No secrets at all?"

"Everyone has secrets," he snapped. "But I don't mean her any harm."

"And how's she supposed to know that? Have you told her why you wanna help her? Like, your motives?"

"No."

"Why?"

"'Cause they're none of her goddamn business. I do what I do because — just—" Cal clenched his jaw. "I have my own reasons."

"So ... you're doing it for you, like she said."

A heavy sigh, and he glanced at the ceiling. "No."

"What are the reasons, then? I won't tell her," the bartender said with an amused tone.

Cal stared her down, but she didn't even flinch. After a long moment of silence, he shifted in his seat, looking away. "I'm ... fuck. Scared ... for her. I don't want her to end up like her dad. Guess I thought maybe if I was around to help..."

For the first time, the bartender seemed to get that he really *wasn't* talking about a girlfriend. "So who knows what'll happen now that you're gone, if she's really got no idea what she's doing. If she really needs you."

He made a face. "I guess, but ... she started the fight! She treated me like I was plotting against her or some shit."

"Yeah, but how can she know what your intentions really are if you never open up and tell her about them? Trust is a two-way street." The bartender pushed off the counter and grabbed a glass to clean, like she was Sam Malone or something.

"She still talked to me like I was shit. No one talks to me like that," he mumbled to his empty glass, twirling it again.

"Maybe she was using it as a defense mechanism." She quirked a brow. "Like you."

"I don't know what the hell you're talkin' about."

The bartender practically cackled. "Case in point. You've been deflecting and belligerent this whole conversation."

"Yeah, well..." He trailed off and sighed, glancing out the window again. The dad and daughter were gone, and a couple crows were picking around the bench, looking for scraps. "I don't need her."

"Sometimes what *you* need isn't the most important thing. Or, at least, it isn't the thing you thought you needed," the bartender said, setting down the glass she was holding. "Everyone these days is obsessed with *self-care* ... and sometimes you have to get away and do things for yourself, sure. Of course. But then you've got to come back and be with your people."

She sighed and rolled up her sleeves. Cal didn't know if she was just getting warm or if she was trying to show him her scars—either way, he caught sight of them. He looked at her face, then behind her, at the bar mirror. There were a couple of photos of her and another, younger woman there. They could be sisters.

"I mean, that's the real self-care, there, y'know? Being with people. Being open. Seriously!" she insisted when he pulled a face. "Humans aren't designed to be all alone and closed off. It kills us, man. We turn into assholes. Sometimes you *need* someone to take care of to realize your own worth. And those people who return the favor? They're like part of your DNA. You *are* who you choose to be with." She sighed, rubbing her elbows. "Everyone needs someone to keep them from going crazy, y'know?"

Cal was still lingering on those scars. Those weren't from any accident. He didn't even know this woman and he wanted to yell at her for having hurt herself. Christ, if Edie ever did that, he'd kill her.

Wait... He paused when he realized the bartender was comparing him to herself. *Why?* He glanced at his own arms.

"There's lots of different ways to hurt yourself, you know," she said, pursing her lips at him. "It's not all blood and burns."

Shame weighed down his stomach. He was about to tell her she was spouting some bullshit when, suddenly, a gale of panic washed over him. Fear. His head hurt; his vision was spinning. Someone was coming to kill him. Something nearby was dark and wet.

Holy hell!

When he focused hard, forcing the world back into perspective, none of those things were true. He was in a pub at mid-afternoon, arguing with a bartender.

But this wasn't his first rodeo. The vibrations of fear running up his spine and through his brain were familiar sensations. There was only one explanation for what he was feeling.

"I gotta go." Cal slapped a fifty-dollar bill on the bar and grabbed his jacket. "Keep the change."

He stomped down the street toward Ghost, trying to quell the feelings Edie was bulldozing into him. *I get it, I get it, you're in trouble!* But he was too far away to send her any assurances—and too far away to feel exactly where she was and what was going down.

He slid behind Ghost's wheel and fished his stupid phone out of his pocket. He should have texted Satara sooner, so she and Astrid knew Edie was out there alone, but he hadn't even looked at his phone for a couple days. Squinting at the screen, he brought up their conversation.

[1 Unread Message from SATARA]

Well, shit. He was in for it now.

[Satara]: Hi. Astrid, Edie, and I are going to meet with Indriði. She finally said yes.

If Cal's heart had been beating, it would have sped up. He checked the time stamp of the message. Three hours ago.

"Fuck!" He slammed a hand on Ghost's wheel. "Fuck, fuck, fuck, I fucking knew it!"

If he'd been right—if the Norn was what had Edie so panicked at the other end of their connection—they were in deep horse shit.

Ghost started up on cue, and they screamed down the road toward Alderdeen. He circled the block a couple of times before driving slowly down Olive Street.

The pain and fear were real here. He could hardly feel anything else as he cruised past the townhouse.

There was no doubt about it. Edie, and probably Satara and Astrid, were trapped in there. That bitch had been feeding Edie bullshit, training her not to trust them, and she'd led them right into the Norn's web, the fucking *dumbass*. How could she have been so stupid?

Cal gritted his teeth. He was still pissed at the kid, yeah—but was he really prepared to wash his hands of her and let her and Astrid and Satara die?

Cursing, he sped off. If he was gonna go, he couldn't go in guns blazing. He needed backup.

He turned the car around, praying that there was still one person in this town willing to help him.

CHAPTER TWENTY-FOUR

MERCY SIGHED as she slid into the heated pool, tension releasing from her muscles. Slowly, her back, her neck, her aching hips and legs relaxed, unclenching. Though she had slipped into the shallow end, she kept a firm grip on the edge of the pool, not wanting to take any chances.

She didn't need to worry for too long, though. The pool's sole occupant sensed the vibrations of her movement and the change in the water, and he surfaced a second later, a needle-toothed smile on his face.

At the sight of Fisk, Mercy grinned back, and she let herself be scooped into his arms. She could already feel the heat melting the pain away, and the salt in the water had made Fisk's scales vibrant and healthful again. Tilda had really outdone herself. Not only was the vampire dedicated to taking the greatest care with her charges, she was also really fun to hang out with.

"Ready for today's session?"

"I am ready," the vættr replied. "Let us get this bread!"

Mercy giggled. She'd explained the phrase to him the other day, but clearly, he hadn't fully understood the context. Still, his foibles were endearing. Talking to him was like talking to someone from an entirely different planet, and in a lot of ways, that was refreshing.

Thanks to the brunnmigi medicine, Mercy's casts had come off much quicker than anyone thought they would, but herbalism could only do so much. She still needed physical therapy. The pain in her hips, legs, and now back made her want to sit still and not move, but sometimes, that exacerbated the horrible muscle cramps.

Pool therapy wasn't only a decent solution; she was starting to find it downright pleasant. She had always swum like a fish, and Fisk was familiar with hydrotherapy as something his people did.

And maybe it helped—maybe, a little—that his affection was, *perhaps*, growing on her.

Mercy pulled away from Fisk, retrieved the kickboard she had left at the edge of the pool yesterday, and floated closer. She avoided looking at him as she did, trying not to admire his built chest. It was silly—he was a giant fish man, for god's sake—but she couldn't deny that she'd been noticing him a lot lately. And considering they now spent almost every waking moment together, that was quite often.

"Can we work on my legs again? Those stretches we did the other day made them feel so much looser."

"Certainly." His tone was cheerful as he carefully pulled her farther from the edge of the pool, so that she could stretch her legs out. In a movement as fluid and natural as the water around them, he slipped behind her. "May I?"

She nodded and relaxed forward, letting her legs float up. As he maneuvered between them, she rested her head on the kickboard and let her whole body relax, weightless. She found herself almost dozing as Fisk slowly stretched her legs, taking his time to work the muscles of her thighs and calves. He continued until she could comfortably stretch them all the way out by herself, then began to gently massage her lower back, her hips, down to her thighs, up her glutes.

Mercy closed her eyes tight and hid her face in her hair, fighting a grin. She tried to tell herself that the warmth beginning to course through her was only a side effect of being in a heated pool. Really, she knew better. She kept her legs stretched out.

Behind her, Fisk emitted a low, relaxed purr, stroking her sides and tracing the mermaid scale tattoos going up her thighs and flank. Some of them had been lost in surgery, but some remained, criss-crossed with scars. Fisk's warm hands roving over the scar tissue, gentle and reverent, felt nice.

His hands slid downward again until he was framing her butt, thumbs stroking a little too close to her crotch to be just a friendly touch. She swore she could feel his heartbeat through his palms. It was almost as though he had sensed her body reacting to the massage.

Mercy knew she should stop him. She was a human, and he was essentially a fish. Then again, she'd dated a lot of other humans, of all different varieties, and no one had taken care of her like this—diligently, gladly, as though it was his purpose, the only thing he ever wanted to do. Hell, Drake had literally kicked her out.

And really, Fisk was better looking than most of the humans she'd dated, not to mention more intelligent...

He pushed himself a little closer, spreading her legs, and a jolt of pain went through her right hip. She gasped, her whole body shuddering.

In a fraction of a second, Fisk had pulled back, removing himself from between her legs. With a sweeping movement, he floated in front of her again, his large, webbed hands on her upper arms. "Forgive me. Did I hurt you?"

"Just my hip." She looked away, her face burning. It had only been a temporary shot of pain, but this moment highlighted what they had been doing.

Thoughtfully, Fisk extracted the kickboard from under her upper body and pulled her upright, flush against his chest. "Perhaps we should try a different exercise."

Was that a come-on? Or was he actually suggesting something different? When she peered up at him to gauge his meaning, his face was close, head ducked to meet her eyes properly. He wore the most earnest expression, now practically cradling her.

Mercy felt herself relax into him. "Maybe..."

With another purr, he ducked his head lower. For a second, she thought he was going to kiss her neck, but instead, he nuzzled his jaw against hers. The action was foreign, but clearly a display of intimacy, and it sent a shiver through her. His hands found their way back to her thighs. Carefully, he pulled her closer until she had her legs wrapped around his waist.

Mercy pressed her mouth and nose into the crook of his neck, tracing his onyx markings. Maybe it was useless to keep denying her affection for him. He might be a mythical creature, but this moment seemed so simple. Everything that needed to be said was passing between them like water itself. Hot tears welled in her eyes. She closed them.

She already liked herself just how she was—it was nice to find someone who felt the same way.

Fisk must have noticed the slight change in her breathing; he cooed and lifted a hand to her cheek. "Why are you crying, pearl?"

"I don't know. You're so ... tender." She tried to blink the tears back, feeling like an idiot. "I'm used to other humans playing games with me, I guess, but you're so honest."

He smiled and hugged her close, and finally, the kisses came. He nuzzled her hair out of the way and placed a dozen little ones just under her ear, along her jawline, onto her cheek.

Mercy's head spun at the light touches. She wanted him. She wanted *this* so bad, but—

Gently but firmly, she placed a hand on his chest and pushed him back a bit. "Hey..."

The vættr stopped, peering down at her. She unwound her legs from his waist, and he pulled his hands back like he had touched something hot. Probably afraid of being devoured—he'd mentioned that sjóvættir tended to make meals of each other at the smallest slight.

Thankfully, it was much easier for her to stand alone in the water. "Fisk ... I like you a lot. And I can't even tell you how much I appreciate your, um, companionship. I like being close to you." She sighed. "But ... I don't think I'm ready yet."

He simply tilted his head.

"I just left a relationship, and I need to focus on healing." Mercy looked deep into his eyes, willing him to understand. "I think— I think I want to be with you, but with everything going on... I need time."

Fisk seemed to mull this over, searching her gaze. At length, he smiled, and hugged her close once more so he could nuzzle her cheek. His voice was raspy as he spoke: "For you, I would wait an eternity."

Mercy blinked. Tears fell down her cheeks, but she was grinning. She wiped them away with the heel of her palm before wrapping her arms around his neck and planting a kiss on his mouth, which he returned *very* eagerly. Sure, she had just told him she wasn't ready, but one little kiss wouldn't hurt, right? She wasn't sure she could help herself if she tried.

Suddenly, the glass door slammed open. Mercy practically jumped out of Fisk's arms, whirling to see who had interrupted them.

It was Cal. Worry was etched on his features as he stomped in, but it was replaced with bemusement, then disgust, as he realized what he'd walked in on. "Well," he grumbled, "this gives a new meaning to the term *hooking up*."

Mercy crossed her arms. "Can we help you?"

"Where's Tilda?"

"She's coming back soon, why?"

Cal jerked a thumb toward the stack of towels sitting on one of the lounge chairs. "You're gonna wanna dry off ... if you can."

She was already climbing out of the pool, with a little help from Fisk. "What happened? Is Edie okay?"

The revenant simply shook his head.

"I knew there was something odd going on," Tilda said as she set a tea tray down on one end of her long dining table. Antoniu was close behind with a plate of tiny sandwiches. "When she was here, I found her going through my things. She was asking all sorts of strange questions."

A glare was plastered on Cal's face as he watched Mercy take one of the sandwiches. He tried to look anywhere but Tilda. She wasn't stupid; she probably knew he'd been avoiding her. He didn't wanna see that hurt look on her face, like their failed relationship was all his fault. He'd gotten enough of that at the party.

Mostly, he ended up looking at her skinny boy-toy wraith. What the hell was with that? She could do better.

"Should've never trusted that Norn," he mumbled. "There was no reason for her to insist on seeing Edie alone. Should've known something was up."

"You couldn't have known it would come to this." The vampire smoothed her skirt out and sat across from him.

The revenant shook his head and said out loud what he'd been thinking earlier: "She was at Zaedicus's shindig. Anyone who goes to a place like that *belongs* there."

Tilda went silent.

"Someone has to go after her," Mercy said, already on her second sandwich. In the time he'd known her, Cal had found out she was a *big* stress eater. "Can you still feel her?"

"Kinda. The thoughts I'm picking up aren't making a fuckin' lick of sense, though. Makes me think she might be unconscious."

Fisk huffed. "How could this be? What has she done to anger the Norn?"

"Herself? Probably nothing." Cal fished his phone out of his back pocket and flashed Satara's message around the table. "The Norn was baiting her so she'd lure Astrid to the house, and the kid fell for it hook, line, and sinker."

Mercy's face was twisted with worry as she devoured another sandwich. She stored it in her cheek like a little squirrel when she spoke. "She has Satara and Astrid, too?"

"Astrid pissed her off like a hundred years ago or something, so it makes sense she'd want to get back at her. But why now? And what the hell is going down in there?"

"We have to help her," Tilda cut in, wringing her hands.

Cal clenched his jaw. *Yeah, we aren't doing anything*, he wanted to say, but kept his mouth shut. Even he had the sense not to bite the very rich, manicured hand that was feeding them at the moment. "I ain't doing shit until I know what's going on in there."

"Who cares what's going on?" Mercy snapped, staring at him in astonishment. "We know everything we need to, which is that our friends are in trouble!"

"And what kinda wards do you think she has on her house?" he returned. "What's her security like, huh? How'd she trap them, and what's she using to keep them trapped? We went into Zaedicus's mansion without a *freaking* clue and look how that turned out." He gestured to her legs.

"What do you think we should do, Cal, find blueprints of her house?"

"Might help!" He growled. "Can you let me do what I need to do? You're not going, anyway."

"I assumed you came to find us because you wanted our help." Mercy crossed her arms. "But fine. What's *your* plan?"

Cal stood and crossed his arms, too, looking around the room in thought. It had been a long time since he had last been in this penthouse. He'd known it would make him uncomfortable, but he'd never imagined being this on-edge. "I wanna find someone who can tell me what I'm up against. Someone who knows the Norn, or can tell me what the hell she had Edie doing for her."

"Wait, what do you mean?" Tilda asked.

"Few days ago, Edie sent me out on some so-called *errands*, and when I came back, she was gone. I found her outside the Norn's place. I think she was having Edie do some of her dirty work, somethin' related to getting revenge on Astrid. Getting something or recruiting someone, maybe."

No one spoke as he began to pace. He walked to the living room and sat down on the couch, holding his head in silence. A few moments later, he sprang back up, quickly coming back to the table.

"There was a kid," he said, stabbing the table with a finger. "When I finally found her, she was coming out of the Norn's building with a girl. Maybe like sixteen. She probably knows."

Antoniu, who had been standing next to Tilda's chair with his arms crossed behind his back, leaned down to whisper in her ear.

Tilda's expression changed from one of confusion to surprise, and she glanced at Antoniu before looking to Cal. "What did she look like?"

"Uh, uh..." He racked his brain, trying to recall details. At the time, he'd been so focused on being angry at Edie that he hadn't looked at her for very long. "Mid-teens, a couple inches shorter than Edie, maybe Asian? No, Native?"

"She could be Inuk," Mercy suggested. "Dumb people mistake them sometimes."

Cal shot her a glare.

Antoniu leaned in to whisper in Tilda's ear again. She nodded, then looked back at the group. "He thinks he knows who you're talking about. She's a young courier he's worked with a couple of times."

Cal looked at Antoniu. "All right, Creepy, where can I find her?"

Maintaining eye contact with the revenant, Antoniu slowly leaned down once more to whisper in Tilda's ear.

CHAPTER TWENTY-FIVE

SISSEL SAT at the kitchen table, watching the TV flashing in the living room. The smell of cooking soup filled her nose, making her stomach growl. Her dad didn't make soup for them very often, because it usually involved vegetables getting slimy and wet and she hated that, but he made do when it came to traditional recipes.

He'd taken the day off for some reason, and she could tell it was bad news. He had been circling her like a vulture the whole morning, wanting to know what she was doing, insisting on spending *time* with her. When she'd finally asked, "Did someone die?" he had seemed surprised, then walked on eggshells the rest of the day.

Parents were so weird. She rested her head in one hand, using her foot to pet Shorts, who had curled up under the table. Dad had turned on the news while he cooked. The metal whisper of the spoon as he stirred the pot was getting to her, so she shot a glare at his back and strained to listen to the TV instead.

"Police were called to a horrific scene at the Freegue Bridge homeless camp late last night, where they found the mutilated bodies of thirty-one men, women, and children. Law enforcement were apparently alerted when workers across the river noticed the

encampment burning and sounds of panic, leading some social media users to theorize that this strike was organized by a group known as 'the Watchers.' Several occupants of the camp are also missing in the wake of the apparent attack..."

"*Takanna!*" Dad said cheerfully, setting a bowl of soup in front of her with one hand and clicking the TV off with the other.

Sissel took her spoon, peering into the soup. "What's this?"

"Suaasat, except I couldn't find any good meat for it, so I used chicken, and ... you don't like cooked onions, so I used onion powder." His nostrils flared, and little lines appeared on either side of his broad chin as he smiled sheepishly.

She spooned a little and laughed good-naturedly as he sat across from her. "So it's chicken and potato soup."

"Ha. How about you enjoy your soup instead of sassing me?"

Sissel tried a couple spoonfuls. It wasn't bad, but it definitely wasn't traditional suaasat. He had absolutely insisted on making this specific dish even though the ingredients didn't really work for them, though, and she was pretty sure she knew why.

She tried to approach it delicately. "So ... what's with all the Greenlandy stuff lately?"

Dad chuckled. "Um ... I'm an Indigenous Studies professor. Not to mention Inuk. *Greenlandy stuff* is what I do."

Okay, maybe too delicately. And maybe not the right words. "Well, yeah, but ... you've been making so much more food, and those documentaries have been on literally non-stop, and the books you gave me ... you've even been speaking the language more often."

He took a spoonful of soup, probably trying to look casual, but the subtle pinch of his eyebrows wasn't fooling her. "What, I can't be proud of our culture?"

"*Daaaaaad.* You know what I mean."

"Okay, okay." He began to fiddle with the napkin at the edge of his plate. At length, he sighed and said, "This was Mom's favorite. I've ... just been thinking about her a lot."

And there it was. Sissel inhaled through her nose. She never *stopped* thinking about Mom, and she doubted he did, either. "Why?"

"Our anniversary. It's today."

"Oh ... right." She was quiet for a while, stirring her soup. "Sorry. I forgot."

Sissel didn't remember much about her mother, but she knew she missed her. She had always made her feel so safe, so understood, and so loved. Dad did, too, but it was different somehow. Sissel longed to feel that connection again. Dad must want to see Mom again just as much as she did, but he didn't talk about it often, and as far as Sissel knew, he wasn't actively looking for Mom like she was. He'd probably given up hope after so long.

Speaking of looking for Mom, she had some people she needed to talk to, soon. Maybe she could find Khenbu again and ask him some questions, or follow up on other leads. She kept them all in a document on her phone, as well as a hard copy in a notebook.

She sighed a little. "I'm probably gonna go out soon. I have some stuff to do."

Her dad responded with silence for a few moments, then: "Sissel..."

Oh, no. Here it came—whatever he'd been waiting to tell her today. She could tell by his hesitation and the tone of his voice.

"I don't really want you going out."

"Today?" She wrinkled her nose. "Why?"

"Er, today, or ... ever." Before she could protest, he continued, "There are crazy people out there. I don't need to tell you that. You've seen the news about the riots and the killings and the attacks, especially on the attuned community—"

"So?" she said, confused and hurt. "You know I can take care of myself. This is how I make money."

"I let you start couriering because I knew how precocious you are, and *yes*, I know you can take care of yourself. But you're a kid. You're not as powerful as you think you are—"

"That's not fair!"

"—and it's not safe." He raised his voice slightly, trying to be heard over her. "There are too many Gloaming running around looking for trouble. You can't control all of them."

"This is dumb!"

"Not to mention it's getting colder out. There was frost on my windshield yesterday morning."

"I don't care about the stupid frost on your stupid window," she mumbled, pushing her soup away and standing from the table. She and Dad might not connect a lot of the time, but they never fought like this, and it made her uncomfortable. Her face felt hot. "This is bullshit."

He remained sitting, but gave her a stern look. "Watch your language."

"I'm *fine*. And you *know* you can't tell me what to do."

He leaned back in his seat, crossing his arms. "Are you really going to manipulate me into letting you out? Are you really going to do that?"

She clenched her jaw. They'd had numerous talks over the years about her powers and how to use them ethically, and she didn't even want to imagine how much trouble she'd get in if she mind-controlled her own dad.

"This is so stupid. They've been bothering people for months and you never said I had to stay home!" She shook her head, brows furrowed. This felt so random and unfair. It was like he had waited to drop this bombshell at the worst time.

"Things have gotten exponentially more dangerous, and you can't trust the police; they aren't doing anything about it."

"I trust myself!"

"You're fifteen years old."

"So, what? You get to control everything I do? Am I just never supposed to have my own money or any freaking friends? I can never go outside, you're gonna lock me away in a cage?"

"Sissel, you are not being fair. You know I'm trying to keep you safe!" He sighed. "You're right, I should have made you quit running a while ago. But I'm doing it now, effective immediately."

Hot, angry tears welled in her eyes. Why was he doing this to her, locking her away like she was a criminal? She hadn't done anything but go about her life, and now she was being punished. She felt like ripping her hair out and stomping her feet like a little kid. The rage was overwhelming, so she tried to squish it down, trap it under a layer of ice. She'd known her dad her whole life, so she knew what made him really angry, and it wasn't tantrums.

Without fully meaning for it to happen, she adopted a snarky tone instead, like she was talking to the biggest moron in the world. "You *literally* can't control me."

"Sissel."

"I don't even know why I'm surprised. All you ever did was try to control Mom and make her *normal*. I'd leave, too."

She regretted going quite that far the moment the words left her mouth, but there was no going back.

Dad flinched, took a deep breath, then stood. His voice was infuriatingly calm when he spoke again. "Go to your room. You're grounded."

Sissel's rage boiled over. As she marched to her room, she screamed, "I hate you!"

She slammed the door. Then, pressing her back against it, she sat, resting her head on her knees. She wrapped her arms around her head, blocking out the sunlight that streamed through her windows. As the tears flowed freely, she tried in vain to stifle her sobs. Maybe he was testing her. Maybe he would come and take back the punishment. He probably wouldn't even care, though. Either way, she'd be vindicated.

Eventually, though, she ran out of tears. The anger drained out of her body, and she was left feeling lighter ... though irritated that she had gotten herself into this situation.

Then, inconveniently, she started to feel bad. She and her dad didn't usually fight like that, if at all—she tended to avoid conflict—but it wasn't fair. It didn't make any sense. She had taken care of herself during that fiasco with Edie; she could take care of herself anywhere. Did he not think she was smart enough to avoid the New Gloaming? 'Cause it wasn't *that* hard.

Or maybe there had been a tiny kernel of truth in what she had said about Mom. He said he'd been thinking about her a lot, anyway. Maybe he'd finally decided that keeping his only daughter locked away was the only way to keep her safe, to ensure she didn't disappear like his wife had.

But it wasn't *fair*. She was her own person. She wouldn't let anyone hurt her. He should have some faith in her.

Sniffling, Sissel dragged herself to her bed and sat down. As she did, her phone vibrated in the pocket of her hoodie.

[1 New Message]

[Antoniu]: I have a job for you. Meet me at the usual place.

A little spark of hope lit up her heart. Her dad was being stupid and unfair, but she didn't necessarily have to do what he said. Might as well go get something done instead of sitting around.

She read the message again, considering this as she crossed the room again to lock her door. Antoniu was kind of a weirdo, but he didn't seem to have a great concept of money, so he always tipped well. It was also kind of cool to talk to a wraith that wasn't enthralled but wasn't feral, either. He was the only one she'd ever known.

She pulled her boots on and laced them tight, then knelt on her bed to open her window. Their apartment was on the second floor, but this wasn't her first time sneaking out. She climbed out onto the roof and scooted until she reached the fire escape outside her dad's window, then dropped down.

Old Town Plaza, where she usually met Antoniu, wasn't that far a walk from here. She texted him that she'd be right there and started on her way.

The first few minutes, everything seemed to be going fine. Every step, she became more indignant that her dad would ever doubt her in the first place. She kept a sharp eye out for any Watchers, and kept her wits about her in case she had to reach out and stop someone in a split second.

But then, as she approached the plaza, she noticed a white car following slowly behind her. Her first instinct was to take a couple of unexpected turns, but the car followed her closely—and the more she looked at it, the more familiar it seemed. It was old, like a muscle car, and she could tell it was a convertible even though the top was up. She snuck glances over her shoulder until she finally got a good look at the person driving it.

The blood in her veins ran cold. She recognized the guy behind the wheel—the same guy that had been waiting for Edie outside of Indriði's house. Edie hadn't given her very much context after the shouting match she'd had with him, but from what Sissel could gather, he wasn't trustworthy.

She started walking faster. She knew this area of the city like the back of her hand. There was a one-way street coming up that he wouldn't be able to follow her down.

She picked up the pace until, finally, she saw the blessed ONE WAY sign. Turning down the street, she watched over her shoulder as the convertible hesitated before roaring around the corner and speeding away from her.

It had been a close one, but he'd probably circle the block and come back. She kept up the brisk pace, crossing the street and starting an alternate route to the plaza.

After a few minutes with no sign of the white car, she began to wonder if she had actually seen that guy or if she'd psyched herself into thinking she had. He didn't seem to be following her anymore. She slowed her pace and relaxed again.

The plaza was in sight. Sissel was about to cross the street when she felt a vehicle rumble up beside her.

"Hey, don't move."

She recognized the voice, and didn't even look behind her before taking off across the crosswalk, away from the car. She could hear the roar of the engine as it sped to catch up with her, and she sorted through streets in her mind, trying to think of the closest place she could lose the stalker.

Like it had heard her prayers, an alley popped up ahead of her, and she turned down it, keeping close to the wall. If she was lucky, he'd lost sight of her for that crucial moment and hadn't even noticed her turning.

The shit thing was, when you were dealing with other supernaturals, luck wasn't exactly guaranteed.

The sound of screeching tires made her jump, and when she glanced over her shoulder, she saw that the convertible had cut through a lane of traffic going in the opposite direction to follow her down the alley. Its side mirrors almost scraped the tight walls, but it fit, and it was trundling after her at a careful pace.

She turned and started to sprint again. At its current speed, she could outrun it—and if her memory served, this particular alley turned a corner. He'd never be able to follow her that far.

Unfortunately, it turned out she had confused this shortcut with one a block away. It did turn a corner, but it was a dead end. Nothing but a couple fire escapes, some discarded cardboard, and trash bins greeted her.

Sissel's heart skipped a beat, then thumped harder in her chest. Could she even turn back? She had to, but he'd be blocking the whole alley.

Breathing fast, she whipped around, her face going cold when she saw that he had gotten out of his car and followed her around the corner. He stopped, huge and scowling, looking her over.

What did he even want with her? Panic began to set in. She couldn't let him touch her, let alone bring her anywhere. When girls who looked like her were taken somewhere, they didn't come back.

Suddenly, she wished she was at home, curled up in bed. She'd tell Antoniu to piss off and then run right back to the apartment. She'd apologize to her dad and hug him and eat his soup even if there were slimy onions in it. She'd do all her chores and homework on time.

The stranger huffed wordlessly and started toward her.

Sissel looked him in the eye and held out a hand. "Stop!"

As she said it, a silvery light flashed in the middle of her palm … but it didn't seem to make a difference. The magic hit his brow and pinged off like it was nothing. He continued to stalk toward her, unabated.

No! What? It had to work. It *always* worked! "Stop now! Don't come any closer!" she tried again—and again, the magic died before it could reach his mind.

When he was finally close enough to touch her, she tried to duck under his arm and run, but he blocked her, movements surprisingly quick despite his size. "Hey, hey! Hey. Kid."

She tried the other side, and he blocked yet again with a sigh.

"I'm real sorry about this, but you gotta come with me."

Sissel screamed and made a last-ditch move to shoulder him out of the way. He caught her by the hood of her sweatshirt and hauled her toward the car.

"That's all I know." The girl threw up her hands and let them fall in her lap, looking around at those still assembled in Tilda's dining room.

The girl—Sissel—had been pretty pissed to find out her mind-control didn't work on revenants. Fortunately, though, she'd started talking when the group had calmed her and explained the situation. And apologized more times than Cal could count for scaring her.

"Is Edie gonna be okay?"

Cal sighed and rubbed the bridge of his nose, not bothering to answer. While the girl didn't have many specifics, what she'd told them had him wondering how Edie could be so goddamn dumb. Not only had she risked her life to bring Indriði a keeper paragon, but she had let the Norn *use* it on her. Tilda had recognized the name of the artifact and explained the implications. Edie was lucky she hadn't been killed, but who knew how long that would last?

"All right," the revenant breathed, dragging his hand down to cover his mouth. He drummed his fingers against his cheek in thought. "All right, all right, all right. I gotta get in there before she decides to use that fucking thing." He looked at Sissel. "Tell me everything you know about Indriði's security system."

She blinked. "Uh, I know she has some security guards, maybe cameras ... before I went up with Edie, I'd only ever been on the first floor."

"There's gotta be something else." He laid his hands on the dining room table and leaned forward. "What kind of wards does she have?"

Sissel's eyes lit up, and she sat straighter. "Yeah, she mentioned them to me one time. She said Roggvi—that's her steward, he's a dwarf—set up a bunch of wards, so he probably has whatever can cancel them out."

"What do you mean by that?" Mercy asked.

Tilda cut in. "It is a little like the system I have, though I'm sure she has more wards. There should be a, eh, particular object or objects that they use to cancel out the wards if need be. Like if they wanted to let a stranger in, or if they turn off certain wards during certain parts of the day, or this or this. Like a ... pass key."

"I'm gonna have to take my chances with the front door and hope it isn't warded," Cal said as he began to pace.

Tilda looked up at him, apparently shocked. "You can't go alone. It's a suicide mission!"

"Well, what the hell d'you suggest I do?" He stopped, gesturing around the room. "Look at us! The only other person here in fighting condition is the fish stick, so I guess that makes two."

She stood, facing him defiantly. "Me. I'm willing to go."

"I can go, too!" Sissel said.

"No!" His face twisted. "I'm not taking you or the kid, it's too dangerous. And Creepy doesn't give a fuck," he added, jerking his chin in Antoniu's direction.

"I can help," Tilda insisted. "I'm six hundred years older than you, Cal. How do you think I've survived this long?"

"No way. No fuckin' way."

She sat back down, crossing her legs and smoothing out her skirt. "I'm coming. You cannot keep me away, and I am not going to let you run off and get yourself killed. Antoniu, will you come, too?"

The wraith nodded.

Cal huffed, seething. He didn't want her goddamn help, even though he probably needed it. Try as he might to disentangle himself from the vampire, Fate kept bringing them together again—and now, on top of that, he had to deal with her boy-toy. He shook his head.

Fisk had an arm linked with Mercy's and was stroking her. "You'll be safe here, my pearl. I will come back for you."

"So that's me," Tilda said, counting heads, "Antoniu, Cal, and Fisk. Hmm ... that isn't enough."

"We need more," the vættr agreed sheepishly.

Sissel groaned and said again, "I'll go!" but nobody replied.

Cal threw up his hands and started to pace again. There wasn't a single trustworthy person in this town who wasn't already in this room, no one who would be willing to go up against a Norn for Edie, Satara, and Astrid. Hell, the three women were literally half of the Reach. He had no time to go out and make new "friends" to recruit, and even if he did, what would he even say? *Hey, I'm having a kidnapping problem. Feel like risking your life for free?*

Fuck. It was a miracle Edie was even still alive at this point. It was a miracle they were *all* alive at this point, after Zaedicus's Prom of Doom. If it hadn't been for—

The revenant stopped pacing, going still. There was one person—one person who maybe couldn't be *trusted*, but could at least be counted on to do the right thing.

Can't believe I'm doing this. That kid better be grateful.

"I'll be back soon," Cal mumbled, and headed for the front door.

CHAPTER TWENTY-SIX

MARIUS TOOK A DEEP BREATH, looking into the pit of the helmet he held in his hand. He had to put it on for his plan to work—Ynga would know something was awry the second she saw his face. But he hesitated. Lying to sneak into a Gloaming party was one thing, but if he went through with this, he'd be tricking another Auroran.

All his young life, he'd been taught that honor was always achieved through honesty. The older he got, the more he realized what a simplistic view of the world that was. Sometimes subterfuge was necessary, especially when you did it to serve the ones you loved.

Still, after being caught going through Tiralda's things, how much more could he get away with before he became a traitor himself?

Deep breath. It would be all right.

It was to protect his father.

He pulled the helmet over his head, securing it snugly.

As he slipped out of the armory and down the hall, he felt a bit bulky in the stolen armor. His usual gear had been painstakingly tweaked and re-tweaked to fit him perfectly. It made more effective armor—better for battle, certainly—but he couldn't wear it. It was imperative that no one realize they were patrolling next to Vivid Marius.

In the past month, Ynga had been assigned to lead city patrols often. Usually, that privilege was saved for vivids or older, more experienced warriors, but the Radiant had apparently taken a liking to her. Besides, now that the Gloaming were constantly causing trouble somewhere in the city, the Aurora had been forced to ramp up the frequency and intensity of patrols. Even experienced warriors had to sleep.

Ynga was still refusing to speak to Marius, and their miscommunication during her proving hadn't done their relationship any favors. When he searched her dormitory, it had turned up nothing. She had barely any personal items. It seemed she only used the room to sleep.

If she was the traitor, the only way he was going to draw any information from her was if she believed he wasn't himself. As a nameless adherent, he could drift behind her, listening closely to her conversations and observing her behavior.

Marius emerged into the courtyard and quickly spotted Ynga near the west gate, leading a group of warriors in warm-ups. The patrols usually included nine adherents, lined up in three rows of three. Thankfully, he had gotten here early, and there were a handful of spots still open for him to slip into.

"Forward." Ynga was demonstrating a lunge before them. "I better not see your knee pass your toe."

Marius hurried over and fell in with the small group, beginning to warm up in time, careful to keep his form decent but not excellent. He was so close to pulling this off; standing out in any way would ruin it.

Eventually, other adherents trickled in, until there were only two empty spots.

"Stance wide, lunge to the side. Lower, all the way! I want you to feel it in your groin."

After a minute, three warriors came jogging up to the group. Two fell into place right beside Marius, while the other lingered. He glanced at the remaining adherent in time to see his expression twist in confusion.

Ynga stood and addressed him. "What are you just standing there for?"

"I had patrol on my schedule, but..." The adherent gestured to the full three-by-three group in front of him.

Ynga seemed unconcerned, hands on her wide hips. "You must have been mistaken."

"But—"

She raised a hand, stopping him. "Take that up with the patrol director. Go on, now."

Marius focused on the ground in front of him. Thank the gods she hadn't bothered to take attendance. He couldn't draw attention to himself. This was necessary. It was doubtful the adherent had really wanted to go on patrol, anyway. Marius was practically doing him a favor.

Ynga joined the warm-ups again, wrapping them up quickly. She lined the adherents up for a cursory armor inspection, then ordered them into rank again. After leading them in a short prayer for Tyr's blessing, she signaled for the west gates to be open, and they marched onto the brick sidewalk.

Marius couldn't help but shiver as the warm light of a cloaking spell enveloped them. They would keep out of sight for a while, until they reached the neighborhood to which they were assigned. Hiding their world from the unattuned had always been a tenuous arrangement, and with the Gloaming's brash attacks and open use of magic, it was becoming impossible. They still tried to do what they could to mitigate the damage. Most humans who happened to look in their direction would find themselves squinting at a strange glare, then looking away and quickly forgetting they had seen anything.

They marched to East End, and upon arrival, Ynga dropped their cloaking bubble with a whispered word.

As they stalked the streets, the adherents watched carefully, heads on swivels in case any Gloaming decided to show their faces. Although the patrol managed to scare a few suspicious groups out of the neighborhood at the sight of them, there was no conflict to be had. After a while, most of the warriors relaxed and broke rank, observing their surroundings more casually as they chatted with one another.

Marius took a risk and cut to the front of the pack so he would be right behind Ynga.

Another adherent was standing beside her now, instead of behind, and they were speaking in Icelandic. Marius was better at Old Norse, but his knowledge of the modern language was passable. He stayed close, quiet as they walked.

The other adherent was asking about the Radiant. "You must have really impressed him. When are they doing Tyr's Rite, do you know?"

"Soon," Ynga replied, inhaling deeply. "We'll see how that goes."

"Are you nervous?"

"More excited than nervous. The Radiant knows he needs more vivids like me, to pick up his son's slack."

The adherent grunted affirmatively. Marius's neck went hot.

"He needs more vivids in general," the adherent added. "The Gloaming are heading the Aurora off at every turn. I think he wants everyone to think we're doing better than we are."

Ynga shrugged a shoulder. "That's what spiritual leaders do. They lie. Even the oh-so-wonderful Radiant."

Marius's ears perked at her tone.

The adherent glanced at her. "You don't like Radiant Eirik?"

"Oh, I know he's only trying to keep up morale," she said with a sigh. "It's not that I don't like him, but the way he lets his son do whatever he wants is infuriating. The boy is his weak spot."

Marius swallowed.

"I bet he'll listen to you," the adherent said. "You'd make a fine commander."

She didn't reply.

After a long pause, he spoke again, his voice lower this time. "Any word of the Gloaming Lord?"

Ynga barked a laugh. "I will meet him on the beach soon enough."

Marius slowed, drawing away from the conversation. He felt almost numb. Had she just admitted to meeting Zaedicus somewhere? Was he insane, or had he mistranslated? No, he was certain that she had said she was meeting the Gloaming Lord on a beach.

It must have been a mistake. A mistranslation, or perhaps he'd heard her wrong. No Auroran in their right mind would ever admit to meeting a Gloaming Lord, especially not to an adherent.

Unless ... unless she wasn't the only traitor.

Was it possible there was a conspiracy?

He replayed their words over and over in his mind as the patrol finished uneventfully, uncertainty shaking him. On their way back, not even the warmth of their cloaking spell could comfort him.

As the other warriors trudged back through the west gate, Marius lagged behind, caught up in his own thoughts. It was stiflingly hot inside the helmet. He took it off, focusing on the bricks below his feet. He could repeat word-for-word what she'd said in Icelandic. If he could find someone who spoke it better than him—

It was only when a car pulled alongside him that he glanced up.

Marius recognized the car immediately, and a scowl twisted his face. Nonetheless, he approached when the driver beckoned him closer.

"What are you doing here?" he demanded of Cal.

The zombie didn't look particularly happy to be talking to him, either. He kept glancing to the side, at the temple. "I got a favor to ask."

The vivid was barely able to hold back an incredulous laugh. "What in the Fosterer's name could you possibly need my help with, again-walker?"

"Not me, really." He was smoking a cigarette, and dropped it in the gutter when he spoke, exhaling. "It's Edie."

A white-hot spark of anxiety lit Marius's heart. Somehow, he already knew what Cal had to say to him. "She's in trouble," he mumbled.

"Yeah." The zombie sighed, looking at Marius like he was cold medicine he didn't want to take. "This Norn she was tryin' to recruit turned out to be Gloaming. Edie's gone. I gotta get 'er back."

The spark burned hotter. Images of Edie in battle flashed before his eyes. Crouched, holding her friend; arms covered in blood, eyes pleading him for help. What state was she in now? Was she even still alive? The dread that question brought with it surprised even him.

Then the zombie spoke again, sharply, refocusing Marius's attention. "So? Are you in or what?"

Marius glanced back at the temple, at the golden dome, the etchings on its frieze. He should go back in there and forget he had ever met the hellerune.

"I'm in."

CHAPTER TWENTY-SEVEN

AN ICE-COLD SMACK woke Edie from her sleep, and she cried out, eyes snapping open. It took her a moment to register that the coldness was everywhere, clinging to her and seeping through her clothes. Wet.

Though her vision swam, she managed to lift her head. A woman in a long velvet dress stood beyond some iron bars, holding a wooden bucket. Edie might as well have woken up in someone else's body, because she had no idea where she was or who was standing in front of her.

The cell door swung open, and a pair of men in dark robes stepped in. Black veils hanging from silver circlets obscured their faces. They descended on her, one of them holding her firmly by the upper arms while the other unshackled her ankle and produced new manacles from within his robe. He clamped cuffs around her wrists and ankles while his partner pulled her to her feet and secured them to another chain around her waist.

The world spun as she was shuffled out of the cell.

"That's enough napping for today, lazybones," said a voice. "You have an appointment to keep."

Scarlet. Scarlet was the woman standing there, and the one coming out of the cell across from her, shackled similarly, was Satara. She was quiet and shaking. They weren't supposed to be here...

The memories trickled back in; terror stiffened her joints as she and Satara were pulled down the dark corridor. Unlike before, there was no distant talking or laughing. Not even their footsteps seemed to make noise as they were led through the labyrinthine passages. The silence coming from the veiled figures was reverent, and they seemed to walk in perfect sync.

Finally, they turned a corner, and an eerie blue light filled the hallway. Not thirty feet ahead of them, a spiked gate separated them from a much larger room. Two of the veiled figures opened the gate, letting the rest pass through.

Stepping into the cavernous stone room was like stepping into a completely different world. The energy shifted significantly. All at once, Edie's body was buzzing with the latent power contained within these four walls. A circular dais rose from the center, etched with thin carvings that shimmered a faint iris color. Blue-white streaks of light rose from the etchings, curling like smoke until they touched similar markings in the ceiling.

Edie felt like she was standing in the presence of someone very important, but no one was here. She glanced up at the ceiling and noticed a hundred little points of light, twinkling and disappearing at intervals like blinking eyes. Wooden talismans decorated with bone and gems hung from the ceilings, too. Some of them had faces carved in them; some didn't. Under their gaze, she felt uneasy.

Even through her haze, she didn't have to be told that *this*—not the room Indriði had shown her to earlier—was the ritual room.

Smaller, lower daises in the floor surrounded the main one like moons. Edie and Satara were led to two near the far wall and forced to their knees, their shackles secured to thick loops riveted in the stone. Once their prisoners were in place, the veiled figures seemed to melt into the shadows. When Edie squinted at where they had disappeared, she was sure she saw movement. Were there more here?

She tried to calm her breathing, focus on slowing her heartbeat. Maybe there was still some way they could get out of this, but she and Satara were too far away from each other to hatch a plan in whispers. She turned her head to the side and tried to catch her friend's eye.

Satara wasn't looking at her. Her eyes were closed, head bowed, cheeks streaked with tears. Between her knees, however, Edie could see her moving her hands, slowly trying to find a way out of her shackles. The chain connecting them to the stone floor tensed and relaxed as she worked.

Edie looked down at hers and tugged a little as well, rattling the chains lightly. The loop was secure, every link strong as could be. She'd break her wrists before she broke these chains.

Just breathe.

But any pretense of calmness, from either woman, was thrown to the wind when the gate opened again and Astrid emerged from the darkness.

"Astrid!" Satara called out, but the valkyrie didn't seem to hear her.

She was flanked by veiled figures, her entire body bound with thick spectral chains that glowed faintly blue. They looked so insubstantial, yet the way she walked—hunched, labored—betrayed how heavy they must be. She was still in her human form, but had been stripped of her armor, wearing only leggings and a tunic. Her face was dirty, her skin and hair matted with both dried and fresh blood. She could barely open her eyes for how bruised and swollen they were.

From behind her, Indriði entered. Edie wasn't prepared for the stab of hatred that went through her body.

When she noticed the keeper paragon around Indriði's neck, the knife twisted even deeper. If this was Indriði's ritual room, then whatever she had done upstairs had been completely fabricated. She had never really planned to empower Edie's fylgja; she hadn't even tried. The "ritual" had always been fake, a ploy to get the paragon.

That hadn't been her only ploy. She'd tricked Edie into thinking that Astrid and Cal were working against her. It was because of Indriði that Cal was gone. Looking back on the runecasting, Edie remembered that the rune symbolizing what she would do in the face of her catastrophic future had been blank. *Fate will decide.* Maybe it had really meant that she didn't *have* a future.

The Norn motioned for the veiled figures to bring Astrid to the central dais, and Edie watched as they secured her spectral bindings to the floor, too. The chains lay heavily on the stone. Astrid's struggling was weak and sluggish.

"Astrid," Satara said again, then looked at Indriði, glare brimming with tears. "What have you done to her? What do you have to gain from this?"

Indriði put a finger over her own dark-painted lips, which curled into a smirk. "Shhh."

Another very familiar person stepped through the gate, pulling Edie's gaze from Astrid and the Norn: Zaedicus. He wore a luxurious burgundy suit, and Scarlet stood next to him, smiling at the scene before her.

Maybe it was the blow to her head, but pieces seemed to be sliding into place. Zaedicus, the Gloaming, Indriði, Sárr, the party... The realization of what was truly going on felt like a slap.

"He didn't recruit you in the past couple months." Burning with rage, Edie looked up at Indriði, who had climbed the dais and was standing above her. "He didn't recruit you at the party. You must have been Gloaming for years. Or at least Zaedicus's friend."

Across the room, Scarlet loosed a laugh.

The Norn sneered down at Edie. "Figured something out?"

"We thought we were safe because he had no way to know we were looking for you," she continued despite their teasing. "Even if he had, he couldn't have known for absolute certain that we would come to his party. Unless he knew someone who could see the future. You."

The room was silent except for the ambient hum of the magical energy.

Edie panted. "He needed us all in one place, so he asked you for help. You were already watching me. That figurine I found in Astrid's shop, the one without a face ... the room I saw while we were scrying.

It was all you, already close to us, looking in on me or Astrid or whoever."

"Maybe— maybe you had a vision that we would find you," Satara said, voice cracking. "Maybe you saw a dozen possible futures where we always sought you out."

"And in one of them, we were *all* together, at one of his parties. So you told him, and you both made sure that would happen," Edie finished, tone betraying her rage. She shook. "'The future isn't so cut-and-dry, *babe*.' You said it yourself. Did you just count on probability, or did you fuck with Fate to make sure we'd come?"

"I guess it doesn't really matter." Indriði calmly crossed one arm over her chest, resting her other elbow in her hand. She brushed a streak of white hair back into place. "We all know how it ended up."

Satara raised her voice, indignant. "You're not supposed to take sides or manipulate time to your own ends. You're not created to. Norns are supposed to weave Fate, not carry it out!"

Indriði's jaw clenched, her pale eyes fixing the shieldmaiden. "Screw what I was created to do. I'm taking my life into my own hands."

"You lied to me," Edie ground out.

The Norn shrugged. "Oh well."

"You made me believe you were my friend, that you were helping me, that you were the only one I could trust. That runecasting ... you made me believe that it was Astrid and Cal who wanted to hurt me, but it was *you*."

"You're too easy, hon." Indriði sighed. "Show you a little bit of affection and you're hooked."

Zaedicus chuckled, and when he did, the Norn seemed to remember he was there. She turned and walked past Astrid, stepping down from the dais to take something from him. When she ascended again, she carried a dark iron dagger in one hand.

Edie's heart pounded. Beside her, Satara mumbled a prayer under her breath.

Indriði circled Astrid slowly, apparently not impressed that the valkyrie had stopped struggling a while ago. "Come on now, really? Already no fight left in you?"

She traced glowing white fingers along the kneeling woman's shoulder, but her fingers turned to talons soon enough, digging into Astrid's flesh. She drew her arm back and thrust the dagger into Astrid's shoulder blade.

The valkyrie's form sparked with white light for a split second. She started awake and threw her head back, screaming in agony. The sound reverberated off the stone walls and shook Edie's bones. Satara shouted wordlessly, straining against her bindings.

Indriði drew the dagger back out with a faint squelching noise. Runes that Edie hadn't noticed before blazed purple-white on the blade.

"To be fair, Edie, it wasn't all lies. The Reach still isn't worth trusting. The only person left in it is a traitor." Her tone was casual as she circled Astrid once more, looking for another place to bury the dagger. "Justice doesn't always come to the people who deserve it, you know? Sometimes you have to make your own."

Without warning, she jerked to the side and sliced through Astrid's tunic and arm. Blood burst, coating Astrid's side and flowing down heavily.

There was silence for a while as Astrid panted in anguish. Then, for the first time since she'd come into the room, she spoke. "This isn't … justice. I committed … no crime."

"Bullshit." Indriði slashed again, and Astrid writhed, growling.

"All humans die … soldiers more often than others. Kolya was … already rewarded. You should be honored … that he went to Valhalla."

With faux thoughtfulness, the Norn withdrew the blade and wicked the blood off between her forefinger and thumb. "That's true. All things do die." She inspected the glowing runes. "I wonder where valkyir go, or if there's nothing at all."

Shouts erupted from Satara and Edie, their words jumbled as they ran over each other's, incoherent in their panic. Their shouts were joined by laughter from the two wights at the other end of the room.

It wasn't until Edie shouted, enunciating each word, "All of this because she killed your boyfriend?" that the room fell silent.

Indriði looked genuinely shocked. She glanced from Edie to Astrid a few times, then squinted at the valkyrie. "Is that what you told her? You told her Kolya was my *boyfriend?*"

"I said you were fixated on him," Astrid mumbled.

The Norn reeled for a moment before erupting. "You bitch!" She grabbed a fistful of Astrid's hair and yanked her head back, literally incandescent with rage; her skin, her eyes, her hair glowed. Edie couldn't tell if it was the odd lighting in the room or some sort of power. "*Fixated* on him, was I? *Is that what I was?*"

Astrid only winced in reply.

"I don't understand," Satara cried out. "If he wasn't your lover, who was he?"

Indriði released Astrid's hair and pushed her head forward, forcing her to bow it. With ragged breath, she took a step back, examining the valkyrie before turning toward the two other captives.

"He was my son," she said, voice thick. She looked at Astrid again. "*Our* son."

Of course. In a horrible sort of way, it all made sense now. The way Astrid had talked about Indriði, so reverently; the way she hung on every bit of news of her. She had been in love with her, perhaps still was, and she had been purposefully vague when telling them about why she and Indriði had fallen out.

"But..." Edie's voice shook. Nothing was making sense anymore. "Valkyir are dead. They can't make babies. How could Kolya be your son?"

Indriði's gaze was flint. "He was abandoned. We raised him in our home, loved him, cared for him just like any mothers. And she"—she pointed the dagger at Astrid—"let him die."

"You're lying," Satara said weakly. "Astrid wouldn't keep that from us."

Astrid raised her head, gaze teary. "She's telling the truth," she whispered. "I'm sorry."

The shieldmaiden looked at her, grimacing, chest jerking as her breath hitched. Her glittery eyes were full of sorrow.

Indriði leaned in close to speak in Astrid's ear. "You are a miserable mother..."

Astrid squeezed her eyes shut. Fat tears slid down her cheeks.

"...and this world will be better off without you."

The valkyrie turned her head to look at Indriði. "There's no need of this. You already had your revenge when you took Daschla from me."

"Ah, yes." The Norn looked at Satara. "I'd say I'm sure you've heard all about the shieldmaiden before you, but now we know that Astrid loves to keep things to herself." She looked back at the valkyrie. "I didn't *take* Daschla anywhere. I told her the truth—more than you ever did for her—and she decided to leave."

"She's doing the Gloaming's work now," Zaedicus added, crossing his arms.

"Hell"—Indriði laughed—"even the Aurora is doing the Gloaming's work now."

That statement chilled Edie to the bone. She knew enough about the Aurora to know that any one of them would die before they worked with the Gloaming. Had someone been tricked like Edie had, or was there some sort of conspiracy?

Indriði shook her head and motioned for two veiled figures to join her. They each grabbed one of Astrid's biceps and hoisted her to her feet.

"I've never felt better about what I'm going to do to you," the Norn whispered, holding the knife above her head. She slashed downward, creating a long gash in Astrid's stomach.

The valkyrie cried out weakly. Now that she wasn't curled up and the light was hitting her just-so, it was clear that the blood Edie had assumed to be deep red was actually a dark amethyst color. It flowed from the wounds more like water, and was practically coating her after all this torture.

Zaedicus eyed her. "If you unveil, we won't be forced to keep hurting you."

Astrid glanced at the paragon around Indriði's neck and gritted her teeth. "You can do what you want to my body. I will never obey you."

The valkyrie steeled herself in time for the Norn's next blow. She thrust the knife into her stomach and twisted, but Astrid barely winced. Edie watched with bated breath as Indriði searched her former lover's face, then pulled away. Was it over?

"She's telling the truth," the Norn finally said, dislodging the blade. For a moment, it looked like she might give up.

Then, she turned back and unceremoniously stabbed the dagger through Astrid's chest.

Edie could hear the resistance of Astrid's flesh; a soft, wet pop as the dagger broke through layers of skin and muscle. Blood surged around the hilt and covered her chest. Though Edie knew the blow wouldn't be fatal, she gasped and had to swallow the bile that raced up her throat.

Beside her, Satara begged, "Stop. Whatever she did, we can find some other way to repay you. Stop hurting her!"

Indriði took a step back, observing her handiwork. "You know what, Astrid? I believe you. Torturing you is gratifying and all, but it's not going to get me what I want, is it? You can take the pain." Those dark lips curled into a smirk, and she looked at Satara. "But, ah ... I wonder if your shieldmaiden can take a beating, too."

"*No!*" The cry ripped from Astrid's throat with such force that it seemed to shake the room. A shard of pain stabbed through Edie's brain, and her ears began to ring again.

"Are you willing to lose another child just to keep running from your punishment, Astrid?"

"*Keep your hands off of her!*"

There was a ghostly shriek—a long, disturbing howl, echoing as though someone down the hall was being tortured, too. Edie knew what was happening before she saw the light burst forth from Astrid; it filled the room, and she had to close her eyes against the radiance of it, her injured head pounding.

After a few moments, she cracked an eye open to see exactly what she had feared. They had coaxed Astrid to unveil. The valkyrie stood on her own, the force of her change having pushed the Norn's lackeys back—a towering figure of white-blue light with flowing platinum braids, gleaming armor, and blade-like black wings. The spectral chains held fast, but she beat her wings, straining against them. The movement kicked up a wind that whipped the clothes and hair of those present and sent pebbles flying.

Indriði turned, eyes shining with triumph. She took the paragon around her neck in one hand, tracing its edges with her thumb.

Dread tickled Edie's innards. Indriði wasn't stupid—she knew that you couldn't kill a valkyrie by conventional means. But Edie remembered something the Norn had said to her: If someone's fylgja died, they died, too.

The paragon had never been for Edie, or to add to her collection. It was for Astrid.

The ambient hum in the room became louder as Indriði took the paragon from around her neck and opened her palm. The prism floated as though it were a balloon she had set free, then stopped between the Norn and Astrid, rotating slowly.

Indriði closed her eyes, and her chanting began. What sounded like a hundred voices chimed in around them, invoking the names of the runes. The strange power in the room surged until Edie's skin was buzzing with energy and even kneeling still was difficult. Beside her, Satara wept in frustration, writhing and straining against her bonds as well.

A streak of midnight blue burst from behind Astrid in a flit of wings. Edie squinted until she could make out the shape of an eagle with a fluffy crest, its form filled with twinkling stars, its eyes electric. It fluttered frantically for a moment, movements perfectly matching Astrid's own desperate thrashing.

Then, Indriði stretched a hand out toward the keeper paragon, and the eagle seemed to almost be pulled into a whirlwind. It could only resist the pull for a moment before it was forced to soar in circles around the ritual room, tighter and tighter, closing in on the prism. Edie shouted as if to warn it, but her voice was drowned out by the chanting.

With an eerie screech and a flash of light, the paragon swallowed Astrid's fylgja whole. The crystal glowed pale blue.

The chanting became faster and deeper, more sinister somehow. They were no longer just invoking runes, but using other words, too, stringing the ancient language into complex sentences. Astrid's anguish echoed in Edie's ears as well as through her body and soul, turning the room cold as ice. Edie could see Indriði's breath as she continued to chant.

The Norn slowly began to clench her outstretched hand into a fist, and as she did, the light emitting from the keeper paragon changed. Deep scarlet began to bloom and spread, whirling, the crimson eddies blotting out every trace of blue until the entire paragon was glaring red. A horrible shriek built up in the room, seeming to come from the very foundations of the earth itself. The prism shook where it floated in mid-air. Then, suddenly, a blazing crack formed. Then another, and another, until it seemed like the crystal was about to explode.

Astrid struggled harder than before—frenzied, pitching, animal. She beat her wings rapidly, feet finally leaving the ground. Her spectral chains squealed like thawing ice as she writhed, her form bursting with light again and again. The wind, the screaming, the light ... it was overwhelming. It was all happening so fast, and Edie could do nothing to stop it. She rocked hard against her chains, crying wordlessly.

Astrid rose higher even though her beating had weakened, wings shuddering. Her bindings strained; the iron rings that attached her to the floor groaned. The valkyrie threw back her head and emitted one last, distant wail as holes began to form in her skin, like paper eaten away by flame.

Eventually, there was nothing left for the chains to hold. They fell to the floor with eerie silence instead of a crash.

What was left of Astrid—nothing more than flecks of ash—dispersed. Soon, the flakes lost their glow and melted into oblivion.

The chanting subsided, but someone was losing their mind, crying and screaming at the top of their lungs. In Edie's dazed state, she couldn't tell if it was her or Satara. If she wasn't screaming, she certainly wanted to. Her ears rang, and the noise became fuzzy as she lurched forward and vomited onto the stone floor in front of her. Her throat burned. She wanted the bright lights and the loud noises to stop. She needed this to be a nightmare.

But the nightmare wasn't done with them. When she finally opened her eyes—puffy, wet, impossibly hot—she came face to face with Indriði.

The Norn sat on her haunches just out of Edie's reach, smiling serenely. "You'll thank me for that someday."

In reply, Satara spat at her feet. "*Fúna í Náströnd*, filthy sow bitch."

"Whatever you say." Indriði's smile became tighter, and she stood, gesturing for four veiled figures to collect the prisoners.

Zaedicus approached. "Take them back to their cells. The Wounded Lord will be here soon to retrieve the hellerune."

"What are we to do with the leftover, my lord?" one of them asked with a voice like whispering cloth.

"He will find some use for her." The high-wight waved a hand dismissively. "Get them out of my sight."

Edie and Satara were hauled to their feet once again, and soon enough, the darkness of their cells swallowed them up.

Edie laid her head down on the stone floor and stared into the void, feeling weightless. This wasn't real. She had to keep telling herself that— because beyond that possibility lay an abyss that would devour her whole.

She closed her eyes. Eventually, Satara's steady weeping lulled her into a fitful sleep.

CHAPTER TWENTY-EIGHT

GHOST'S MOVEMENTS were jerkier than usual as she cruised toward Alderdeen, and Cal couldn't blame her. It wasn't often she had to cart around so many strangers and people she didn't like in one day. He rubbed her wheel as he navigated through the city, teeth perpetually gritted, trying to reach their destination as fast as he could.

Like the car, he was tense, too. Tilda was in the passenger seat, tucked up against the door with her legs tightly crossed so she wouldn't have to touch him, even by accident. Not that he wanted her to. But still.

Her boy-toy and the fish stick were both brooding in the back seat, and Cal glanced into the rearview mirror to examine them. Fisk was just coming off a near-fatal sickness, and Antoniu looked like a strong wind would snap him in half. Tilda could hold her own, but she was still only one person.

Cal was starting to wonder if there was *any* chance they'd make it out alive, but it was too late to turn back now. He'd already told Marius where to meet them, and if one thing could be said for that vivid, it was that he didn't waste any time.

As they turned into the neighborhood at last, a strange thumping noise from Ghost's rear caught Cal's attention. He was running through a mental list of broken parts that made a sound like that when, suddenly, Ghost pulled herself off the road and popped the trunk.

Dread and anger throbbed through his shoulders and up his neck. Cursing, he kicked the driver's side door open and got out just in time to see someone climbing from the trunk.

Sissel. Of course.

"Fuck sake, get in the car," he snapped, eyes darting around the street. It wouldn't be much of a stealthy rescue if they were spotted before they even got there.

The kid practically dove into the back seat, sandwiching herself between Fisk and the wraith. Her cheeks were flushed, but she flashed a shit-eating grin at Cal when he climbed back in and turned to look at her.

"What in the flame-roasted fuck do you think you're doing here?" he demanded.

She fiddled with the sleeves of her oversized hoodie. "I wanted to come, but I knew you wouldn't let me. Soooo, I hid. It was kinda getting claustrophobic back there."

Cal turned forward and glared at the steering wheel, addressing Ghost. "Were you in on this?"

She rumbled underneath him.

"Bitch."

"Soooo," Sissel said, looking around at everyone. "Can I come?"

Tilda gave her a deeply disapproving look. "We asked you to stay behind for a reason. It's going to be very, very dangerous. You could get hurt. You could die!"

The teen shrugged. "I mean, I'm already here. You can't just take me back, right? This is all kind of time-sensitive."

Cal groaned and rested his forehead on the steering wheel. "Why are you like this? Fuckin'—" He raised his head and looked up at the rearview mirror, fixing her with a glare. "You're staying in the car, got it? No *freakin'* way I'm letting you step foot in there."

Sissel crossed her arms. "Come on, bro. You keep Edie alive on the regular, and we all know I'm more useful than she is."

He couldn't argue with that. But then again, he kind of *had* to keep Edie safe. Sissel wasn't his responsibility, and he didn't want to *make* her his responsibility. He pulled back onto the street, mumbling, "It ain't my fault if you end up dead, *bro*."

Beside him, Tilda sighed hard and shook her head.

The street was quiet as they pulled up to the Norn's townhouse, but bright yellow lights flashing in the vestibule windows betrayed the fact that Marius had arrived before them. Cal pulled the car to the curb and stormed out and up the front steps. As he yanked the double doors open, he could hear the others following.

Marius stood in the center of the sleek lobby, in front of a security desk. His glittering half-plate was splattered with blood, and in his left hand, he clutched a dying security guard by the collar. The bodies of a couple others littered the floor, singed and thrown in awkward positions.

When the vivid noticed them entering, he turned and dropped the security guard at his feet.

"I see you started without us, Sparky," Cal said.

Marius rolled his neck. "I figured you'd be joining me soon enough." He gestured to the guards. "I was able to take them out before they could sound an alarm, but more may come if there are monitored cameras."

Tilda came to stand next to Cal, looking up at him. "Can you sense Edie?"

He closed his eyes, trying to focus on the connection. It was much stronger now that he was inside the building. She was cold and wet, her brain throbbing. Pain, confusion, anger all mingled with a gut-wrenching sense of loss.

It was a bad feeling. Raw. Cal wasn't a praying man, but he hoped to all the gods that they were all still alive and in one piece, 'cause it sure didn't feel like it.

After a moment, he exhaled slowly and opened his eyes. Their connection was tugging him downward. "She must be in a basement or something." He pointed to the spotless white floor. "Down there somewhere."

Marius nodded and wasted no time, turning to jog to the shining elevator on the left-hand wall. The others watched as he lingered in front of it, waving his hands—or hand and wolf-head-gauntlet-thing, Cal supposed—like he could feel something in the air. After a few moments, he turned back again with a noise of frustration. "The elevator is warded. I'll need the *skjǫld-lykill* to break it without alerting anyone."

"In English, please?" Sissel said from somewhere behind Cal. "Literally?"

"Jesus Christ, I told you to wait in the car!" the revenant snapped.

She shook her head. "Nope, you said it wasn't your fault if I ended up dead. I'm cool with that responsibility." Before someone could protest, she added, her tone more agitated, "And I don't need to be parented. I'm here to help, so let me."

"A ward key," Marius clarified as he eyed Sissel, clearly growing impatient.

Cal crossed his arms, still glaring at the teen. "We haven't gotten it yet, but *apparently*, the Norn's steward is in charge of all the wards. So, we just need to find the bastard—or wherever he keeps his shit—and we're gold."

"Fine." The vivid counted heads. "We need to split up into groups and try to find either some stairs leading to the dungeons or a ward key. Which of you have combat training?"

"I'll go with Antoniu," Tilda offered crisply. She probably wasn't the biggest fan of having an Auroran calling all the shots, and Cal couldn't say he blamed her.

Sissel scooted toward Fisk and linked arms with him. "I'm going with the *Shape of Water* guy!"

Oh, brother. That meant...

Cal cringed and glanced at Marius with a huff. The vivid was eyeing him similarly. "I guess that means it's me and you."

The groups dispersed. Once he and Cal were alone in the foyer,

Marius turned toward the staircase. "I doubt they'll find any stairs to the dungeons. That isn't really something you want guests wandering into."

"Where were you thinkin', then, smart guy?"

"I think we should go up there." He pointed. "Better chance of finding the steward's room, and while we're up there, we can look for an office or study. If we don't find the Norn herself, we might find some valuable intelligence."

Cal didn't particularly *want* to run into the Norn, if he was honest. He didn't want to tussle with anything that had managed to capture both Astrid and her shieldmaiden, but snooping around sounded fine. He followed Marius silently up the staircase, thankful that the guy at least had a good head on his highfalutin shoulders.

The two were quiet as they roamed the halls, giving every room a cursory glance. On the second floor, they didn't find anything that looked like a study. Most of the doors were warded, or else the rooms plain and empty; in fact, it wasn't until they reached the fourth floor that there were any signs that this place was actually lived in.

The set of back stairs they had been using led straight to a hallway with a tidy bedroom at their end. Tidy, but weird. Most of the furniture looked like it was made of stone, the fireplace more a reservoir for coals than a traditional hearth. Cal could feel the heat of the glow from here.

Marius looked back at him, brows knit tightly. "Does a dwarf live here, by any chance?"

"Uh..." A sudden memory; his spirits lifted. Yes! "The kid said her steward was a dwarf. Roggvi."

"Perfect." Marius slipped inside.

Cal glanced down the hallway, feeling exposed now that he was the only one standing there. "I'm gonna look for a office," he mumbled, then slank off, one hand on his shotgun.

Turned out, this stupid place was insanely confusing. It was like it had been designed to turn people around, and he almost found himself lost a couple times before he finally located more rooms. At the end of the dim hall, the familiar platinum elevator stood between what looked like a lounge and a study.

Jackpot. These rooms were empty of people, like the rest of this damn house. He was beginning to wonder what the deal was with that. If it *was* some kind of ambush, they were really biding their fuckin' time. But if it was an ambush, what about the others?

Antoniu wouldn't let Tilda get hurt. Cal had *witnessed* Fisk biting a guy's *actual* head open, once. They'd all be okay.

He took a deep breath and slipped into the study.

It was a surprisingly modern room for someone who was a billion years old or whatever. He was used to ancient pricks like Zaedicus who liked writhing around in animal furs, caressing antique chalices and wingback chairs. For some reason, the stark difference in Indriði's style— not to mention the spider tanks around the room, *fuck*—made him nervous. Now he wasn't sure what to expect from her at all.

Carefully, Cal crept over to the desk. Seemed like any information worth having would be there. A state-of-the-art desktop computer gleamed back at him, and he felt weird clicking the mouse to wake it up. It didn't ask for a password, just opened onto a screen full of documents. But, hell, he'd never used a computer before. Even if he knew what he was looking for, he probably wouldn't be able to find it.

He ignored the computer for now, focusing on the desk instead. The papers resting on top of it were financial documents of some kind, like Indriði had been doing taxes before deciding it would be fun to kidnap a valkyrie. He rifled through the drawers, but it was more of the same— miscellaneous papers having to do with assets or whatever the hell.

The last drawer, though ... something was off with the last drawer. He took all the papers out, frowned, then glanced at the front of it again. It looked way bigger on the outside than it did on the inside. Either it was a big empty space in there, or...

Cal set the papers aside and peered into the drawer again. Pushing on the inside of it caused the bottom panel to rock and thump quietly as it shifted.

Gotcha. False bottom.

He grabbed a letter opener from the desk and pried it open.

Inside was a mess of papers, mostly handwritten. They were in a weird language—Icelandic, he thought—but if they were hidden, they had to be important. He leafed through them, trying to see if he recognized any names, but most of them were unsigned.

And then— *Scarlet.* Seeing her name made him stop in his tracks. That bitch. If there was info to be had about her, he was definitely taking it. He pulled the paper out, scanning the lines of gibberish. The name Zaedicus popped out at him, too, and—

And a third name. One he hadn't heard in a long time. Daschla.

"Astrid's shieldmaiden?" he mumbled to himself.

Movement in the study doorway caught his eye, and he looked up to see Marius slipping inside.

"Any luck?" Cal asked.

The vivid shook his head, expression twisted with frustration. "Only personal effects. He must keep the ward key on him."

"Guess we'll just have to find him, then." Cal took as many sheets of paper as he could comfortably fit in his jacket's inner pocket, folded them, and tucked them away as he stood. Sparky might be able to read them, but he wasn't about to drop info in the Aurora's lap. Best to take them along. Astrid or Satara could translate it for him.

Hopefully, they were still alive.

Marius gave him a once-over. "What did you find?"

"Nothing important. Let's get the hell outta here."

"Couldn't agree more." The vivid turned and left the room.

They navigated the dark halls, Cal taking up the rear, and between the two of them managed not to get lost on their way back to the servants' stairs.

But as they rounded a corner, Marius stopped abruptly and dug his heels into the floor. Cal cursed, barely side-stepping him to avoid a collision. "What the hell's your problem?" the revenant began.

Then he looked up.

Standing at the top of the servants' stairs, flanked by two angry guards, was a very unimpressed nickel and copper dwarf in a suit. His gaze was stony as he stared the two intruders down.

"Men," he said to the guards beside him, "tell the mistress we have guests."

CHAPTER TWENTY-NINE

BEFORE EITHER CAL or Roggvi could react, Marius darted down the hallway. The dwarf barely had enough time to raise his arms and block a hit from the vivid's plasma blade. When the blow struck his arms, no blood came gushing out, but the skin glowed angrily like ore heated in fire, dented now.

Of course. He was made of freakin' metal. Cal pulled his revolver and put down one of the guards right off the bat, but he'd have to be careful none of the bullets ricocheted off the stupid dwarf.

Roggvi shouted something in Norse and raised an arm. The hallway began to shake. In a split second, the plaster cracked, and a huge chunk dislodged and went flying at Marius; more fell from the ceiling above Cal as the fissure spread in no more than a couple of seconds.

Marius followed Cal's lead and danced past Roggvi, narrowly dodging a bullet from the other guard's pistol before tackling him. Blood painted the shuddering walls as he sliced through the man's jugular.

Fuck it. Cal shoved the revolver back into his waistband holster and dove forward, driving his shoulder into the dwarf's broad form. Hitting him was like hitting a brick wall. He was so damn *dense* that the blow only staggered him for a moment before he twisted around to strike Cal with a spell—

A booming, vibrating sound. Without him really knowing what had happened, every muscle in Cal's body contracted, so intensely and quickly that he was flung down the hall. Spasms flew up and down his arms and legs, and an intense thirst suddenly gripped him.

He skidded across the waxed wood floor, scraping his skin raw and drawing blood, before his sharp revenant instincts kicked in. He had picked himself off the floor and was barreling back into the fray before he even registered that he'd been hit with a lightning spell.

Roggvi had picked his way past the plaster in the wall, and Marius was now deflecting a volley of brick and wood with his glowing shield. Worse, the closer Cal got to the dwarf, the slower he seemed to be moving. The bastard must have had a stone aura up, slowly paralyzing anyone close to him.

Sure enough, Cal spotted a rock the size of a child's fist orbiting the dwarf's head and leaving a little streak of stormy gray in its wake. It was probably the focus of the spell, but Cal wasn't sure he'd be able to get close enough to snatch it out of the air, or what would happen to his body if he did. He could barely move, now. Sunshine didn't seem to be faring any better.

To his surprise, though, Marius glanced up at him and snapped through gritted teeth, "Go!"

Fucking hell. Cal knew he was right. If he'd been able to use his guns, he could keep his distance while still doing damage—but bullets weren't only useless here, they were dangerous, and there was clearly no chance of taking Roggvi in hand-to-hand when he was practically turning into a statue. He'd be more useful in the foyer.

Marius covered Cal as he pushed past the stone aura and rushed to the stairs, but the revenant stopped short.

An idea sprang into his mind, and he fumbled for his revolver again. His body trembled as his lower extremities were paralyzed completely. In front of him, Marius was seizing up in the same way, no longer able to move his legs. In a few seconds, they would both be turned completely to stone.

He only had one shot.

He raised the revolver and aimed for the stone focus, exhaling slowly.

Bang.

The bullet hit the little rock, and they ricocheted off each other with a whine. The bullet thumped into the adjacent wall, and the rock dropped to the ground once it was thrown off its orbit, cracked and powerless.

Cal raced down the stairs, leaving Marius alone.

Marius ducked to the side and rolled down the hall, putting some distance between himself and Roggvi. The dwarf wasn't happy that Cal had destroyed his stone focus, and was stirring up another, more powerful spell now.

As the dwarf wove his magic, a whirlwind of fire and flashing lightning appeared suddenly, roiling next to him. With a thunderclap, a burly form made of rock and black clouds emerged from within, its eyes two crackling sparks of pure white energy.

Storm elemental.

Though he'd never fought one, Marius knew about them. They were pure chaos. One man was no match, and the vivid was smart enough not to try. If he could put Roggvi down first, though, the elemental's connection to Midgard would be severed, and it would disappear.

Mustering light from within, Marius summoned a full-body shield and dispelled the one at his right wrist. Against something as powerful as a storm elemental, such a large shield would only last a second, the light spread just a little too thin. The elemental was already trundling toward him, veins of lightning crackling across its form, but it was so large that it barely fit in the hallway. Marius's agility would be his saving grace.

He only had to avoid getting hit.

The vivid skated past the elemental, its electric atmosphere making his hairs stand on end. He ground his teeth, sprinting toward Roggvi. As he summoned a ball of golden energy between his hand and wolf vambrace, he prayed it would find its mark.

When he released it, it shot down the hall, careening into the dwarf. A hissing sound cut the air, and Marius's heart lifted as he saw the dwarf falter, clutching his white-hot face.

While he was distracted, Marius summoned a gleaming lance. Every second he spent fighting with this dwarf was another second uncertain of Edie's fate. If the Gloaming had her, it was only a matter of time until Sárr showed up to take her. Marius wouldn't let that happen.

Roggvi sped toward him, and the vivid roared, lunging. The lance flashed as he buried it in the dwarf's chest. Marius could hear the dense metal sizzling as the weapon seared through.

Without warning, something struck him in the side of the head, making his vision spin for a brief second. When things came back into focus, the lance had been dispelled, and he was already instinctively pulling himself to his feet. Roggvi now held a large, square hammer in his hand, the head of it wreathed in fire.

Marius could tell from the static in his toes that the storm elemental was upon him. He was literally between a rock and a hard place.

Annoyance boiled over. It was time to end this.

With a growl, the dwarf raised the hammer and swung. The corner of it clipped Marius's shoulder, dangerously close to his head. Heat licked the vivid's heart. Then, audible rumbling and vibrations in the roots of his teeth alerted him that the elemental was a half-second from attacking.

With nowhere else to run, Marius rolled to the side, into Roggvi's open room. When he looked back at his opponents, he couldn't help the crazed grin that came to his face.

The elemental was too big to fit through the door.

He had bought himself time, but no doubt the elemental had lightning at its disposal. Roggvi needed to die. Now.

"Come here, dwarf," Marius rasped, "so I can send you back to the stone."

Roggvi, surprisingly nimble for someone in a three-piece suit, charged. The storm elemental swelled and rolled, preparing a spell, and Marius's heart burned. Sunlight coursed through him, one with him, streaming from his hand and eyes.

When the dwarf pitched forward to crack Marius's knee, the vivid seized his head with a snarl. The incandescent magic writhing in his gloved hand surged, melting through the dwarf's copper hair, allowing Marius to dig his fingers into his skull.

Roggvi thrashed, but he wasn't dead yet. Marius held fast, clutching him harder and harder until molten metal poured between his fingers in rivulets.

Before the heat and power could overwhelm him, the vivid dislodged his fingers from Roggvi's skull. The dwarf stood for a moment, head misshapen and concave. A handprint blazed yellow on the side, his metal skin sagging and melted.

Then, he toppled over, stiff as a statue.

The storm elemental fizzled out of existence in a rain of static.

Breathing heavily, Marius knelt and began to search the dwarf's body for the ward key. It didn't take long—it was a thick, flat stone covered in runes, hanging at the end of a watch chain.

Marius pocketed it and quickly left the room. If the alarm hadn't been sounded before, it definitely was now. He had to get back to the others.

When he finally reached the imperial staircase, the ragtag group of Reach had just picked off half a dozen guards. Marius's heart darkened when he noticed that they weren't security officers like the others had been; they were clad in black, silver, and raven feathers. New Gloaming. An audible alarm was beeping somewhere in the house, faintly.

"You get the key?" Cal asked, eyes on Marius. He didn't have to look at his shotgun while he reloaded it.

The vivid held up the key and hurried down the stairs, to the elevator. He activated the runes with a touch of magic, and when he waved the stone over the ward, it shimmered and disappeared.

With a slow exhale, Marius pressed the elevator call button. It lit up, and the floor indicator began to count down. Victory.

Thump, thump, thump, thump, thump. For a moment, he couldn't tell where the vibration was coming from—then a huge black mass appeared on the staircase landing.

He didn't have time to see what it was. It pounced and tackled him to the ground, sending him sliding across the tiles. A sizzling sound rippled through the foyer, and a horrible, caustic smell invaded his nostrils.

Marius was able to prop himself up on his elbows in time to see the thing dig its claws into Cal, who it had apparently plowed into in one fell swoop along with Marius. Black scales gleamed like an oil slick and yellow eyes glared, panicked, around the room.

Dragon. No, not big enough to be a dragon. A drake. And judging by the smell, one with poison powers.

It hopped over Cal, thundering toward Antoniu, Matilda, Sissel, and Fiskbein with its huge jaws open. A rumbling growl shook the room, and a noxious, greenish-yellow cloud poured from its huge mouth.

The wight and wraith dodged, and Fiskbein clutched the girl, pulling her out of the way of the toxin. Meanwhile, the revenant recovered with startling swiftness, raising his shotgun. Marius pulled himself to his feet as well, but when Cal's bullet hit home, the drake wheeled around, smashing them both with its powerful tail. They hit the floor again, and Cal's gun skidded away from him.

The drake turned, hissed at Fiskbein, and crouched, getting ready to spray its venom again.

Without warning, Sissel pushed the vættr roughly to the side, putting herself squarely in front of the beast.

"*No!*" Cal's voice.

Despite the chaos, the girl's mind seemed to clear, her body eerily still and expression serene. She raised her hand, and for a moment, Marius expected a volley of magic to come screaming from her palm.

But it didn't. Instead, the drake ceased hissing and slowly stood from its crouch. Girl and dragon stared at each other for a long time. Then the drake crept closer, lowering its head.

The room was silent, except for a bizarre grunting noise issuing from the beast. The group watched in awe as Sissel stroked its nose, its tiny crest of horns. After a moment, she opened her arms and hugged its whole head to her body.

Hesitantly, Marius pulled himself to his feet.

"What the hell was even that?" Cal breathed, following suit. The front of his chest was coated in dark maroon blood.

"Huh?" Sissel blinked, seeming to come out of a trance herself. "He was scared. I just told him it was okay and that he had to stop."

Marius shook his head. Mind-controlling any kind of dragon was immensely difficult, something *masters* sometimes never learned to do, but... "That's impossible." He glanced at the others over her shoulder, then back at the drake. "It looks like a Venomgut drake. Even juveniles like this *can't* be mind-controlled. It's why they're so sought-after as guard animals."

Sissel pet its head. After some thought, her expression screwed up. "But it ... it didn't feel like I controlled him. It was different."

Cal retrieved his gun and gave her and the drake a wide berth as he walked back to the rest of the group.

"You're bleeding," Matilda said as he approached, her white brows knit in concern. Marius observed as she tried to reach out to the revenant.

He waved her off. "I'm fine." Then, glancing back at the drake, "At least now we have a dragon to guard the elevator while we do what we need to do."

"Do you think you can keep the beast controlled for that long?" Fiskbein asked, peering at the girl.

She rolled her eyes. "He's not a beast any more than you are. And I told you, guys, I'm not controlling him. Not really..." She looked as confused as everyone else, though, and shook her head. "We'll stand guard up here."

"Antoniu," Matilda said, turning to the lanky wraith. "Let us see what we can do about disabling any security cameras while they're downstairs.

We don't need more guards sneaking up on us while we are up here alone."

"You're staying here?" Cal asked her, then quickly added, "Good. We'll need to move fast down there."

Her expression withered slightly, and she muttered, "I'll take the east wing; you take the west."

Antoniu responded by shedding his human skin, melding into the skeletal, ghoulish form of a wraith. He crouched on all fours and bounded off like a starved, twisted dog. Matilda, too, was gone in an instant, dashing to the east wing at an inhuman speed.

Marius barely suppressed a shudder. That was right—he was working with creatures of darkness. Why *was* he doing this?

He was still squinting at where Matilda had disappeared when Cal trotted past him, pushing the call button to open the elevator doors.

As Marius, Fiskbein, and Cal piled in, Cal addressed Sissel. "All right, kid. You stay here with the dragon. We'll be right back up... hopefully." He ran his hand along the panel of buttons, brow creasing. "Shit. No basement button."

"It must be one of these other ones," Fiskbein suggested.

The revenant's mouth moved, counting the floors silently before pausing and crouching. "Right here. There's a button for the sixth floor, but there's no sixth floor."

He jammed it with his thumb, but it didn't depress.

A growl. "Jesus H. Christ, we don't have time to stand around here and figure out how to work this shitty freakin' Wonkavator!"

"Let me see," Marius muttered, switching positions with Cal. He crouched and examined the button, tapping on it himself.

Hollow. It was probably supposed to be opened and *then* pressed. His eyes traced the shape of it, catching on an irregular detail—a small lip on one side. He managed to get his gloved finger under it enough to pop it open with a metallic crack.

But there was no button, only a round, empty hole.

"Fuck me," Cal grumbled behind him.

"No, wait," the vivid said thoughtfully. "There has to be some way ... they wouldn't hide this for no reason."

It could be an opening for something, but what could possibly—?

He opened his palm to look at the ward key, then held it up to the hole, looking between them. Perfect size.

With a deep breath, he lined the key up and pushed it in.

For a few seconds, nothing. Then the runes on its surface lit up.

Marius stood and exhaled slowly, allowing himself a smile. Another victory. Now they had only to ride down to the basement, grab Edie, and leave.

The doors closed with a soft *ding*, and the elevator jerked to a start.

Then it began to free fall.

CHAPTER THIRTY

THE SMELL of fresh night air stirred Edie from her deep sleep. Had she gotten free, somehow? Was the nightmare finally over?

When she opened her eyes, her heart sank. Surrounding her were familiar inky shapes against a familiar gray background. Snow fell silently before her, the only sound a slight ringing in her right ear.

Slowly, she stood and dusted the snow off her clothes—the same cloak she was always wearing when this dream began. There was no reason to wait for the wolf to appear. She left the clearing and stepped into the forest, picking up her pace the farther she went. If she could get this over with, get to the point of the dream where she always woke up, she could get back to the waking world.

The second she thought it, she couldn't quite remember why that was so important. Something was happening there. But what?

It hurt to think about. She'd think about it later...

Someone was whispering nearby. No, not someone. A river. Yes, she remembered.

Somewhere far behind her, the wolf howled. Usually, when she had this dream, she felt the urge to follow the howl, to find the wolf or call it to her. Usually, she felt slow and confused. It had improved the more she'd had the dream, but nothing like this. She now felt as focused as if she were awake. She *knew* the dream was almost over. It must be. There was no need to worry about the wolf.

The river was getting louder.

The snow was falling heavier.

The laser focus told her to keep going forward, forward, even when it seemed like the forest didn't want her to go any further.

When something screeched in her ear, she stopped dead, gasping instinctively. Something soft and strangely muscular, like a shadowy hand, beat against the side of her face rapidly. She ducked and covered her head. It didn't hurt, but the sound was startling and bothered her ears.

With a *whoosh*, the sensation was gone, and when she uncovered her face, she saw a bird flying away from her. A crow. Her dad had taught her the difference between a crow's and a raven's tail once, a long time ago.

The crow fluttered onto a nearby tree branch and tucked its wings neatly. It stared at her, expectant. Waiting for her?

She crept forward, and the crow took off again, flying ahead.

Less than a minute of walking later, the trees suddenly cleared, and she found herself on the grassy bank of a loud river. Fifteen feet or so to her left stood a small arched bridge. Far off in the distance, she could see the faint lights of a village.

The crow fluttered onto one of the bridge's pilasters and looked between her and the river with that same expectant look. Did it want her to get closer? Was there something in there? She took another step.

Before she could approach the water, though, growling reached her ears. She spun around.

There, in the treeline, was the wolf that she had heard but never seen before. It was big, white, with cold steel eyes—and it was looking at her like she was dinner.

Edie's breath caught in her throat. The dream wasn't ending, but she didn't know the next part.

The wolf bared its teeth, lips trembling, and sprinted forward.

Without quite knowing she was doing it, Edie planted her feet and spread her arms at her sides, inhaling the frigid night air deeply. There was power here, all around her—and, all at once, in her. A strange, overwhelming pressure raced up her arms; the kind she always felt when she was fighting, right on the edge of something more. It always made her fight harder, trying to reach that crescendo, but it never amounted to much.

Until now.

As the wolf dove for her, she thrust her hands forward. The pressure burst, an icy numbness enveloping her hands and sending shivers through her shoulders and down her back. A bright blue flash filled her vision, engulfing her.

She woke with a jerk.

For a moment, Edie was confused at why the world around her was so dark. She was lying on her back, and skimmed her hand across the rough stone below her. Wet. Freezing.

Oh.

Anger crept up her back, tightening every muscle. Now she remembered. *Now she remembered.* They had chained her and her friends up like animals. They had *killed* Astrid, and chances were Satara was dead, too. Now they planned to throw her to the Wounded like a hunk of raw meat to a wolf.

Edie's arms shook, though whether it was with anger or the lingering power from her dream, she couldn't say. Her stomach ached so fiercely and deeply that she could feel it in her heart and spine, like something rotten was spreading through her. She clenched her fists, trying to calm the tremors.

God, she didn't even know how to describe what she was feeling now. Hopeless, angry, frightened—those words didn't seem adequate. The only phrase playing in her mind, over and over, was *fucked up. Fucked up, fucked up, fucked up.* It was all fucked up.

There was some kind of commotion, all around. Edie lifted herself a few inches off the gritty stones and peered dazedly through the cell bars.

Familiar veiled figures were rushing objects covered in black sheets through the passage between hers and Satara's cell. Some of the items were small or pushed along on trolleys; others were much bigger, having to be negotiated through the narrow space by two or more people. In the opposite direction, New Gloaming guards wove between the encumbered figures. Some were still in the process of donning their armor, pulling on gauntlets and helms as they trotted by.

A voice down the hall was so loud so suddenly that it stunned her eardrums for a moment. "The house isn't fortified well enough to survive an Auroran raid, okay? Just get all madam's shit out of here before they storm the place! Go!" Someone mumbled in response; then there were more indistinct shouts, talking over one another. And all the while, the Gloaming walked back and forth.

An Auroran raid?

She closed her eyes tight, trying to clear her head. As she slowly came out of her daze, she realized that some of the thoughts tumbling inside her head weren't her own. She had a sense that something cool, grounding, was nearby; a kind of spark in the periphery of her consciousness...

Cal.

Why the hell was Cal here with an Auroran raid? He hated them almost as much as he hated the Gloaming, and she knew no self-respecting member of the Aurora would ever associate with an undead. Still, he was here—though with all these Gloaming insects swarming the place, who knew how long he'd last, even if he had backup?

Edie knew she had to think up something to meet him halfway. She wasn't about to just sit here. Beyond that, she was *tired* of sitting here. She was tired of being powerless, tired of being manipulated, lied to, thrown around, taunted, used.

In the beginning, she had only been doing what was asked of her. Following along and trying to find her place. Desperately hoping to do the right thing. Above all, fighting for survival.

Now, she had a score to settle.

For Mercy, for Astrid, for Satara, every single New Gloaming bastard was going to pay.

Edie rose to her haunches and rocked forward, gripping the wrought-iron bars. She peered past black-clad legs as they rushed by. Standing diagonally from her cell, directing the two-way traffic in the corridor, was the young man Scarlet had brought to Satara earlier. A breathstealer, but he was still wearing the baby-faced warrior's skin.

Hanging on his belt was Scarlet's keyring.

A bizarre combination of heat and cold ran through Edie's body, making every hair stand on end. She clutched the bars tighter to quell the shaking. He would be the first to die.

"Psst." She pressed her face to the bars, trying to regulate her breathing. "Hey."

He heard her and glanced over, then did a double take. With a confused frown, he pointed at himself.

"Yes." She didn't even sound like herself. The word came out like she was possessed, a low hiss. Slowly, she stood, though she still leaned heavily into the bars. "I stole something from Scarlet on her way by. Do you think she'll want it back?"

The breathstealer paused for a moment before looking both ways down the corridor and approaching.

Edie shook her head and motioned for him to come closer still. He did. Evidently not very smart creatures, breathstealers.

As he neared, he glanced at her lips; and like that, his features blurred and shifted until he was her father again. Asshole. He had only been looking for an excuse to suck more life from her.

A voice slithered in the back of her skull. *We'll see who sucks the life from whom.*

Edie waited until he was close enough to reach a hand in. Then, one of hers darted out. She seized him by the collar and jerked him forward, thankful for the strength training and the icy magic numbing her muscles. His face struck the bars with a dull clang, and blood sprang from his nose.

Die.

He recovered quickly and reached both of his hands in, clutching for her throat.

Keeping a tight grip on his collar with her right hand, she used the other to try and twist one of his wrists away from her throat. But he was strong, pulling her hair, trying to jab at her eyes. He breathed raggedly and snarled like an animal, drool dripping from the corner of his mouth, spittle flying as he grunted.

All she had to do was call the magic.

In a second, the tide of the scuffle turned in the breathstealer's favor. He yanked his wrist away from Edie and grabbed one of her jacket's lapels, pulling her against the bars, flush with his chest. With teeth bared, he forced his hands onto either side of her neck, pressing into the base of her skull, trying to bring her mouth closer to his.

All she had to do was call the magic. In panic, she gulped down a mouthful of air and waved her arms around, trying to find purchase on his shoulders or his clothing. But she could only find his face—his snarling, grinning face.

The breathstealer pressed his thumbs into her windpipe, and she choked and slapped a hand over his mouth, pushing as hard as she could. If only she were stronger...

Warmth. Warmth under her fingers, a lively spark that shot up her arm. Edie watched, wide-eyed, as blood dripped from his nose onto her knuckles. *Yes, bleed. Bleed.*

She didn't need strength. She had blood.

Edie gritted her teeth into a hideous smile of her own and looked him in the eyes. Cold, slate gray. Her father's eyes. Her own eyes.

Blue fire ignited in her hand. With an icy spark, clothes turned to ash, flesh to bone. The figure in front of her rotted away in an instant.

.   .   .

The sound of the elevator screeching on its rails filled the air, so loud Marius could barely hear himself think. The lights flickered, everything rattling and shaking like existence was about to come apart at the seams.

They were going to crash. And, considering his companions were a deathless revenant and a sea spirit, *he* was the most likely to perish when they did.

There wasn't even time to scream in horror. All three men wavered, lowering their center of gravity and waiting for impact. With ragged breath, Marius uttered a small prayer, hoping to mitigate at least a little of the damage with a shield of light. It flooded the car.

But they didn't crash. In fact, they didn't even come to a hard stop. One second, they were free falling; the next, the car was sitting neatly at the bottom of the shaft. The floor indicator dinged pleasantly, and the doors opened.

It defied the laws of physics and time as Marius knew them, yet there it was.

"That shit ain't right," the revenant breathed as the group stepped out.

A collective exhale washed over them as they stared into the dark room in front of them. It was mostly pitch black, but at the far end, some torchlight glowed under the crack of a door. Marius could see just fine—he'd always had keen night vision—but he wasn't sure about the others. He summoned a ball of energy in his hand to illuminate the room.

It was a stone basement with low arched ceilings. Tables and chairs were staggered around the room, littered with bottles. A couple stools had been tipped over, and there was a heavy, yeasty smell in the air. As Marius shone his light around, they even spotted a robed figure passed out drunk in the corner, breathing slowly and evenly.

The Gloaming had been celebrating down here. That didn't bode well.

When he looked to his left, Marius noticed that Fiskbein had disappeared. He turned and was about to call out when the door in front of them opened.

Torchlight poured into the room, and with it, a group of perhaps eight New Gloaming soldiers. They stopped short for a moment when they saw Marius and Cal; then the biggest one shouted, and they all drew their blades.

The vivid released his ball of light, letting it bob above his head as he summoned his weapons. The Gloaming were already upon them, and his shield glimmered into existence just in time to deflect an axeman's blow.

Cal fired his revolver one, two, three, four times, putting down three warriors in one fell swoop and making Marius's ears ring. Fiskbein leapt from behind one of the stone pillars and tackled two more opponents. With those dealt with, Marius could see there were three left: the axeman, a swordsman, and an unfortunate mage carrying a runic staff.

The vivid dove for the mage first, skirting around the other two. He slashed for her throat, but she deflected his blows with ward spells, and his blade spat yellow sparks each time it scraped against them. Thrusting his left hand forward, he called up a shield. He'd let her throw a few spells at it while he dealt with her friends breathing down his neck.

He turned to the side to face them, summoning a whip of light from his right wrist. The golden rope whistled from the mouth of his wolf vambrace and wrapped around the axeman and the swordsman with a *crack*. Marius shortened the rope, jerked his whole arm, and heard the crunching of bones.

He dispelled the whip, letting the two warriors reel with pain. A second later, they both had bullets in their heads.

The mage had been fighting through the vivid's shield with huge torrents of dark purple shadow spells, but watching her companions fall had made her abandon that endeavor. Now she dodged to the side, trying to manipulate the darkness in the corners of the room to escape.

Marius lunged after her, but someone beat him to it. A huge webbed hand shot from the darkness.

As his ball of light wheeled around the room, he only caught glimpses of Fiskbein grappling with the mage, whose hair and face had somehow become soaked; then she was gone. When Marius called the light back to his hand, he finally got a clear picture. The sjóvættr had her by the ankles and was using her to beat one of the other guards to death.

Gruesome. But clever. The Reach were a strange people.

"All right, all right," Cal said as he crossed the room, reloading his revolver and shouldering open the door. "Come on, Free Willy, we got shit to do."

Indeed. Marius followed him, with Fiskbein taking up the rear. Now they were in a stone corridor. It was lighter here, so Marius dispelled his ball of energy, but there was still only a torch every twenty feet or so. As they went farther in, more corridors branched off, and more, until he was sure this was a network of some kind—probably leading to other exits all over the house, perhaps even the neighborhood. They trod quietly, following the torches and ignoring the darkened halls.

Distantly, he thought he could hear some argument going on. He could only pick out a few words: *quickly ... retrieve ... other way ... all costs.*

He was listening so hard that it was a complete surprise when, as they passed a perpendicular hallway, their flank was slammed by two robed figures.

The figures—wearing circlets and veils over their faces—were unarmed. Both toppled over when they ran into Cal and Marius respectively, and something they'd been carrying between them crashed to the ground, shattering. Both figures looked up at the intruders but seemed more concerned with crawling around on their knees, trying to pick up the pieces of whatever they had dropped.

Cal cranked his leg back and kicked one of them in the head, causing him to immediately slump to the side. The other, he grabbed by the collar, forcing her to look at him. "Where's Holloway?" he demanded, his voice even more gravelly than usual.

The veiled figure said nothing.

Sounds of fighting, very faint, turned Marius's ear. He looked up ahead. About forty feet in front of them, the corridor they'd been following turned sharply, and he could see lights pouring from it, flashing. Shouting, screams, and the sound of metal on metal raced down the hall toward them.

"Answer me!" Cal barked.

"Cal." Marius nudged him and pointed to the strobing battle lights. "There."

Cal dropped the veiled figure, and the three men sprinted down the hall, closer and closer to the invigorating scent of magic. Marius's hairs stood on end. Was someone using it against Edie? If so, she was helpless.

When they were barely ten feet away, there was a sudden, eerily silent explosion of color, and the screaming ceased. Bright blue light pulsed faintly from somewhere around the corner.

They rounded it and stopped dead in their tracks.

Before them was a hallway of cells with a narrow passage between them. Standing in the middle of it, facing away with her hands engulfed in blue flames, was Edie.

At least ten bodies—though the way they were piled made them hard to count—lay at her feet, in various stages of decay. Some had their faces rotted away to skulls; others were only partially putrefied; some were simply withered and hollow-faced. One, slightly off to the side, had turned completely to dust and bone. The grisly pile glowed with a faint blue aura.

Edie wavered on her feet, and Marius could hear her breathing harshly from where he stood. Slowly, she turned to face them, looking like an entirely different person—one that wanted more bodies, more death.

The moment, however, was brief. As the power faded from her body, she only looked exhausted. In one of her hands, a keyring hung limply from her fingers. She gazed down at it like she hadn't noticed it before. Then, her knees began to shake.

Marius rushed forward, and she slumped into his arms, letting the keys fall to the stone floor.

A flood of heat filled his chest and mingled with concern as he hoisted her up, trying to help her stand on her own once more. He barely noticed as Cal picked up the keyring and went to unlock the adjacent cell. A moment later, Satara shuffled out, her fine dress dirty and rumpled. She looked even more exhausted than Edie did, and surprised to see the vivid.

"Where's Astrid?" Cal asked, helping the shieldmaiden over the pile of bodies. He patted her down as though looking for injuries.

"Dead," Satara murmured, letting the word drop from her lips like an anchor; then, "We have to leave. Now."

Fiskbein hissed as Satara began to struggle down the hall. He scooped her up bridal-style, then started back where they had come from.

Dead? A valkyrie, dead? They died now and again, but mostly in otherworldly battles. Marius had been under the impression that it was nearly impossible to kill a valkyrie in Midgard.

Then again, perhaps "impossible" was just a challenge for Norns.

The hellerune was still in his arms, eyes closed, breathing irregular. He looked down at her and brushed her hair from her face, shaking her gently to try and bring her back to the waking world. The hollows of her eyes looked bruised, her face pale, nostrils crusted with blood. She was a mess.

The warmth in his chest spread down his arms, dutifully healing her. "Edie ... you have to wake up. We have to leave this place. It's over," he murmured, tracing her chin with his thumb. "Wake up for me."

Cal lingered for a moment, glancing between the two of them before following Fiskbein.

After a few moments, Edie's eyes fluttered open—those eyes he wished he could stop noticing, the color of rain on stone and storm clouds. Her face twisted in pain, and she pulled away, holding her head. "Ugh, shit..."

So eloquent. Marius's mouth twitched, but his concern for her only grew. He wanted to reach out and steady her, but what if she pushed him away? Their relationship wasn't exactly warm.

"How? How did you do all that?" He clenched his jaw as he gestured to the pile of bodies. It was obviously death magic—powerful death magic, at that—but he thought she didn't know how to use it.

Edie turned her head, looking at them as if for the first time. "I ... I don't know." She shook her head like she was trying to shake the image from her mind, locking eyes with Marius. "You ... *you're* the Auroran raid. You ... came to help. You helped Cal."

Marius nodded, finding that he couldn't look away. She looked so earnest.

Swallowing, she rasped, "There's ... there's a traitor in the Aurora. Indriði said."

"I know."

"Wha ... how?"

"It's a long story." He reached forward, but hesitated. "Are you going to be all right?"

She wiped her nose and tried to avoid the skeletal remains scattered around the hall as she stepped forward. "I'm ... I'll be fine. We gotta— we should—"

"Hey, guyyys." Cal's voice echoed from down the hall, in a tone that set Marius's teeth on edge. "Better come quick. We got a problem here."

CHAPTER THIRTY-ONE

THEY LEFT the cells behind together, with Edie at the front and Marius following close behind in case she felt faint again. It took them a minute to navigate the winding halls, but eventually, the trail of lit torches led them back into the room with the low arched ceiling.

Fiskbein and Satara stood beside the closed elevator doors, while Cal stood in front, hammering on them with a fist.

"What's wrong?" Marius asked as they approached.

The revenant groaned. "What do you think? The goddamn doors won't open." He threw his hands up, then let them smack against his thighs. "The bastards probably cut the freakin' power to trap us when they figured out we were down here."

Marius frowned, watching Cal kick the doors as though they would bend before sheer anger. "No doubt more guards will come once they find the bodies and the empty cells. We may be able to find another route through the tunnels, but it could take a while."

"I have an idea," Satara whispered from where she was leaning on Fiskbein. She crept forward, touching the elevator's platinum doors. "Can you pry these open?"

Cal looked around at their group. "Between the five of us, probably. But we'll never get it working."

She sighed, "Just do it," and backed away.

Marius came forward, summoning a lance. "I'll need some help." The tip was thin enough to wedge between the doors, and he moved it back and forth as he eased it deeper in. At least they knew it wouldn't break.

Fiskbein planted his hands on top of Marius's, and Cal gripped it from the other side, mumbling something snappy about holding hands. Edie and Satara joined, limbs shaking with effort. Together, they were able to pry the doors open enough that they could shove them apart.

Satara went in first, looking up at the ceiling. She pointed at a small hatch there. "If one of you can break the lock on that, we can climb out. This building is old; there may be a ladder up."

Cal peered up, frowned, and placed his hands on his hips. "Where the hell'd you get that idea?"

"*Die Hard*," she answered simply.

The lot of them looked at her strangely, but she didn't seem to notice.

Fiskbein was the only one tall enough to use all his strength against the hatch, and it only took a few blows for the lock to break and the hatch to pop open. He helped Satara and Edie out first, then made way so Cal could climb up himself.

As Marius waited, his hairs stood on end. They weren't alone.

Sure enough, a second later, footfalls reached him. When he turned, the basement door burst open, and a large group of guards came pouring in. *Dammit.*

Just as he was about to summon his weapons, Fiskbein laid a heavy hand on his shoulder, pushing him toward the elevator. "Go, Vivid. I will take care of these fiends."

Marius looked over his shoulder one last time to see the vættr turn, puffing himself up to face the guards. The vivid hesitated, mumbled a quick prayer, then jumped and hoisted himself through the hatch.

The inside of the elevator shaft was sheer concrete, though there were rails along both sides and lips of metal edging all along the walls at intervals. To his right, a thin, treacherous-looking ladder with rungs barely big enough for one person to plant their feet side by side was riveted into the concrete. It trembled as Satara and Cal climbed it.

Edie must have noticed this, because she was still standing on top of the elevator car, staring wide-eyed up at her friends.

Marius watched his step as he went to her. "You need to go up."

"Are you crazy?" She looked at him. "That thing is going to collapse!"

"We can't go back, unless you want to surrender and let Sárr take you to gods-know-where." He looked from her to the ladder. "Go. I'll be right behind you."

"That doesn't make me feel better," she mumbled. Still, she reached out and, after a moment of hesitation, climbed up. Marius followed closely to make sure she wouldn't fall, his breastplate nearly touching her lower back.

They both paused when, with a *boom*, Fiskbein flopped onto the top of the car below. His obsidian eyes were gleaming, his front covered in gore that poured from his mouth. When he looked up, Marius could see little bits of human flesh stuck between his sharp teeth.

Dread filled the vivid, though for another reason entirely. If anything was going to cause the ladder to collapse, it was the sjóvættr's seven feet, three hundred pounds of densely packed muscle.

But fortunately—and astonishingly—he forewent the ladder, using the rails, metal edges, dents in the concrete, and his own inherent stickiness to scale the wall. He was so quick that he arrived at the lobby doors before any of them. Hyped up on bloodlust, the vættr managed to wrench the doors open on his own, then hung precariously on the edge to help the others make the big step out to the lobby.

Marius held his breath as the sounds of fighting reached his ears.

The sight that greeted him when he turned and leapt from the ladder and into the lobby was not exactly a welcome one. The clean white floors were coated in venom and blood, the chandelier cracked and swinging. Antoniu, Matilda, Sissel, and her drake were all engaged in a fierce battle against a group of Gloaming guards.

The air was thick with a coppery scent. Marius's eyes caught on Antoniu as he was thrown and slid across the room, leaving a streak of blood on the tile. Matilda was clutching her wounds as she fired her handgun, and the dragon had to fight twice as hard to protect the teenager behind it. He could tell from the bodies riddling the floor that the Reach fighters had made significant headway, but more simply replaced those Gloaming that fell.

Cal hurried forward, supporting Satara with one arm while he picked off Gloaming with his revolver. "Get the fuck out of here!" he shouted without slowing. "There's too many. Move it!"

Spells were still flying, steel clashing as the guards rounded on those trying to retreat. Marius's heart caught in his throat, and he pushed Edie in front of him, hurrying her along. The drake charged to the front, spread its wings, and roared. Under its cover, Fiskbein dashed forward, then Matilda and Antoniu in uneven limps.

Would there be more opposition waiting on the street? Marius stopped short, momentarily forgetting the battle, his eyes darting as he counted heads. Almost everyone had made it to the getaway car, he thought—

Something whined through the air, reaching him too quickly for him to react. Blistering heat slammed into his shoulder and neck, and he was thrown forward, hitting the floor hard and twisting his wrist. Pain raced up and down his arm as though he'd shattered the bone.

Whoever was wielding the fireballs assaulted him with another volley. The tiles around him cracked, the flaming debris trapping him in. The fire only burned the small amount of skin not protected by his armor, but the force of the magic kept bowling him over. He tried to pull himself to his feet, but every time he did, another salvo would knock him down again.

With the right timing, he could throw up a barrier and break the pattern, but he couldn't seem to get the hang of it. Was he going to die here, surrounded by Gloaming? Helping the Reach?

The ground trembled, accompanied by a bone-shaking roar.

Something wet ripped, and there was a scream of agony. A second later, Marius felt a huge, foul-smelling form stomp over him.

The drake. Had it broken from Sissel's control?

He looked up frantically, but was surprised to see a small brown hand reaching down to him from the beast's back. The teen had mounted her new friend.

Her dark eyes shone. "Come on, before someone puts that dude's arms back on!"

The vivid huffed and pulled himself forward, thankfully able to dodge the other spells being thrown at them. Sissel pulled him up behind her, and he held her waist tightly as the drake barreled toward the open doors.

"I'm not sure this is such a good idea!" Marius cried as they neared.

"Don't be such a baby," she returned with a grin. "Hang on!"

The drake pinned its wings back and crouched as it charged toward the doorway. If the Gloaming didn't kill them, being crushed against the door's casing would. Marius held the girl close, ducked, and summoned a shield of light.

The doorframe whistled above their heads, close enough that it ruffled his hair. Then the drake was back to its full height, thumping down the street, its wings spread in triumph. It raised its face to the sky and bellowed joyfully.

They were out.

Edie was so happy to be safe and dry at Tilda's house that she didn't even mind that Mercy was fully in her lap. She sipped soda from a straw while her best friend hugged her neck tightly, cheek pressed to hers.

"I can't believe you turned a bunch of men into skeletons," Mercy mused. "You're, like, a feminist icon now."

Edie knew it was supposed to be a joke, but she couldn't even muster a laugh. "I don't understand. I was having such a hard time doing anything with my powers, and that suddenly changes?" She paused for a moment, then added, "I'm not sure I could even do it again if I tried. It felt so ... weird."

Cal leaned back in his nearby chair, folding his arms behind his head. "Well, you are supposably meant to just *have* your powers and know how to use 'em. Maybe the gods decided to throw you a bone."

For the first time in a while, Marius spoke. "It could be because you started with no grasp of magical theory," he said softly. He had spent the last couple hours hovering near Edie but had taken a break to go watch the rain through the floor-to-ceiling windows. Now he approached her again, brows knit. "You had no context for what you were supposed to do, but now that you have a better idea and are being exposed to others using magic..." He trailed off with a shrug.

"I thought of that." Edie rolled her bottom lip between her teeth. "Whatever was wrong, I guess I'm happy it's coming along now. Slowly."

Marius looked tired, but she wasn't surprised. She had been able to use necrohealing to restore the undead members of the party, and bloodmending on herself, but the other humans—including him—had been his responsibility. Nearby, Augustus was folded into a loaf shape, with Sissel half-asleep against his side. Miraculously, rest was all the drake needed to regenerate. Antoniu had left the second he was well enough, apparently tired of the lot of them; Tilda was making a big pot of tea, and Fisk sat on his haunches a few feet away, watching the rain.

The only person she couldn't touch with her eyes was Satara, who had isolated herself on the terrace despite the rain. Cal had given her a bunch of papers to translate, but she probably wasn't working on them now. Edie's heart ached for her.

With a sigh, she finished her fancy soda—some weird European brand Tilda had handed her—and set it aside. "Marius..."

He looked up.

"How did you know there was a traitor in the Aurora?"

"It's a long story," he said with a sigh.

Cal snorted, crossing his ankle over one knee. "We got all the time in the world now, Sunshine."

"Maybe *you* do." Marius rolled his eyes, but told them anyway: "As her proving, my father assigned a vivid hopeful a mission to retrieve some runepriest's artifact from a troll. It was a mirror that shows the future when you look into it. I saw my father being assassinated, and the word *traitor*."

Edie frowned. "Has he found out who it is yet?"

"That's where the problem lies. He has foresight as well, and he either believes that the vision doesn't mean anything or is confident that no one would be able to assassinate him. But if they were close enough—" The vivid shook his head. "I can't afford to lose him. None of us can, not now. I laid out my leads to him, but he shot them all down."

Damn. If Marius was concerned, Edie was concerned, too. As much trouble as the Aurora had given her, they were the only thing really holding the Gloaming back at the moment. "So now what?"

"Now ... I don't know." Marius paced to one of the couches and sat down. At some point, his right ear had gotten singed, and he fingered the burn thoughtfully. "I suppose I keep looking until I find out who it is. I think I'm getting close."

Outside, thunder cracked. Augustus looked at the window with sleepy eyes and lifted a wing, covering Sissel with it.

"Ack! I'm all good, buddy, I'm good," the teen complained, easing into a position that didn't require she be tucked in the drake's armpit.

Edie glanced at them, then looked beyond, toward the terrace doors. Through the frosted glass, she could see Satara's hunched and shivering outline. Why did she want to be out there, soaking?

The room was silent as Edie untangled herself from Mercy and walked to the terrace.

Quietly, she stepped out, closing the door behind her. The terrace was big enough to fit a bar, a long electric fireplace, lawn chairs, and a daybed under the awning. She was surprised at how heavy the rain had become, but Satara seemed unaffected, standing at the edge of the terrace and clutching the parapet. Her head was bowed.

Edie cleared her throat lightly and came closer until they were standing side by side, looking down at the city together. It felt so strange to think that Astrid wasn't out there somewhere.

At length, Satara spoke. "I lost the shield and spear again. She took them. After everything..." Her voice was so thin that the sound was almost lost in the rain.

"It's not your fault," Edie said, feeling unhelpful. She remembered how strange it had been to lose her father. Incomprehensible. Dad was supposed to always be there, and then he wasn't. Satara's situation was a little different—she hadn't lost a parent, exactly—but the hurt was probably similar. It was a helpless, clueless kind of hurt.

"I have to get them back."

Edie straightened her shoulders and nodded. "I promise we will."

No words passed between them for a while. Edie found her mind going back to the ritual, replaying it over and over again in her head. She was sure Satara was doing the same.

Eventually, the shieldmaiden sniffed, raising her head. Her eyes were puffy, deadened. "I need to see the shop. I need to make sure they didn't send people to upturn it, and I..." She inhaled shakily and turned her face away. "I have to go see it."

Even though she knew Satara couldn't see her, Edie nodded.

"Will you go with me?" She turned to look at Edie again, her expression open. She looked almost scared that Edie might say no.

"Yeah. I'll go with you."

God, she wanted to hug Satara. They hadn't known each other for very long, but Edie cared for her, and they had been the only ones to see Astrid die. Her last moments lived with them. That was a hell of a thing to have in common.

But she sensed that Satara needed space for now, so she stepped away from the parapet. "I'll tell the others."

Satara dismissed her with a silent wave, and Edie reentered Tilda's apartment, happy to be back in the warmth. A conversation had been going on between Cal, Mercy, Marius, and Tilda, but when Edie stepped in, it died. They all looked at her expectantly.

She took a deep breath. "Satara and I are going to Astrid's shop first thing tomorrow morning. There are some things we need to take care of."

Cal hoisted himself out of his chair with a grunt. "Guess I'm goin', too, then."

"I'll come," Marius said, his tone brooking no argument. "If there are Gloaming there, you'll need the extra hands."

Cal smirked. "You mean extra *hand*?"

The vivid shot him a look.

Sissel yawned. "I'll come—"

Before she could even finish her sentence, Tilda was shaking her head. "Not under my watch, young lady. It's late, and your dad is probably sick with worry."

Sissel rolled her eyes and groaned at the ceiling.

"Don't roll your eyes at me." The wight—who now seemed to be making cookies to go with their tea—was waggling a spoon at her like a proper Romanian grandma. "We kept you alive all day and this is the thanks? *Pe dracu'*! *You* will be the one to tell your father where you've been all day and night."

The teen sighed and looked down at Augustus, petting his big, blocky head. "But I don't want to leave. Augustus needs me."

"You could always take him with you," Edie suggested. It probably wasn't the best idea she'd ever had, but Sissel couldn't stay here and never see her dad again—that was ridiculous.

"I guess that would be okay." Sissel looked at him thoughtfully, screwing up her face. "Dad said I couldn't have a ferret, but he didn't say anything about a dragon."

CHAPTER THIRTY-TWO

IT RAINED ALL NIGHT, and when Edie woke the next morning, it was still raining. All the beds in Tilda's penthouse were downright luxurious; Edie had slept so soundly that she woke up dazed, not quite remembering where she was. She relaxed when she glanced over and saw Mercy on the other side of the queen-sized bed, cocooned in blankets like a princess.

Careful not to wake her friend, Edie padded softly into the hallway. The clock there read 6:03. Yikes. No wonder the apartment was so quiet.

She knew vampires and zombies didn't have to sleep, but she didn't spot Cal or Tilda as she crept down the long glass staircase to the living area. She did, however, spot a familiar face passed out on one of the couches.

Marius was sprawled, still sleeping, his armor carefully resting on the other end of the sectional. Edie felt oddly scared—like if she woke him, he'd burn her to a crisp—but maybe she was just terrified of how freaking *awkward* it'd be to be the only two people awake in the house.

As quietly as she could, she navigated the kitchen to get herself a glass of water and some human food. She wasn't surprised to find the fridge filled with blood bags, but they were opaque, and carefully separated and labeled. Of course, she'd expect nothing less from Tilda.

Her heart clenched when she heard stirring behind her. She let the fridge close and looked over her shoulder as Marius sat up, gazing around blearily.

Then his eyes fell on her, and his focus sharpened considerably.

"Morning," she said. She felt a little ridiculous, standing there in Mercy's pink pajamas with little witches all over them.

Fortunately, he didn't seem to notice. "Good morning."

Edie took a sip of water and approached, glancing around the room. Where the hell was Cal? Marius had helped save her, it was true, but she still wasn't 100 percent on him. Most of their dealings had involved him telling her what an abomination she was, after all. "How come you're sleeping down here?"

"I couldn't double up with ... you know, a girl."

He was definitely less intimidating when he talked like a five-year-old. "Have you got something against *girls*?" she asked with a laugh.

"No." He looked away, then stood and went to his armor, starting to put it on. He was wearing a thin shirt and leggings, and Edie found herself staring as he geared up.

He was... *What? No. What? It's just the ... mail is so shiny. Very shiny mail.* Her glass of water was suddenly extremely interesting.

"I'm sorry—do you mind helping me?"

Edie looked up, blinking. "Huh?"

Marius had armed himself as best he could, but was still missing some key components. He held up his breastplate and pauldron.

"I wouldn't know what I was doing," she mumbled, though she set her glass down.

"I'll tell you what to do."

He beckoned her over, and she responded numbly, walking around the sectional until she was standing in front of him. His eyes were literally gold, huh? She'd looked into them before, obviously, but it was a shock every time. She wondered what gene *that* was, the golden-eyed gene, or if it was a vivid thing. It could be some kind of mutation, one of those harmless ones. Her eyes were technically a mutation of blue eyes, which were a mutation in and of themselves, and—

He fitted the breastplate on himself as best he could, then turned, taking her hands and placing them on the straps. She fumbled her way through as he calmly explained exactly what to do.

"Sorry. Fuck," she said when she pinched him a little too tight. "Sorry, I'm dumb."

"You're not dumb." He glanced over his shoulder at her. "It's your first time. But you'll get it. The pages and squires who do this all day are considerably younger than you are."

Edie raised a brow, loosening the strap and trying again. "The only way I'll *get it* is if I'm practicing it a lot, and I'm not sure I'm gonna be helping knights get dressed every morning."

Marius didn't respond.

After what felt to her like a painstakingly long time—though he didn't lose his patience, thankfully—they were done. He moved his arms, shoulders, and neck, testing the fit. "Not bad for a beginner."

Edie smiled and looked him over. He looked how he always did when wearing his armor, so there was that, at least.

The sound of Tilda's front door opening made her jump. She turned to see Cal paused in the doorway, peering at the two of them.

"Morning," she said hurriedly, going back to her glass of water.

"Uh ... morning." Cal stepped in and slowly closed the door.

"Where were you?"

He strode into the kitchen and unclipped a key from his sparse keyring, setting it on the dining room table. Tilda must have lent it to him. Weird that he didn't want to keep something that would be so convenient. "Out."

No elaboration, and Edie figured she probably wouldn't get one—especially not around Marius.

Soon, the house started to wake. Tilda emerged from her bedroom first, her hair and face already made up; Satara came next, looking like she hadn't slept a wink, which was entirely possible; and finally, Mercy joined them, already showered and changed. Fisk was the only one who came *up*stairs, firmly patting himself with a fluffy towel after a night's sleep at the bottom of Tilda's pool.

Though Edie longed to pretend this was a regular morning with old friends, what had happened yesterday had sobered everyone, and there wasn't much conversation. As soon as Tilda had coaxed the humans into eating something, Satara was ready to leave.

It was still raining when Satara, Edie, Marius, and Cal stepped out onto the sidewalk. Cal would drive to Shipshaven, but the other three would be taking the much faster route.

Satara fished Astrid's glass whistle from one of her deep pockets and called the spectral wolf. For a moment, Edie was afraid that since Astrid was gone and it was bound to her, it wouldn't come at all. But fortunately, it did, leaving a bloody wound in the universe as usual. The smell of the battlefield overwhelmed Edie, and she was the last one to climb on. She hated that smell so damn much.

When they arrived at Harbinger Trinket & Tome, the lights were off, the CLOSED sign still in place. Satara drew the spare key from under a shrub and whispered a short spell to activate it. When the door unlocked with a tiny spark, she led Edie and Marius inside.

The place was empty and untouched, looking like it had been abandoned for a year instead of a day. Satara walked to the ironbound door at the back of the shop, then stopped, breath hitching.

Edie was silent for a moment before touching her arm. "Are you going to be all right? We can always come back here some other day..."

The shieldmaiden shook her head and reached down to unlatch the door. When it opened, the smell of fading incense and herbs washed over them—a calming scent, but one distinctly Astrid. The valkyrie's living quarters were just as she had left them. Satara moved through them like a ghost, brushing her fingers over things as she went.

Edie glanced back at Marius. His expression was disturbed, and she wondered what he was thinking. About his father's death, perhaps? The one he'd seen in the mirror?

Satara left the hearth room behind and stepped into the short hall. There was a door at the end—Astrid's workshop—and one in the right-hand wall. She stopped at the right-hand door as she had the ironbound one, taking a deep breath. It was almost like she was preparing herself to face a particularly powerful enemy. Maybe, in a way, she was.

Slowly, she opened it.

Astrid's room was simple and clean, a picture of rustic Scandinavian design. Her scent was even stronger here. Marius and Edie stood just inside the door as Satara went to her battlemother's wardrobe and opened it, rifling through the clothing there for a moment.

Edie wondered what she was looking for, but didn't dare break the silence. After a few moments, Satara went instead to a trunk at the end of the bed. She unlatched it and began taking out carefully preserved books, papers, artifacts wrapped in cloth. She looked at it all, touched it, but didn't explain herself. It was almost like she was searching for something more.

At length, Edie ventured a question that had been on her mind since the night before, her voice barely above a whisper. "Is she really gone?"

The shieldmaiden didn't raise her head, but she nodded. "Yes," she said, her voice equally as soft. "I can feel it in my soul. I … I can't describe it. Grief always leaves an emptiness, but it's … more."

Her face crumpled, then, and she sank to her knees next to the bed, head in her hands. Her shoulders trembled.

Edie practically leapt over the bed to go to her, kneeling beside and putting her arms around her. "It's okay." She smoothed a hand over Satara's braids as she cried, and rested her cheek on the shieldmaiden's cold shoulder. "It's going to be all right. We're still here. We'll figure it out."

She wasn't sure if any of those things were true. Astrid had been the nucleus holding what remained of the Reach together. Would they all drift away, now?

"I can't do this without her," Satara managed through fits of tears. She went from kneeling to sitting, and leaned into Edie's chest. "She wasn't supposed to leave me like this. I *can't*..."

The way Satara said it, it sounded like Edie was missing something. "What do you mean?" she asked slowly.

Satara inhaled shakily, raising her face to the soft morning light streaming in through the bedroom's sole window. She tried to steady her voice, but it was thick and uneven as she spoke.

"When someone becomes a shieldmaiden, there is always a chance that they may become a valkyrie one day. If they show great valor, if they sacrifice themselves in battle." She twined her hands together and looked down at them. "There are some politics to it. Becoming a valkyrie is a high honor for followers of Odin and Freyja, and— and most people vie for it."

"But not you," Edie murmured. She'd known that since Satara had first opened up about her past, how her parents had sent her away to Astrid when she was sixteen. They hadn't had the opportunity to talk about it since.

"Not me," Satara echoed, a bitter smile twisting her gorgeous features. "But there are ancient rules, edicts put in place so the valkyrie army can only grow larger. The gods' laws say in the rare event that a valkyrie is truly obliterated, her shieldmaiden must take her place."

Edie blinked, automatically looking to Marius, who was still standing in the doorway. He bowed his head, but his expression told her he had already known this.

She pulled away slightly so she could look Satara in the eyes. "But ... you'll need to die."

The shieldmaiden shrugged one shoulder. The bitter smile tried to return, but it was fooling no one, trembling then turning to a grimace. "This is what my family was hoping for me when they had me begin my training. I was supposed to— my brother—" She stopped dead and clamped her mouth shut.

"You don't have to do this." Edie took both of her shoulders, frantically searching her face. "You can help the Reach in some other way, if you want."

Satara shook her head. "No one defies the gods."

Gently, she brushed Edie off and stood. Edie watched in astonishment as a pair of black wings unfolded, fanning out behind the shieldmaiden. They were noticeably smaller and fluffier than Astrid's, more like a real bird's, but weren't entirely opaque. The sunlight from the window filtered through them slightly, especially at the ends of the feathers.

Edie stood. She felt the strange urge to reach out and touch the wings, but refrained, simply gazing from them to Satara. "Have you always had these?"

"No." They relaxed and shifted forward slightly, almost like she was cradling herself with them. "They appeared after..." She trailed off and sighed. "They symbolize my becoming a fledgling valkyrie."

"But why? Won't you just get new ones if you, uh, change?"

Satara combed her fingers through them. A feather came loose in her hand. "They're more of a warning than anything. If I don't transition like I'm supposed to, they'll start to decay, and I'll die of the infection."

Edie's face went numb and cold. Blood drained to her heart.

"I've already pledged myself to Freyja, and the gods don't take oaths lightly. If I don't do this, I could get sent to Náströnd."

"Na-what-now?"

"The Shore of Corpses," Satara said. She folded her wings back, and they disappeared. "A castle made of snakes, with rivers of venom and a rotting dragon that chews on the inhabitants."

Okay, well, no wonder she didn't want to go there.

"I've heard tales of fledglings who have died and gone there before. Ghost stories from where I grew up. They become horrible, twisted creatures."

Edie bit her lip thoughtfully. "I— I guess there's no choice, then." After a deep breath, she added, "But if there's anything I can do to help, I want to do it. So, what's next?"

Satara sat on the bed, and another surge of tears came. She shook her head so hard her braids flew. "I don't know! That's the problem. I *can't* do this without Astrid. She never prepared me for this, never told me what it is I have to do."

"Why would she do that?"

"I don't know. Astrid was very proud. Perhaps she thought she would never need to? That she would live forever?" She turned up one palm. "*I* thought she would."

Edie left briefly to get her a tissue, then returned. Satara's shoulders sank as she wiped her nose and eyes.

"I … I suppose the first step would be to journey to the gods' World, Asgard," she said, at a loss, "but I have no idea what happens then. I'll have to find someone who can get me that information."

"I'll do it," Marius said abruptly. Both women looked up at him, and he shuffled in the doorway. "My father has a vast personal library. If it doesn't hold the answers, the mages' library might."

Satara bowed her head. "I would appreciate that. A lot."

Silently, Edie held Marius's gaze. Saving her, and now this? Since when had he become so decent?

After a pause, she took Satara's hand and helped her off the bed. While Marius busied himself with research, she'd treat Satara to the modern woman's proper cry-fest, pint of ice cream and all.

"Come on," she said, "let's put this stuff away so we can go check on the cats. I'll even put on a *Die Hard* movie for you."

CHAPTER THIRTY-THREE

TIME WAS OF THE ESSENCE, so Marius wasted none. The distance from Shipshaven to Anster was an hour by car, but on his lightsteed he made the trip in forty minutes. It was almost noon by the time he trotted into the Temple of the Rising Divine and made a beeline for his father's office.

Radiant Eirik himself stopped him outside the oak doors. "Ah, Marius. I was just about to send someone to go looking for you."

"Your Grace," the vivid said with a bow. "I came to use the library."

The Radiant sighed and came closer, putting an arm around his son's shoulders. "You really don't have to call me that when it's only us. I *am* still your father."

Marius blinked, a little confused. Eirik had never taken issue with that before. Regardless, he nodded. "What was it you wanted me for?"

"Congratulations are in order. A new vivid is about to join your ranks."

He could only be talking about Ynga. Marius nodded again, stiffly.

"I expect you to be there for her Rite. It will take place tomorrow, when the sun reaches its zenith." The Radiant smiled tiredly and patted his son on the back, then passed him, his voice echoing more the farther he walked. "I have some business to attend to. The library is yours. We'll talk more tomorrow. I love you."

Ynga had proven herself, but to undergo Tyr's Rite so soon... His father *must* be desperate for more vivids. Or she had manipulated him in some way. And Marius was expected to be there?

Oh, he'd be there—to reveal her as the traitor, or at least demand answers.

He walked into the library, deep in thought. Ynga was a strange case. If anyone had good reason to hate the Gloaming, it was her; they had killed her family and taken her as a child slave. So then why would she betray the Aurora to them? Was she being blackmailed or threatened? She'd never allow it. It didn't make any sense—but he had heard her talking about meeting Zaedicus with his own ears.

Marius tried to put it out of his mind for now. He was here to help a friend, maybe, if he could call Satara that. She seemed decent. If nothing else, she was a devout follower of the gods, set to be a valkyrie, and it was his duty to help her any way he could. Both to adhere to the gods' laws— he was a Blade of Tyr, after all—and because, frankly, he didn't want her to die. To turn into one of those twisted fledglings she had described. Even if she was Reach, she didn't deserve that.

The library was vast, but Marius had had his whole life to familiarize himself with his father's system. He peered into the section designated for knowledge of ancient rites. It was doubtful that anyone had written a glossary of the thousands upon thousands of investitural ceremonies associated with their Pantheons. It could take days to find the right book, and if it was written in another language, it would take even longer to then read.

Carefully, he selected a few books about Odin. Freyja was the Mother Valkyrie, their commander, but Odin ruled them. Plus, if Marius was going to find an ancient ritual anywhere, it would be in a book about the god of secrets and magic.

He flipped through the first few pages of the first one, mood souring.

He liked reading fine, but only on his own terms, and he could already see that the text would be dry as kindling.

As he was mustering the will he'd need to get through even a page, one of the library's huge doors creaked open, and he looked up.

Standing there was a young woman wearing a sweater dress, leggings, and an oversized scarf. Her skin was the color of bark, and her voluminous curls were woven with baby's breath and pink blossoms. Her pointed ears told him she was not human. She looked around the library nervously.

He lowered his book, turning. "Can I help you, miss?"

Her gaze darted to him, and she nodded and produced an envelope from a well-loved leather shoulder bag. "Perhaps? I'm sorry. I have this letter..."

"For whom?" Marius set his book on a nearby table and went to meet her at the door. She was easily under five feet tall, and now that he was closer, he noticed faint emerald moss highlighting her cheekbones and hairline. The blossoms in her hair were closing and blooming at intervals, and her eyes matched the pale pink of the buds. Definitely a landvættr, then.

"It's for Radiant Eirik. It's very, very urgent." She shuffled from foot to foot as she offered him the letter, eyes darting around the room.

Marius took the envelope slowly, searching her face. Why was she so nervous?

"Please, can you make sure he gets it? As soon as possible. It's very important he read it at once." She was already backing out of the room.

"Uh ... yes, I'll see he gets it right away."

He peered at her. With a quick farewell, she was gone, leaving a gentle floral scent behind her.

What on earth?

Marius looked down at the envelope in his hand. It was a sunny yellow, and scrawled on the back in a shaky hand were the words *to Eirik*.

They used his father's first name. There were very few people left alive who still used his father's first name without his title. *Could this be connected to the traitor?*

He had to know. He climbed one of the spiral staircases to his father's desk and carefully used a letter opener to extract the leaf of paper from the envelope.

It was a short letter:

Eirik,

I'll try to make this brief and clear, because it hurts me to have to hurt you. But I can't bear the guilt anymore.

As you know, it's not much longer now until I go to the gods. Since I can't go in battle, I want to go with a clean conscience. You've taken good care of me for the past couple of years, and I appreciated your money, but I can't take any more.

People need to know what really happened at the runepriest monastery that day. I will tell anyone who will listen. Gods forgive me for not saying anything sooner. Gods forgive us both.

I'm sorry.

-Tara

Marius's mouth was dry as he set the letter down. The runepriest monastery—the place his mother had died, along with hundreds of Odin's faithful. His father had been the only survivor ... or so he'd always claimed.

Apparently, there was one other. Tara.

He had to find her. He had to know what was going on.

Edie closed her eyes and took a deep breath of fresh air, letting the late afternoon sun warm her face. With her legs crossed at the ankle and an ice cream cone in one hand, she sat on a bench overlooking the Shipshaven docks.

The world was falling apart around her, but damn, she sure was finding a lot of time for ice cream.

Satara had decided that she needed to stay in town for a couple days to get Astrid's affairs in order and take care of the shop. When she wasn't doing that, she mostly stayed indoors, trying to keep herself occupied with hobbies or reading. For Edie's part, sitting inside and wasting away with grief was enticing, but she needed to keep it together. It hadn't even been a full twenty-four hours since Astrid had died, and yet she had to put it out of her mind. Thinking about the entire experience sent her into a spiral, and there was no time for that. For now, she had to push it down as best she could. Sever it from herself. Compartmentalize.

It was also nice to hang around outside, something she wouldn't dare do in the city—though, of course, she still had to be cautious. The locals seemed to mostly be supernaturals or attuned folks who minded their own business, but even this small town could be crawling with Gloaming spies. Or Aurora, for that matter.

Sitting here, watching the sunset and licking an ice cream cone, Edie echoed a thousand of her own childhood experiences. She hated herself for it, but this made her miss her dad terribly. At least when he had been a normal dead dad, no necromancer shit, she'd had memories. Now even those were tainted.

Maybe it was selfish, especially after seeing Satara lose Astrid, but she mourned the loss of those memories. What would Dad think of what had happened yesterday? Would he have cared as much as she did?

The wind coming off the ocean drowned out the sound of footsteps on the grass behind her, but she could feel a familiar presence approaching. Cal appeared to her left, hands in his pockets, and stood watching the sun for a few moments.

Edie cocked her head, looking him up and down. "It's freezing. You should probably put your coat on before you freak someone out."

"You're the one eating ice cream, sister."

She shrugged. "I'm just saying, there are kids walking around in parkas right now."

"Eh ... no one's lookin'."

He sat beside her.

In the past couple of months, she and Cal had spent so much time together that silence between them felt comfortable. But not now. This was different. This was the first time they'd been alone together since their fight, and she could tell from the way he'd been acting that he was still hurt. Even if he wouldn't admit it in a million years.

Edie finished her ice cream quickly, then tossed the cone to a nearby pack of seagulls, who started ripping it apart. Best not to have it melting all over her knuckles while she tried to apologize.

"So..." she began.

Cal sighed in response and drew a pack of Newports from his back pocket, lighting one up.

"Thanks ... for coming to rescue me. After..."

He side-eyed her and said nothing. He wasn't giving her a damn thing to work with, but maybe she deserved that.

A strong wind blew through, throwing hair into Edie's eyes and mouth and making her teeth chatter. She brushed the strands away, then tucked her hands between her knees. "Listen. I'm ... really sorry I treated you badly, and gave you the runaround. I should have asked you about stuff instead of yelling at you." She chuckled humorlessly. "I pretty much knew that the second you left."

Cal stayed quiet.

"I should've known, after ... everything, that I could trust you. It's just, she was so *convincing*. Like she really was telling me those things for my own good." She looked down. "I was dumb."

Silence.

"You're— You're not selfish. I am. I told myself I'd appreciate you, but I've been ... pushing people away." She paused. "Letting their support go to waste. Maybe— maybe I'm afraid of letting you down and, like, if I don't try, I can't fail. Or maybe I don't think I deserve your ... loyalty or something, so I ignore it, and try to leave it alone, and hope people will get tired of me and stop caring."

He still hadn't said a word, and tears filled Edie's eyes. She wasn't saying anything right, was she? Was it possible that he'd only stuck around to rescue her and was going to leave again? The thought made her whole body ache as a wave of sadness crashed through it.

She clenched her fists. "You've already done more for me than my dad ever did. I'm— I'm sorry I thought you were lying. I promise I won't do it again..." *Just don't go*, she added internally. Another deep wave of misery hit her, and she was barely able to hold her tears in.

Cal exhaled slowly, smoke circling his head. He was quiet for a while before surprising her by saying, "No ... you were right."

Edie blinked, letting the tears fall before wiping them away quickly. "What?"

"You were right." He sighed. "There's somethin' I haven't told you."

"What?" She looked him over. Her train of thought had been cut off completely, and her mind felt like it was hanging in midair, stalled, directionless.

He cursed under his breath and dropped his cigarette, crushing it in the grass. When he raised a hand to rub his brow, Edie could see how tight the muscles of his jaw were. Then again, she could always kind of see the muscles of his jaw.

"Your dad did a lot of bad shit, but he was good at what he did..."

Edie's heart sped, her tears drying. Even as they'd gotten closer, Cal had refused to go into detail about her father beyond what she already knew. After her awkward conversation with Tilda, she'd almost wondered if he had lied to her about some of it. But here he was, actually opening up!

"Far as I know, he started out working for other people. Making magical things, mostly. Amulets, rings, scrolls, whatever. He was good at that, like no one I've ever seen." Cal spread out a hand and mimed casting a spell. "He could, like, put his own spells into things, so people who didn't know how to use magic could do shit like raise corpses or make your blood explode.

"It made him huge. Then, of course, he became the guy you went to see if you wanted someone dead. Then, he started doing the killing and cursing himself, for a price. Had so much money he started dealing it, lending it, investing in stuff so people owed him favors. And he made a lot of enemies."

Cal sighed, putting another cigarette between his lips but not lighting it.

"That's around the time he raised me. He was almost like a— a Don, you know? And I was his … fixer."

So that was why he'd been in those pictures with her dad, looking like he was hanging out. He'd been a thrall, but he hadn't *just* been some servant; he was an enforcer, part of the operation. Edie'd had a feeling there was more to their relationship. She had already pieced most of it together but had been missing a crucial piece of the puzzle. Now it all made sense, though it certainly didn't cast her dad in any better light. Cal obviously still hadn't had a choice in the matter.

"How much did my mom know about this?" she asked.

"I couldn't tell ya. She'd have to be pretty dumb not to know he was into some shady shit—and I'm sure she saw some crap she couldn't explain—but I never heard nothin' about her finding out the whole truth."

"The fact that he made you hurt people," she murmured, "that can't be what you're talking about. I already guessed that. That doesn't change anything."

"Shit, kid…" The revenant sighed and rested his head in both hands, taking a while to find the right words. "Holloway was smart, okay? Knew what he was doing. He made an assload of money over the next decade and didn't blow it on crap he didn't need."

Edie chuckled humorlessly. "Yeah, my *mom* did that after he died."

"Nuh-uh." The little blue spark in the back of his eyes bored into her as he looked up. "Not all of it."

A pause. "What are you saying?"

"He— *fuck*. Y'know … he had his tax money, and then his real money, stashed away. He took some whenever he needed it." Cal closed his eyes and cursed again. "And when he died, I … I took it with me. Okay? The money and Ghost. I've been scraping off the top for the past ten damn years."

Edie's heart fluttered. His nervousness and guilt told her he had taken a huge sum of money, but she refused to be optimistic. "Exactly how much are we talking, here?"

Cal looked away thoughtfully. At length, he leaned back and murmured, "Eight, nine? It's been a while since I counted it all out."

"Thousand?" She held her breath. Nine thousand dollars would take a huge chunk out of Mercy's medical debts, if he let her have it.

The revenant looked at her like she was the stupidest person he'd ever spoken to. "*Million*, kid. Million."

Edie's thoughts stopped floating and started racing at a thousand miles an hour, wheeling around her brain. A million dollars felt like more than she could ever use in her whole life. *Eight or nine* of those was a whole different ballpark. He had to be joking.

"Come on," she finally managed to sputter, "how much really?"

"I am not kidding," he said flatly.

She reached down their connection, probing for answers. He was telling the truth.

Edie wasn't sure what to do with herself. She wanted to jump up and start celebrating, but the feeling was short-lived. It wasn't even assured that she would be getting any of the money. It was Cal's. If he was leaving again, he'd be taking it, too.

But what if...? Thoughts clambered over one another in an unending wave. She looked down at her own shaking hands.

"It's yours," he said, perhaps sensing her uncertainty. "You need it more than I do."

She still shook, astonished at how little joy she felt. The money didn't mean anything if it wasn't given freely—and it didn't make her any happier if he wasn't staying. "But you earned it. Everything he did to you... Why give it to me?"

"I don't need your money. I can take care of myself. And you'll need it all to get the Reach off the ground without Astrid. Besides," he added, looking over and cocking a brow, "I *assumed* you'd share it with me."

Edie's heart lifted a little, and she searched his face. "You're staying?"

"Kid, if I didn't want to come back, I'd be in Vegas right now."

Finally, she stood, bouncing on the balls of her feet and practically tackling him in a hug. Mercy would be okay. Things would be so much easier. Money couldn't buy happiness, but it sure could buy stability and security, and that went a long way. Edie squeezed Cal as tight as she could.

"Whew." He squirmed. "Why the hell are you huggin' me?"

"I'm happy you're staying."

"*Why?* I'm the bastard who stole nine million dollars from you. You oughta be strangling me."

Edie shook her head, mumbling into his shoulder, "You needed it more than I did. I'm just ... I'm happy we have it now. I'm not mad." She breathed a laugh. "Not at *all*."

After a moment, he huffed and put his arms around her, too.

Edie relaxed, letting more tears come. The past couple days had been so overwhelming that she was toeing the line of hysteria constantly. To have someone like Cal—who didn't do *touching* or *affection*—hold her felt like a triumph, and she definitely needed a win. This particular rush of euphoria was a very specific feeling; one she'd been deprived of since her dad had died. Hugging Cal felt like family.

"All right, okay, that's enough," he finally said, pulling back and wiping the tears from her face. He sounded exasperated, but his expression was gentle. "Quit it with the crying, you're getting yourself all upset. We can think about the money some other day."

With a hard sniff, she pulled back and wiped her nose.

"Now, uh, there's something else we gotta talk about."

She exhaled sharply. "I'm not sure how much more I can take. Are you pregnant?"

"I *will* punch you," he warned, pointing at her. Then his expression shifted until he looked almost nervous. "Those bastards you dusted at Indriði's. You remember anything about it?"

If she was honest, Edie didn't remember much, only that it had been so easy at the time. It had felt natural to rot their skin away and suck their life-force into her own, but hell if she remembered how she had done it.

"I dunno," she answered. "It just kind of— I got really angry, and it kind of exploded out of me."

Cal cringed. "Yeesh. Death magic isn't the best thing to be spitting everywhere willy-nilly."

"I don't know how to control it. Indriði warned me that I was like a balloon waiting to pop, but we never found someone to help me." That was the one thing she still blamed Astrid for, after everything. She had wanted Edie—and Satara, for that matter—to do all these great things, but hadn't deigned to actually prepare them for any of it. "Indriði tried to make it out like Astrid was doing it maliciously, but maybe she thought we had more time."

"For the love of—" Cal sighed and looked out at the ocean, taking the unlit cigarette from his mouth and fiddling with it. "All right, so ... I'm sure you noticed Astrid and I weren't exactly happy with each other."

"When we were trying to plan out how to find Indriði at the party?" She wrinkled her nose. "Yeah, I remember. I thought it was pretty odd."

"Hmph. Well, she and I were ... we didn't see eye to eye about how you should be trained. After you found me in that alley, I left in the middle of the night, drove out to her place by myself. I wanted answers, y'know, about how I could get my memories back. But it kind of escalated into a fight about ... everything. About your dad, about how she didn't help me get away from him back then.

"I asked her how exactly she was planning to handle another hellerune, and an untrained one, at that. Pretty fuckin' dangerous." He huffed, shaking his head. "She said she had assumed *I* would do it. I told her to take a long walk off a short pier. But it looks like we don't have a whole lotta options now."

Edie frowned, knitting her brows. She had almost suggested that to him over a week ago, before Percy had interrupted. "Can you ... do that?"

"There are some things I can teach you, yeah. I don't know everything. Magic isn't really my thing, and it's not like Holloway and I had long discussions about it. But I was *around* him for a long time—him and more mages than I can fuckin' count. So I know some things. The mechanics or whatever. I'm good at figuring out how things work."

"Like when you talked me through saving Mercy."

Cal nodded. "Sparky was right about that part. I think all you need is a little help learning to call it up and get it out. You can figure the rest out yourself."

Edie looked down at her hands thoughtfully. Every cell in her body screamed that she couldn't possibly do this. Magic was too hard, like she was trying to move a building through sheer force of will. She was the first defective hellerune. She'd be wasting her time, and, more importantly, Cal's time.

But— *Kid, if I didn't want to come back, I'd be in Vegas right now.*

She took a deep breath. Cal didn't waste his time with anyone.

"Would you really do that for me?" she asked, looking up.

He cocked a brow. "Are you kiddin' me? I wanna see you stand on your own two feet more than anybody. If we're gonna stick together, you're gonna have to hold your own in a fight, sister."

Tears came to Edie's eyes again, but she quickly blinked them away. This dumbass revenant had gone through so much in his short un-life, and he'd still come back and helped her. He wanted to be a part of her life, even after everything. And he *still* put up this front like he was the most selfish person in the universe. She didn't know what he was trying to protect himself from, but maybe someday he'd bring those walls down for her.

For now, she shook her head at him. "You are really a piece of work, you know that?"

To her satisfaction, her words made him grin wickedly. "And don't you forget it."

CHAPTER THIRTY-FOUR

IT HAD ONLY TAKEN an evening of asking around and a bit of digging to find out where Tara lived, but Marius had barely been able to sleep that night. All he could think now, as he stood in front of the brick apartment building with the morning sun on his face, was that he hoped this was the right place.

He had considered wearing street clothes, but with all that had been happening, he wasn't confident that it would be safe. Perhaps Ynga had realized he was on to her and the letter itself was an ambush. Best to be prepared, so he had donned a long gray overcoat to keep most of his armor concealed.

The building itself was nice. Not posh or anything, but it looked well taken care of and the neighborhood seemed quiet. When he entered, he stopped before the stairs, eyes wandering over the mailboxes in the vestibule. *Apartment 9, Tara Farhansdóttir.* An odd name, Arabic and Scandinavian mixed into one. A good portion of Odin's runepriests were Arabs. She had to be connected to the monastery.

His heart hammered a furious tattoo against his ribcage as he climbed the stairs to the apartment. The number nine glared like a beacon at the end of the hall, and he almost felt like he was floating toward it. Was he really knocking or was that someone else's hand? He gritted his teeth hard to try and keep himself tethered to reality.

He had to know. The answers were just beyond that door.

Something shuffled inside the apartment for a moment before a tiny voice asked, "What do you want?" He recognized it as the vættr's voice.

"I'm here to see Tara," he responded evenly. "I didn't deliver her letter. I have questions."

There was a period of silence, and he wondered for a moment if she wouldn't let him in at all. Then, metal slid against metal and the door opened a crack. A familiar, pale pink eye looked him up and down. Then, the door opened more fully, revealing the landvættr he'd spoken to in the library.

"You *need* to deliver her letter," she said, almost in a whisper.

So she wasn't Tara. Marius put his hand on the door, praying she wouldn't try to slam it. He wasn't going to leave until he got answers, but the last thing he wanted to do was scare this already nervous person. "I will deliver it, but I need to know what it means first. Please. She said she would tell anyone who would listen."

The vættr looked him over warily again before taking a step back and opening the door a little more. Once he was inside, she closed the door behind him quickly. "Come with me."

As she led him down the hall, he took in his surroundings. The apartment was cozy but well-appointed, and smelled like fresh rain and moss. Lush plants—from vibrant flowers to cacti—decorated the floors, walls, and ceilings everywhere he looked. Watercolors and cross-stitch of cute animals and affirmations hung at intervals. Something was baking in the kitchen, and as they passed it, he spotted a big, fluffy white dog curled up in one corner.

Eventually, they entered the living room. Two large windows looked out onto a garden with the city in the skyline. A home hospital bed sat in front of them, hooked up to a blinking machine.

Curled up in the soft-looking blankets was a woman wearing an oxygen mask. Short black hair framed a tired face with slender brown eyes. Her ochre skin looked sickly and sallow, and her frame was so limp that he didn't have a hard time believing she was on death's doorstep.

She raised her head, and he was surprised to see how young she was— no more than five or six years older than him. She removed her oxygen mask to speak. "Hello?"

The vættr passed him and went to the other woman's bedside, checking the machine quickly before leaning down to kiss her. "This one is a vivid, Tar. He wanted to ask you about your letter."

Tara's eyes lit up, and she looked over the vættr's shoulder to study Marius. She whispered something to the vættr, who nodded in response and left the room, closing the door behind her.

Awkwardly, Marius came closer and pulled a seat up to Tara's bedside.

She sighed and sank into the blankets. "It's nice to meet you, Mister...?"

"Harald," he lied.

"I'm Tara. The one who let you in is my girlfriend, Harper." She looked out the window, and Marius wondered how she would even find the strength to tell him anything. "What do you have questions about? Eirik didn't send you to kill me, did he?"

"No. I didn't give him your letter at all."

She turned her head and frowned at him, waiting for an explanation.

"Before I start something, I want to know what happened," Marius said.

"At the monastery?"

Slowly, the vivid nodded. "Yes ... but I don't understand. You can't be much older than I am. How...?"

"How am I dying?" She smiled thinly. "Thyroid cancer. I've been in remission three times, and this is the fourth time it's come back."

"I'm sorry."

"I'm about to tell the doctors I'm done with medicine. I'm tired of being sick." With a mournful smile, she added, "And so the little girl who survived a Gloaming sacking succumbs to human illness."

He shifted uncomfortably in his seat, not meeting her eyes. "How *did* you survive?"

"Do you really want to know?" she asked. "Once you know, you can't un-know. Trust me, I've tried."

Marius paused for a moment, but ... of course. He had to know. He nodded.

"All right." Tara turned her face away, closed her eyes. "I was only a little girl when the monastery fell. It was after a long stalemate between the Gloaming and the Aurora protecting us. The Gloaming suddenly pushed. The priests tried to gather the apprentices and the few children in the relic room with one of the vivids, but I wanted my mother, so I slipped them.

"I went looking for her. There was fire everywhere, beams and stone falling, arrows flying over the walls. I was terrified. Eventually, I found my mother's body in the courtyard, near a pile of other priestesses. I crawled under it ... out of some sense that I needed to hide, and I wanted to be close to her, and she would protect me."

Tara stopped, putting her oxygen mask back on. Marius's arms warmed with light, and he wondered if he could do anything to help her. Would that be rude, if it was even possible? He could almost feel the spark of life within her, and it was still salvageable.

After a few deep breaths, she continued.

"The Radiant came charging out with a troop of Aurorans. He had shut everyone else away. They fought for a long time, but ... I— I don't remember. I only remember how hot and loud it was, and how badly it smelled. Eventually, the fighting stopped. Everyone was dead or dying. Gloaming rushed past my hiding spot.

"I remember peeking out and seeing the Radiant lying face-down. I thought he was dead, too, but then a lady appeared. I remember that the way she looked scared me. Pale skin, hair as orange as flame, red lips. She sent the Gloaming away so that she and Eirik were alone.

"She brought him up to his knees"—Tara mimicked the movement —"tipped up his chin, and ... she seemed to know him, but he didn't know her. I didn't understand until later that she must have been his dís."

A spirit of Fate. A Norn. His father's Norn, the one he had always said had given him foresight. Marius swallowed hard, voice sandpaper as he asked, "What did she say?"

"She said that if he promised to serve her when she called for him, she would spare his life and give him powers that would make him a legendary Radiant. She said if he refused, she would tell the world his son's secret."

Marius's extremities turned numb.

Secret? He had no secrets to keep.

"I had to tell," she rasped, "because now I understand. Now I can see that this is ... this is bad, something he didn't want anyone to know. She must have been someone dreadful, and he made a deal with her. And now the resurge of Gloaming has taken root in Anster so fast ... even if the other Radiants sent their best tomorrow, they'll never quell the rise in time. It's too late. We're already at the flashpoint."

Marius's mind reeled, barely registering what she was saying. He was still focused on the last part of her story. His voice was barely above a whisper. "The son. Did she say what the secret was?"

Tara only shook her head. She looked exhausted from the stress and trauma of recounting her story. She took another few breaths from the oxygen mask, then let it drop. "I couldn't tell you."

Silence fell between them as he tried to process this new information. Things were starting to fall into place like some sort of horrific puzzle, painting a picture that filled him with the most spine-tingling dread. He felt like he might vomit.

One piece, however, was still missing.

"Do you speak modern Icelandic?" he asked softly. "Can you translate something for me?"

Tara seemed surprised, but nodded. "What is it?"

Taking a deep breath, he recited what he had heard Ynga say about Zaedicus a couple days before. "*Ég mun finna þig í fjöru.* I thought it was *I will meet him on the beach,* but she can't possibly be meeting this person."

"Ah." Tara smiled sagely. "I see. No, you translated it well enough, but it's not what you think it means. *I will find you at the beach* is a promise of violence, back from when punishments and trials were held seaside. Basically, she was saying she's going to kick his ass."

Marius frowned at the floor. He'd been misled by a godsdamned *idiom?*

As he sat there, trying to collect himself, Tara turned her head. Her tired eyes searched the vista out her window like she was looking for someone. When she spoke next, her voice was quiet. "You know ... I often wonder about that secret. What happened to the Radiant's son, what he's hiding." She looked back. "Do you know him, Harald?"

Slowly, Marius raised his eyes. "I don't know anymore."

Edie gasped as yet another ball of death magic destabilized, exploding in her face.

That made, what, seventeen? Across Astrid's hearth room, Cal was regarding her with increasing boredom and irritation, arms crossed. But god help him, he was trying.

Breathing raggedly, Edie doubled over with her hands on her knees. "Can't I practice something else? I haven't done any plague or shadow magic yet."

"You're not touching any of that shit with a ten-foot pole till you get a hang of this," he scoffed. "You humans have enough trouble with preventable diseases as it is, never mind a new plague."

She inhaled and exhaled sharply like she was in labor, shaking the excess energy out of her system. "How about blood magic?"

Cal shook his head. "Death magic was what cropped up when you were pissed off, so we're starting there. Besides, I'd rather have you accidentally boil a guy's blood than rot him into a skeleton. Easier to explain."

"Fuck you, man." Edie groaned and held her hand out again. It felt like it might be easier to practice *on* someone, but people's bodies weren't exactly disposable. "Could I maybe practice on you and then necroheal you all better?"

"That's a big fat no." He gestured for her to conjure the magic again. "The ball."

"Are we training a necromancer or training for the NBA, here?"

"Show me the ball, Holloway!"

Another, longer groan. She took a deep breath and closed her eyes, trying to put herself back in her dream. In her mind's eye, she envisioned the wolf coming at her, and let the now-familiar icy sensation race down her right arm and into her palm. When she opened her eyes, ghostly blue light swirled in her hand.

Cal maintained a safe distance, watching her skeptically. "Okay, now let it kinda ... flow out and over."

"I'm not really sure how to do that, *Cal*," she said through gritted teeth. It took enough effort to keep the magic from exploding again. It really wanted out, and wasn't happy with being slow and steady.

"Well, stop trying so damn hard."

Stop trying so hard. Easy! She tried to loosen her mental grip a little.

The spell vibrated in her hand and flashed, then burst in a shower of blue sparks. Edie moaned as the embers hit the wooden floor and died.

Cal sighed and came closer. "Listen, you need to relax. Just let it come."

"If I do that, I'm afraid I'll blow the whole block up," she mumbled, taking her leather jacket off and shaking her arms again. "It's not that easy."

"You gotta work the magic, not force it. Like the heavy bag, remember? Jab and flow."

"Easier said than done."

"It's a little like ... like playin' an instrument." He strummed an air guitar. "Do you force it this hard when you're playing bass?"

Edie wrinkled her nose at him. "No, but it's different. First of all, I know I'm not going to hurt someone if I mess up. Second, I know where my fingers have to go. I have a rhythm. This is ... chaos. There is no rhythm."

Rolling his milky eyes, he returned, "Then you'll just have to make your own."

The sound of the shop door's bell tinkling gave Edie pause. The CLOSED sign was still in the window, but maybe it was one of the employees coming to check on Astrid. She turned to look over her shoulder as someone threw the private door's latch and barged in.

Her heart stuttered. Marius. And he looked pale, like he was about to puke.

"What's wrong?" Edie asked.

"I have to tell you something." The vivid took a couple steps closer, looking lost. Urgency tightened his voice to the point of breaking.

It took him a few moments to gather his thoughts, but he told them everything that had happened. The letter delivered by the vættr, the hush money, Tara, and the story about Eirik and the Norn. It all seemed too crazy to be true—a Radiant working with the Gloaming? But there were so many little things that were coming together now.

When Marius was done, Cal crossed his arms, rubbing his chin thoughtfully. "It would explain why the Aurora keeps getting their asses kicked whenever the Gloaming riots. He's doing *just* enough to keep the place from falling apart all at once, but he's still lettin' it fall apart."

"Is that why the Aurora was trying so hard to find me?" Edie asked, looking between them. "Eirik didn't want to kill me, he had a job to do. To give me over to Sárr?"

"Could be."

Marius looked equal parts haunted and angry, but angry seemed to slowly be winning out. He paced a hole in the floor. "He knew what he was doing was bad from the beginning. He saved Tara, but told everyone that no one had survived. He warned her never to tell. And then, recently, he was paying for her cancer treatments to keep her quiet."

"Why did she tell?" Edie asked gently. "Did she say?"

"Because she has more honor in her thumb than he has in his entire body?" he snapped, holding his head. "I don't know."

She frowned. "You said that the Norn was his dís?"

"She must be. *Must* be. No one but your own spirit of Fate can give you such a strong talent like that, besides maybe a god. I always assumed he'd had it since birth, but... The Norn must have been planning this for centuries, waiting to line up the perfect string of events."

Cal crossed his arms, glancing over. "White skin, orange hair, red lips, likes fucking with people, works with the Gloaming—?"

"It must be Indriði," Edie finished.

Marius cursed and stopped pacing, his voice a murmur now. "The mirror wasn't warning me about a traitor trying to assassinate my father. It was trying to tell me the traitor *was* my father, and that he had to be brought down." He seemed to pant for a moment, as though he was struggling for air. "Why would he do this?"

In that moment, Edie wanted to reach out to him. She could feel the pain radiating from him—pain she had felt herself. To suddenly find out that your father had lied to you was a feeling she knew better than anyone else. But she refrained. Comfort wasn't what he needed now; she could see that in the way his golden eyes burned, the way every muscle in his body was tight and ready to *go*. He needed to act. He needed answers.

She turned and slipped her jacket on again, which seemed to shake him from a reverie.

"You don't have to—"

"I'm not letting you go alone," she said. "Where is the Radiant now?"

He loosed a puff of air, searching her face. Then, suddenly, his eyes were wide. He looked at the ceiling and said one word: "Ynga."

CHAPTER THIRTY-FIVE

THE PORTAL in front of Indriði blazed azure against the stones surrounding it. The vibrant color was cut off at intervals as her veiled servants walked through with her belongings. The artifacts had been saved first; now just her spiders, her furniture, and her documents and books remained. She was prepared to close the portal at a second's notice, but she wanted her creature comforts if she was to start fresh in another city.

It had been two days since the "Auroran raid" that had turned out to be a false alarm, infiltrators trying to retrieve the hellerune and the shieldmaiden. They had also stolen her drake, but the idiots could have the lot; she had met all her goals. All that was left of Astrid were her shield and spear, nothing but valuable trophies—finally hers, no thanks to Lylirion *Dead*-Shadow.

Without the valkyrie, the universe was a better place, and the Reach would finally crumble to dust.

"Ahem."

Behind her, Zaedicus, the annoying little worm, was supposedly helping her supervise the transport. What he was really doing, however, was standing off to the side, getting drunk off blood and criticizing her. If there was one thing mediocre men liked to do, it was criticize people who were more successful than them. Elves were no different.

"Do you think leaving Anster on such short notice is really wise?" he intoned skeptically, swirling his goblet like the Anne Rice reject he was. His pet human-wight, Scarlet, was almost as egregious, but at least she wasn't a coward. "Did you not put years of effort into cultivating your Auroran?"

Indriði crossed her arms, not bothering to turn around to address him. "I did. But Anster was only the start. I've got bigger things in the works."

Did Zaedicus really care about her leaving? Ha. Chances were what he really cared about was not having her around to ask for favors and guidance. He was useless, and he knew it.

"I stayed this long mostly to watch the hellerune and bring her close to me. And to kill Astrid." She shrugged one shoulder. "Now I'm done."

She was done with Eirik, too. For years, he had been easy to control through blackmail. Funny that the secret he was protecting was one she and Sárr had also worked hard to keep under wraps—best for everyone that Marius stay clueless—but Eirik hadn't needed to know that.

It had begun with one little favor: look for the hellerune and bring her to me. She had escalated it from there. Now he had outlived his usefulness and was beginning to disobey her subtly. The crisis the Aurora found itself in was his problem now. Eventually, his excuses wouldn't be enough, and he'd be exposed. Without her, he'd face the full backlash of the Aurora; and without him, knowing their Radiant was a traitor, the Rising Aurora would crumble and the New Gloaming would swarm in.

"Are you not concerned what the Wounded will think of your little stunt?" Zaedicus scoffed. "Yes, you killed the valkyrie, but you lost the hellerune."

Indriði closed her eyes and smiled against the tone in his voice. He thought her a silly idiot for losing Holloway when he had done the same, what, three, four times? "No, honey. Believe it or not, I let her go." She looked over her shoulder at him. "You really thought you got me with that one, huh?"

The high-wight's face twisted sourly. "The Wounded is going to—"

"I *honestly* couldn't care less."

All at once, the colors of the portal before her shifted. A streak of blood red invaded the blue, becoming bigger as it whorled until the entire thing glowed crimson. A familiar figure clad in leather and steel stood stark black against it.

"Speak of the Devil," Indriði whispered to herself. He had been on his way to retrieve Edie. Well … oops.

The Wounded stepped away from the portal, features becoming clearer now that he wasn't back-lit. His seething expression heralded death. Maybe they'd be lucky and it would be Zaedicus's—although, after all his failures, the Wounded saw Zaedicus as so inconsequential that he probably didn't even notice his presence. Indriði had to agree with him on that front, at least.

"Welcome, my lord." She scanned the area behind him. "Where are your pets?"

"Busy. And they are not my pets." Then came the question of the hour: "Why did you allow Holloway to escape?"

Indriði spread her hands calmly. "I'm cutting my losses. After talking with her, it's obvious to me that she's not even half as powerful as she's supposed to be. Even if she was, she'll clearly never join us. We should shift our direction and kill her on sight instead. Shouldn't be hard."

The Wounded set his jaw, the bridge of his nose wrinkling in fury. "We chose her for a reason, Norn."

He couldn't scare her, though. He should know that. They were practically equals in this operation, even if he was their master's golden boy, so to speak.

"Listen, hon," she returned, relishing how the term of endearment made him twitch. "It's not gonna happen, and you and I both know she isn't the only hellerune available to us. That's part of why I'm moving my operation here. There's another one nearby, and he can't hide from us forever."

The Wounded was silent, gray eyes searching her face, probably trying to find a weak spot. He still wouldn't let this go. Pathetic.

The Norn bridged her hands. "I don't have to remind you that there's more at stake here than ... whatever it is you want her for." A smirk. "You're being greedy."

He growled, his fingers twitched—and for a moment, it seemed like he really would reach for his claymore and try something. But he stopped, eyes wandering.

Something behind Indriði seemed to have distracted him. She thought it might be Zaedicus, but no ... something high up, a point near the ceiling. The Wounded's expression melted from fury to a blank, haunted look.

The Norn glanced over her shoulder, but there was nothing. *What was he seeing?*

"Very well," he said abruptly, drawing Indriði's attention back to him. His jaw was clenched, eyes alight, but his face was devoid of emotion. "Daschla will no doubt benefit from having you in the area. I give you Scarlet and her Watchers as well, to command as you see fit."

"*What?*" Zaedicus sputtered. "My lord, I— need Scarlet here!"

Sárr ignored him. "You have my blessing, and my permission to hunt for the other hellerune."

Indriði's smile was tight. "Bold of you to assume I needed your permission. Or wanted it, for that matter."

The Wounded stared at her for a moment, huffed a low laugh, then turned and left.

The chapterhouse was bathed in honeyed light, but the tone in the room was somber. Across from Eirik, standing behind a bloodied altar, was Ynga. She clutched the bleeding stump of her wrist to her chest as a pillar of light engulfed her, turning her glacial blue eyes to rings of glittering yellow for a brief moment. A golden halo wreathed her head; then the pillar expanded, filling the whole room with warmth before slowly fading.

He was supposed to be left with a feeling of joy. He had done this time and time again, but this felt different. Had it finally happened? Had the gods forsaken him?

When the intruders burst in, he heard them, but couldn't seem to turn to confront them. A great clamoring like a thousand bells ringing at once filled his head, and the vision shook and turned to white all around him. He sensed the end. His knees buckled, the world rushing upward in a blur, then—

Nothing.

Eirik opened his eyes. The vision was over.

He stood on the battlements surrounding the temple grounds. Before him was the main building of their order's hub, its golden dome shining in the late morning sun. Most people who looked up at the Temple of the Rising Divine assumed it was some sort of campus, and that was true enough. Masquerading as a religious college and sending money to the right places had kept them safe and unmolested thus far.

How long could that last now? His heart ached at the thought. Indeed, how much longer could *any* of them live in secrecy?

Snow had begun to fall, light and delicate on the breeze. A thin layer of it coated the stone, slowly melting when it made contact with the sun-warmed surface. Some day soon, it wouldn't melt at all. Eirik's stomach was a hollow void. He knew what this snow meant, and he knew his hand in bringing it upon them. It took all his strength not to collapse to his knees and wail his grief into the sky.

Marius. He had to remember. All the horror, the pain, the death was for Marius.

At first, the Norn had simply asked for the hellerune. That had been one thing. He didn't know and didn't care to know what the Gloaming wanted with her. Then the favors had become bigger and bigger, until he was working against his own people. Until he was a traitor.

But it was all for Marius. He was only doing his duty. Tyr, of all people, must understand.

Marius knew; Eirik could sense it somehow. He found himself scanning the vista before him, trying to pick out his son's righteously furious form. His son knew what he had done, and he would no doubt kill him for it.

Perhaps that was what the gods wanted—blood. Perhaps it didn't matter whether he was really a traitor or not.

Regardless, whatever happened, Marius—that brilliant child, the light of Eirik's life, the only thing that mattered anymore—was ready to become Radiant. It was up to him how he wanted to achieve that.

"Your Grace," said a voice from behind him. He turned to see a vivid standing at the top of the battlement steps, helmet under their arm. "The chapterhouse is prepared for Tyr's Rite. We're ready to begin whenever you are."

With a heavy heart, Eirik nodded and turned from the parapet. It was time to face his fate.

CHAPTER THIRTY-SIX

THE GROUP at Shipshaven had piled into Ghost as soon as they could explain the situation to Satara. They'd contemplated taking faster modes of transportation, such as Marius's lightsteed or Astrid's spectral wolf, but Edie had argued that there was no better use of the hour drive than putting their heads together and coming up with a solid plan.

However, considering they only had four people and little idea of what they were up against, a solid plan soon proved to be nearly impossible.

"How the hell are we supposed to take down a whole stronghold of Aurora?" Cal asked as he turned onto the highway. "Not even the Gloaming go near that place."

"We don't have to take down a whole stronghold. Only my father." Marius's tone was dark, his fist clenched.

Edie, sitting next to him, tried to keep her tone gentle. "We shouldn't just waltz in, then. Where can we find your dad?"

"In the chapterhouse. He's inducting a new vivid today." He scrubbed his face and sighed. "It'll be packed with vivids, but I'm ... hopeful they'll see the truth. They have to."

"Do you really think they'll listen to you over him?" she pressed.

He said nothing. Edie could practically hear the wheels turning in his head. Learning your father had been lying to you for years *and* having to test your people's trust in you all in one day had to be agonizing. Marius kept shaking his head, whispering to himself at intervals.

She let him alone for now. He had an hour to come up with how he was going to convince the other vivids. At this point, Edie was starting to think it might be better for them to just assassinate Eirik and go, but Marius probably wouldn't consent to that until his back was to the wall. He wanted his moment.

They discussed the layout of the temple, what other forces they might be met with, and how they might escape. When they finally reached Anster, Marius directed Cal to a street around the side of the temple.

The building was huge, though Edie had been expecting something more churchlike. Tall stone walls obscured what she assumed were the grounds, and the only entrances seemed to be the main one and four or five doors around the perimeter.

The place Marius had instructed them to park was near a public square. It wasn't until he brought them to one of the square's far-off, lonely corners that Edie noticed a lower portion near the temple's wall, mostly hidden and cordoned off with a gate and an iron fence. When she peeked beyond, she could see a spiral staircase leading underground.

Satara examined it skeptically as they approached. She was holding together well, considering the ordeal they'd been through only a couple days before. Edie worried for her, but if focusing on the task ahead helped her cope, that was valid. "Where does it lead?" asked the shieldmaiden.

There seemed to be no latch or lock, but Marius whispered a spell to open the gate. "The undercroft. The chapterhouse only has one door in use, but there is a secret entrance in the wall. We can get in from here." He dragged the gate open and ushered the rest of the party in first, checking the square before locking the gate again and following them.

The stairs only went down a floor, but after the first turn, they disappeared completely underground. Edie put one hand on the stone wall and carefully felt her way until they were at the bottom, standing in front of a door bound and riveted with iron. Marius whispered another spell, and a golden barrier that hadn't been visible before flashed and melted away.

The undercroft was even darker than the stairwell. Edie's time in Indriði's dungeon hadn't exactly endeared her to darkness, and to boot, she could hear water flowing nearby. She hugged her jacket close. "Is there a river down here?"

"It's a canal," Marius's voice answered, so close behind her that it sent shivers down her spine. "It cuts the temple grounds in half."

"Great. Does anyone have a light?"

Up ahead, Cal flicked open his lighter and waved it around, probably trying to find a torch he could ignite. It didn't seem like there were any sconces down here, though, let alone torches.

"Don't bother," Marius said. He went to the front of the group and summoned a glowing yellow ball, letting it float above their heads. "The dark is part of how they make sure non-Aurorans stay out. Most of us know at least one rudimentary light spell."

He started forward, and the rest had no choice but to follow closely. Edie pumped her legs harder to keep up with the others, all of whom were taller than her. Even though it was freezing down here, she was sweating with anxiety.

"We need weapons," Satara said, an irritated edge to her voice. "Walking in with a necromancer is not likely to soothe your people."

"I know."

Edie liked Marius fine, but the idea that he was willfully leading them to their deaths did not sit well with her. In the dim light, she exchanged looks with both Cal and Satara. If things went south, they might have no choice but to bail. It was Marius's choice to come with them or not.

"Satara's right," she said. "We won't attack them if they don't attack first, but we need to be armed."

"I know," Marius repeated, harsher this time.

She gritted her teeth and pressed, "So, what's the plan?"

After a lull, their procession stopped. The arched ceiling of the undercroft had become lower as they reached a wall of doors. Marius touched the one he was standing in front of, then started walking again, much faster. "That's the chapterhouse. The main entrance is guarded during ceremonies, so we'll have to use that one."

"We, uh, kinda missed it," Cal grumbled. "Where the hell are you taking us, Sparky?"

The sound of flowing water intensified as the ceiling got higher again. The ball of light above their heads split into two, and one left, bathing the path ahead of them in light.

Up ahead, Marius was already crossing a stone bridge with no parapets. The canal rushed under it, frothing as it flowed downhill. Edie's heart seized at the sight. The bridge was so *skinny*. With nothing to hold onto, the only way she was getting across that thing safely was on her hands and knees.

Satara crossed quickly, then Cal followed suit. Edie halted stiffly at one end. Why did everything have to be a fucking trial?

Cal stopped in the middle of the bridge when he noticed she had stalled. "Get a move on, kid."

"It's— I ... listen. Give me a sec."

The revenant cocked a brow at her, then looked at the water rushing below them and rolled his eyes. Leaning forward, he took her arm, and though his grip was gentle, he dragged her across the bridge with a strength she couldn't even hope to resist. "How are you supposed to fight witches and werewolves if you can't even cross a freakin' footbridge? I'm asking!"

As they reached the other end of the bridge, Marius finally spoke. "I was thinking about how I'll get the others to believe me. You're right; with Edie here, they'll think she bewitched me or something. But then I realized that they don't have to believe me—they only have to believe their gods."

"What are you talking about?"

As if answering the question itself, one of the balls of light rushed ahead and perched on the casing of a huge golden door. Even in the dim light, it shone like a beacon. Its marble frame was large, intricately carved with the likenesses of what must be famous Auroran warriors. In its center was a three-dimensional crest emblazoned with a sun.

"We're under the inner sanctum now. This is the Golden Crypt. It holds the corpses of past Radiants dating back ... a long time. Several centuries."

Marius studied the marble carvings for a moment before pointing to one of the figures depicted there—a slender woman in a white hood, carrying a staff on her back and a knife in her left hand, held at an impractical angle that Edie could only guess was symbolic somehow.

"It's said Radiant Hærfríðr the Puretongue never told a lie in her entire life, such that the iron knife she wielded as an adherent turned to silver and adopted her virtue. Supposedly, anyone who holds the knife is only able to tell the truth. Not only truth as he knows it, but the absolute truth."

Edie blinked. "Does it actually work?"

"I don't know," he replied quietly. "They only need to believe it does."

Marius inhaled audibly and touched the door's crest. In an instant, magic poured from his palm, into the door. The crest slowly filled with light until it hurt Edie's eyes to look at; then it rotated, separating into four parts that shifted to the side and allowed the door to open. The massive, bassy creak alone set Edie on edge; the icy wind that flowed out from the room beyond downright frightened her.

"Sounds good," Cal rasped, apparently unaffected. "Let's get 'er done."

Marius entered first. The balls of light coalesced into a single ball once more and hopped from sconce to sconce, lighting their way as they entered the crypt.

Edie was unable to hold back a gasp as over a dozen grinning, glittering faces lit up in the darkness above their heads. It took a moment for the lights to brighten, and for her to realize exactly what she was looking at.

Skeletons, and not of the spooky Halloween display variety. Standing in individual alcoves and powerfully posed, these skeletons were dressed to the nines in fine gilded robes and polished armor designed to show off their bones. The bones themselves seemed to be covered with delicate fabric, every inch of it embellished with gold and jewels. It was stretched across their skulls, their eyes replaced with gems and silver filigree; their teeth were lustrous pearls, jaws encrusted with emeralds, sapphires, and diamonds.

Despite being decorated similarly, they were all distinct. Eygísl the Vengeful—so said the plaque at his feet—wore completely different but equally as extravagant armor as Petronia of Swift Wind. Even though these Radiants were long dead, Edie felt watched under their eyes.

"Auroran gilded corpses," Satara said in awe. "I never thought I would get to see these in person."

She sounded like she'd just been ushered into paradise, but Edie wasn't as convinced. The skeletons were beautiful, no doubt about it; and under normal circumstances, if they were visiting a museum or something, she would have been gaga over them. But in the dark recesses of a centuries-old crypt, under a temple full of old god worshipers who wanted her dead, they struck her as a little more sinister.

"How did they … do this?" she asked. "And why?"

"Younger Norse burial customs dictate people of importance should be buried with grave goods." Marius gestured around the room as they walked. "This is how we honor that tradition while still preserving our Radiants. When they die, they're stripped of their flesh, their bones coated in wax. Then acolytes wrap each bone in thin silk lace, for protection and as a surface to decorate. It's been years since any of them were on public display, but they still need tending to from time to time."

Cal snorted and jerked a thumb toward one of the corpses. "Hey, Holloway, I think you owe me some bling."

"Sure. When this is all over, I'll take you shopping."

"Here." Marius stopped in front of a skeleton toward the back of the hall. Her plaque read *Radiant Hærfríðr the Puretongue* in runes, Icelandic, and English.

Her pedestal had to be taller to compensate for her short height, and she was posed with her left arm swept to the side, the other—missing a right hand, of course—pinning an ornamented tome to her chest. Her gaping eye holes had been covered with sapphires circled with diamonds. The gossamer robe draped over her shoulders was cut to reveal her rib cage which, outside and all the way in, had been coated in filigree and pearls. Almost every vertebra was visible, and all decorated with a bejeweled golden cuff. Her long silver hair had been preserved and crowned with a gilded wreath and a gold-plated nimbus behind her head. Not one finger was unadorned, nor one speck of her robe plain. At her hip, a silver dagger was sheathed.

Cal whistled. "Well, she's a looker, I'll give her that."

Marius ignored him and stepped up to the pedestal, stretching to reach her sheath. The dagger hummed faintly as he drew it out, its blade twinkling pure silver. He held it aloft for a moment.

"How does it feel?" Edie asked, itching to leave this place. "Truthy?"

Marius's golden eyes were wide. "It feels—"

Without warning, the corpse's free arm dropped. Edie started, wondering if removing the dagger had destabilized the Puretongue in some way, and she would come crashing to the floor and break into a thousand little pieces.

Then, her ring-heavy hand shot forward and gripped Marius's wrist.

The vivid inhaled sharply and tried to pull his arm away, but her grip tightened. With the horrible groan of scraping bones, the Puretongue leaned forward and slowly lowered into a crouch, then slipped off her pedestal, to her feet.

All around them, rattling and clanking filled the air. Edie whipped around and watched in horror as the other gilded skeletons climbed out of their alcoves with heavy, deliberate movements.

Marius's cry cut the air as he wrenched his wrist from the Puretongue's grasp: "Run!"

Edie didn't need to be told twice; she was off pronto. But as the group sprinted toward the exit, the heavy doors swung shut with a resonating

BANG. Edie watched in horror as a glowing barrier sprang up from the floor and blanketed the entrance.

She was the first to reach it, and she pounded against the doors, trying to force them open. In a second, she was joined by the other three, but even their combined strength wasn't enough to open the magically-sealed exit.

"No!" she screamed, beating her fists in time with her flailing heart. "Fuck, fuck, fuck, *no!*"

There was a loud clang, too close by, and she turned just in time to see one of the skeletons nearest the entrance step down from his pedestal. His plaque said *Radiant Geir the Tempest,* and he was dressed in full plate armor, a gold nimbus similar to the Puretongue's attached to his silver helm. Two filigreed oval holes in his breastplate revealed his ribs, and the handle of his falchion sword was shaped like a comet's tail.

The rubies in his skull seemed to glow as he stood at attention before them. Behind him, the other Radiants fell into rank, drawing their weapons. The longer they were animated, it seemed, the faster they moved. They were almost as fluid as living people now.

And there were so many. Edie and the others would never be able to take them all down, not without weapons.

"This is impossible," Marius whispered, looking as transfixed as he did disturbed.

The group backed up as the skeletons began to advance, but could only put another foot or so between them before their backs hit the door.

Edie's mind reeled. The torches were beginning to go out, row by row. If she could just— But there were *so many.*

Panic suffocated her, but the Aurora's honored dead didn't care.

One of the skeletons toward the front—a man with a jewel-encrusted jaw and silver doublet—raised a flail and swung it toward Cal, startlingly quick. The revenant ducked a second too late, and it connected with his jaw. A sharp *crack* rang through the crypt; his gun clattered to the floor. As he darted to retrieve it, the skeleton reared back for another strike.

"Cal!" With a cry, Satara dove forward, pushing Geir out of the way and seizing the other's arm. A corpse with glaring emerald eyes and a platinum crown practically leapt onto her back, wrapping her braids around its hand and yanking her to the ground. She hit the floor hard and immediately went limp.

Edie screamed, "*NO!*" and tried to summon power in her hands.

Marius slid across the floor to cover Satara, summoning a shield of light around them both. But where was his blade? He wasn't hitting anything. *Now* was the time to *hit* things!

The icy feeling built up her arms. *Time to kill.*

Something whistled through the air. It was a sound that haunted Edie's nightmares, and she knew what it was before she saw Radiant Swift Wind's raised light bow. She jerked to the side just in time, but the plasma arrow still grazed her ear, taking a chunk of the lobe in its deadly clutches. Hot, sticky blood suddenly coated her neck, and pain tore through her body in a sudden, pulsing, screaming, excruciating wave.

Time to die.

"*Enough!*"

CHAPTER THIRTY-SEVEN

EDIE WAS sure it was her father's voice booming through the crypt, but she couldn't see him. All at once, a cloud of blue light formed around her and burst forth like a wave, blanketing the room.

As it hit each skeleton, they became subdued: Eygísl the Vengeful turned his head toward her and lowered his lance, Geir stood at attention, Swift Wind returned her light arrow to its non-existent quiver. The one in the silver doublet stopped whaling on Marius's shield.

Death is my domain. You were stupid to think you could use it against me. The voice in Edie's head almost didn't sound like her own.

She gritted her teeth, breath coming faster and fogging in the suddenly chilly air. She clenched her fists, and the Radiants fell robotically back into rank.

Stay.

It was a moment before the haze over her mind lifted and throbbing pain replaced it.

Without thinking, she raised a hand to her bleeding ear, hissing when she found that the lobe was mostly torn off. Only a small piece was missing, but the radiant arrow had torn upward and nearly severed it from the rest of her ear.

She turned away from the Radiants. For some reason, what they were doing wasn't important ... she just wasn't sure why right now.

Carefully, she extracted the still-summoned arrow from the door, and the chunk of her flesh along with it. The arrow flickered and dissolved in her hand, and she quickly forgot about it. Edie worked mostly on instinct as she pieced her ear back together and called up her blood magic. As it whispered through her, she let her eyes drift closed.

What felt like a couple seconds later, she could feel that the skin was fused back in place, the bleeding staunched. There would be a nasty scar, and she might be lopsided, but she refused to leave flesh on these grounds.

What a creepy thing to think, she realized a second later, then shook her head and turned.

Her three companions stood there, staring at her. Satara was conscious now, her body glowing faintly from Marius's healing magic. The looks on their faces gave Edie pause.

"What?"

"You..." Marius began uncertainly. "You were turned away, swaying and muttering to yourself for nearly five minutes."

"Nothing we said could get your attention," Satara added.

Edie glanced around the crypt. The Radiants stood watching her, too, though their gazes were less intelligent. Subtle blue light glowed in their eye sockets. Slowly, the realization of what she had done crept up on her. Her whole body started to tingle with equal parts glee and terror. "I... Well, that's— good," she managed.

"Turning someone else's zombies into yours is, uh ... pretty advanced," Cal mumbled, rubbing his jaw. "Even if whoever cast that spell is a billion years dead by now. Kudos ... I think."

"There shouldn't be undead down here at *all.*" Marius took a step forward, looking at the neat regiment of undead Radiants. "The Aurora has never used necromancy. I don't understand..."

Cal shrugged nonchalantly, but his expression was grim. "Looks like Eirik isn't the only one keeping secrets."

Eirik. They still had something they needed to do—and now they had a little more help to pull it off. Edie glanced at her small army of skeletons and turned to the crypt doors. "We need to leave. Can one of you open this?"

With a good deal of clattering, one of the Radiants—Something-or-other the Mournful, she thought she remembered, whose breastplate seemed to be a reliquary for his own gold-encased heart—stepped up beside her. He swept his velvet cloak to the side and produced one gloved hand. His palm glowed as he laid it against the door, and with another bright flash, the barrier dissolved and the doors croaked open once more.

Marius left first, breezing past the Mournful with his head down.

Edie followed him closely, reaching out to touch his arm. "Marius, it's okay—"

He pulled it away. When he turned, his expression was ... there was no way to describe it other than *broken*. And like any broken thing, there were edges too sharp for her to touch: "An army of undead Aurorans may be okay for you, hellerune, but not for me."

She shied away. Yet another reminder of what an abomination she was in his eyes. Great.

He'd need to get himself together before they could confront his father, but that was his problem. She turned to focus on getting her newly acquired army out of their crypt.

As she did, however, she noticed that the floor beneath them was ... shaking? For a moment, she wondered if it was vibrations from the temple above, or the canal, but no. The sound, the timing—

Footsteps.

She turned her head and squinted into the darkness down the hall. Marius must have heard the thumping, too, because he conjured another ball of light in his hand.

At first, they couldn't see anything but blackness beyond the scope of the glow. Then, slowly, the light reached something in the dark—something silver. It gleamed here and there as it paced closer, and though

Edie couldn't make out its form, she could tell it was massive, towering at least four or five feet above them.

"Oh," Marius breathed. In a second, he had conjured his sword. "I forgot about him."

"*Him?*"

Slowly, the huge silver thing stepped into view. It seemed less like a creature and more like a construct, a metallic being almost resembling a human but not quite. Its waist was a little too thin, its arms and legs a little too long, its head a little too small. Its mouthless face was smooth, with two tiny, glowing orbs where eyes should have been. A pair of wings formed of metal layered to look like feathers stretched from a foot above its head to the backs of its armored calves. It held a spear as silver as itself.

As soon as the light fully illuminated it, it stopped and leaned forward slightly, scanning their forms. An eerie, resonant, almost robotic breathing sound issued from it.

"The Crypt Keeper." Marius spoke fast. "I've never seen him awake before. I always thought he was a guardian statue or something symbolic, not something that could actually walk."

The Crypt Keeper emitted a strange, low belch, like it was trying to say words but the necessary parts had long fallen into disrepair.

It straightened up, and its white orbs turned red.

Even faster, Marius continued, "It can't be reasoned with. We're going to have to fight it."

Cal, who had come out of the crypt after the Radiants, growled at the construct. "Great, another fucking metal thing I can't shoot at. You're gonna owe me a drink after this, Sunshine."

The Crypt Keeper gave a grinding, mechanical roar and raised its spear. Runes etched on its surface flashed as it brought the spear down at their feet, the head of it barely missing them. The flagstones cracked, and debris flew.

Edie staggered back, adrenaline surging through her veins. She threw her hand forward as orders flew wildly through her head, hoping her horde could understand her. *Go, go, attack!*

They did. Blue and gold flashed together in a glorious wave, light and death working as one within the Radiants' bodies as they charged the Crypt Keeper's legs. Marius conjured his glowing shield and joined the charge, and to Edie's surprise, so did Cal; holstering his gun, he wove in between the construct's legs and began to climb up its wings.

And speaking of wings, behind her, Edie was surprised to hear a pair unfurl. Wind beat her back for a moment, and before she could turn her head to make sense of what was happening, Satara had lifted into the air. She darted toward the Crypt Keeper's head with one of her magical battle-cries. An azure flare enveloped her, bolstering her defenses; then she made impact, kicking the construct hard enough to leave a dent in its face. Thank god wooden shields weren't the only kind shieldmaidens knew how to wield.

Edie swelled with pride, then confidence. Her friends—two of them without weapons—were taking this thing down like experts. She looked down at her hands and willed the icy magic to fill her. The chances of her being able to hurt this thing with death magic seemed slim, but she had to try.

Blue fire engulfed her hands like it was nothing. Astonished, Edie reeled back and flung the magic at the Crypt Keeper as hard as she could. A blast left her palm and struck the construct in the chest, leaving a scorch mark.

Its torso spun 360 degrees; it waved its spear wildly, trying to shake Cal off its back or knock Satara out of the air, but to no avail. Edie could see that Cal was dismantling it piece by piece, tearing off the slats of its wings and letting them fall to the stone floor. Before her, Marius and the gilded army were deftly avoiding its stomping feet— she'd only seen one Radiant get crushed and one kicked into the canal so far.

They were going to *win*. This thing had walked straight out of her nightmares and into its own doom.

Edie reeled back for another strike. Jab and flow, find a rhythm. More blue flame, more scorch-marks. She did it again, and again, until—

No ... but that wasn't right. It wasn't real fire; it shouldn't leave any scorch-marks.

Holy shit. I'm decaying it.

A plan sprang into her mind suddenly, and she cupped her hands to shout, "Guys! Ease it toward the canal!"

Her friends' tactics shifted. Satara, who was drawing most of the Crypt Keeper's attention, swung around and ducked so that she was hovering just above the rushing waters. Edie called off her Radiants, and the lot scurried out of the path of the stomping construct to stand behind her.

Stay!

She rushed into the fray, weaving around Marius and smacking her glowing hands onto the Crypt Keeper's closest knee. Before her eyes, the silver tarnished, then rusted and grew brittle. The longer she held her hands in place, the more it spread until the entirety of the construct's right leg looked like the hull of an abandoned ship.

Above her, it groaned and wavered.

"Cal, get off!" she shouted upward.

"One sec..." The revenant kicked, the thick heel of his boot connecting with a spot he had been working on for a while. He'd stripped the metal away and revealed the bolts that riveted the construct's right wing to its back. "A little help here?!"

Edie backed up and shot a blast of magic under his foot. The next time he struck it, the wing twisted off with a groan and slammed to the stone floor.

Cal hopped off, landing next to Edie. Behind him, urged on by repeated blows from Marius's shield, the construct swayed and screeched as it staggered to the edge of the canal.

Satara had been hovering just out of reach, but dove forward once she saw it teetering. As the Crypt Keeper tumbled into the frothing water, she was able to snatch its spear.

She touched down next to Edie, twirling the weapon in her hand triumphantly. "I'll be having this."

"Let's get to the chapterhouse right away," Marius said, already trotting past the crypt and toward the bridge they had crossed earlier. "We've already wasted enough time, and I'm sure someone has heard us down here."

They'd done it. *She'd* done it, and not by improvising, but with actual magic.

After fighting the Crypt Keeper, crossing the bridge didn't seem so scary. Edie just made sure to walk straight and avoid looking down.

Marius tried to ignore the sound of Edie's sacrilegious army clattering behind him, instead rushing to the back door of the chapterhouse. He found it blessedly unlocked, and opened it to reveal a narrow stone staircase. At the top, gold light shone through the barest cracks in the hidden doorway.

Motioning for the others to remain silent, Marius padded up the stairs and pressed his ear to the wall. The others gathered behind him, the Radiants' armor and weapons clanking softly.

His father's voice floated through the door, speaking familiar words. "We invoke Tyr's fortitude and bravery, and ask for strength, and for him to be present during this sacred rite. God of battles, may we strive to match you in valor and virtue. Pantheons, grant Adherent Ynga Sól's power as she remakes herself in the Wolfbinder's image."

Marius closed his eyes. In his mind, he could see himself in the chapterhouse those few years ago, surrounded by at least forty other vivids. His father shone in the sun, gesturing for him to kneel and hold his arm out on the altar. He heard the whisper of a blade being drawn, the ceremonial blade used only for Tyr's Rite. Marius remembered it—a saber with a hand guard shaped like a wolf's jaws.

"With this blade," recited the Radiant, "let your child feed the wolf as you did. Let her sacrifice please you. Let her strengthen Fenrir's bonds with her blood. Ynga, may Tyr grant you the righteous light of justice."

"I pray he may grant me this."

His father whispered a few ancient words, and the light pouring through the secret door's cracks grew more intense. Marius braced himself for what came next.

A whistle, then a crack and *thump*. Squelching. A long, strangled groan of pain. Marius shivered as he recalled the moment in his own memory. It had been the worst pain he had ever felt in his life. Every time he thought of it, it was almost like he was experiencing it all over again. The pain had been intense at first, but it had built and built until his mind had fogged, face and limbs going numb. He had been suddenly certain that he was going to collapse and die.

Then, something had filled him. A strange, foreign fortitude; an intense burning sensation to fight off the numb cold. Painful still, but different than the blade—seething, deep, cleansing. Dizziness had turned to raw power surging in his chest.

He sucked a breath in through his teeth as the waking world mirrored his lifelike memories: "Do you welcome the righteous light of justice into you, body, mind, and spirit?"

I do. "I do."

"Do you promise to wield proudly Sól's light in the name of Tyr, striving to bring justice to the Nine Worlds and honor to your people?"

I do. "I do."

"Do you swear to purge or bind the wicked for the sake of the innocent, the gods, and, as Tyr did, for the sakes of the wicked themselves?"

I do. "I do."

"Do you vow to spill blood, or give your life if you must, to uphold and protect the ideals of our people?"

I do. "I do."

"Do you swear complete devotion to the Aurora and the Pantheons it serves?"

Marius gritted his teeth. *Do you?*

"I do," said Ynga.

"Finally, do you promise never to disgrace yourself with treachery, especially perjury, on punishment of death?"

"I do."

Fire licked Marius's aching heart. How long had his father been giving this oath, threatening others with death when he had been doing the very thing they were swearing not to do? The hurt, the anger, was almost too much to bear.

There was no more time to wallow over this. Eirik had taken the oath. Marius had taken it, too. *Punishment of death.*

His soul burned as he kicked open the secret door and stepped into the mellow amber light of the chapterhouse.

Ynga and his father stood in the center of the room, bedecked in gold and bronze. Forty vivids sat on benches set into the chapterhouse walls, along with Tiralda, who looked rather bored with the whole ceremony. Every head turned to behold Marius's blinding fury.

They want righteous justice? They'll have it.

From behind him, as if she had read his mind, Edie's Radiant army spilled into the room.

A number of vivids stationed near the door jumped up with cries of surprise, but were cut down before they could even summon their weapons. Blood washed the stone floor. More vivids leapt to their feet, conjuring swords and shields, but their attackers seemed to give them pause. Some looked distressed; others simply looked confused.

"Stay your blades!" Eirik turned, eyes touching Marius briefly. As he scanned the skeletons, it seemed like he didn't quite believe what he was seeing. "What is this?"

Radiant Geir dropped the bleeding vivid he'd been holding, wiping his falchion on his white cloak. He rolled his neck as he squared up to Eirik, blue and gold lights shimmering around him.

Eirik glanced at the corpse in disgust. Then he stopped and looked again, recognition dawning on his face. "*Geir.*" He gaped at Marius, then Edie. "The crypt. What in the gods' names have you *done*, Marius?"

Ynga was no longer clutching her wrist stump to her chest, as she had been when they'd entered. The fire powering through her veins had already staunched the bleeding. "How could you let that monster do this?" she demanded. "Why are you with *them*?"

Marius's stomach soured. Snapping his gaze to Ynga, he raised his voice loud enough that the whole room would hear the truth.

"The hellerune did not raise the honored dead. I tripped a booby trap in the crypt, and they woke by themselves. It was only because she was able to gain control of them that I'm still alive." He narrowed his gaze at Eirik. If only a glare alone could burn a hole through him. "Charms of necromancy on our honored dead? How long has this been going on?"

Eirik didn't respond. His face remained stoic.

"But that's not the only secret you're keeping, is it?"

"Marius—"

He held up his hand, blood racing, breath coming hard. "No more lies! I found the last survivor of the attack on the runepriest monastery, the attack that supposedly only *you* survived. She told me what she saw. You broke your oaths and betrayed the Aurora."

For a long moment, Eirik said nothing, staring at his son in sober silence. It wasn't long, however, before the room erupted in groans and curses and boos in Marius's direction.

Tiralda stood from her seat and pointed at him. "That child is lying. He is a menace. I've caught him snooping around in my room and all over the temple. If anyone is the traitor, it is him!"

"He saved the hellerune's life and then released her at the Gloaming Lord's party," Ynga added. "And now here he is with her again."

Before Marius could say anything in his own defense, the vivids were yelling again. "I don't suppose you have any proof of what you say," said one, venom dripping from his every word.

"Traitor!" Tiralda spat. "Liar."

Do you promise never to disgrace yourself with treachery... As the crowd closed in, readying their weapons, Marius thought of the vow; an oath never to lie to their people. An oath to which he was sworn. An oath to which all the Radiants who had come before were sworn, too. He reached for his belt.

The silver dagger sang when he drew it, and as he held it high above his head, it began to glow.

CHAPTER THIRTY-EIGHT

EDIE WATCHED in awe as the vivids' expressions began to change. Anger was replaced with awe and uncertainty. They all knew what they were looking at, just as they had all known whose skeletons she controlled.

In front of her, Marius swelled, his confidence renewed as the blade's light washed over him. He took several deep breaths.

"He who bears the Puretongue's blade cannot dishonor himself with a lie. He must tell the truth; not the truth as he knows it, but the absolute truth," he reminded them. He leveled the blade at his father, who still stood before him. "You made a deal with a Gloaming Norn in exchange for your life. You've been feeding her information and doing her bidding for gods know how long. You betrayed the Aurora."

"I would never put my own life above the Aurora," Eirik replied in a whisper.

"The dagger doesn't lie. She gave you foresight. She told you you'd be great."

"I know." He sighed. "But that was not why I did it."

A confession. Silent heartache filled the room, and Edie's stomach sank. She couldn't help but feel bad for these people. They were watching the Rising Aurora crumble before their eyes and they knew it.

The vivids looked to Tiralda, the eldest being among them, for help.

After a few moments, the vættr sorceress stepped forward, eyeing the back of the Radiant's head. "We shall soon deal with Eirik ... but now is not the time to stand divided. We know who our enemy is here." She pointed one claw at Edie and bared her teeth.

Marius aimed the silver dagger at Tiralda, now. "She is innocent. I won't let you lay a finger on her."

The sorceress looked at the blade, sneered, and smacked it out of his hand. It flew across the room and clattered to the floor, lifeless once more. "Then you'll perish with her."

Edie wasn't sure who struck first, but in an instant, the room erupted in battle. She dropped to the floor, ducking a blast of energy someone sent her way. *Spread out, go! Take down! Kill!* She barely had to think the orders and her army of undead Radiants plunged themselves into battle.

She watched as the Mournful and another skeleton with a huge silver hammer cut a swath through the vivids in front of her. A large man wove between them and dove for Edie, but one of Swift Wind's arrows whistled over her shoulder and slammed into his forehead. Her little army shone. Many of their opponents hesitated to hit their honored dead, and that hesitation usually meant their deaths.

But not all the vivids were so torn—the Radiant army was still suffering losses. An Auroran archer at the far end of the room had felled the Vengeful and one or two others, and was now was aiming for Geir, who flanked Tiralda with Satara.

No!

Fresh blood coated the stone, and as Edie pulled herself up, it coated her hands, too. Her gaze flew over the bodies bleeding to death at her feet.

I'd rather have you accidentally boil a guy's blood than rot him into a skeleton...

Why not both?

Beside her, Cal's shotgun boomed, and she took off at the sound, sprinting like it was the start of an Olympic dash. An icy blue mist enveloped her as she ran. She could feel the power building up her arms.

The archer didn't even have time to lower his bow before she slammed into him. The blue wove with scarlet, flourishing up her arms as she grabbed the archer's hair with one hand and gripped his face with the other. Her fingertips dug into his skin as it decayed, and the blood coating her palms sizzled. Edie watched in sickening fascination as his veins were laid bare, bubbling. His blood revolted against him.

He was dead almost as soon as she touched him. When she dropped him, she felt invigorated, renewed with the life she had sucked out of him. It was a beautiful and horrible feeling.

Boom! She spun when she heard the chapterhouse doors burst open. Several adherents stood there, their mouths agape. Three rushed into the small vestibule, and one scrambled to run down the hall.

Kill them all.

The Mournful, the skeleton with the hammer, and the skeleton with the flail drove them back. Swift Wind bolted after the deserter.

Edie looked over her shoulder, careful to be aware of her surroundings. On the far left-hand side of the room, Satara was turning Tiralda's own magic against her with some sort of reflective spell. Cal's bullets were breaking the vivids' shields of light quickly, and he was picking off a good amount, but had to keep stopping to reload.

Cover him! She sent the Mournful and the Puretongue over to help.

Just beyond the altar, Marius dealt with Ynga. She had conjured her own lucent weapons, and hers were wilder, less controlled and bursting with light. Flares of plasma sparked off them and flew this way and that, hitting friend and foe alike.

That left one person unaccounted for. Edie's eyes darted around the room until she spotted his bronze armor. He was backing away from the fray, toward the secret door through which they'd come.

No way. They might not have to kill him like Marius had said, but she sure as hell wasn't letting him get away.

She conjured flames of death in both hands and barked, "Eirik!"

He couldn't hear her over the battle, but he must have felt her watching him. As she sprinted around the altar, their eyes met; in the split second before they collided, his flashed gold.

Pain blossomed in an instant, exploding through her body. She didn't need to look down to figure out that he had drawn his blade across her chest—the burning told her all she needed to know. Her vision wavered. *Mistake.*

Eirik slashed again, grazing her chest and leaving a screaming gash on her stomach. Then his glittering blade dissipated and coalesced into a blast of energy that knocked her back. Her jacket was torn from her body as she skidded across the floor, the broken stone and grit shredding her back and shoulders.

She lay there for a moment, the sheer intensity of the pain taking her breath away. Even minuscule movements made it feel like fire was coursing through her veins.

Suddenly, she was obscured, closed off from the rest of the battle by a wall of vivids. They had rallied and were cutting through her Radiants. She wanted to give her army orders, but she couldn't seem to focus...

Eirik broke through the wall of vivids and stood above her, looking down with a stern expression. "Why are you doing this?" His voice was soft; she could barely hear him. "You *know* the Reach will never be able to defeat the Gloaming."

The initial shock of her pain was wearing off, and she mustered enough strength to pull herself into a sitting position. She tried to scuttle backward, but her hand slipped on something cold and sharp, and she tumbled down to one elbow again. "Wh ... why do you care who fights it off? Doh— don't talk to me like I'm the one ruining things. *You* betrayed the Aurora, not me."

His expression wavered slightly. "In the end, it's not the Aurora I answer to."

"You ... you lied to Marius. You let innocent people die so you could have power."

"No," said Eirik. "It wasn't for power. It was never for power. I knew from the very beginning that my only reward would be disgrace—and death."

Slowly, so as not to alert him, Edie reached behind herself, groping for the thing she had slipped on. Finally, her hand closed around it; her mind cleared.

Eirik followed her the half-step she'd scuttled a moment earlier and knelt beside her, searching her face. "But you... Who do *you* answer to? Why allow all this fighting for your sake, abomination? What is it you want?"

Edie looked back at him and mouthed something, but her voice was too small for him to hear. He leaned closer until her mouth was almost touching his ear.

"I just want to survive the fucking afternoon."

She gripped the silver dagger and swung forward, jabbing it into his armpit.

His chainmail stopped it from piercing his skin, but he cried out as she struck him, the blunt pain stunning him for an instant. It was enough of a distraction that she was able to roll away and onto her feet.

I'll show you an abomination.

Edie sucked in a breath, and with it, the energy buzzing around her. Death spun, twisting, tangling within her until it reached a fantastic crescendo. The golden glow around them dimmed, the room turning dark and icy in her very presence. She dragged her clenched fists up from the ground as though she was pulling power out of the earth itself.

Then she dropped it. Hard.

Ynga lashed Marius with wave after wave of her unstable magic, beating him until his back was against the wall. Her onslaught was relentless; when she didn't need her shield, she summoned two swords of fire.

She was talented and precise, and her fury was as volatile and boiling as her light. Marius was starting to wonder if he would survive this encounter.

He watched his flank as he fended her off, waiting for a weak spot. Edie's gilded army was slowly falling around him, and nearby, hand-to-hand had left Cal worse for wear. In addition to his guns, he'd stolen one of the gilded skeleton's weapons, but he wasn't particularly skilled in melee. Vivids were beginning to overwhelm him. Satara helped where she could, but Tiralda was a formidable enemy. Between her water, light magic, and viciously sharp claws and teeth, she required most of the shieldmaiden's concentration.

Marius himself had already had to buck off a dozen other vivids trying to join their stand-off. They had cut the number of vivids down, but there were still too many, and they were overpowering the Reach.

"How could you side with her over us?" Ynga raised her flaming blade. "Traitor!"

He was barely able to lift his shield high enough in time to deflect the strike. "Edie is innocent of whatever crime you're accusing her of."

"You may as well be Gloaming yourself."

He gritted his teeth. He couldn't spend more time fighting Ynga—he needed to help the others. She needed to be dealt with *now*.

"Are you brainwashed or just stupid, Marius?" she taunted.

"I could ask the same of you!" He bolstered his shield and pressed her unexpectedly, knocking her off balance.

When she clattered to the floor, the room seemed to dim suddenly, as if someone had knocked out a light bulb. The only problem was, there was no electricity in the chapterhouse, and it was midday.

Marius lowered his weapons slightly at the sight in front of him. What was left of the vivids had created a wall to face their enemy undivided—but now they were keeling over, falling to their knees or collapsing completely. His gaze was drawn to the floor, where a curious circle of dark blue flame smoldered. As he glanced around the room, he noticed Cal and Satara shying away from it. It had to be...

"Edie?" The word left his mouth like a prayer, and he watched in awe as the collapsing vivids revealed her standing there, shrouded with crisp blue smoke.

Her eyes and the runic tattoo on her right wrist blazed the color of the magic surrounding her, her raven hair floating as if lifted by a strong wind. She was moving her hands rhythmically, almost as though she was weaving the spell to maintain it.

At her feet was his father, lying still on his side.

It was over almost as quickly as it had begun. The darkness and the magic shrank back into Edie, and she fell to her knees.

Marius's heart skipped. He dropped his weapons to go to her, and—

A fiery blade dug itself into his shoulder, the untamed magic cutting right through his armor.

Agony exploded, his vision turning white. Ynga had recovered from her fall and from whatever Edie had done. As she lifted herself up by the hilt of her blade, it spat plasma and sank deeper into him.

His mouth open in a silent scream, Marius collapsed to the chapterhouse floor. Blinding points of white light, like the end of a child's sparkler, danced in front of his eyes as he sank further. They exploded, threatening to fill his vision... *Damn. Damn, damn, damn.* He had been distracted, and it had only been a second, but it had been enough. *Stupid.*

Ynga stood above him for a moment, breathing hard. Fire ravaged his veins, his skin, and just when he thought he might pass out from the intensity of the pain, she yanked the blade out. It hissed as the blood on it almost immediately evaporated.

"Two traitors for the price of one," she said mournfully.

Around Marius, the dying sounds of battle became muffled in his ears. Only the thump of his own pulse and Ynga's words reached him now. He had been forced prostrate, his forehead against the bloody flagstones.

"I don't understand," the new vivid whispered, sounding like she was trying as hard as he was to stay upright and conscious, "how you could let this happen. Look at all of them ... *us* ... dead. Because of you!"

From above him came a whine and a wave of heat. He didn't have to look to know that she was raising her sword for the killing blow.

This room was too small for him to unleash his aura. He would defeat

Ynga, but hurt Edie and Cal and Satara along with her. He closed his eyes. If he could muster the strength to *get up...*

Without warning, a desperate roar rose from somewhere in front of him. The skin on the back of his neck stung as a giant blast of radiant magic flew over him and slammed into Ynga. There was a loud *clang* as she hit the back wall and toppled over.

Marius's heart was pumping slower now, the stink of his own flesh in his nose. It was only through sheer force of will that he was able to look up to try and find his savior.

The fighting had all but died. In the corner, Satara impaled Tiralda on her spear, digging the head of it into the wall so that the sorceress was pinned like a twitching insect. The Radiant army had fallen, but Cal was picking off the few vivids who had managed to survive Edie's deathtrap. Edie herself lay on the floor, half-awake and breathing evenly.

And in front of him ... his father.

Somehow, though he had been hit with the full force of the hellerune's death magic, Eirik was still alive. He lay on his side like a dying fish, tear-filled eyes staring at his son. Radiant magic still glowed in his palm as he dropped his left hand.

Marius's heart ached. His father, the traitor, the *liar* ... in that moment, he couldn't understand. He almost wished he didn't know.

Were they going to die here? Why all this fighting just to die? What had they gained? As Marius struggled to his knees and crawled closer, he didn't know whether to slit his father's throat or hold him.

The vivid gripped the central altar and pulled himself to his feet ... but after a couple limping steps, he stopped. A strange twinkling sound had begun to fill the room, like a million little bells. He watched in awe as an arched doorway filled with glittering orange-gold light opened behind his father.

Eirik searched his son's expression, then craned his neck to look at the doorway, too. When he saw it, his whole body relaxed. Marius watched his father's profile practically glow with awe, surprise, and ... relief.

He dragged himself up, as if called by something unearthly, and faced the doorway.

Marius glanced between them, frantic. His father was trying to *leave*, to run. "Stop," he rasped, his entire body shaking from the effort it took to keep standing up. "Tell me ... tell me where Indriði is."

Eirik had turned to look at him, equally as ashen as his son. "She's gone. Done with me, I imagine."

Marius shook harder. His eyes, cheeks, and the tips of his ears had become unbearably hot, almost matching the wound in his shoulder. Warm tears spilled. He didn't want them, he hated them, but they didn't care. They came thick and fast, burning his neck and wetting his collar.

His father still hadn't moved. Tears streaked his cheeks, too, as he searched his son's face, trying to find words.

Finally, Marius ground out, "Why?"

"I love you," Eirik whispered. "I'm so sorry."

"No. That's not enough. You made an oath. You have to ... you have to pay, like a traitor pays."

Eirik took a deep breath and looked him dead in the eye. "Marius, your father is not a traitor." He glanced over his shoulder at the doorway, then back, new tears welling in his eyes. "Thank the gods, I am not a traitor."

Marius's heart beat hard in his throat as a wave of pain washed over him.

Wait—

The secret.

He had to know.

His voice was thin and wavering like heat. Darkness was closing in. "Who am I?"

In response, Eirik closed his eyes, turned away, and stepped through the portal.

No! All at once, adrenaline surged through Marius's body. The pain turned into panic, darkness into desperation; his vision tunneled to focus on the portal alone. The orange-gold doorway was enveloping him almost before he realized he was sprinting towards it.

Beyond the doorway, there was nothing but warm, coruscating yellow light. It was so bright that he couldn't make out anything around him, but every muscle instantly relaxed. He could feel the heat skate across his skin and become absorbed, healing all his injuries. A sweet, ghostly hum filled his ears. Welcoming. Right. *Home.*

He started to close his eyes.

Then, something blossomed from the light. A figure. It was broad and wore a winged helmet, but the features were washed out, obscured in the blinding light. A glowing man.

The man took him by the upper arms. For a moment, Marius thought he was going to embrace him.

Then, with inhuman speed, the man pushed him away. Marius was lifted off his feet by the force of it. In less than a second, the light and the humming disappeared, and he was soaring backward out of the portal.

He hit the stone floor next to Edie. The last thing he heard before he was swallowed by darkness was the clamor of the temple guards bursting into the chapterhouse.

CHAPTER THIRTY-NINE

W ARM LIGHT BATHED Marius's face, and the smell of clean, fresh linen surrounded him. His limbs were heavy after a dreamless sleep that felt like it had gone on for a year, and he kept his eyes closed, hoping to drift back into it. He didn't want to wake up. He didn't want to face whatever came next.

Then—something warm stirring beside him. Some*one*, in bed with him, their back barely touching his bare arm. He didn't have to open his eyes to know who it was. Like always, when he turned and reached for her, she was there. He hugged her close to his chest, perfectly content.

Slowly, however, the memories began to come back; and with them, dread. It shook him, making his heart beat faster. His eyes flew open, and he sat up.

He was in his bedroom. At first glance, everything looked normal. Was it possible that all the horror had been a bad dream?

But no, his aching muscles told him otherwise. Ynga's fiery blade had seared his flesh to the bone, and though whoever had grabbed him within that portal had healed him, they'd still hurled him onto a stone floor after. He had so little energy that his muscles trembled as he sat up straighter and moved to get out of bed.

GENEVRA BLACK

He stopped short when he noticed that things were out of place. The drawers of his dresser were pulled out; the trunk that belonged under his bed had been opened, its contents strewn along the floor. A weight settled in his stomach when he glanced over at the small table adjacent to his bed and saw a solitary issue of *Rolling Stone* smacked across its surface.

They'd gone through his things.

As he stood and crossed shakily to his dresser, someone knocked on the door—a forceful knock that demanded an answer. He pulled on a shirt and called out, "Come in."

A man in gold-and-bronze armor entered, and for a brief second, Marius thought it might be his father. Then his eyes darted to the man's face. He was white but tan, with piercing blue eyes and a trim gray beard. The man was familiar; they had met before.

"Radiant Oddfreyr." Marius bowed his head. After everything, he didn't know what else to say.

"Marius," Oddfreyr grunted tiredly, crossing to the small table and sitting without being invited. He gestured sharply for Marius to take the seat across from him.

He sat. The fact that the Radiant hadn't called him *Vivid* was a bad sign.

"A bit of light reading?" Oddfreyr asked flatly, picking the magazine up between his thumb and forefinger. "Did your new friends give this trash to you?"

Marius said nothing.

The Radiant's nostrils flared. "You know why I'm here."

"You are the Radiant of the Mid-Atlantic Divine, sir," Marius replied slowly, trying to keep his voice calm. "But I assume you're here on behalf of the Divine Assembly."

"Indeed I am."

The international council of Aurora would not be pleased—about any of this. Marius hadn't thought about what might happen after he fought his father. Then again, he hadn't been expecting his fellow vivids to attack him. He closed his eyes, a sudden wave of grief washing over him. Ynga had been right. All that death, all those warriors. Gone, because of him.

"Do you understand the gravity of what you've done, Marius, or shall I remind you?" When he didn't answer, Oddfreyr continued. "Bringing a hellerune on hallowed ground. Bringing undead on hallowed ground, for that matter. Stealing and destroying holy relics. You killed *forty* people— that cuts the number of vivids in this province by nearly half."

"Who told you that?"

"Ynga Widearms. One of the only ones you didn't slaughter."

"She lives?" Marius asked.

Oddfreyr replied with a snort. "Barely."

Marius took a long, deep breath and exhaled through his mouth. "Then what happens now?"

"No decision has yet been made. I leave for the Alltemple this afternoon. There, we will review and discuss whether you should be exiled, or executed, or..." Oddfreyr paused, tipping his head strangely. "Or made Radiant of the Rising Divine."

Marius clamped his jaw shut to keep it from dropping open. "What? Why would you do that?"

"I never said there was a good chance of it, but the chance is non-zero." Oddfreyr huffed. "You did root out and kill an oathbreaker. A Radiant, no less. Then again, he was your father. You *could* become the most powerful man on the East Coast ... but chances are your family will languish in dishonor."

"Where is my father?" Marius asked tersely.

"As far as anyone knows? He has been exiled."

He knit his brows. "But that's not true. I saw him leave through some sort of portal."

The Radiant looked at him pointedly. "You saw nothing."

Marius's body tingled with anger. There *was* an explanation. There was more to the story, and the Aurorans were more interested in covering it up than telling people what was going on. How could it be that the very people who preached speaking the truth were such heinous liars?

"And the hellerune?" he muttered.

Oddfreyr clenched his fists tighter. "She and her friends escaped, unfortunately—and left you behind, at the mercy of the Aurora, I might add. But there's what you get for trusting Reach scum. They have no conviction. No loyalty."

Marius's heart sank. They had abandoned him? Of course, the temple was a wildly dangerous place for them to be, but he would have pulled any of them out were he in their shoes. He'd have found a way to bring them with him.

Still, Oddfreyr thought Edie was evil, and Marius knew that wasn't true. "The hellerune isn't a threat to you."

"Hellerunan are a threat to everyone."

Marius kept every muscle in his body tightly controlled. "I don't understand why. They were created by Hel. She's a goddess; the Old Ways revered her."

"Yes," Oddfreyr snapped back, "*she* is a goddess. Her hellerunan are mortal, and too powerful. We've seen time and time again, for centuries, that their power drives them to evil. They can't be trusted and don't belong in this universe."

Finally, Marius stood. "How you can say that when the Aurora uses necromancy, too?"

Oddfreyr crossed his arms tightly, remaining seated. "Oh? Enlighten me."

"The bodies in the Golden Crypt were animated. They came back to life."

A pause. "That is not necromancy."

"Necromancy by another name, then! I saw them come to life, and she was able to save us by taking control of them. That's death magic."

The Radiant stood abruptly. He had been speaking at a normal volume before, but all at once, he was shouting in Marius's face, cheeks red and spit flying. "Keep your mouth shut when you don't know what you're talking about! It is not the same, and if you can't understand that, you aren't fit to be Aurora!"

Marius took a step back. The yelling was a shock to his system. His father never yelled, and he hadn't had a mentor yell at him in years. For a brief moment, he wondered if Oddfreyr would draw his blade and kill him right then and there. No one would be able to stop him before it was over. The look in the Radiant's icy eyes said he knew that.

But thankfully, Oddfreyr pulled back. He regarded Marius with disgust as he spoke. "During the review and investigation period, you will be confined to this room. Good day."

He left quickly, and Marius was alone, his chest slowly filling with dread and heartbreak. He had found the tarnished underbelly of the Aurora's golden façade. After an argument like that, he had little doubt as to what his sentence would be.

Oddfreyr was right about the Reach. They had abandoned him. He had nowhere to turn. But he wasn't about to sit here, imprisoned and waiting for death.

There was only one thing he could do.

As he crossed to his dresser again, there was another knock on the door, softer this time. He turned and mumbled for them to come in.

A young servant entered the room. She didn't look at him, didn't say anything as she walked to the table and set a tray down beside his magazine. The tray was stacked with clean linens, of which he already had plenty. She left before he could say anything to her.

Marius turned back to his dresser, grabbing a leather bag from nearby and starting to fill it with what few street clothes he had. Something gave him pause, though, and he slowed. After a moment, he turned to look at the tray of linens.

Everything about them was strange. The time of day, the fact that the servant hadn't stayed to change the sheets, the fact that they were on a *tray*. He set his bag down and went to the table.

It only took a moment of searching to find what he was looking for.

Tucked into the folds of the middle sheet was a leaf of notebook paper, folded in half. Hope lifted his heart as he opened it.

Marius,

I hope you're okay. The temple guards pulled you out before we even knew what was happening, and we had to run out the back way. I wouldn't have left you if I had the choice.

Cal wants you to know he shot four of them, though. He says "you're all right by me, Sparky" :)

You know where to find us.

-Edie

He stroked the note with his thumb thoughtfully. Maybe there was still somewhere he could go. After a few minutes of thoughtful silence, he picked up the issue of *Rolling Stone* and shoved it into his bag.

CHAPTER FORTY

EDIE SQUEALED as some of the water from Sissel's hose overshot Augustus's back and sprayed her in the face. She hadn't expected to be up and about so soon after an exhausting magical battle, but the sun was out, the snow had melted, and she felt like celebrating being alive.

Almost everyone had congregated in Tilda's rooftop garden. Edie and Sissel were hosing down their new drake friend and watching him dance around in the water. Nearby, Mercy was trying to salvage the snow-dusted flowers in a big planter while Fisk wove her a spring crown with flowers from another. Cal was sulking inside, avoiding Tilda as usual, and Satara was using the computer to translate the papers the revenant had stolen from Indriði.

Most notably, on the morning deck, Tilda and Nils—Sissel's dad—were discussing his daughter's future over coffee. With a Venomgut drake dropped in their laps, Nils needed help—and with no errands to run, Sissel needed something fun and independent to occupy her time. Tilda had some ideas, and it was good for Sissel's dad to meet her new, safer friends.

Well ... slightly safer friends.

He glanced over at Edie and Sissel and waved. Edie thought he seemed like a nice guy, if a bit cautious when it came to the supernatural. But she supposed that was probably a normal reaction, especially when you had a kid to worry about. Extra-especially when that kid had a penchant for getting into trouble.

Edie spritzed Augustus's face with the hose, smirking as he snapped at the water. "Your dad seems to be getting along well with Tilda."

The teen scratched the drake's side. "Yea! But she's been dead, like, a billion years and she's still the most normal out of all of you, so I'm not surprised."

"You think she'll be able to change his mind about the couriering thing?"

"I dunno." She wiggled her nose thoughtfully. "He was trying really hard to pretend we were normal before, but now that that's off the table..."

"With a drake living with you? Yeah, I'd say so."

Sissel's eyes lit up. "Oh, bro, maybe he'll join the Reach! He's really good at languages and research and a bunch of other random stuff. I bet he could really help."

"We'll see," was all Edie said, though the thought of having a researcher on their team was pretty damn appealing. If Astrid being dead forever meant Edie was now the Reacher, maybe it would be her job to convince him—but who knew how that would go?

Edie sat on a nearby bench, turning her hose off for the time being. As she watched Augustus and Sissel play, she thought of Astrid. It had only been a few days since she had watched her die, but somehow, it felt like years. So much had changed since then.

The loss still hurt, of course. When Edie wasn't sleeping the dreamless sleep of exhaustion, she lay awake at night, replaying the scene in her head; otherwise, nightmares woke her. Astrid's face, her pain, her desperation toward the end ... warriors weren't supposed to die like that. The images were burned in Edie's mind forever.

She couldn't imagine being in Satara's shoes. Not only had she lost a friend and mentor, she had lost her connection to the valkyir. None of them had any idea what the next step to becoming a valkyrie was, and Satara only had a limited time to sort herself out before those wings turned her into a twisted, evil demon. Edie assumed Marius's offer to help them had been rescinded—she doubted he'd still have access to his father's library. They'd have to figure it out themselves.

The shieldmaiden had been coping mostly by closing herself off. When she wasn't translating Indriði's papers, she was on the terrace two floors below, staring out into the city. Astrid had left her without a clue, and she seemed to be floating, knowing what she needed to do but not how to start. Edie could only speculate on why Astrid had neglected to teach her.

And though she mostly felt sad for Satara's loss, she also found herself feeling angry. Angry that Astrid had been so careless, that she had left Edie and Cal and the Reach flat, too. Edie barely knew how to do her taxes—how was she supposed to run an entire faction and stop a war at the same time?

A strong breeze blew some mist from Sissel's hose into Edie's face, bringing her back to reality. She looked up in time to see Satara walking through the glass-paneled sunroom, holding a stack of notes. Her hair was still silk-wrapped, and she wore a T-shirt and leggings as pajamas. Either she hadn't slept at all last night or she had been working on translating Indriði's papers since first thing this morning. The bags under her eyes suggested the former.

Edie stood to go meet her at the glass door of the sunroom, and the shieldmaiden silently motioned for her to follow.

Downstairs, Cal was already waiting for them in the living area, sitting uncomfortably on the couch and focusing a little too hard on his smartphone screen. When the two women approached, he stood. "Any good news?"

"I finished translating the papers," Satara said with a sigh. She set the original copies and her typed notes down on the coffee table. "I'm afraid that's the end of the good news."

Cal picked up the stack and scanned the first page. "What was the hold up?"

Edie cut him a look, and he backpedaled hard.

"Uh ... I mean, not that it was a problem, considering what's been— I'm just curious." He pulled a face and shrugged at Edie.

"I can speak Icelandic fine, but they aren't Icelandic." Satara sat heavily on the shorter part of the sectional, pulling one knee up to her chest. "It's a similar language called Faroese. I could guess some of it, but a lot of it, I had to look up."

"Okay." He scanned the page again before setting it down anxiously. "Give me the short version?"

Satara sighed, squeezing her tired eyes shut for a moment. "The letters spoke of something happening in New York City, some sort of gathering of people, like a faction or an army. Indriði's contact didn't give specifics—they speak mostly in obscure references—but I know that Daschla is leading them ... on behalf of the Gloaming, I assume."

Cal grunted in recognition.

"Just like Zaedicus said she was," Edie mumbled.

"Besides that, there were a couple of things they mentioned that I think we should look into, for the Reach's sake." Satara slid the papers closer to herself and flipped through them. "There's another hellerune in New York."

"No shit?" Cal raised his brows.

"Their plan is to recruit him, but he's been lying low for years, and they can't seem to find him. They don't even know his name or whose son he is." Satara pointed. "Then, here, Indriði's contact mentions there is a 'Reach problem.'"

Edie snapped her head up to look at Satara. "I thought Astrid said she was all that was left of the Reach."

"Maybe she thought she was. Or maybe she was keeping what she knew close to the vest."

Edie sighed. Yeah. Apparently, Astrid really had a habit of that.

"But it would make sense that there are remnants of the Reach there.

The hellerune would have to have a network of people to hide him away."

"And it makes sense there'd be pockets," Edie added, scanning the page. "I mean, if it was really as big as Astrid said it was, all those years ago, there'd have to be more people than just us."

Cal took out a cigarette and gnawed on the filter. "That's probably where Indriði pissed off to, then."

"I think we should follow her." Satara stood and went to the window. "She has Astrid's shield and spear, she knows where the Wounded is, and she's planning something awful in that city. We have to go stop it."

"But what about here?" Edie gestured around. "We can't abandon Anster. The New Gloaming is still fucking everything up."

Cal snorted. "Nothing short of the National Guard is gonna stop those assholes from fucking everything up, kid."

"We'll set up a network," Satara said. "Matilda has already been talking about it. She knows who she can bring over to our side from the Gloaming and Aurora both. She has the money to start building the Reach here as soon as we give her the go-ahead. I think the hellerune situation is worth looking into."

Edie huffed unsurely, scrubbing both hands across her face. When she looked back up, Satara had turned to her. Her eyes were intense.

"Edie, I won't hold you to your promise, but I'm still going, with or without you."

There was a long pause. Satara was right—she had promised. And after everything the shieldmaiden had done for her, it was only fair. "All right, I'll come."

"I'm always up for a road trip," Cal added, standing. "Let's not get Watchers in New York, of all places—that city's enough of a batshit garbage fire."

Edie snorted. "It's not your sweet Vegas, anyway."

"Exactly."

The doorbell rang, and Edie got up to answer it, if only to distract herself from the conversation. She tried to shake off her nerves. Things were changing so quickly. What had seemed like a wild ride at first had turned into her every waking moment. Magic, mythical beings, and avoiding grisly deaths at the hands of her enemies were now part of her life. It was a weird thing to have to get used to, but she found that she worried less and less about herself and more about the world she'd leave behind if she died.

When she opened the door, there he was.

Marius was in his armor as always, but he carried a huge leather bag under one arm; and, notably, his hair was out of its usual stiff style, curling around his ears and forehead like a cherub's. When he looked up, his golden gaze was earnest. His expression was vulnerable and unsure, like he thought there was a chance she might slam the door in his face.

They stared at each other for a moment before he said softy, "Hi. Can I come in?"

Edie stepped aside, then remembered to say, "Uh, sure. Come in."

When he entered, he glanced around the room, his anxious gaze landing on the others. "Can we speak privately for a moment?" he mumbled to Edie.

She didn't even have to say anything. Cal and Satara were already starting to leave, though Satara lingered for a moment, eyeing the vivid warily before stepping onto the terrace and closing the door.

"Uh ... sit down, I guess." Edie gestured to one of the couches, and Marius eased onto it, setting his bag down on the floor beside him.

She hesitated before sitting next to him. Somehow—maybe it was all the radiant energy she'd been hit with recently—she had become more aware of the strange magical aura he possessed. All her hairs stood up on the arm closest to him. "Did you get my note?"

He bowed his head, looking at the floor. "I did."

She gnawed on her bottom lip, squeezing her hands between her knees. "So, how are ... things?"

"Not good."

"Did you get in trouble?" she asked.

The vivid took a deep breath. "The Divine Assembly is going to vote on my fate. They're a select number of Radiants from around the globe who come together to make decisions like this."

"You don't even get to go and plead your case?"

"No." He sighed sharply. "They wouldn't listen anyway. I already know what my sentence will be."

Edie remained quiet. There was no doubt that whatever it was, it was bad.

"Now that I know about their lies and the necromancy in the crypt, they'll all want me gone before I can ruin their image. Even the good, merciful Radiants will likely vote against me to keep the Aurora's unity."

"I'm sorry," she whispered, wanting to touch his arm but refraining.

A lull fell between them. Marius searched the floor between his feet like he might find a solution to his dilemma there. When he spoke again, his voice was so soft it was almost a whisper. "I don't want to leave my people behind ... but they're not my people anymore. They aren't who I thought they were, and I..." He looked up, meeting her eyes. "I'm not who I thought I was, either."

Edie held his gaze. "And your dad?"

Marius simply shook his head and looked away again.

Gone, then. "I'm sorry. I ... know what it's like to lose your dad—and to find out that he had been keeping secrets from you." She shifted and sighed. "I guess my dad didn't betray me, though."

Marius shook his head again, like he was trying to scramble jumbled thoughts back into order. "I've been thinking about the mirror, and what he said. He kept saying he wasn't a traitor, that he was doing it all for a good reason. I ... I think I believe him."

"But why? He confessed to working for the Gloaming."

He shook his head a third time, harder. "No. In our culture, breaking a vow is comparable to murder. He would never break the oaths he made unless there was a good reason. Unless someone above him commanded him to."

He looked ahead, out the window. He was drawn, his expression haunted. Edie knew the look; she'd caught it on a lot of her friends' faces recently. Marius was seeing something she couldn't see, in a place she couldn't go.

"What if the traitor the mirror warned of wasn't my father?" He turned slowly to look at her. "What if it was me?"

Edie frowned. "That can't be true. You were doing what was right. The Gloaming hurts people." In truth, she didn't know the answer, but she could see that this question would torture him.

"And now I'm leaving the Aurora," he continued. "Running away from my punishment. I made a vow, too, Edie."

Finally, she dislodged her hands from between her knees and laid one on his arm, turning her body toward him. "Marius, you said that they weren't the people you thought they were. You aren't obligated to stay and take shit from people you don't believe in or trust anymore 'cause you were born into this ... duty."

Marius rubbed his forehead, loosing a puff of air. "Trust or duty or whatever, if I leave, I'll be breaking an oath. People go to Náströnd for that."

Ah, beautiful Náströnd. Murderous monsters, rivers of snake venom, and a dragon that gnaws on your bones. It didn't sound like a nice place, but Edie wasn't convinced it was real. And here, now, Marius was killing himself over a decision that should have been simple: leaving the Aurora and being happy, or execution.

She rolled the dilemma around in her head for a moment. "But you said that sometimes there are good reasons to break an oath. Tyr broke an oath, remember? You told me so once. He gave Fenrir his word that the gods wouldn't bind him, and he lied."

"He's the god of law and justice," Marius replied miserably. "He gets to decide where the law stands."

"And he decided that sometimes rules have to be broken for the greater good."

Marius was silent for a while, and Edie let him ruminate on her words. She couldn't make him believe something he didn't want to believe; all she could do was offer another perspective.

Eventually, though, curiosity got the best of her. She pointed to the bag at his feet. "What's in there?"

"My belongings," he mumbled, nudging it with his foot. "Just a few things I could use besides my armor."

Edie's heart sank. Good god, there wasn't much, was there? It was a big bag, but not *that* big. Her own bedroom back at the apartment could probably fill a dozen boxes. He had so little to call his own.

That reminded her: "Hold on, I have something for you. Stay there."

She jumped from the couch and ran up the stairs to the room she was sharing with Mercy. Pulling open the drawer of her bedside table, she grabbed a cloth-wrapped object, then headed back downstairs.

"What is this?" Marius asked as she approached and laid it in his hand.

"Open it."

He eyed her warily for a moment before unwrapping the cloth. As the silver dagger was revealed, it hummed softly, as though it was greeting Marius. He blinked and looked up at Edie. "You ... *stole* ... Radiant Hærfríðr the Puretongue's ancient silver dagger of truth."

She spread her hands. "Surprise!"

He shook his head, looking between her and the knife. "You are *full* of surprises, Edie Holloway."

"Good." Edie smiled, then sat next to him again. "Oh. There's this thing I keep wanting to ask about and then forgetting with all the crap going on. Since you owe me"—she smirked—"maybe you can help?"

"I suppose," he said dubiously.

She took a deep breath and tugged up the left sleeve of her shirt. Tattooed on her left wrist in stark black was a new rune, one that looked a bit like the letter M. It seemed familiar, but she couldn't place it. "I woke up in the middle of the night last night, and this had appeared. Do you know what it means?"

Marius set the dagger aside and seemed to hesitate before taking her wrist in his hand, investigating the rune. "This is ehwaz, the horse."

She thought she remembered that from Indriði's runecasting. "What does it mean?"

"Ah ... it's been a while since I needed to know that." He managed a small smile. "But if I remember right, in some cases, I think it means betrayal."

"And in others?" she pressed. "Give me some good news."

Marius chuckled a little. "It also means moving forward, development. Teamwork, people you can believe in. Trust."

"That's not so bad." She smiled. "And now we're even."

He nodded, releasing her wrist with a sigh. "Thanks for the dagger, but I'm not sure how much help it will be to me. I have nowhere to go. The Aurora doesn't forgive and forget. I'll spend the rest of my life running from them."

"Well..." Edie looked away, touching the papers Satara had left on the coffee table. "There's some stuff we need to take care of in New York, me and Satara and Cal. You could come, too."

"You want me to work with the Reach?" he asked, blinking.

"Why not? We make a pretty good team." She peered up at him. "Will you go with us?"

Marius tilted his head, regarding her thoughtfully for a moment. His eyes probed her face, and she kept her expression open, honest and unguarded. He might have been told she was an abomination, but she could tell he didn't believe it, especially not now.

Earlier, she had wondered when he'd become so decent, but the truth was, he always had been. Even when they had been on opposite sides, he'd healed her friends, helped them through trials. Breaking laws to help vulnerable people—it didn't get much more decent than that.

Finally, he answered her: "If you'll have me, I'll follow you."

CHAPTER FORTY-ONE

THE CHURCH WAS dark as the priest stepped out of the sacristy and headed down the nave. As he walked, he adjusted the buttons on his clerical shirt—all in the right rows for once. His head was such a mess these days, it was a wonder he even remembered to dress himself, let alone how to lead mass. And things were only getting worse.

He stopped in the center of the nave and half-turned to look back. Behind the sanctuary's altar, an enormous wooden crucifix cast its shadow over him.

If only the guy hanging up there could help him now.

The narthex smelled of sunlight and stuffy incense, but it was a familiar smell, one he'd come to love to hate. A well-lit staircase to the immediate right of the double doors led him down to the basement—a community area, though no one was there now. Exactly how he needed it.

A small room with tiled floors had become his emergency ritual room. There was probably something deeply screwed up about that, but he didn't have the time or energy to have a crisis with himself over it. It wasn't like Christ was going to come down from that cross and stop him.

He locked the door behind him and drew the curtains. The specially-mixed bottle of ink he had hidden away was right where he had left it, the substance inside thicker than it looked like it could possibly be. It only took a few dips of his finger to draw an entire circle of runes around himself.

After, he took a step out of the circle and drew three interlocking triangles in its center—a symbol of his patron god, but one he didn't particularly like drawing anymore. With what had been happening in the city lately, the sight of it left a bad taste in his mouth … though he supposed one could say the same thing about the crucifix.

"All right," he mumbled to himself, screwing the cap back on the ink bottle. "Let's get a move on."

Slowly, the already-dark room became darker. The shadows deepened. Eventually, little points of light appeared, the darkness twinkling like the night sky. A cool breeze enveloped him as if he really were outside.

At length, one particular point of light shifted. The figure in front of him could only be distinguished from the darkness by the way that single light moved, and the fact that it occasionally passed in front of the other lights and blocked them out. The shuffle of pacing feet accompanied the figure's appearance, and with it, clicking—a spear being used as a walking stick.

"Good of you to finally show up," said the figure. "I was beginning to think you had forgotten me."

The priest rolled his eyes. "How could I forget when you have a flock of blackbirds practically attacking my church windows?" Then, in a more playful tone, "You know, for a guy called the Hawk, you need a lot of help keeping track of your stuff."

The figure barely breathed a laugh. "I am also called the Blind, and I have nine Worlds to cover. So, what's your report?"

"The Blood Eagles are rising in numbers." The priest spread his hands. "I have *literally* no idea how they're doing it. They're just a bunch of humans. The growth is unprecedented!"

"Unprecedented?" the figure asked skeptically.

"All I'm saying is it's looking grim, jefe."

The figure heaved a great, irritated sigh. The wind that followed almost knocked the priest's glasses off his face. "I want them gone." Its voice was louder now. "I don't let fools use my symbols. Their ignorance is the antithesis of my existence. Anyway, you'd think they would have learned."

"I'm doing all I can." The priest cocked a brow. "It's probably an internet thing. There's got to be someone I can talk to about it."

"Good. Look for someone who can help you with the ... *internet*, then, and let's be done with this." The voice huffed a laugh. "Any news of the hellerune? You've been keeping an eye on him as I asked?"

The priest sighed. Again with the stupid hellerune. "Yes, but I'm not the only one. I've been at this for a long time, but I'm still only one guy. If the Gloaming's calling in the cavalry, it's not gonna take them long to close in."

"Just keep your eye on him." The figure clicked the butt of its spear on the ground rhythmically, slowly backing up into the darkness once more. A smile appeared in its voice as it said, "I have a very strong feeling you'll receive some help soon."

The priest sighed as the darkness melted together, then faded.

Help? More like trouble.

GLOSSARY

I USE a lot of crazy words in this book that you might not know how to pronounce, so here's a small list of all of the Norse words in *No Earthly Treason* and how to say them.

Some things to keep in mind before you read this guide:

1. Some words have been adapted from Old Norse rather than taken from Old Norse, so their pronunciations are different. It's also important to note that any "authentic" Norse pronunciation is reconstructed.

2. Some words are pronounced different contemporarily, so they aren't widely pronounced the way the Norse would have said them. In fact, I mix and match a lot—sometimes I use the legit Old Norse words for things, and sometimes I use the more contemporary forms. In the case of **valkyrie/valkyir**, I literally just made up the plural "valkyir" because it sounded cool.

3. I've had to cobble together words like "**hellerune**," etc., from other languages, so their pronunciation is a little

fudged. As for the full sentences, I'm absolutely fudging vocab and grammar. If you know someone who can hook me up with an authentic Old Norse translation, I'll take all the help I can get.

4. Pronunciation basics: the Norse almost always **rolled their r's**. The letters f and v, when they don't start the word, are pronounced as a v sound and a w sound respectively. The "aw" I've written to express the letter á is a round-mouthed almost-o sound like the au in the English word "**maul**" as opposed to "ow." The letter j is pronounced like y is in English. The letter thorn (Þ, þ) is pronounced like the "th" in "Thor," while the eth (Ð, ð) is pronounced like the "th" in "father" or "this." I've expressed the eth sound as "**dth**" because that's what it sounds like to me.

CHARACTER NAMES:

- Sárr – SAWR-ur (a very hard name to say, I've come to find...)
- Marius – MAH-ree-us
- Eirik – EY-rick
- Fiskbein – FISK-bane
- Indriði – INDRI-dthee
- Hati – HA-tee
- Sköll – skohl
- Roggvi – ROGG-vee
- Ynga – ING-ga
- Freyja – frey-ya (Or, with reconstructed Norse pronunciation, "FROY-ya.")
- Odin – OH-din (Old Norse "Óðinn" or "OH-dthin.")
- Skuld – skoold
- Sváfa – SWAW-va

- Tiralda – teer-AHL-da
- Geir – gair (like "air" with a g at the beginning.)
- Daschla – DAHsh-la
- Hærfríðr – HAir-free-dthir (with "HA" said like you're starting to say "had," so it's really more like "haaihr.")
- Eygísl – OYE-geez-il
- Oddfreyr – ODD-froy-r

RUNE NAMES:

- Ingwaz – ING-wahz
- Perthro – PAIR-thro
- Laguz – LAH-gooz
- Merkstave – MAIRK-stahv
- Thurisaz – THU-ri-sahz
- Ehwaz – EH-wahz
- Berkana – BAIR-ka-nah
- Isaz – EE-sahz
- Hagalaz – HAH-gah-lahz
- Ansuz – AHN-sooz
- Kauna – COW-nah
- Raidho – RIDE-ho
- Mannaz – MAH-nahz
- Algiz – ALL-geez
- Othala – OATH-a-lah
- Dagaz – DAH-gahz

MISC:

- Ván – vawn
- Hellerune – HELLA-roona
- Hellerunan – HELLA-roonen

- Vættr – vaa-tur (where "æ" is pronounced like the a in "had" or "mad.")
- Brunnmigi – BROON-me-gi (hard g, short "ee" sound.)
- Wight – white
- Griss – grees (Translation: *piglet*. Used as an insult.)
- Dvergr – DWARE-gur
- Dís – dees (longer "ee" sound than in "griss.")
- Heimdyrr – HAYM-dyur (the y sound makes a rounded "ee" sound like the u in "tune," but it's difficult to say.)
- Vanaheim – VAH-nah-hime (Old Norse "Vanaheimr," or "VAH-nah-haym-ur.")
- Landvættr – LAHND-vaa-tur (where "æ" is pronounced like the a in "had" or "mad.")
- Mimir – MEE-meer
- Andi-stelari – AHN-dee-STEL-ah-ree
- Valkyrie – VAL-kur-ee (in reconstructed Old Norse, "valkyrja" or "VAUL-keer-ya.")
- Valkyir – VAL-kyeer
- Alfheim – AWLV-hime (Old Norse "Álfheimr" or "AWLV-hay-mur")
- Aesir – ICE-eer (Old Norse "Æsir" or "ASS-eer," which for obvious reasons doesn't sound as cool...)
- Vanir – VAH-neer
- Valhalla – VAL-hal-la or VAHL-hah-lla (Old Norse "Valhöll" or "VAHL-holl.")
- Niðavellir – NEE-dtha-vell-ear
- Yngvi – ING-vee
- Fylgja – FYULG-ya (where the y almost makes a rounded "ee" sound like the u in "tune". Plural "fylgjur" or "FYULG-yur.")
- Gátt-krít – gawt-kreet
- Fuglfolken – FOOgl-vole-ken (plural "fuglfolk" or "FOOgl-volk.")
- Sjóvættr – SYO-vaa-tur

- Seiðkona – SAYdth-conn-ah
- Seidr – SAY-dur (Old Norse "Seiðr" or "SAY-dthur.")
- Njord – n'yord (Old Norse "Njörðr" or "N'YOAR-dthur.")
- Ljósálfr – LYOES-awl-vur
- Valmey – VAUL-moy (Translation: "Maiden of the battle-slain.")
- *"Fúna í Náströnd"* – FOO-nah ee NAW-strohnd (Translation: "Rot in Náströnd.")
- Náströnd – NAW-strohnd
- *"Ég mun finna þig í fjöru"* – yea mun FIN-ah THIG ee FYur-oo
- Tyr – teer (Old Norse "Týr," where the y makes a rounded "ee" sound like the u in "tune")

NON-NORSE WORDS

(I'm not an expert on any of these languages, so take these with a BIG grain of salt!)

- Zaedicus – ZAY-di-cus and ZAI-di-cus (I made this name up and use both, which I'm sure he'd despise.)
- Izem – EEZ-im (Berber/North African; I always imagined some of Satara's ancestors being from there.)
- Ardelean – ar-DELL-yan (being Matilda's last name, this is Romanian, of course, not Norse.)
- Antoniu – ann-TONE-eoo
- Lylirion – lie-LEER-eeyun
- Khenbu – KEN-boo
- Inuusuttoq – inoo-oo-sutt-ok
- Kolya – COAL-ya
- Mulțumesc – mool-tzu-MESK (also Romanian, translation: "Thank you.")
- Kalaallit – kahla-al-eet

- Takanna – tahk-ah-NAH (Greenlandic. Translation: "Enjoy your food/dig in.")
- Suaasat – SOO-aah-ahh-set (A Greenlandic stew.)
- Pe dracu' – pe DRA-ku (Romanian. Translation: "On the Devil! / No way! / Bullshit!")

ABOUT THE AUTHOR

Genevra Black is an author, a video game and movie nerd, horror buff, and lover of all things odd. She lives in Maine with her partner and her pitbull. She has always been enamored with mythology, folklore, and the paranormal. Her favorite pastimes include playing Dungeons & Dragons; gaming; watching slasher films; and designing and creating costumes/cosplay. She loves spending time in epic, exciting worlds, and each and every one of her stories is a personal invitation for readers to join her!

Find her at:

genevrablack.com
fb.me/GenevraBlack
twitter.com/GenevraBlack
genevrablack@gmail.com

And if you join her mailing list at GenevraBlack.com you can download the exclusive short story "Night Vet of the Living Dead"—the tale of exactly what happened to Hervey at the emergency vet.